Love in the Lowcountry

A Vacation Collection

Addie Bealer | Paula G. Benson | Victoria R. Benson
Janie Gordon | Robin Hillyer-Miles | Linda Joyce
Elaine Reed | J. Lynn Rowan | Suzie Webster

Poe Substitute by Paula Gail Benson

Analysis of Love by Linda Joyce

Forever After at the Ever Rest Inn by J. Lynn Rowan

Work, Play, & a Folly Vacay by Addie Bealer

Consider it Done by Victoria R. Benson

Moonlight in Moncks Corner by Janie Gordon

IOP Connection by Elaine Reed

The Blue Victorian by Robin Hillyer-Miles

Finally Found by Suzie Webster

Stories included are ranked by spice level

CONTENTS

Introduction

I am honored to pen the forward for Love in the Lowcountry, Vacation Collection, an excellent anthology written by members of the Carolina Romance Writers, all talented authors from up-and-coming to bestselling. Ultimately, we all want to be whisked away to worlds in which we can lose ourselves in stories that allow us to feel good and dream about what might be. This anthology does just that.

The Carolina Romance Writers is particularly special because it consists of writers at different stages of their journey who have become a community dedicated to the art of writing about romance. They support one another from beginning to end. Their writing community is integral to the success of their anthologies.

Together, they share the good and the bad through partnership and encouragement. They are committed to continuously learning and refining their talents which culminates in this anthology of stories that will make you swoon in all the best ways.

Each story is a delight, ranging in spice level from peppermint-sweet to sizzlingly heart-pulsing. You'll find the story for whatever your heart desires.

So, my reading friends, consider this your personal invitation to escape to South Carolina, where you will travel from warm sandy beaches to small quaint towns with a promise of laughter, love, and maybe a tiny bit of strife… that only a Lowcountry story can provide.

Read well!

Yasmin Angoe
Best-selling author of *Not What She Seems*

Poe Substitute

by Paula Gail Benson

Poe Substitute

by Paula Gail Benson

With a successful Charleston tourism business, a daughter excelling at Ashley Hall, and a Labor Day Sullivan's Island house-sitting gig next door to a captivating director scouting locations for his upcoming film about Edgar Allan Poe, Fleur Brawley seems to have it all. Except, it's not the life she wanted. She may be losing her beloved daughter to her ex-husband and his fiancée, and a pesky actor wanting to play Poe is stalking her. When Fleur and the actor are caught moving backward in 15-minute historical time loops, can they escape to the present and a chance to find love?

Chili Pepper rating: 0.5

Chapter One

Fleur Brawley parked in the gravel lot and tried not to step on the tiled gold bug embedded in the sidewalk as she passed it to enter Poe's Tavern. Some folks dismissed the place as a tourist trap, but she loved the ambience with portraits of the mustachioed, sad-eyed Edgar Allan Poe looking upon the diners. She appreciated that for a brief time, Poe had lived in and been influenced by Charleston, even though her personal experience with the writer was not always a happy one. Fleur blamed that on her ex-husband, Will, returning to college for a second graduate degree to become a Poe scholar.

Her friend Pam had lucked into a booth against the back wall. Fleur waved and made her way through the packed room, taking a seat on the opposite bench.

Pam raised a hand before Fleur could speak. "I know this may not be your favorite spot, but while you're spending the Labor Day holiday on Sullivan's Island, you know you'll encounter Poe."

Fleur leaned across the table. "I may have given up Poe's interpreter in the divorce, but I don't blame Edgar. His time in the military enlisted under the name Edgar Perry makes him part of Charleston history."

Pam circled her glass with her straw. "How are Will and his fiancée?"

Fleur shrugged. "I didn't see them when I dropped Belle Deveau off at the engagement party."

Will's last name was Wilson, but Fleur insisted their daughter also carry part of her family's name, her mother's maiden name, too—hence, Belle Deveau Wilson. Fleur loved using both her daughter's first and middle names together. Will had shortened it to B. D., which made Fleur cringe. Of course, Fleur delighted to see Will squirm when Belle Deveau called Will's fiancée Mel by her full name of Melangell, after a Welsh nun who protected rabbits.

"I saw B. D. on the soccer field at Ashley Hall. She's grown so tall."

Fleur sat up. "What were you doing at Belle Deveau's school?"

Pam smiled. "I've been dating the guy who coaches the team. They practice right across the street from where I work at the medical school. I can walk over and blend into the crowd. It makes it easy for me to see my guy and his daughter on neutral ground."

Fleur rolled her eyes. "With his ex watching from the stands, no doubt."

Pam sighed. "She's not quite an ex, which is why we're taking things slowly, being discreet." She pointed her dripping straw at Fleur. "What's your excuse for *not* being there. Are you avoiding Will and Mel cheering B. D. on?"

"Don't call her by her initials."

"Okay." Pam put her straw back in her glass and took a sip before asking. "So, why weren't you there?"

Fleur fingered the clasp on her purse. Both she and her mother had been Ashley Hall alumnae, along with a host of well-known women. Fleur insisted that Belle Deveau continue the tradition. "Someone in this broken family must work to pay Belle Deveau's tuition at Ashley Hall. It's not inexpensive, you know."

Pam stirred her drink. "I know, but Will makes a decent salary from the Charleston Library Society not to mention royalties from the books he's written about Poe, and I'm sure Belle Deveau would qualify for an academic scholarship if she needed one."

"Brawleys pay their own way." Fleur hated she was echoing the words her father often said.

"Maybe, but Belle Deveau is a Wilson, not a Brawley."

Fleur straightened her shoulders. "The better part of her is Brawley."

"Will might object to that."

Fleur pushed away from the table and stood. "Thanks a lot. Nothing like having that thrown in my face twice in a day."

Pam motioned with her hands. "Calm down and sit, honey. I know today's been tough for you."

Fleur collapsed into her seat, putting her elbows on the table and sinking her face into her open hands. Maybe a bit melodramatic, but that was exactly her mood. "Belle Deveau wants to stay with Will and Mel."

"Permanently? She told you that?"

Fleur tried to recall Belle Deveau's exact words as she left the car to go to the engagement party on Gold Bug Island: "I'd just as soon spend the Labor Day holiday weekend with them, if you don't mind, Mother. There's lots to do before the wedding, and this would give us a chance to shop for my bridesmaid dress. I don't have much more time off from school this fall and the wedding is the day after Thanksgiving."

So many things Fleur might have said in reply: *What about us spending time together as mother and daughter? I took this housesitting job on Sullivan's Island for the holiday weekend because I thought it would give us the perfect setting to bond and share each other's dreams.* Instead, she'd told Belle Deveau, "Don't let Mel talk you into anything green. Not even mint or aqua. Those colors look terrible on you."

That was the last thing my daughter heard me say. How she shouldn't wear green.

"Hey," Pam interrupted Fleur's thoughts. "Did Belle Deveau ask for a change in custody?"

Fleur shook her head slowly. "No, although that may be coming. She was talking about things she, Will, and Mel needed to do together. The kind of plans you make as a family."

"Look, she's verging on being a teenager and is excited to be part of the wedding. Right now, everyone's being extra respectful of each other's feelings, but after Will and Mel are married—when Belle Deveau feels excluded by the couple—she'll be happy to have you to turn to."

Fleur looked at Pam's encouraging face. "Do you really think so? I hope that's true."

A server limped up to their table. Dark hair, dark eyes, and a drooping mustache, he wore a black tee with the restaurant's name and location on the left side of his chest.

"Hi!" The word came out as a whoosh, as if the journey to their table had winded him. He leaned heavily on the table's edge and gave them an endearing smile. "My name is Ali, and I'll be your server." When his eyes turned to Fleur, they lingered—like he wanted to take in all her features.

His scrutiny unnerved her a little. Something was familiar about him. Fleur glanced at the portraits. Must be his resemblance to Poe.

"I'll have a Negroni," she said.

"Ah, we've got a new bartender . . ."

Fleur pushed the menu out of her way. "Make it Long Island Iced Tea, then. A pitcher."

"Bring her a glass, not a pitcher," Pam told him.

Fleur leaned back and crossed her arms. "Spoilsport."

Ali gave Fleur a flirty grin before tilting his head and making a note on his pad. "How about an appetizer?"

Fleur glanced at the menu. Almost every item featured the basic Southern food groups: fat, grease, fried breading, and melted cheese. A carb catastrophe she needed to avoid, but she was tempted today.

Pam asked the server, "What do you recommend?"

"I'm partial to the chili cheese fries or the Edgar's nachos."

Ordinarily, Fleur would object, but those selections sounded comforting.

"You really don't want to miss Edgar's drunken chili," Ali continued. "It's on the nachos."

Pam nodded. "Okay. We'll try them. And I'll take a refill on sweet tea."

"Coming right up." Ali turned and limped away. Fleur noticed his hair flipped up in a ducktail at the back. Again, it reminded her of someone.

"Our order will take forever."

Pam pursed her lips. "Why does it matter? Your next stop is your Labor Day retreat. Chill. Let the relaxation begin now."

Fleur stretched her neck and shoulders. "I hate waiting around when I could be doing something."

Pam was silent for a minute before asking, "Is that why you don't come to Belle Deveau's games?"

Fleur sat up very straight. "What do you mean?"

Pam sighed. "Look, I've watched her play and talked with the coach about her. She's a great, gung-ho team player, but no natural athlete."

"Learning good sportsmanship is the goal, not excelling at the game."

"Belle Deveau is a great kid. She's smart, friendly, polite, and kind. You've set high standards for her and given her a wonderful example. Maybe she needs more from you than just being a role model."

"I have never demanded that Belle Deveau pattern herself after me."

Ali set a tray down on their table, handing Fleur her drink and Pam the nachos. "Yeah," he said. "You kinda have."

Fleur grabbed the glass, taking a long swallow before demanding, "How do you know anything about my daughter and me?"

"You hired me last Thanksgiving to be your chauffeur and to entertain the Japanese tourist group you hosted."

Fleur's eyes widened in recognition. No wonder she remembered the back of his head. "You were playing Ebenezer Scrooge at Dock Street in *A Christmas Carol*."

Ali bowed. "I was."

"I thought it was a coincidence that your name was Alistair, and Alistair Sim played the role in the black-and-white movie. I promised you a costume upgrade and hourly wage for driving the group around and presenting a one-man-show version of the novel."

Ali smiled broadly. "Correct. And you never paid me."

"Because you disappeared. I tried to contact you, then I heard another actor played the role in the Dock Street production."

He lowered his head. "True. I was trying to get the set ready and fell from a ladder. I spent a few days in the hospital and am still having to take physical therapy."

"I'm sorry." Fleur tried to remember the time they had spent together. "When were you with me and Belle Deveau?"

Ali pressed his lips firmly together beneath his mustache before replying. "I drove your car when we picked her up from the library the night before Thanksgiving. She had been with her father and the lady who became my ex."

"That's right." Fleur took another sip. "You had been dating Mel, who's now Will's fiancée."

Ali huffed. "I wish I'd been a better boyfriend. Mel and I met in Columbia. Then, I relocated here with her when she was accepted in graduate school. She focused on her studies, and I became obsessed with being an actor. Eventually, we lost each other."

Fleur emptied her glass with one swallow. "I'd like a refill."

Ali seemed lost in his memories. "After my injury, I had a lot of time to think. Mel came to see me in the hospital, helped me to find ways to pay my bills. Every time she visited, she talked about how close she had grown to Will as a personal and intellectual soulmate and how much she loved B. D."

Fleur pushed her glass toward him. "I really need another drink."

The manager came over to the table. "Is there a problem, ma'am? May I help?" He looked uneasily at Ali.

"No, thank you," Pam replied. "We've just realized where we met before."

"Ali, why don't you get this lady her drink?" the manager suggested.

"Of course." Ali gave another brief bow before scooping up his tray. "I hope you enjoy those nachos," he said before limping away.

The manager watched him go before saying, "He's new and adjusting to this work, but please let me know if I need to send you a different server." With a quick head nod, he left.

"Listen, Fleur," Pam said. "Maybe it's a good thing you'll be on your own this weekend. This is not just a housesitting gig or a minivacation, but a business opportunity."

Fleur pinged her nails against the empty glass. "I don't need a business opportunity. I have plenty of those."

"Not like this one. I didn't tell you before, but the man renting the house next to the one you're housesitting is Darryl Maitland."

Fleur shrugged. "So?"

"The film director?"

Fleur rolled her eyes.

Pam shook her head. "I thought you knew what was happening around Charleston. Darryl Maitland just optioned the novel about Poe's time on Sullivan's Island, *A Man Called Perry*. He's here to check out locations and get a feel for Poe's real experience."

Fleur thumped the glass harder. "He should talk with Will."

"He doesn't want a researcher, but a Charleston expert who can show him the heart and soul of a place that touched Poe's life and changed it forever."

"Quote the raven, 'Nevermore.'"

"Don't be morose."

Fleur sighed. "It wasn't my life's dream to work in tourism." That was what she had been hoping to talk with Belle Deveau about this weekend.

Pam took her hand. "But, honey, you're brilliant at it. The best. That's why all the groups book you. You know Charleston, and you understand how to market it in a way that honors its heritage."

Fleur wondered if Pam had taken her hand to comfort her or to keep her fingers from knocking against the glass. She withdrew from the grasp. "Growing up, I wanted to be an architect. Daddy always told me it wasn't a job for a lady."

Pam snorted. "Well, you know better than that."

"I didn't at the time." Her eyes glistened. "Do you know who I idolized? A man you probably never heard of: John Henry Devereaux. An Irish immigrant who married a French immigrant, served in the Confederate army, and became a prisoner of war, then returned to Charleston where he built the post office, numerous churches including Mother Emmanuel, entertainment venues, a distinguished girls' school, and his own lavish summer home on Sullivan's Island. 1914 Middle Street. Only the gatehouse remains today, but when it was built, it was the grandest, most opulent residence with a whale's jawbones leading to the front porch and a ship's wooden female figurehead in the garden. How I would have loved to have visited."

Pam reclaimed Fleur's hand and gave it a shake. "See, honey, this is why you are so good at promoting Charleston. You know all the stories the rest of us have never heard."

"She's right. You have phenomenal skill." A limping Ali brought her another drink. "It's a real gift you could capitalize on."

Fleur looked into his eyes. He seemed sincere, but he obviously played the most advantageous angles. "Why are you being nice to me?"

He shrugged. "Maybe because you gave me a chance once. Not your fault I made a mistake and blew it. I heard you had a great reputation. I figured if I could impress you, perhaps you would have other work for me. People love Charleston. With your background and knowledge, you could develop all kinds of touring programs. Get a photographer and do a coffee table book featuring great black-and-white photos. Then, make a walking tour based on the locations in the book." His eyes grew wide. "It would be a natural to turn into a one-man show. 'Finding the Real Charleston.' I could represent historic figures through the centuries."

Fleur grunted and took a swallow of her new drink. "All it takes is a financial backer."

Ali, caught up in his own dream, ignored Fleur's comment. "I can see it being picked up by some PBS producer and turned into a documentary series. I could intersperse dramatic snippets."

"Go away," Fleur told him.

"He's got a point," Pam said. "You may want to take it up with Darryl Maitland."

Ali's eyes grew wider than saucers. "You know Darryl Maitland?"

Fleur shrugged. "Most folks have heard of him."

"But do they know he's in Charleston scouting out locations for *A Man Called Perry*?"

Fleur squinted at him. "Is that why you wear your hair like Poe? Hoping he'll spot you?"

Ali smiled. "I've been slimming down so I would be perfect for the role. What better place to be discovered than Poe's Tavern? No doubt he'll visit here."

Fleur laughed. "He's more likely to go to The Obstinate Daughter."

Ali frowned. "Why do you say that?"

Fleur was about to blurt out its proximity to where she was housesitting when Pam interrupted. "I imagine he'll be keeping a low profile with a private tour guide and catered meals to keep his dealings for the film incognito." She gave Fleur a silencing stare.

"What have you planned?" Fleur asked.

"Yes, what?" Ali echoed.

"We need to go," Pam told him. "I'll take the check."

He eyed the nachos with longing. "Shall I box these up for you?"

"Take them," Pam said. "We'll get something later."

Ali took the dish and limped away. Watching him go, Fleur commented, "What do you want to bet he eats them himself?"

Pam shrugged. "He looks as if he hasn't been eating regularly. Not just for a role."

Fleur reached to finish her drink. "If he hasn't been, it's his own fault."

Pam took the glass from her hand. "Don't be too hard on a guy for dreaming out loud. Remember, you have dreams too."

Chapter Two

While Pam waited for the bill, she sent Fleur to fix her face in the restroom. "You need to be looking good if we run into Darryl."

Fleur went reluctantly. She splashed her cheeks with water, lightly toweled them, then strategically reapplied blush. She assessed her image in the mirror and touched up her mascara with a flick at each eyelash. Her eyes could convey a flinty glimmer as well as clear discernment. She was always on her game. Had to be to succeed in the Charleston tourism industry.

Daddy always said she'd inherited her mother's good looks (well, at least a reflection of them—as Daddy put it, "Nobody's ever been a match to your mama's beauty."). "Make Southern charm count," Daddy encouraged her. "Don't compete with men. Wind them 'round your little finger."

"But, Daddy," she'd protest. "I don't want to compete with them. I want to work alongside, to build something lasting, beneficial, and beautiful."

He'd practically chuckled at her words. "Oh, darlin', I hope you can figure out how. I've seen too many women ruin their chances for finding a mate by insisting on succeeding in the workplace."

Maybe that was what her parents' relationship had been. Fleur would never know for certain. Her mother had passed away when she was four—before Fleur had had much time with her. Fleur's frame of reference was mostly based on her father's descriptions, but she did have a few memories of a strong, resilient soul who'd loved her with a fierceness that permeated Fleur's being. Even as a tiny child, that lingering warmth and assurance had made Fleur feel as if she could accomplish anything.

Fleur remembered her mother's soft whisper: "My delight, my sweet love, I will always be cheering for you."

The recollection of that voice pushed Fleur to achieve, despite her father's cautions. Her attraction to Will had been a form of rebellion. Will was everything her father seemed not to be: kind, scholarly, respectful of women's capabilities, and a natural collaborator. They'd eloped while Will was in graduate school, and Fleur became the breadwinner while he pursued his degree. She'd worked for many years as an administrative assistant with the state's tourism office before opening her own business as an event planner and tour guide for companies seeking to locate in Charleston.

By the time Belle Deveau was born, her father had become bedridden. With great pride, she'd taken her newborn daughter to meet him.

"Doesn't she look like Mama?" Fleur had asked.

Slowly, he'd shaken his head. "Too bad she'll have to depend upon you to support her."

Fleur had held the baby tightly as her eyes filled with tears. *You don't understand, Daddy. Will and I have something you and Mama never knew.*

But had they? As the years had gone by, after Daddy died and Fleur found herself alone with Will and Belle Deveau, she'd felt more and more used. Her salary paid for the lifestyle to which they had become accustomed. That became even more clear when Will had announced his intention to pursue a second Masters in English so he could concentrate on Poe's work. While she loved Will's devotion to his scholarship and their daughter, she hated having to be the main financial source. In a way, their divorce had proven her father right.

Pam pushed open the restroom's outer door, breaking Fleur out of her thoughts.

"Ready to roll?" Pam asked.

Fleur took the extra time to reapply her lipstick. Maybe Darryl Maitland was the kind of man she should be after—someone who had made his own way and could afford to give her and Belle Deveau the life they deserved. It would be nice to throw that in the face of Will and Mel's future happiness. Perhaps Belle Deveau would see a relationship with her mother could be as beneficial as one with her father and his new bride.

Snapping the lipstick container shut, Fleur tossed it in her purse and took one last look in the mirror. "Of course," she replied. *Game on.*

Chapter Three

They managed to escape Poe's Tavern without another Ali encounter. Fleur followed Pam's car traveling down Middle Street. Again, she wished she could have convinced Belle Deveau to spend the Labor Day weekend with her. They might have walked the quiet streets and headed to the beach. In the relaxed surroundings, maybe Fleur could have convinced her daughter they could spend quality time together, just as Belle Deveau did with Will and Mel.

If Belle Deveau had been with her, Fleur would have explained who John Henry Devereaux was and how he had inspired her to be an architect, even though she never achieved that goal. She would let Belle Deveau know that she worked hard so Belle Deveau could follow her own dreams.

Pam pulled into a residence that appeared stalworth and imposing. Fleur parked beside her and got out of the car to survey her weekend retreat. She remembered many of Sullivan's Island houses started out as military facilities and wondered if this one had that history.

"How do you know the owners?" Fleur asked.

"I work with them," Pam replied. She was one of the information officers for the Medical University of South Carolina. "The husband's an oncologist and the wife's a neurosurgeon."

Fleur nodded her head. "High-powered careers."

"Yes. They're vacationing with the couple that lives next door." Pam pointed to the neighboring house. "A lawyer and a financial advisor. I don't know which spouse is what. Anyway, the lawyer and financial advisor learned through connections that Darryl wanted to visit so they offered to rent him their house. I told the doctors I knew someone who could housesit for them. With the proceeds Darryl paid, the two couples are now sailing around the Bahamas."

"Good there are no hurricanes on the horizon."

"Exactly." Pam pulled out a ring of keys. "They have the original locks as well as a security keypad. Let me show you around."

Fleur approved of the neat, logical organization she would have expected to find in the household of two medical professionals. They saw so much suffering, so many cases they couldn't save. They compensated by controlling their living space. That was something Fleur could understand. She did the same.

Leaning in to inspect a photo that hung in the hallway, she saw a joint graduation, a male and a female student, with surrounding family and friends smiling in support. This wasn't a father who'd advised his daughter not to compete with boys.

"Glad you find everything acceptable," Pam said as they stepped back out on the front porch after the brief house tour.

Fleur glanced across the road and saw a beat-up vehicle parked there. The driver hid behind an open newspaper.

A voice sounded from the yard. "Is this the friend you've been telling me about?"

Fleur looked to see who was speaking and encountered the most startlingly expressive blue eyes she had ever seen. They were set in a face that successfully combined boyish and rugged features and enhanced by a smile that captivated, as well as framed by cute ears that appeared perfect to whisper sweet nothings into. The man took her breath away for a moment.

"I wondered when you might show up." Pam went purposely down the steps, approached him, and gave him a loud smack on the cheek. Turning back to Fleur, she said, "Meet my cousin, Darryl."

"Your cousin?" Fleur found she had to take the steps down cautiously to avoid stumbling. She tried to channel runway model but couldn't shake the image of awkward stork.

Get your act together. Make slow and sensuous work for you. Don't want to mess this up.

"Every so often, she claims me," Darryl admitted. "I'm glad this is one of those times." He extended his hand. When he clasped hers, tingles filled Fleur's insides.

Her flirt engine revved up. "The pleasure is all mine."

Another male voice intruded. "And I am similarly delighted to make your acquaintance." Ali limped toward them with a to-go bag in his hand.

"Who might you be?" Darryl asked.

"Name's Ali, but you can call me Edgar."

Darryl shook his hand but looked skeptical. "I'll stick with Ali."

"He's a server at Poe's Tavern," Fleur explained, feeling her flirt engine stalling.

"Former server. By the way, here are your nachos." Ali handed the bag to Pam. "My current unemployed status means I can devote myself full time to your project, Mr. Maitland. Previously, I worked as an actor."

"Feel free to send your resumé and headshot to my office," Darryl told him. "Now, if you'll excuse us . . ." He reached to take Fleur's other hand. Holding both, his piercing blue eyes focused on her face, and his slow grin invited her into their own private world.

Yes. She felt as if she were floating in anticipation.

"Actually." Ali pushed against their clasped hands, breaking the connection. "Ms. Brawley and I are a package deal."

Fleur recoiled from the intrusion. "What?"

Ali winked at her before focusing on Darryl. "You know she's a fabulous tour guide."

"So I've heard."

"Take my word for it. She will regale you with the hidden histories of the Holy City as I drive you to the locations she describes. Nearby are Gold Bug Island, Fort Moultrie, Poe's Tavern, and the Edgar Allan Poe Library. On the Isle of Palms at Wild Dunes, which may have been named after a Poe work, the rumored Gold Bug tree is on the golf course. And in Charleston proper, we can visit the Unitarian Church's graveyard where the inspiration for Annabel Lee may be buried in a secret grave."

"Conjecture," Fleur protested. His knowledge of Poe haunts was impressive, but that grave story couldn't be confirmed.

Ali pointed to her. "You see how wise she is? She should write a book. It would be a great documentary tie-in to your movie."

"We are not a package deal," Fleur insisted.

"Absolutely true. But we could make a great team." Ali inserted himself more forcefully between Fleur and Darryl, keeping their hands from touching. "Ms. Brawley is the genius, the mastermind, the true and valid authority. I am simply her faithful and earnest interpreter. Hers is the vision."

"You've sold me." Darryl raised his hands in surrender. "The thing is, currently I only need a tour guide, not a driver. You can send your acting credentials to my website."

Fleur noticed the prominent watch band around Darryl's left wrist. The watch face had a digital display of 19:14.

John Henry Devereaux's address number on Middle Street.

"I'm not asking just for myself." Ali refused to move. "I truly believe in your project. Ever since I read *A Man Called Perry*, I knew it had to have cinematic treatment. So many people don't understand how the short part of Poe's life spent here under a different name influenced his future and writing career. That book spoke to me. I want to be part of bringing it to the screen."

Fleur couldn't believe what she was hearing. Ali spoke about Poe the way she felt. She and Will had never shared that kind of intellectual affinity.

Darryl was not impressed by Ali's connection with the book. "As I said, submit your documents to my office for review. Now you need to leave."

"Please." Ali limped forward. Darryl pushed him back. Ali fell against Fleur.

She was still pondering the coincidence of the digital numbers matching John Henry Devereaux's address when Ali's dead weight sent her plummeting to the ground. Her head hit something sharp. She heard Pam cry out. Then, darkness.

Chapter Four

As she came to, Fleur thought it was odd for the sky to be so dark at 7:15 p.m. The sunset usually did not occur until after eight. The time hadn't come to change from Daylight Saving.

Her head ached. Turning to look at the ground behind her, she noticed an imbedded stepping-stone. It had a sharp edge. Must have been what she hit.

In the distance, she heard a methodical sound. Something heavy was hitting something that sounded like metal. She struggled to rise.

"Take it easy. Your head hit that rock hard. You'll likely have a bump on your noggin'."

Placing a hand against her forehead (as if she could somehow subdue the throbbing), she rubbed gently. Ali knelt beside her.

She looked up into his brown eyes, seeing sincerity tempered with concern. Ali's face didn't have the swoon-ability of Darryl's gaze and features, but his expression conveyed kindness and caring.

Of course, he should care. She wouldn't have fallen if Darryl hadn't pushed Ali into her, which sounded like Darryl was more at fault and made her head hurt worse.

"Your friend and Darryl must have gone for help. They've vanished."

She sensed it was just herself and Ali on the lawn, but the constant noise wasn't as far off as she originally thought. Struggling to sit upright, Fleur felt Ali's hand gently supporting her back.

"Are you sure you should be moving around with a head injury?"

"Yes."

Glancing at her outfit, she saw it was no longer the one she wore to meet Pam.

"Why am I wearing this costume?" she asked. She had never seen the pastel blouse and dark skirt that fell to below her knees. They reminded her of 1940s clothing.

Looking at Ali, she discovered he also had changed clothes, now sporting a white short-sleeved shirt and slacks. "If this is some kind of game you're playing, I don't think it's very funny," she told him.

Ali seemed as confused as she was. He shook his head. "I'm not playing a game. I don't know why we're dressed like this or what happened to the clothes we were wearing."

Fleur pulled away from him. "What is that infernal beating noise? It's giving me a headache."

Ali looked around. "The boy across the street is throwing rocks at that house."

"Please ask him to stop."

Fleur looked in the direction of the noise. As her eyes focused, she couldn't believe what she saw. Ali's beat-up car no longer sat parked in the street. An elaborate mansion had somehow replaced the smaller residence she remembered seeing. The mansion was familiar, yet in a state of disrepair.

"It looks like," she began, then shook her head. "That can't be."

"What?" Ali asked.

"The Devereaux mansion. It was razed years ago. Only the gatehouse remains."

Ali looked at her, then back at the mansion. "That's more than a gatehouse."

She grabbed the lapels of his shirt. "It wasn't there when you parked, was it?"

He shook his head slowly, but said, "It must have been."

"No, it wasn't. I'm sure of it."

"Are you saying we're imagining the mansion? That I'm seeing it, too, even though I didn't hit my head?"

Fleur gazed at him, bewildered by this place where they found themselves. Her hands loosened their grip on his shirt. She could feel its texture against her fingers. Cool and steady as he seemed to be. Not at all the flake she remembered hiring last Thanksgiving.

Then, she spotted a figure on the street, a teenaged boy winding his arm as if he were aiming to pitch a high fast ball. He sent the object in his hand skyward where it bounced against the mansion's dome.

"Hey!" Fleur found she had the strength to pull herself up. "Stop that!"

Startled, the teen glanced in their direction, then turned to run. Amazingly, Ali caught and tackled him. How did Ali manage to move so quickly with his limp?

The teen wiggled under Ali's weight. "Let me go, mister. I didn't cause the damage. Everybody uses it for target practice. I'm not the only one."

Ali remained seated on the teen's torso. "I believe you, and I'm going to let you up, but first I need to ask you something."

"Okay." The teen stopped moving.

"What year is this?"

The teen looked as if he couldn't believe the question. "Are you joshing me?"

"No. I need to hear you say it."

Fleur reached them. "You'd better be truthful."

"1941," the teen gasped. "Now will you let me go?"

Ali stood and offered a hand, but the teen dashed off as soon as he was free. Ali called after him, "No more rocks!"

"Is it possible?" Fleur asked. "Have we gone back in time?"

"So it would seem."

"But how? And why just the two of us? Where are Pam and Darryl?"

"I don't know." Ali bent to pick up the remains of a sign. After looking at it, he held it out to Fleur. It read: 1914 Middle Street.

Chapter Five

Suddenly, darkness surrounded Fleur again. From somewhere beyond, she heard Darryl saying, "You've sold me," and Ali arguing his case to be a driver. She glimpsed a flash of Darryl's watch face showing 19:14. Then, Pam cried out and Fleur lost consciousness a second time.

When she awoke, she saw the twilight sky. Again, what had happened? Was she still in 1941, or had she returned to the present?

Her head throbbed as she struggled to sit upright. Once more, she found herself in unexpected garments. The hem of her dress touched her ankles, and she saw black-laced shoes on her feet. Looking around, she hoped she wasn't alone.

"Ali?" she called hesitantly.

"Here," his voice answered.

She looked toward him, this time seeing the Devereaux mansion as it must have looked when the family had occupied it.

"Look!" Ali pointed toward the entrance. "It's a whale's jawbones!"

The magnificent mandibles added both grandness and oddness to the building. One could almost imagine a hapless Jonah being drawn into the interior of the sea giant's gullet.

Ali's outfit had changed too. He was no longer in shirt and slacks, but rather in a suit reminiscent of the late 1800's or early 1900's.

"What's happening to us?" she asked.

"I think we're caught in a time loop."

"Time loop?"

"You know," Ali said. "Like that Bill Murray movie *Groundhog Day*, where his character kept waking up to find he was reliving February second in Punxsutawney, Pennsylvania."

Leave it to Ali to find a theatrical tie-in. He had probably convinced himself this was some elaborate audition for Darryl's movie.

Standing, she dusted off her clothing, feeling self-conscious in such elegant garb. If this *were* an audition, she didn't want to be accused of damaging the costumes. And she planned to demand to know how her dress was being changed without her being aware of it. If Ali were involved, he would learn a Southern belle's vengeance was both bitter and deep.

Walking to stand beside him, she observed, "It isn't really like *Groundhog Day*. While we may still be on Sullivan's Island, we've also gone back in time."

"You're right. Haven't I been saying you're the brain power?"

His body blocked her view from the item upon which he focused his attention. She gently punched his shoulder. "Hey, how do you explain the shift in time, and why we're the only ones caught in it?"

As he turned to face her, she saw his hand rested at the top of a sign affixed to the fence. The sign they'd previously seen in disrepair with the address 1914 Middle Street.

"Wasn't that . . . ?"

"Yes," Ali answered before she could finish the question. "Now we see it in pristine condition. Minutes ago, it was only a remnant."

"Minutes?"

"Yes. If I'm calculating correctly." He looked for his wristwatch and finally had to settle with consulting a pocket watch. "We seem to be shifting every fifteen minutes."

"Every fifteen minutes? Why do you say that?"

He showed her the pocket watch. "See , it's seven o'clock now. At seven fifteen, we'll reset."

"Why seven fifteen?"

"The numbers in the address. One plus nine plus one plus four equals fifteen. If I had to guess, I would say this is likely 1914."

Like the logic Alice might find in Wonderland. "Why is this happening?"

His voice took on almost a professorial tone. "In literature, a time loop story usually occurs when the protagonist has acted badly and needs to learn a lesson. The weatherman in *Groundhog Day* must figure out how to become a better person and express true love." Ali paused in thought before continuing. "I guess the same thing happened to Ebenezer Scrooge."

"A story with which you have some connection."

"True." Ali smiled at her remembering. "Scrooge's experience is more like ours than Bill Murray's. We're experiencing shifting time periods, while he relived the same day over and over. As to why you and I are the only ones experiencing the shifts . . ." He gave her a halting glance. "I guess Pam and Darryl didn't need to take corrective action about their lives."

Fleur had to admit Ali was demonstrating some brain power too. "So, how quickly can you improve so we can get back to our own time?"

He faced her. "Don't just look at me. We're in this together. Besides, visiting the Devereaux mansion is your fantasy."

"Something you only learned by listening to my conversation with Pam."

"You weren't talking quietly, which I might add led to my losing the job when the manager came over to check on you."

"I think once you heard we had a connection with Darryl Maitland, you voluntarily quit so you could stalk us and track Maitland down."

"You flatter yourself. I could have found him easily enough through my own connections."

"Then, why were you hiding behind a newspaper in your car spying on us?"

From behind them, they heard a discreet cough. Turning, they saw a compact man wearing a bowler that he amicably tipped in their direction.

"Beggin' your pardon." His voice carried a hint of Ireland. "But when I come upon a couple so intent in their discussion, I'm loath to interrupt and even less wanting to appear as if I'm eavesdropping. Since I have disturbed, perhaps you can forgive the intrusion if I ask you to partake of a cool beverage to better enable your continued talking?"

Fleur recognized him immediately from the World's Fair photo that appeared on his Wikipedia page. "Mr. Devereaux."

He nodded. "One and the same. And who might I have the pleasure of meeting."

"Fleur Brawley."

Unexpectedly, he took her extended hand and brought it to his lips. Looking up at her, he smiled. "My wife's family was from France. She taught me proper form." He relinquished her hand and turned. "And you, sir?"

"Ali." He offered his hand to shake Devereaux's.

Fleur realized she didn't know Ali's last name, and Devereaux didn't press to learn it. Maybe he assumed they were both Brawleys.

"Shall we go into the house?" Devereaux asked, leading the way.

Ali offered her his arm. She placed her hand at his elbow. As they passed through the whale's jawbones, Fleur suspected she was entering a wonderland of her own making.

Chapter Six

Walking up the steep stairs to the welcoming porch, Fleur couldn't help but smile when she noticed a joggling board at one end. How pleasant it would be to sit swaying as the ocean breezes kept the air cool and sweet.

She entered a hallway that could have doubled for a ballroom. Seeing windows overlooking the backyard, she rushed to them, the long skirt hindering her legs' movements. But she had to try to look at the garden, if darkness had not engulfed it yet.

Her eyes squinted as she tried to make out the landscaping. Fortunately, a servant was in the process of lighting torches along a path, and Fleur spied what she had hoped to see: the rumored ship's figurehead was real and featured a saucy red-haired wench in a bright blue dress that emphasized ample cleavage. Mr. Devereaux must have had it painted. The true surprise was the figurehead's face—Fleur could have sworn it was her own mother's.

"Is it all you imagined?" Ali's voice came from close behind her.

"More." She felt the warmth in his words and for a moment was glad to be here with someone who seemed to appreciate the place as much as she did. Then, she turned to face him, crossing her arms. "I knew you overheard my conversation with Pam at Poe's Tavern."

He held up his hand in a boy scout salute. "I've already admitted my guilt. I'm always listening out for a potential character to portray. John Henry Devereaux sounded as if his life was perfect for dramatic treatment."

She gave his body a slow once over. "Not to mention a good reason for you to add some weight to your frame." His looks would improve with a few added pounds. She experienced a wave of domesticity, thinking it might be pleasurable to make Ali a hearty home-cooked meal and watch him joyously devouring it.

He leaned closer. "Good idea."

Momentarily, she was shocked to think he somehow overheard her thoughts.

"I wouldn't mind bulking up a bit," he said. "Even Poe wasn't as thin as I've become. I hope Pam doesn't polish off those nachos before we return."

Moving away from him, Fleur shook her head to clear away the random thoughts and refocus on the getting back to the present. If she must feel inclined to take care of anyone other than her daughter, it should be Darryl Maitland, whose heart-stopping good looks and easygoing personality had overwhelmed her. Darryl could offer her and Belle Deveau a happy future. Ali was a freeloader, simply hoping for a chance at another acting job.

Yet thoughts of Ali had driven Darryl from her mind.

She walked stoically toward the front of the house, not even taking the time to admire its grandeur. "I've got to get back to Belle Deveau." She couldn't let her last words to her daughter be criticism about clothing.

John Henry Devereaux's voice called from a room off the entrance hallway. "Won't you join me in the parlor?"

Ali, who had followed her, whispered in her ear, "'Said the spider to the fly.'"

She batted her hand against his chest, part playfully, but more to break the spell he was weaving—their forced collaboration was beginning to be an aphrodisiac. "You're terrible."

"One of my more endearing qualities." Unexpectedly, he took her hand. "Look, remember Bill Murray's character in *Groundhog Day*? Once he learned how to be a better person and truly love, he got to return to his regular life. That'll happen for us too."

She eyed him skeptically. "Us?" she asked.

He shrugged. "We're here together, aren't we? Just us." His expression grew more serious. "You're not alone with Darryl Maitland or . . ." He paused as if he was lost in thought.

"Pam. My friend. Darryl Maitland's cousin."

Ali smiled and slipped her hand in the crook of his arm. "Good to know the connection. Meanwhile, let's not keep our host waiting."

With what Fleur considered stately decorum, they retraced the entrance hallway, entered a sumptuous receiving room, then passed into a smaller, more intimate parlor. John Henry Devereaux had glasses filled with lemonade and motioned for them to take a seat.

A silver set displayed on a shelf caught Fleur's eye. She walked over to it, her fingers lightly touching the tray. "Is this the gift from St. Matthew's congregation?"

"That it is. Are you one of the parishioners?"

Fleur blushed. "No, but I admire your work and heard of the congregation's gratitude."

Devereaux sipped his beverage. "I'm fortunate to have fared well in this time. Some criticized my taking the federal government's money to build the post office, but it helped establish my reputation and keep my family afloat."

"You have a son and daughter and care for your mother," Fleur noted, remembering at the last minute to add, "I believe?"

His eyes twinkled. "We let my mother think she cares for us. She has been a fine influence for my daughter who lost the mother for whom she is named."

"I also lost my mother at a young age," Fleur said.

Devereaux paused before continuing. "I dare say you carry your mother's essence with you."

Fleur nodded. "I hope so."

"Loss always comes too soon. I was commissioned in the Confederate army not long after we married, then taken prisoner of war soon after my service began. My survival was fueled by determination to return to my family." He took another sip, as if washing away bad memories. "My son was born during my incarceration. My daughter came a year after I returned. My wife died the day my daughter was born."

Fleur wanted to reach out to him but wasn't sure if the gesture was proper. She kept her hands in her lap. "How difficult it must have been."

"Yes. Almost one defeat too many." He looked at Fleur and smiled. "But I have a very stubborn Irish mother."

Ali lifted his glass. "God bless them, everyone."

Devereaux chuckled. "A paraphraser of Tiny Tim's author, are you?"

Ali nodded, putting his glass down without drinking. "A poor player enchanted by greater men's words."

"My mother always said the poet immortalizes loving relationships with words. I didn't have the skill with language, but I sought to create monuments of love with my buildings."

"I love that image," Fleur said.

"That is my legacy for my lost love," Devereaux explained. "Buildings she will never see but that make the world a welcoming place for her descendants."

Fleur closed her eyes and sighed. "That's what I long to do."

"You've done it." Ali took the glass from her hand and put it down. "You've built memorials by teaching people forgotten history."

She looked deeply into his eyes. She'd often longed to hear such praise. Could he really mean it?

"Are you an educator?" Devereaux asked, downing the remaining beverage in his glass.

"Of sorts." Fleur reached for the glass Ali had taken from her.

Ali caught her hand and held it tight while shaking his head. "People come from far away to hear her lectures," he told Devereaux.

"Why?" she whispered, not understanding the reason he kept her from drinking.

"I think folks will never tire of hearing Charleston's history," Ali said, still speaking to Devereaux and not letting her hand go.

"Good," Devereaux replied. "I feared no one would want to remember the South after the war." He leaned back against the sofa, his eyelids fluttering as if they had grown heavy.

"I suspect it will always be a source of curiosity," Ali speculated. He turned to Fleur, saying quietly, "Did you notice? He seems to be fading away."

"That's absurd." But even as she spoke the words, she realized she was wrong. Devereaux's image was only a trace of what it had been. His eyelids completely closed, and a gentle snore came from his lips.

"Our fifteen minutes are almost up," Ali told her. "If we eat or drink anything, it might trap us here."

"You don't know for certain."

He squeezed her hand. "What if I'm right? Do you want to be here forever?" He looked at her glass, then picked it up. "If you're staying, I am too."

For a moment, it was so tempting. To stay here with Ali's support and Devereaux's friendship would be a dream come true. Then, her mind flooded with the image of Belle Deveau.

"No," she cried, pushing his hand to put the glass down. "I want my daughter."

Chapter Seven

Fleur sensed the darkness coming over her and the cycle beginning again. She tried to maintain consciousness, to be aware of everything happening around her. When she exited the rollback, she would be outfitted for a different time period on Sullivan's Island. If the two previous times offered guidance, it would be a year with its digits adding up to fifteen—just like 1941 and 1914.

When she opened her eyes, the houses were gone. Instead, waves lapped upon the shore where they once stood.

Her clothing had changed again, but it was similar in style to the outfit she'd worn when visiting Devereaux's mansion. Hopefully, she had not gone back further than the nineteenth century.

In the distance, she heard men calling out a military cadence. A marching song. Fort Moultrie's history went back to 1776, including a time when it was under British domination. She had to figure out the time period, and she was frustrated she could only hear the cadence's rhythm and not its words. What were those soldiers saying, and what had happened to Ali?

Twisting around, she saw him standing with his back to her. This time, he was wearing dark clothing and a flat hat. A uniform. He also seemed focused on the cadence.

"Do you recognize it?" she called to him.

"Yes. It's from Poe's time in the military. I memorized it, thinking it would give me an edge in auditions."

He turned to face her. The uniform he wore made him look more like Poe.

"Your resemblance to him is uncanny," she said.

Ali spoke with assurance. "He's not here yet."

Fleur blinked. "How do you know?"

"I would feel it if he were close by. No. He's in Richmond or Charlottesville. He's suffered a broken engagement and a flood of gambling debts. His uncle who had supported him refuses to send any more money. He's beginning to think the army is his only resort."

"How can you be sure?"

"From the digits in the year. Poe doesn't arrive at Fort Moultrie until 1827. One plus eight plus two plus seven equals eighteen, not fifteen."

"Maybe our time loop is extending, giving us more time in each historic period."

Ali shook his head. "That would be a bit ominous, don't you think? Wouldn't you expect that longer time periods mean it's less likely we can return home?"

"No!" she cried out. "That can't be. I must get back to Belle Deveau."

He kicked at the sandy beach with his boot. "I'm guessing it's 1824. The military was here, but it also had become a summer retreat for Charlestonians. Staying here might not be so bad, particularly considering what I have to look forward to in the present."

"What do you mean?"

He shrugged. "Maitland's not going to choose me for a role in his film, certainly not Poe. He'll have to offer that to an actor with star power to make the whole project bankable."

"Maitland will need consultants to make it more authentic. With all you've studied and learned—"

"And, he'll have his pick, maybe even at no cost. You can introduce Belle Deveau's dad to Will, so maybe he can at least get a mention in the film's credits." He gave her a rueful smile. "All the knowledge I've acquired makes me better outfitted to stay here, watch for Poe's arrival, follow him through the rest of his life, and figure out the answers to the mysteries that surround him."

"What value would that knowledge be if you couldn't share it with our time?"

Again, he shrugged his shoulders. "Who knows? Maybe it would give me the peace I seek, to answer my questions and live out this time with him, perhaps as a footnote in history."

The cadence sounded more strongly. He turned back to it, as if summoned.

"No, no!" She threw her arms about him. "Your place is in the present as an actor and interpreter, helping audiences understand the fascination about Poe comes from the mysteries surrounding him. You can't stay here. You must return with me."

"I'll only drag you down."

"No. We'll learn how to support each other. You'll help me be there for my daughter."

He struggled in her embrace. "I don't want your pity."

She pulled back but held on to his arms. "You don't have it. But I want to know, when you praised my skills, was it to use me—to flatter me so I would do what you wanted?"

He thought a moment, then shook his head. "Maybe it started that way, but I really do admire you. That's why I agreed to be your chauffeur almost a year ago. I saw you going after what you wanted and getting it. I wished I could use my own talent in the same way."

She smiled, her face relaxing. "Thank you. No one has ever said anything like that to me."

He brushed the toe of his shoe against the sand. "Pam seemed complimentary toward you."

"Pam's been a good friend," she agreed. "But her belief in me is usually linked to a favor she's about to ask."

"Maybe if she didn't sense you were so needy, she could focus on your friendship without constantly worrying about how to buck you up."

Her lower lip sagged into a pout. "So, you think I'm needy?"

"Yes."

The answer surprised her. She opened her mouth to respond, and he placed his finger across her lips.

"I think you are needy in the way that people who are looking out for their families and future have needs. You want your daughter to be proud of you and of herself and to be certain no doors are closed to her."

"That's true."

"And you realize that you may not always have been able to depend on others for the support you craved, but that's in the past. No matter how much you regret it, you can't change it." He dropped his voice. "And I wouldn't want you to if you could."

"Why?"

He wrapped his arms around her. "Because I wouldn't have a chance to make things right for you now."

She looked up at him. "How can I believe you?"

Ali held her more tightly. "I don't know. I have no record to point to. I just know I want to be with you. To help you find your dreams while I search for mine."

"My daughter and I are a package deal."

"An added bonus. I would love being part of Belle Deveau's life."

Fleur sensed he might be fading away. "I can't see you clearly."

"Hold on. Keep your arms around me."

She tightened her grip. "Don't let me go either."

"Nevermore."

Chapter Eight

Fleur opened her eyes. Her head felt as if it were splitting apart. She heard voices, one talking over the other.

"Call an ambulance," Darryl said.

"Is she conscious?" Pam asked.

Ali seemed close by. "Do you think we can get her to the hospital?"

"What happened?" she asked.

She looked at Ali, who held up his watch. The digital display read 19:15.

"We passed it," he told her. "We're back in the present. No longer in the time loop."

"How?"

"I don't know," he replied. "Maybe by being honest with each other. Who cares as long as we're back."

"What if we can't remain honest?"

His grin turned flirty. "Maybe we get sent back."

"No." She threw herself into his arms.

He embraced her back. "Look, it'll be okay. We'll figure it out as long as we're together."

She pulled back. "How do I know I can count on you?"

He scrutinized her face. "You can't. How does anyone know another person's heart unless they work on trust together."

She nodded. "Like creating monuments of love."

"Exactly," he agreed.

Darryl watched them suspiciously. He turned to Pam, "I think they both need medical attention. Neither one of them is making any sense."

"Fleur." Pam shoved a cell phone at her. "You need to talk to Belle Deveau. I called to let her know you'd had an accident. She wants to hear from you directly."

Sitting up, Fleur took the cell. "Sweetheart?"

Belle Deveau's voice sounded worried. "Pam said you were unconscious."

"Just for a second, sweetie. I slipped, fell, and hit my head."

"I want to go with you to the doctor."

"That's not necessary."

"Yes, it is. You might have a concussion and need someone to stay with you."

"I don't want to take you away from the engagement party."

"Dad and Mel understand. I want to be with you. Can Pam drive us?"

Fleur looked at Ali, who had been watching her carefully. "Actually, someone else may be able to help. Do you remember Ali?"

"Mel's Ali?"

"Yes."

"I thought you didn't like him."

Fleur smiled. "I may be reconsidering."

Belle Deveau paused before replying, "If Mel saw something good in him, he can't be all bad."

Fleur laughed. "You can help me decide."

"Hurry, Mom. I'm waiting."

"We're on our way." Fleur promised. As she disconnected, she looked at Ali. "Aren't we?"

His lips curved in a smile never seen on portraits of Edgar Allan Poe. "Evermore," he answered.

The End

About Paula Gail Benson

A legislative attorney and former law librarian, Paula Gail Benson has short stories published online in the *Bethlehem Writers Roundtable* and *Kings River Life* as well as in the electronic and print anthologies: *Mystery Times Ten 2013*; *A Tall Ship, a Star, and Plunder*; *A Shaker of Margaritas: That Mysterious Woman*; *Let It Snow*; *Fish or Cut Bait: a Guppy Anthology*; *Love in the Lowcountry: A Winter Holiday Collection, Volumes 1 and 2*; *Heartbreaks and Half-truths*; *An Element of Mystery*; Malice Domestic's *Mystery Most Diabolical*; *A Death in the Night*; *Dark of the Day*; *Smoking Guns*; and *Season's Readings: More Sweet, Funny, and Strange Holiday Tales (A Sweet, Funny, and Strange Anthology)*.

In *Killer Nashville Noir: Cold Blooded*, she co-authored "A Matter of Honor" with New York Times Bestselling thriller writer Robert Dugoni.

Her work appears in four of the Red Penguin Collection's publications: *The Empty Stage*; *Once Upon a Time*; *Stand Out: the Best of the Red Penguin Collection, Volume 2*; and *My Robot and Me*.

In addition to short stories, she writes and directs one act plays and musicals for her church's drama ministry. Her article on how to promote short stories is in *Promophobia: Taking the Mystery Out of Promoting Crime Fiction* (a Sisters in Crime publication that won the Agatha Award for Best Nonfiction). She regularly blogs with others about writing mysteries and romances at the Stiletto Gang and Writers Who Kill.

Find Paula Online:

Blogs: http://littlesourcesofjoy.blogspot.com/
http://www.thestilettogang.com
https://writerswhokill.blogspot.com/
Email: paula@paulagailbenson.com
Facebook: https://www.facebook.com/paula.benson.161
X: https://twitter.com/PaulaGBenson
Website: http://paulagailbenson.com
Instagram: https://www.instagram.com/pollygail/
Amazon:https://www.amazon.com/Paula-Gail-Benson/e/B001KCLXI0

Analysis of Love

by Linda Joyce

Analysis of Love

by Linda Joyce

Career-driven Olympia Grant Hughes believes in compromise and respect, which has earned her a sterling business reputation, a hefty bank account, and the condo of her dreams, but her life's portfolio lacks love. Love requires vulnerability—a risk she'd not been able to take.

Noah Rutledge is his own man. Runs his own company. Carved his own path, not relying on his family name or connections. His gut is his guide, the wind that fills his sails. When he meets Olympia, it's love at first sight.

Can Noah persuade Olympia to open her heart to the possibility of forever love?

Chili Pepper Rating: 0.5

Chapter One

Hartford, Connecticut
Mid-November

Pia pushed her reading glasses on top of her head, then gently rubbed her tired eyes. Soothing jazz floated around her. Sitting in the dining room, folders spread out before her, she sipped the last of red wine from her second glass since dinner. With every tick of the clock, her career, her pride, her future imploded.

"Enough." She slapped her hand on a folder. "Ten o'clock on a Saturday night and again my date is a spreadsheet. Life is different than I imagined it'd be at thirty-nine." She paused when the image of her father popped into her mind. "Yes, Dad, I'm grateful to be alive."

She pushed her laptop away, folded her arms on the table, and rested her head. Months ago, she'd warned the board of directors about potential doom. Now, internal reports, economic forecasts, and the Fed's reaction to inflation offered a picture that had the company's senior management acting like ostriches with their heads in the sand. "Nothing more to do but call Dixon for a stiff drink."

Bzz. Bzz.

Pia opened one eye. Patted around the table, found her cell phone, and answered, "Olympia Graham Hughes speaking."

"Pia, it's only eleven p.m. Did I wake you?" Her mother's voice broke through Pia's haze. "Are you with Dixon?"

"No, I'm home." Dixon was her "surrogate" boyfriend. No romantic attachments. However, relationship details had been painted differently to her mother to keep her worries at bay.

"Home? You're working, aren't you? You work too much. Anyway, Pia, I need your help."

"I'm at your service." Her mother rarely asked for anything, other than for Pia to be surrounded by love, hence the Dixon white lie.

"I've booked you a flight for Monday evening into Charleston—think of it as a vacation with your sister. We'll meet at the airport. You'll take care of Carolina here while I go to Rome."

Pia sat up. Where had she gotten lost in the conversation? "What?"

"Baby, I've got to go," her mother whispered. "Hunter and I are working on reconciling. I can't tell Carolina why I'm going. Can't get her hopes up. And I can't leave her alone—especially during the holiday."

Pia sighed.

When I was sixteen and Dad died, you had no problem leaving me alone...

While she and her half sister weren't especially close, she never wanted her to feel abandoned. In Carolina's case, her father had left, but he was still very much alive.

"I have a ticket for Christmas. But you want me to come now?"

"Well...I want us all to be together then. But I need you now—I don't know how long I'll be gone. After all, it's not like there's a formula for reconciling with a husband."

Her and her mother's relationship was separate from Hunter, separate from Carolina. Pia stood outside that family bubble and gazed inside, like watching life inside a snow globe.

"Mother. My job—"

"Olympia Graham Hughes, I need you. Your sister needs you. What's the point of power and money if you don't use it? A millionaire at twenty-five? A hedge fund manager at thirty-two? A million-dollar condo in Connecticut?" Her mother's voice steadily rose. "I never taught you to measure success in dollars and cents. Love is what's important."

Dealing with facts, numbers, work was infinitely easier than dealing with her personal life. Over the years, love had proven to be messy.

Pia sighed. "Mother, I'll be there." She couldn't possibly refuse.

"Thank you, baby. I knew I could count on you."

Pia set her phone down. "Company Director to Babysitter—a significant title change. And a job for which I possess no qualifications."

At sixteen, she'd thought by now she'd be in a committed relationship, maybe married or a mother. Yet she had none of that. She wasn't unhappy being alone, but it wasn't what she wanted for the rest of her life.

Her therapist had told her love required vulnerability, compromise, respect. "You have this ideal you cling to that a man can never live up to. You try to tightly control all aspects of your life. Consider this, if your ideal man walked through the door right now, would you be his ideal woman?"

That thought had haunted her for the last four years.

She could handle respect and compromise. Vulnerability held her back. And now she wanted more than a surrogate boyfriend. Maybe it was finally time to take a risk on the advice she'd paid for.

Maybe.

Or maybe not.

Chapter Two

Charleston, South Carolina
Thursday before Thanksgiving

The South Carolina sunlight winked at Pia through pine and palm trees. She released her tight grip on the steering wheel, flipped her sunglasses off her face, and repositioned her hands on the wheel. After quick glances in the mirrors of her new Lincoln Navigator, she drew a deep breath, exhaled, turned the steering wheel for a third try at backing in.

"How in all that's holy does this school expect a parent to park a vehicle in these tight spaces?"

She snorted. Painted white lines caused the parking problem. She'd solve that easily.

Warning beeps blared. Red lights flashed on the dash. She slammed on the brakes to avoid crushing the convertible in the next space, her composure now crushed. "Parking lessons. Is that what I need?" She slammed her hand on the steering wheel, which activated the horn. Startled, she jerked her hand away.

Honk. Honk.

Outside the Navigator, other drivers punctuated their displeasure.

Pia glanced at the rude drivers producing noise pollution and caught movement to her left. A man exited a white pickup. He rushed in her direction—T-shirt with the school's logo, cap on his head, sunglasses hid his eyes, his mouth quirked to one side.

"Lady!" he shouted on his approach. "If you'll get out"—she lowered the driver's window as he continued toward her—"I'll park your boat. Then we can all go about our day."

"What?" Then she noticed all the cars stopped behind the man's truck.

"Please, lady." His tone carried impatience. "I'm needed at a jobsite in thirty minutes. Name's Noah. Everyone knows me." He motioned to the school's logo on his shirt. "You can trust me."

"Absolutely not." Her anxiety soared. It had been years since she'd owned a vehicle. Months since she'd driven anything other than a golf cart. Let someone else take the wheel of her brand-new SUV? No. No. And no.

Beep. Beep.

She took a second survey of the parking quagmire. Cars four deep to her right. She couldn't pull forward without hitting one of them. She'd failed three attempts to back her "boat," as he'd called it. And she was about to be late for her meeting with the principal.

Pia looked him over. Early thirties, a little younger than her. Tanned, but not like he spent all day, every day in the sun. Taller than her—she could wear heels.

She shook her head at that thought. Where did that come from?

"Ma'am, I'm asking nicely. Please, help me help you. Let me park this thing."

His "help me help you" had her opening the door and sliding out. Those were the very words she'd used in her email to her boss about the business. Yet her boss had rejected sound analysis. She would not do the same.

She went to his truck. When she turned back, the man had parked the SUV between the lines, windows up. He exited and moved in her direction.

"Thank you." She stepped aside.

He waved her off. "Just ask Principal Phillips. She'll be happy to sing my praises and dish on my faults."

Once inside his truck, he drove farther into the campus.

Pia headed for the school's entrance. Palmetto Prep was her high school alma mater. Inside the office, a man at the front desk motioned for her to sign the visitor's register.

"Olympia Graham Hughes to see Principal Phillips." She scribbled her signature.

"Ms. Hughes, welcome. Dr. Phillips is expecting you. Please, follow me." He ushered her into a sunlit office. A large desk sat in the middle of the room. Bookcases lined the side walls. A couch and two chairs created a comfortable sitting area. The potted plants added a calming touch.

"If you need anything, Principal Phillips, please let me know." The man closed the door behind him.

"Pia, I'm so happy to see you!" Dr. Jordan Phillips scooped her into a hug. "It's been too long, cousin. I'm glad you're here. If anyone can help Carolina through this, it's you."

Pia hugged her older cousin; little had change about her smile and warm personality.

Jordan released her but gripped her arms. "It's ironic. You lost your father when you were sixteen. Uncle Chandler was a gentleman and scholar. I know Carolina's situation is not the same, but the absence of a father is still felt."

"Thanks, Jordan. Help me deal with Carolina. At work, I handle deals worth millions. In my private life, I can't handle a sixteen-year-old."

"Trust me, being a parent and making good decisions is no different from assessing risk and making an informed decision." Jordan's tone offered compassion.

"But she's blood and flesh and hormonal. Money bears no resemblance to those characteristics." Pia sighed.

"And she's in the new infirmary, waiting for you." Jordan stepped back. "She had a meltdown during the Student Council meeting, but the cause of her tears is the result of someone saying something mean about her father being away for Thanksgiving."

"I remember how painful gossip was at her age. Were we this cruel then?" Pia asked. Jordan had been a senior when Pia started her freshman year.

Jordan shrugged. "Teenagers of every generation are…teenagers. You can't predict Carolina's emotional state. Maybe it's good she came to school. You suggested she stay home. You let her make a decision, a decision she now regrets. Going forward, maybe she'll take the time to consider your input before being stubbornly insistent. Maybe this will create a bonding moment between the two of you."

"I guess the difference between Carolina and me is that I know I'm clueless," Pia whispered. "And my mother said this was a vacation."

Jordan chuckled.

Pia did not. "By the way, Dr. Phillips, this guy, Noah, ended up parking the Nav for me. Who is he?"

"Besides eye candy?" Jordan winked. "He owns NR Construction. Now, follow me. Let's go help Carolina."

Chapter Three

Pia followed Jordan to the infirmary. The outer door appeared the same as when she'd attended Palmetto Prep, except for new white paint. Inside, the oak-paneled room had been transformed into a clean white infirmary. Now, curtains hung from ceiling tracks and offered privacy for each of four beds. One of them sheltered her sister.

"You're finally here," Carolina whined. "By all means, move at a glacial pace. You know how that thrills me."

"Good luck," Jordan whispered. "I still want a plaque with your name on the door. We'll discuss that later."

Pia felt a slight shove before her cousin departed with the school nurse in tow.

Striding across the room, Pia stopped beside a bed. "That's Meryl Streep as Miranda Priestly in *The Devil Wears Prada*." She and her mother had seen it in the theater when it was released. "The 2006 movie is two years older than you."

"Mother watched it with me for my sixteenth birthday." Carolina's tears spilled down her cheeks.

Pia sighed again. Carolina's father had been a no-show to celebrate her sixteenth birthday. Their mother, Shelley, had tried to give her younger daughter a memorable experience. A spa day. A nice meal. A movie. Just the two of them. Pia had been invited, but work had kept her away.

Well…she let work be the excuse.

Pia's heart felt weighed down with iron anchors. Had she come, she and her sister might have created a nice memory. However, memories of her own sixteenth birthday and the news of her father's death had overlaid Pia's decision. Carolina's father had left—not died—there was no true comparison.

She sank onto the bed beside Carolina and reached for her hand. The teenager flinched, scooting away as though burned.

"Carolina," Pia said softly. "I'm very sorry I wasn't here, last month, for your birthday."

Carolina stood, smoothed imaginary wrinkles from her school uniform, and then picked up her backpack. "Let's go," she ordered.

"Yes, let's." Pia was grateful for the about-face. "I need to stop at the grocery store. You can stay in the boat or come inside with me."

"Boat?" Carolina pushed open the infirmary's door. Noise from students in the hallway filtered in—giggles and shouts and the banging of a bouncing ball.

"Well, some guy called it my Navigator "a boat," but he was kind enough to park for me in those tight spaces out front."

"You're supposed to park big vehicles by the gym. Didn't you read the sign?"

"OMG!" squealed a voice coming from the hallway. "Did you see Coach Rutledge?"

"Olympia." Carolina turned back to her. "Ignore these childish girls. They do not represent the standard of a true Palmetto Prep student." She crossed the threshold into the vortex of a gaggle of gossiping girls.

Her sister's presence quelled the roar swirling in the hallway. Students parted as though a red carpet had been laid out for Carolina.

Pia followed several feet behind, impressed by the maturity her sister displayed in front of her classmates. Where two halls intersected, Carolina navigated to the left, heading toward the school office and then the front doors leading to the parking lot.

A handsome young man—Pia guessed the student to be a senior—walked toward Carolina. He stopped. She stopped. His face remained unreadable. But…a look about his eyes when he gazed at Carolina blazed with tender affection so intense that Pia glanced away.

When she looked back, Carolina had handed him her backpack. He took her hand. The two walked through the school's front doors and into November's sunlight.

Stunned, Pia stopped and gazed at the pair beyond the doors, still holding hands, standing side by side. The scene had to be the most touching display of love and support she'd ever witnessed.

Who is he?

A tap on her shoulder pulled her back to her surroundings.

"Hello again. It's your friendly boat captain."

Pia lifted her gaze, locking onto deep brown eyes that appeared lit from within.

"Your boat's trapped," he continued. "I'll get you out, if you'd like."

"Trapped?" She was. In his gaze. Stunned at that realization, she stuttered, "Y-you're Noah, right? More-than-eye-candy Noah."

"Excuse me?"

Her cheeks heated. "Ah. Sorry." She offered her hand. "I'm Olympia Graham Hughes. I'm Carolina's sister. You know her, yes?"

"You're Pia?" He took a step back and looked her over. "Not exactly what I expected."

She drew back. Was there something wrong with Japanese custom-made jeans, Italian black leather boots, a T-shirt, and a Burberry plaid jacket?

She perused him. Gone was his cap. His dark brown hair, no longer hidden, had been scooped behind his ears. His sunglasses dangled from the neck of his shirt. His jeans fit—not too tight, not baggy. His work boots appeared appropriately worn. He was…too athletic, too toned, too much of everything that wasn't her type. He probably didn't own a suit. But she couldn't shake the feeling of being drawn to his eyes.

"This is awkward." She looked down. "Yes, I'm Pia. But only to my family and friends."

"Ahh…that's the Pia I heard about."

She locked eyes with him again.

"I was told she's a bit prickly around the edges." He grinned. His brown eyes sparkled. "I'm Justin Rutledge's uncle." He pointed to the young man still holding her sister's hand. "And part-time soccer coach."

"Noah. Rutledge. Of the Rutledges?" Their history was deep and long in South Carolina, going back to when it was a British colony.

His demeanor shifted at the mention of his family's reputation. She caught his slight wince.

"You're blocked," he said. "Cars on either side of you are so close you can't open a door. If you'll open the sunroom—I mean sunroof—I'll climb in and pull your boat forward."

She would never have thought of doing that, instead would've called a tow truck for assistance. However, he pointed out an obvious problem. Offered a reasonable solution. He had an analytical mind. Intelligence. That she found sexy.

Never had she ever thought she'd need a knight in shining armor. Yet twice, Noah had come to her rescue. Some folks might call it fate.

She called it embarrassing.

It demonstrated her lack of skills in simple matters of everyday life. At least his demonstration would be educational in case the "boat" was ever sandwiched again.

"Thank you." She reached into her purse and pulled out her keys.

His fingers lingered on hers when she offered them to him. He stared into her eyes as though trying to communicate something.

Her heart expanded. Contracted. Fluttered. "Keys?" she asked.

His fingers still lingered.

"Something wrong?" Her heart raced when he still didn't take them.

Noah's eyes blazed with humor. He winked.

He was flirting with her!

She couldn't remember when that had happened last.

But this was not fate.

Only a nostalgic response to a guy at a high school.

She pointed to her SUV. "Mr. Noah Rutledge, I'm in your care. Show me what you've got."

He was a good-looking guy. Really good-looking guy. Even if his brawn wasn't her type.

Chapter Four

Pia waited beside Carolina and Justin as Noah pulled the Navigator forward, allowing room to open the doors. He hopped out and held the door for her. Jordan was right. Eye-candy Noah.

"Thank you." She emphasized the words; it was a sincere response of gratitude.

"You're welcome. And I know you want to return the kindness. Let's do a double date tomorrow. We'll take Justin and Carolina to dinner at Shem Creek."

Pia blinked. Had he just asked her out? "Ah…"

"I'll take that as a yes." He waved, then walked toward the school's entrance.

She forced herself to turn her attention to Carolina and Justin.

They knew more about romance than she did, and Pia took note of every move Justin made. After putting Carolina's backpack on the backseat, he tucked her into the front passenger seat, then clicked her seatbelt into place. He wasn't treating her like a helpless child. His gentle care resonated with chivalry. A knight taking care of his lady.

Pia shook her head. Where had he learned to do that? Some British etiquette class during a semester abroad?

He backed away from the SUV and closed the door. Throughout the entire interaction, neither he nor Carolina spoke. Yet it was obvious they communicated, as though reading each other's minds.

Justin waved as Pia pulled away. A stab of jealousy irritated her. How had Carolina, at sixteen, found someone so endearing, yet Pia's love life was lacking?

"You can't date Mr. Rutledge," Carolina said, breaking the silence.

"What are you talking about?" Pia checked for traffic before changing lanes.

"Coach Rutledge, my soccer coach. Noah Rutledge. Justin's uncle. All one in the same." Carolina's gaze remained straight ahead. Her speech, too straightforward.

"I just met the guy."

"Don't sound incredulous. Love at first sight, first touch, first eye contact, can happen. Plus, he's only thirty-four."

"I really don't know what you're talking about." Pia focused on the traffic. "How about we do something after dinner? Ice cream? Maybe a movie—at a theater?"

"I want to go to the beach." Carolina folded her hands in her lap and hung her head. "I won't go back to the house."

"Carolina, I'd like a beach break, too. But sweetheart, we have responsibilities and obligations to attend—"

"That's how you think of me," she shouted.

Pia sighed. "I didn't mean it to come out all businesslike and clinical. I'm explaining we need groceries and to organize the schedule for next week—a vacation week."

"Sorry for yelling. My feelings are jammed up. I don't understand why my dad took a job in Italy. I feel guilty because I refused to move. Look what I did to my parents' marriage. What am I going to do?" Carolina choked out a sob.

Pia pulled into a parking lot and stopped, hoping her sister's crying would subside. Heart aching, no longer able to wait—uncertain if her sister would reject her again—she steadied her shaking hands before she reached across the console and pulled Carolina close. "I'm so sorry. You need Mama right now. You could use your daddy, too. But I'm afraid I'm it. I promise I'll do the best job I can while I'm here." She stroked her sister's hair. "I love you."

"Job?" Carolina asked, sniffing, pulling away. "That's what I am to you. Do I have to go into the grocery store? Can I stay in the car?"

This was one of those times when Pia wished she'd spent more time in therapy, then maybe she'd know how to comfort her sister. "You can stay, though grocery shopping is a very adult activity. I could use your help. Let's do this together."

To her surprise, Carolina followed her into the store, grabbed a shopping buggy, and began selecting fruit. They walked up one aisle and down the next. Pia stopped by several items and shared a memory about eating it for the first time—like a full bag of chips when studying for a college final. In the next aisle, Carolina joined in the game.

Pia hid her smile. Jordan had been right. A bad day could turn into a bonding one.

After checking out, Pia pushed the buggy outside. She met, head-on, Justin and Noah. Carolina motioned for Justin to follow her. Confused, Pia watched them walk toward an ice-cream shop two doors down, then she turned at the clink of glass. Noah, cap and sunglasses back in place, had placed a bottle of white wine and a six-pack of beer into her buggy.

"What?" she asked.

"For later. I'll come by and have a drink. I told Justin he could borrow my truck and take Carolina to the beach. But they'll be back by ten."

"What?" she insisted.

"I think we need to get to know each other better. For the sake of the kids. They can hang out for a while tonight. They're good kids—no worries." He walked around the buggy, came up beside her, leaned in, and whispered close to her ear, "Besides, Dr. Phillips told me I have you to thank for the infirmary job."

Pia wasn't sure if it was his warm breath on her ear or the sultriness of his voice, but a shiver ran up her spine.

Noah Rutledge was as unusual as he was attractive. She was intrigued. Her instant analysis said they had respect for each other—she'd accepted his help twice that day. There was compromise—she wouldn't permit Carolina to date on a school night, but she'd allow it with Justin. It was vulnerability that prevented her from allowing giddiness from Noah's attention to surface. Carolina was right. She could not think about dating Noah Rutledge. Yet she couldn't not think about it.

"Great! It's a date." Noah stroked his finger down the outside of her arm, then jogged toward his truck.

His touch surprised her. Excited her. Panicked her.

"No," she said. "No. No means no."

However, Noah was out of earshot.

Chapter Five

Sunset ushered in a cool November evening. Pia and Noah stood in the driveway at her mother's house and waved. The deep bass thudding from the truck's stereo could be heard until Justin turned onto the main street. The truck disappeared into traffic, taking Carolina to the beach.

Pia looked at her watch. Six p.m. The kids were due back by ten o'clock, the curfew Noah laid down and Justin agreed to.

But what would she and Noah do for four hours?

Noah shoved his hands into the front pockets of his jeans. The bump of his elbow against her arm, the tilt of his head, and the cut of his eyes toward the house conveyed his suggestion of going inside.

"Glass of wine time?" She pointed to the door.

"Won't turn down a beer." He grinned.

His smile was as beguiling as it was persuasive. "He's totally not my type," she muttered, leading the way. But then again, at thirty-nine, single, and her employment status teetering on unemployment, did she even know what her type was anymore?

In the kitchen, she pulled two bottles of beer from the fridge, popped the caps, and handed one to Noah. "Cheers." She clinked her bottle against his. Had she had beer straight from a bottle?

"Would a movie or talking get your mind off whatever is keeping those cogs in your brain turning?" Noah asked.

"What kind of movies do you like?" She had no intention of sharing her inner thoughts regarding anything personal. "You want the conflict and confrontation of thrillers or war movies? Or are you a sci-fi fan? Or will you shock me and confess to liking rom-coms?"

"Well…what was the last rom-com you saw?" His tone carried a challenge.

"I read. I rarely watch movies or TV."

He glanced from the family room to the back door. "Plan B. It's cool enough for a fire in the pit, and we could talk, since I get the feeling you'll do a character analysis about me based on my movie tastes. If I'm going to be judged, I want it to be based on something other than eye candy and movies."

Her cheeks heated. The man could read people. And he was right about the analysis. Besides, she didn't want him judging her based on what other people had told him.

He went to the desk and pulled out a box of long matches. "I'll start a fire."

"You sure know your way around my mother's house."

"Yeah." He nodded. "I've spent my share of time with Hunter, though he doesn't seem to know much about you. Your mother is a proud mama. Carolina tows the line, sticking to facts about you, doesn't get off in the emotional weeds—usually. Her meltdown worried Justin."

"I'm at a disadvantage." Not being on equal informational footing made Pia's internal vulnerability dragon rear up and want to defend. But what? Noah wasn't a physical threat, though his good looks could be a secret weapon. He was intellectually interesting, very sexy. Emotionally, she hadn't gotten a good read on him.

"Then let's level the playing field. I'll make a fire. You grab a couple beers and join me in fifteen minutes. I'll answer any and all questions."

"Alcohol on an empty stomach? I'll get snacks."

Noah saluted and left, taking his beer with him.

Pia admired the hug of his jeans as he turned toward the sliding glass back door.

He might not be my type, but he is nice to look at. He's like art. I wouldn't buy a Jackson Pollock, my tastes run more to a Monet. However, I can appreciate a Pollock.

"Are you staring at my butt?" Noah called out, pointing to her reflection in the window beside the door to the backyard.

When the door closed behind him, Pia paused. "Does he wear Calvin Klein undies?" Her cheeks flushed. She took a draw on her beer. "Where did that thought come from?"

After raiding the fridge, Pia put together an appetizing charcuterie platter. She finished her beer and grabbed two more before picking up the platter and heading to the back door. As she approached, it opened. Noah took the platter, then the beers from her.

"It's a little cool. I'll be back with a couple of blankets," she said. There was something relaxing about a cool South Carolina fall and a fire. And because Noah had stayed for the evening, she wasn't worried about Carolina. The idea of sitting by the firepit, drinking beer with a sexy man, made her giggle. She covered her mouth to muffle the sound.

Pia returned with blankets and settled onto the couch. Noah stoked the fire, then draped her lap with one of the blankets. He moved a side table and the charcuterie platter close enough for her to reach.

Then he sat beside her.

She raised an eyebrow at him.

He raised an eyebrow back—a question but also a challenge.

She shrugged. For goodness' sake, she was five years older than him. Their lives were worlds apart.

But then he scooted closer and tugged on her blanket to cover his lap, too.

If she didn't know better, she'd think he was flirting with her.

Seriously flirting.

Her heart fluttered. A little flirting never hurt anyone.

Or at least that was her less-than-solid analysis.

Chapter Six

Now this was a vacation.

The fire crackled in the unusually cool autumn air. Smoke curled, lifting upward. Pia took tiny sips of her beer to distract herself from her rising awareness of the man beside her. He appeared to be completely at ease with their closeness. Dang if she didn't feel like a high schooler. A never-been-kissed schoolgirl.

She needed the tension within her to melt before it exploded—she wanted him to kiss her. What if she leaned in, but he turned away? What if he wasn't experiencing the same heart-fluttering appeal?

She took a gulp of beer.

There was a lot to be said for old-fashioned attraction.

Noah reached for the platter and offered it to her. "I don't want to be accused of trying to get you drunk before I take advantage of you." His grin let her know he was teasing. Maybe it was his way of letting the air out of her ramped-up tension. "Tell me about the cheese selections."

She pointed. "This is Manchego. Made of sheep's milk. From Spain."

"And this one"—he plucked a slice and placed it onto a cracker—"goat cheese with blueberries."

After he ate, he licked his lips.

She stared. She'd seen a man eat before. She'd seen a man lick his lips before. She'd never been mesmerized by that simple action.

She lifted her gaze and caught his. His eyes spoke of seriousness, interest, and desire.

He leaned closer.

Her eyes still captured by his, her brain spun, her body leaned in his direction. His lips parted. Her heart raced. He was about to kiss her.

Time slowed.

The crackle of the fire grew softer.

The thudding of her heart grew louder in her ears.

Bzz. Bzz.

"Grrrr," Noah growled and reached for his phone in his pocket. "Justin's calling me?"

Bzz. Bzz.

Pia reached for her phone in her jacket.

"Hello?" Pia and Noah said simultaneously.

Carolina's wail came so loud, Pia moved the phone away from her ear. She rose and walked toward the back door. "Carolina, honey, take a deep breath. Go slow, sweetie." She couldn't understand her sister's garbled words. Tension shot through Pia's body like a rocket lifting off.

"What? How? Where?" Noah's voice rose with each word.

Pia turned when he popped up from the couch.

"Pia, they won't…won't let me go in the ambulance…with…with Justin. He's hurt!" Carolina's words came between sobs.

"Where are you?" Pia asked. "I'll be right there. Breathe."

"Isle of Palms." Carolina drew in a breath, then exhaled. "Waterway Boulevard near the public boat dock."

"How bad?" Pia heard Noah ask.

"They're taking Justin to the emergency room in Mt. Pleasant," Carolina wailed.

"Are you hurt?" Pia asked her sister, her concern soaring.

"Banged up, but the hit was to the driver's door." Carolina's voice warbled. "A truck hit us. I think that driver's drunk."

"Devin, listen to me. Put her in an ambulance, too." Noah's voice was steel and stone. "Just because she's not bleeding doesn't mean she isn't injured."

Pia felt the heat of a hand wrap around her wrist.

"We've got to go. Now." Noah opened the back door and pulled her into the house. "Where are your keys? I'll drive."

Later that night, Pia sank onto the couch in the family room. The room was dark except for the light from the gas log dancing in the fireplace. Heat from a mug of hot chocolate, the marshmallows melting, warmed her hands. She'd be taking Xanax instead of sipping cocoa had it not been for Noah's calm and commanding presence when the evening had taken a hard turn into scary territory.

From the moment he grabbed her wrist until his friend drove her and Carolina home, Noah had been a pillar of strength. His concern for Justin and Carolina overshadowed any talk about damage to his work truck.

Trying to make sense of the emotional overload, she replayed the events in her head.

She'd stood in the hallway, about twenty feet from Noah, when her sister was taken for a CT scan. Nearly trembling from the shock of Justin covered in blood and Carolina in a neck brace, she observed the interactions of hospital staff and overheard conversations—insights into Noah Rutledge.

"He's the boy's uncle and adopted father. I'll tell you later about that situation," a nurse said to another nurse.

"What would Justin do without Noah? And what will Noah do when Justin goes off to college next year? He's raised that boy into a fine young man," another nurse replied.

An EMS driver approached Noah. "Man," the EMS driver said, grabbing him by the shoulders. "This isn't like Austin and Amber's accident. I was at that accident, remember? I held your brother while he died. I know Justin will be fine. Head wounds always bleed."

A male nurse joined Noah and the driver, handing Noah a cup of coffee. "You can wait in the waiting room, or I'll get you a chair and put it in the hallway, so you know when Justin is finished in radiology."

"Two chairs, please," Noah said. Then he walked toward Pia and opened his arms.

She ran to him. He embraced her, cradling the back of her head. She clung to him. He was sanity in the insanity of the moment.

Noah stroked her head. "They'll be fine."

To muffle her cries, she buried her face in his neck.

"They'll be fine," he murmured over and over until she was weak from crying.

The doctor arrived and explained Carolina's injury: a mild concussion, whiplash, and bruises could be expected. She needed rest. Carolina wasn't to push herself. Pia could take her home.

The doctor turned to Noah. "Justin is receiving a few stitches to his head. He has a concussion. Whiplash. No herniations found. No strenuous activities for at least three weeks. I'll give him something for headaches. He sustained a left fibula fracture. He'll be in a boot for about six weeks. Dr. Lloyd will follow up with his care. We're going to keep him overnight. See how he's doing in the morning."

"Thanks, Doctor," Noah said.

Pia watched the man beside her take several deep breaths. His steel backbone flexed with relief.

"Could I have a recliner brought into his room?" Noah asked. "I'll be staying with him."

Carolina was released before Justin finished his treatment.

"I don't want you to drive," Noah told Pia. "I called friends. They'll take you and Carolina home in your car."

"Thank you. I'm too shaken to drive." She clasped her hands together to steady them.

Noah waved goodbye in the hallway when she followed the nurse pushing Carolina's wheelchair to the front doors.

Turning just before Noah would be out of sight, Pia waved back. He had nodded.

However, what she had wanted was to run to him again and hug him and comfort him like he'd comforted her.

His final wave good-bye felt lonely.

But she had her own patient—Carolina—to care for.

This was not the vacation she'd imagined.

Chapter Seven

An hour later, Pia remained still planted on the couch, soaking in the comfort of the fireplace and the blanket covering her lap. Hot cocoa comforted her, but it hadn't erased her anxiety.

How shocked would her mother be when she learned of the accident?

Several times, she'd picked up her phone and considered calling Rome. Yet that would startle her mother awake, and she didn't want her mother to think her incapable of caring for Carolina. Yes, it was a significant accident. Yes, Carolina sustained minor injuries. Yes, she'd been terrified for her sister. Thanks to Noah, her meltdown was private.

"I'll see how Carolina is in the morning." She'd "mother up" and wait until Carolina woke. It would be best if the two of them did a video call to assure Carolina's parents of her condition.

It was nearing two in the morning when Pia's phone vibrated. Noah's name flashed.

A surge of concern flashed within Pia.

"Hello?" she answered quickly.

"Hello." Noah sounded tired. "Sorry to intrude so late. I intended to leave a message. Just wanted to let you know Justin is finally in a room and resting."

She heard concern, hesitation, exhaustion, and love for Justin in his voice.

"Prognosis is the same?" She wanted to ask about Austin and Amber's accident—what had happened to them. But now wasn't the time.

"He's not going to like the haircut he's got, but that's the least of my concerns. He's resting comfortably. We'll see how he does throughout the night. He might be released tomorrow. How's Carolina?"

"Asleep. She cried about Justin. I'm sure she'll want to see him in the morning, if that's okay with you."

"Sure. And Pia, I'm sorry about the accident. I hate that Carolina was injured. I'm not sure how this will impact Justin beyond his physical condition. That worries me the most."

"Noah, neither you nor Justin caused this accident. An irresponsible drunk driver did. I am so grateful it wasn't worse." She wouldn't tell him how shaken she'd been when she'd seen Justin, bleeding and so still, lying on the gurney. "What exactly do you mean by 'beyond his physical condition'?"

He sighed. "I'll explain that another time. I think Carolina knows… Anyway, I hope you'll get some sleep."

"Good night, Noah." She didn't tell him that she had planned to sit in Carolina's room in case her sister woke up during the night. Not knowing how the accident affected her sister beyond her physical condition, she didn't want her to be alone.

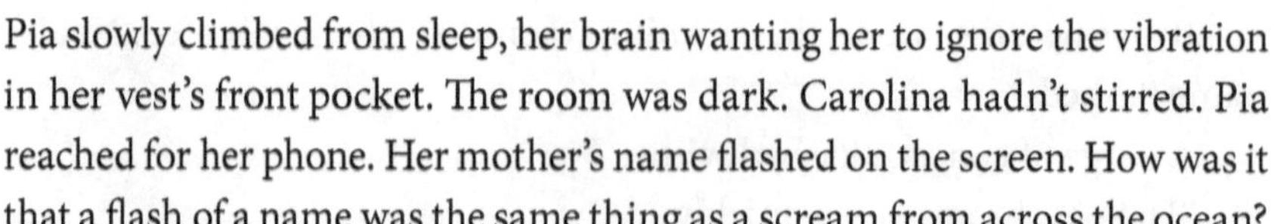

Pia slowly climbed from sleep, her brain wanting her to ignore the vibration in her vest's front pocket. The room was dark. Carolina hadn't stirred. Pia reached for her phone. Her mother's name flashed on the screen. How was it that a flash of a name was the same thing as a scream from across the ocean?

She quietly headed for the family room.

"Mother," Pia whispered. "It's five a.m. here. What's up?"

"Olympia Graham Hughes, what happened? Devin called Hunter. Carolina was in an accident? How's is she?"

"Devin? Who?" Then Pia recalled Noah on the phone with someone named Devin after the accident. "A friend of Noah Rutledge?"

"Yes. He's with EMS. Please, how's Carolina?"

"Well, right now, I'm trying not to wake her. I slept in the chair in her room."

"Is it that serious?"

"She has a mild concussion. Mild whiplash. Probably have bruises. Overall, she's more upset about Justin."

"My baby and Justin could've been killed! How's he doing?"

"Noah let me know Justin is doing okay. Overnight in the hospital. Hopes to be released today."

"I'm headed home on the next flight. I'll get someone to pick me up. You stay with Carolina. No leaving the house until I get home."

"Mother, do you think I can't take care of her? Are things situated with you and Hunter? I think you need to stay there. I didn't mention this before, but isn't part of the issue between you and Hunter about you smothering Carolina and…neglecting your husband? A man, who I believe, is a good husband and father."

"Pia, I never knew you felt that way."

"Well…Mom, truth is, it's none of my business. I only want y'all to be happy."

"Y'all? Olympia, I haven't heard you use that expression since you left for college. So you can handle Carolina? Teenager. Drama queen. Patient? But still a girl, trying to grow up too fast."

"I'm saying I believe I have the support I need to take care of her here. There's Jordan, if I need her. There's Noah. And it appears he knows every-one, so should I need advice or help, I believe I have it."

"Well…just so you know, Hunter agrees with you." She sighed. "As soon as Carolina is up, call me. After I see her, I'll make my decision about coming home. But know this, my decision isn't about whether or not you're capable but more about my mama-heart fear."

"Video call. A sound strategy, Mother."

"And Pia…I'm so proud of you. Thank you. I love you."

Pia's eyes filled with tears. "I love you, too."

After the call, Pia sat on the couch. The house wasn't her family home. Hunter had bought it when Carolina was born. As for the family, maybe she needed to try fitting in. She never gave Hunter any consideration. He was the man her mother married when she unexpectedly got pregnant. It had surprised her to learn Hunter agreed with how she wanted to handle things now.

He could never be a father to her, but maybe they could be friends.

And maybe it was time to consider moving home to South Carolina.

Chapter Eight

The morning dawned with cooler temperatures. The outside world felt untouched by last night's events. Pia ended the video chat with her mother, Hunter, and her sister with a feeling of mission accomplished.

"That went well. You're a good actress," she told Carolina. "You showed Mother your maturity. She and Hunter looked happy. However, for the next few days, you're going to rest."

Carolina saluted. "Yes, ma'am. So you're cooking breakfast?"

Pia chuckled. "My breakfasts are usually yogurt and coffee."

Carolina scrunched her nose. "I want pancakes, please."

"Pancakes it is." She headed into the kitchen.

"Then will you take me to see Justin?" Carolina sat at the breakfast bar.

"As long as Noah says it's okay."

Pia's cell phone rang. It was as though he'd heard his name.

"Good morning," Noah said. "How are you? How's Carolina this morning?"

He was always thoughtful.

"She's hungry, a good sign. After pancakes, she wants to see Justin, with your permission. I could bring pancakes to the two of you." A spring of urgency surged in her chest. She wanted to see Noah.

"Justin will be released this morning, so pancakes tomorrow? I have a favor to ask. Your mother, stepfather, and Carolina were invited to spend Thanksgiving with us—us being whatever Rutledges show up—at the IOP—Isle of Palms—house. Thanksgiving school break starts on Monday. It's a vacation and a holiday week. It's a good time with family. It's a good opportunity for you to meet my family."

Meet his family? A ripple of anxiousness spun through her. Her mind whirled. "I haven't been away so long that I forgot that IOP stands for Isle of Palms. However, I'm not certain what favor you're asking."

Noah cleared his throat. "Would you and Carolina come to IOP today and stay through Thanksgiving? Family members will start to filter in and out, but I'll need help with Justin."

His "well" had made her pause. The Justin part was fine. But a week at his family's vacation home?

"Well…" She mirrored his hesitation. But could she politely decline?

"It's a big house," Noah continued. "Beach front. Six bedrooms. You'll have your own room. Carolina can stay with Justin and the rest of the cousins on the enclosed sleeping porch—she's stayed there before. Or she could share a room with you."

Pia assumed the "she's stayed there before" part was to make her comfortable with the sleeping arrangements. How could she say no to his request? Justin would need help, and caregiving worked best with several people on the team. But to stay at the beach in a house with Noah and his family for a week? The uneasy ripple grew to a wave washing through her.

The intimacy of being a houseguest felt odd. But Noah didn't feel like a stranger. A could-have-been-fatal accident involving children they both loved had knitted them together. She understood what he felt. He understood her feelings.

But how did she feel about him?

"Are you sure we won't be intruding? We can commute. We don't need to stay—"

Carolina waved at her. "Yes. We. Do! It's so fun there at Thanksgiving."

"Sweetie, this is a decision between adults."

"You have never been on a vacation with me." Carolina pouted. "You're my surrogate mother now. We need to bond. No better place than the Rutledge beach house. And I get to be with Justin. Pleeease," she pleaded.

Pia wanted to halt another Carolina meltdown.

"How about a compromise," she said, returning to the conversation with Noah. "We'll meet you and Justin there today. I'll see how today goes—but not spend tonight, and then I'll decide." She respected that Noah had asked for help, not many men would do that.

"I'll take that offer," Noah said. "I'll call you when Justin's released. Meet you at the house. I'll text you the address, and so you can prepare, know that I plan to use every tool at my disposal to convince you to stay."

Pia looked at her phone. He'd gotten the last word in. Ended the call. And made her heart flutter.

For once, she refused to question her feelings, instead choosing to feel the sweetness of the attraction blooming in her heart. Was this what vulnerability felt like?

The sun warmed the afternoon. Pia stood in front of floor-to-ceiling windows, looking at the Atlantic Ocean. Sunlight glinted off water with whitecap ripples caused by gentle waves. She'd never spent a vacation, let alone a holiday, on IOP. Never spent Thanksgiving with a man who was only a friend—and Noah had become that. Never said yes to her heart when her brain was screaming, "What are you doing?"

"A dollar for your thoughts," Noah said.

Startled, Pia turned. He was so close, she nearly tripped.

"A dollar? That's some inflation." She laughed.

"I never understood 'penny for your thoughts' because I have so many, and a penny is too cheap. You were deep in thought. Tell me about it?"

"Hmm…what's next on the schedule?"

"Justin and Carolina are listening to music. I believe they'll both rest. They'll be fine for a few hours. How about if we go Thanksgiving grocery shopping?" He reached for her hand and began to tug her toward the elevator.

"Thanksgiving grocery shopping?" She rarely grocery shopped. The grocer near her home delivered, putting her groceries in the mudroom, where she kept a small refrigerator.

"Simple process. You walk up and down the aisles, greet your neighbors, taste some irresistible snacks, and buy food."

She'd forgotten about southern neighborliness at a local market. "Well…"

"It's an adventure. When was the last time you went grocery shopping for Thanksgiving dinner?"

"Well…"

"Olympia Graham Hughes. You've never been grocery shopping for a Thanksgiving dinner?"

She grimaced. "My mother did that when I was a kid. I was always studying or practicing the piano."

His grin spread wide. "Let's go! I'm excited to be the one to introduce you to this adventure."

Noah, she mused, was an adventure. He stirred within her long-buried feelings of family, food, and fun. Feelings she'd buried when her father had died.

———————— ♥ ————————

They crossed from the packed parking lot to the packed grocery store. Everyone on Isle of Palms must have started their holiday shopping. Pia read Noah's handwritten grocery list while he pushed the buggy.

"We're getting fresh pumpkin for pie?" Pia asked. "There's no frozen pie crust on the list. Shall I add it?"

"We'll make it together." Noah continued down the aisle.

"You make pie crust? I've never even made a pie. That's what bakeries are for."

"Consider me a baker."

"Dad. Soccer coach. Construction manager. Baker, too." Clearly, there was a lot to know about Noah Rutledge.

"Hey, Noah!" a man coming down the aisle called out. "How's the brick warehouse renovations coming?" He stopped to stare at Pia. "Only you would bring a pretty woman on a date to the grocery store." He punched Noah's arm.

"Oh," Pia said. "We're—"

"Thompson, you don't know what a good date is," Noah interjected. "Besides, I would only bring a keeper with me to shop."

The man's eyes grew wide, as did his smile. "He's going to cook for you?" he asked Pia.

Not certain how to answer, Pia looked from the man to Noah and back. "Well, he told me he was going to make pumpkin pie, so I guess that counts as cooking."

Noah grinned and nodded as though she'd answered correctly and made him proud.

"I'm Thompson, by the way. Nice to meet you…" He held out his hand.

Pia shook it. "Olympia Graham Hughes."

"You're Hunter's stepdaughter. Heard a lot about you. Big success up north."

He'd heard a lot about her? Stepdaughter? From Hunter? "You know him?"

"Thompson knows everyone," Noah said.

"Listen, how about cocktails and roasted oysters at my place? Tonight good? Or when?" Thompson pointed at the calendar on his phone.

"Actually, we'll take a rain check," Noah told him. "Justin is under the weather. Maybe in a week or so. I'll call you."

"You can only come if you bring the charming Miss Hughes." Thompson winked at Pia.

"Is this a meeting?" A woman in perfect makeup and with girl-next-door beauty, looking like she'd stepped out of an Orvis outdoor women's catalog, approached.

"Casey!" Thompson shouted. "This is Olympia, Hunter's stepdaughter, and Noah's new girlfriend."

Pia caught Casey's flinch at the word girlfriend. Was she interested in Noah?

"Charmed." Casey gave a slight tilt of her head. "You're Carolina's sister. She's a handful, that one."

Pia wasn't certain how to take the comment. Yes, Carolina could be a handful, but that was none of Casey's business and certainly impolite to speak of it.

Stepping between Pia and Noah, Casey covered Noah's hand on the buggy's handle with her own. A stab of something too close to jealousy stung Pia.

Pia stepped back. "It was nice to meet you both. I'll get back to the list while you visit with Noah."

When she turned to step away, Noah plucked the list from her hand. "Not so fast. This is a dynamic duo's job. I need you to help me." His grin was charming. "Thompson, I'll call you about that roast. Casey, as always, it was nice to see you." Noah turned the buggy around and reached for Pia's hand, entwining his fingers with hers. "This is a buddy system. I can't let you go off the rails and buy stuff we don't need." Noah tugged her away from his friends.

Pia kept pace with him until they reached the end of the aisle and turned from sight. The moments-before conversation zipped through her mind. Feelings zipped through her body. One word grew louder and louder, over and over: girlfriend.

She stopped. "Why didn't you correct Thompson?"

"What?" He looked around as though the answer to the question could be found floating in the air. "Why, indeed. Let's finish our job. We have pumpkin to cook."

Returning to the beach house, Pia had never laughed so much as during the drive. Noah was as smart and witty as he was handsome. When he reached over and squeezed her hand, she felt as though she'd come alive in a new, different way. There was freedom and joy in laughter with him.

"We're back," Noah announced, exiting the elevator on the second floor.

He'd promised to convince her to stay at IOP and help him care for Justin, and she was ready to ink her signature on the bottom line of that contract, if for no other reason than her heart had softened like dark chocolate in the sunshine of Noah's smile.

"Olympia Graham Hughes!" Carolina called from the beachside porch. "A word, please."

She joined her sister on the porch. Carolina had been waiting for her—a cup of hot tea and a plate of cookies had been laid out on the table.

"Sit." Carolina pointed to a chair.

Pia held up her hands in surrender.

"Look"—Carolina stood with hands on her hips—"I warned you about dating Noah. One, he's too young for you. Two, you don't seem to comprehend he's my soccer coach. I don't want your personal life mucking up my social life. Three, Casey Sumpter is interested in him. She's my best friend's aunt. You getting involved with Noah will upset the balance of everything."

Frustration shot through Pia. Who did Carolina think she was? Pia drew a breath and paused. She needed to deflate the tension.

"I hear what you're saying. I can give you more reasons. Olympia Graham Hughes lives in Connecticut. Doesn't date men who don't wear suits. Doesn't date men who drive trucks. Doesn't date men who prefer beer or who think the best table service is at a backyard oyster roast."

Carolina sighed deeply. "Good. We understand each other."

"I don't," came Noah's voice from behind Pia.

Chapter Nine

Panic hit Pia in the gut. She rose from the chair, fearing what she'd see when she turned to face Noah.

His smile disarmed her. He'd heard every word. She fought back tears. Never would she intentionally hurt him. But he had to admit they had different lifestyles. Did they even want the same things in life? Dating? Did she even know how? The words she'd uttered were for Carolina's sake and Carolina's sake only. Would he understand?

Noah's smile softened. "Ladies, I'm starting dinner." His tone was calm and quiet. "I could use your individual expertise. Olympia, please help Justin. He needs a snack, some meds, and to be moved to the living room. Carolina, you're on cooking duty with me." He did an about-face and left Pia and Carolina alone on the porch.

"Now you've done it!" Carolina spewed. "For some reason, he's interested in you. Did you have to put him down that way?" She was on the verge of bursting into tears.

"Sweetie, I love you. However, whether I'm here or in Connecticut, my personal life is none of your business."

"Until you involve my life!"

"How about we discuss this later, when you're calm and I've had a glass of wine?" Without a glance back, Pia entered the house.

Minutes later, from the third-floor family room, Pia watched Noah stoke a fire in the outdoor firepit. Night would soon erase color from the sky. Carolina joined Noah, carrying a platter of oysters. Together, they placed oysters on the grate over the fire.

"I can manage by myself, Miss Olympia." Justin lumbered into the room on crutches. "You can join them."

"I'm here to assist you, Justin. We'll go down in the elevator together."

He stood beside her, and they watched Noah and Carolina.

"You haven't asked, but I want to tell you, Carolina means well," he said. "Hunter leaving… She feels as though it's her fault. She's worried she's ruined her parents' marriage. Then just when she was sorta getting used to her dad being so far away, her mother takes off. Plus, you got dragged down here. She knows you don't like being here."

"Justin, I know you haven't asked, but I want to tell you, this is my home. I wasn't dragged down here. I volunteered to come."

"How do we make her understand that?" Justin implored her.

"I love my sister. I love my mother. I love Charleston. I like…Carolina's father. And this trip has opened my eyes."

"Well, it's not good to go through life with your eyes closed." He grinned, looking so much like Noah that she understood why her sister could be in love with this young man. "Let's go."

When the elevator opened, Carolina was there to help Justin. The loving expression on her face was returned with Justin's heart-melting grin. They radiated waves of the purity of first love. It was as though the rest of the world didn't exist.

Pia accepted being persona non grata after the verbal lashing Carolina had given her.

The evening cooled with the sea breeze and setting sun. A fire blazed in the pit. Dinner was full of lively conversation and good food.

Afterward, Pia rose. "Carolina, we'll be leaving in a little while. But tomorrow, we'll come back to stay the rest of the week." Her sister gave her a forced smile.

Noah held the door for Justin and Carolina, who retreated inside to watch movies. Then he motioned to Pia to follow him.

"For someone who doesn't like backyard oyster roasts and beer, you did a fine job of concealing any disdain." Noah chuckled, handing Pia a plate with warm bread pudding.

After a bite, Pia said, "Who made this? I love it!"

"Interesting. Bread pudding is often considered peasant food. Leftover stale bread, extra-ripe fruit, nuts for texture. Not haute cuisine."

"Oh…this is in response to what you overheard earlier. Well, Mr. Rutledge, you don't know the rest of the story."

"I'm interested. Want to share? But, before that, I'd like to ask you for a date. A proper date. Tomorrow evening. I'll pick you up here. Five thirty. I have an evening planned."

Pia cut a glance at him. "Hmm. You sound pretty sure of yourself. Confident that I'll agree. And you'd be right. I accept."

Chapter Ten

Pia and Carolina spent the morning packing for the rest of the week. Carolina loaded their luggage into Pia's Nav, then they set out for Isle of Palms and a Thanksgiving vacation with the Rutledge family. Pia gripped the steering wheel. It had been years since she'd worried about making a good impression. Years.

"I'm curious." Carolina turned down the radio. "If you don't intend to be here long, why did you buy this "boat"? Is something more going on?"

"Interesting. You think so?" She didn't want to discuss it.

What is going on?

The morning had dawned with an email from her CEO. They were shutting down Pia's line of business. There might be a position for her in the reorganization, but no guarantees.

Carolina waved her hand in front of Pia's face. "People don't give teenagers enough credit for understanding."

When Pia remained quiet, Carolina put in her earbuds. Pia was thankful her sister could take a hint.

The drive took longer than expected. Pulling into the parking courtyard, Pia navigated to an end spot, away from the three other vehicles.

Noah appeared and waved. Beside him was a wagon. He pointed to an upstairs window, which framed Justin standing with crutches and waving, too.

"Lunch is at noon. My cousins are here. I'll make introductions. Then I need to leave. But…Miss Hughes, I'll pick you up at five thirty."

Carolina rolled her eyes and headed for the elevator.

"A youthful disease—teenage-itis," Pia grumbled.

"Lucky for us, it'll only last a little longer." Noah chuckled, unloading luggage into the wagon. "She's wise beyond her years about some things."

"I can't describe how I feel when I watch her and Justin together. They make me believe love is the single most important ingredient in life." Pia grabbed her purse and locked the Nav.

"Interesting. You think so?" Noah mused.

Pia wasn't sure if he wanted to avoid the topic or talk about it.

They rode the elevator upstairs, where the Rutledge cousins welcomed Pia with a lunch buffet. Justin and Carolina were already seated at the table, enjoying their meal.

Noah surprised Pia when he kissed her cheek. "I'll see you later."

He left before she could blink, though she caught Carolina's eye roll and Justin elbowing her with a scowl.

After lunch, Pia walked the stairs to the third floor and stood in front of the window where she'd stood with Justin the evening before. The backyard and the sand dunes with the walkway to the beach spread before her. It made her think of future possibilities. It was as though, while gazing at the view, a door opened her mind and heart. Ideas she'd previously discarded as futile or impossible came into focus, like a ship at sea moving toward her, growing in scale and size, becoming recognizable.

She'd changed since coming to South Carolina—buying a land yacht was a notable departure from her life in Connecticut. She could permanently change her address. She could change her career and chase a new dream. She could change her family dynamics, accepting Carolina's father into her life.

And she could change her notions about love.

Couldn't she?

———————— ♥ ————————

After a shower, Pia opened the door from the bathroom to the bedroom. Carolina, clutching a black purse, and Noah's cousin, Delia, sat on the bed, whispering. Pia glanced to where they'd pointed. A black dress hung from a hanger on the closet door. A pair of new black shoes were on the floor below it.

"We're sorry to intrude." Delia took the purse from Carolina and offered it to Pia as though it were something delicate and treasured.

Pia drew closer.

"A gift from Noah's grandmother," Delia said. "The shoes are from his mother. The dress is from me and Carolina."

Confused, Pia tilted her head. "What?"

"It takes a village to raise a child." Carolina stood beside Delia. "We're hoping your date with Noah goes well."

Pia drew back. "Interesting."

"A person can change their mind, can't they, Carolina. Look at a situation from a different perspective," Delia replied. "We'll help you dress for your date. I'm great with hair and makeup."

Delia and Carolina fussed Pia into perfection. When she descended the stairs to the second-floor living room, a wave of applause from a group of women startled her.

"Um…thank you." She wasn't sure what to say.

A woman stepped forward. "We want you to have a splendid date with our Noah."

She guessed this woman was his mother.

The woman draped a black velvet wrap around Pia's shoulders. "So you don't get chilly." She went to the elevator and pushed the button. The door opened after a ding. The woman motioned Pia inside. "Have fun."

The elevator descended, as did her stomach. This was the oddest start to any date she'd ever experienced. Ever.

The giddiness in her chest danced the flamenco. After the elevator opened, Pia exited and walked to the driveway. Her heels tat-tatted, a drumbeat of anticipation.

A black limo waited. Noah stood beside the long, stretched car, door open, and he held a red rose. His hair had been styled perfectly, his black suit fit him perfectly, his smile perfectly lit his face. Her heart fluttered. Her emotions burst like fireworks.

"Good evening, Miss Hughes." Noah offered the rose.

She accepted it and nodded when he gestured for her to enter the limo.

We have a reservation in Charleston." He settled beside her.

When the driver pulled away from the house, Noah reached for her hand, lacing his fingers with hers. She grinned, knowing it was a stupidly happy grin.

Candlelight. Moonlight. A tiny flashlight—from the waiter to read the menu. It all enchanted her. And when it came time to order, Noah asked her what she might enjoy, though he did let her know he had planned a special dessert.

Soft piano music floated around them. The lightest fragrance of roses scented the air. Dinner began with champagne and an amuse-bouche, then ended with a fraisier for dessert. From the way he held a glass to how he cut with a knife to dabbing his mouth with a napkin, Noah's manners were impeccable. And he displayed the utmost formality of mannerliness. He asked polite questions, inquiring about her mother, Pia's college alma mater, and if she liked dogs or cats. He spoke of the weather—hurricane season was ending soon. He made her laugh when he shared about naming his first sailboat H2O Dreams.

She openly stared at him. It was as though she'd waited all her life to meet this Noah. Tonight was the pinnacle of perfection. Resisting falling in love with him was futile.

In the after-dinner moonlight, he guided her for a stroll in Waterfront Park. The warmth from his hand radiated to hers, sending pulses throughout her body.

"I have something serious to discuss with you." Noah covered her hand with both of his.

"Nothing ominous, right? No bad news tonight," she told him.

"People often seek tradition in life. I don't subscribe to that trend, and you need to know that about me. We don't know each other—yet. But I completely trust my instincts. My inner voice is my guide. For example, I was advised not to adopt Justin, yet I legally became his father when his parents died. He's my nephew. And he is my son."

"I'm a tad envious," Pia said. "I'm relegated to half sister."

Noah stopped, her hand still in his. "I would like us to date seriously." He solemnly delivered the earnest words.

The words date and seriously sent a tremble through Pia. Her mind scrambled with analysis in rapid succession, creating a list of reasons why dating Noah would never work.

But her heart had its own logic.

A long pause hung between them.

"I'm not sure I understand." Her heart kicked out the negative mental gymnastics her brain tried to cling to. Her heart wanted what it wanted. Wanted what she'd lost hope of ever having—true love.

Yet, with Noah, how long would forever be?

Her heart whispered, "As long as it lasts."

She'd risk all and accept that forever could be a day, a week, a year. Or years. With Noah, she could risk being vulnerable.

"It's simple. I want a committed relationship with you, Olympia Graham Hughes. I want to learn everything about you. I'm falling in love with you. And when you love me, when you're ready, I want our dating to lead to marriage. I believe that's when the deepest connection will happen for us. I don't want to scare you or rush you. However, it's important that you fully understand my intention from the very start. I want forever."

She gulped. "Forever?"

"Yes. Forever. But if you're not willing to give it a chance, take a risk, then I'll take you back to IOP. We'll have a great family vacation…and I'll stop all pursuit. But I won't be able to be your friend…at least not for a while."

Her heart beat with deep resounding thuds. She was certain he could hear them. Emotions came too fast, too much, too different, too strange. But Noah made strange seem magical and adventurous. He wanted all or nothing.

Pia faced Noah. She lifted her chin to meet his mesmerizing gaze.

"Noah Rutledge, let me give you Pia's analysis of your plan. Planes, trains, and automobiles travel to and from Connecticut and Charleston, making dating exciting. You look as good in jeans as you do in a suit. Trucks are a practical mode of transportation for work. I'll always prefer a good wine to beer. And I was wrong, a backyard oyster roast holds equal weight to a six-course meal."

Noah moved his hands to cup her cheeks. He ran his thumb across her lips, sending a tremble through her. Slowly, he lowered his lips to hers.

His kiss took her to a magical place. Warm. Sincere. Full of positive possibilities.

Her mind gave up all fight. Her heart melted. Her body relaxed.

"Noah," she whispered against his lips. No name had ever sounded so romantic.

"Pia," he whispered, his voice carrying a note of impatience. He hugged her closely. "Thank you for your analysis. It would help me now if you would say a simple yes to my plan."

Pia stepped back, threw up her arms, and shouted for anyone to hear, "Yes! Noah Rutledge, I say yes."

What a vacation this had turned into!

The End

About Linda Joyce

Award-winning author Linda Joyce writes contemporary romance, women's fiction, and she's working on a cozy mystery series. Also, her short stories appear in multiple anthologies.

Linda married her college sweetheart, and they are dog parents to Jake, Max, and Sugar. They all travel together in their RV. Linda's most daring exploit was learning to fly a plane. Now, she reserves piloting for ziplines. Everyone has a weakness and Linda's is gumbo and sushi.

While New Orleans is her hometown, Linda has lived in many different places, including in Japan. She's improving her conversational Japanese and is learning Kanji. She enjoys discovering the uniqueness of every new town she visits.

She's a member of Carolina Romance Writers. She looks forward to meeting readers and learning about their book passions.

Find Linda online:

Website: http://www.linda-joyce.com
Newsletter: http://www.linda-joyce.com/newsletter/
Facebook: https://www.facebook.com/LindaJoyceAuthor
X : https://twitter.com/LJWriter
Instagram: http://instagram.com/lindajoycewrites
Amazon: http://www.amazon.com/Linda-Joyce/e/B00BODDROS/
Goodreads:http://www.goodreads.com/author/show/6950241.
Linda_Joyce
BookBub: https://www.bookbub.com/authors/linda-joyce

Forever After at the Ever Rest Inn

by J. Lynn Rowan

Forever After at the Ever Rest Inn

by J. Lynn Rowan

Disillusioned with his career and reeling from a breakup, Max Andersen heads to a Lowcountry bed and breakfast near Georgetown, South Carolina, for time away to relax and determine the next steps in his life.

The Ever Rest Inn isn't only a bed and breakfast. It's Vivian Ravanelle's family legacy. She's inherited more than just the property. The inn comes with financial problems that must be solved if she doesn't want to lose everything.

Vivi never forgot the boy who helped her overcome a lonely summer twenty-two years ago. But the boy has become a man—a handsome one who seems to reciprocate a new attraction. During Max's stay, the two share more than family stories and personal problems. Perhaps Max's next steps are tied to Vivi, who may find not only hope for the inn's future, but happiness and love.

Chili Pepper rating: 0.5

Chapter One

Max leaned back and draped his left arm across the back of the park bench, his midday coffee half-finished in his right hand, letting his attention wander from his office buddy's ramblings. Noise from Uptown Charlotte's latest high-rise construction site drowned out most of his words anyway, and Max was almost more invested in the pick-up game of soccer some college-aged students were playing on the other side of Romare Bearden Park.

Tucker gave Max a light punch on the shoulder. "You don't give a crap about my IT issues, do you?"

"Not during my lunch hour." Max took a sip of his coffee and grimaced. It had gone cold, and he lowered the cup with a sigh. "We should probably head back. I have a meeting at three and still need to finalize the account reports."

"Do you want to stop off for a fresh coffee on the way?" Tucker gathered the wrappings from his food truck lunch and stood.

Max shrugged, then retrieved his own paper bag from the ground and plopped the cup inside. "I think I can manage with the office pot if I need another jolt of caffeine before my meeting." As he dropped his trash into a nearby receptacle, his smartwatch buzzed. He glanced at the alert, then pulled out his phone with a frown.

"What's the matter?" Tucker asked.

Opening the notification, Max let out a slight groan. "I totally forgot."

"Meeting time changed? We can make it if we run. It's only three blocks."

"No, nothing work-related." Max pocketed his phone again and gestured for Tucker to start walking. "I had booked next week at a bed-and-breakfast down in the Lowcountry. It was supposed to be a romantic getaway with . . . well, you know."

"Ah, yes. She Who Shall Not Be Named." Tucker pressed the crosswalk button when they reached the corner. "Mid-March is kind of a weird time to take a trip to the coast."

Max pulled a face. "I didn't want to do it at Valentine's and have a bunch of expectations tied to it. It would only have been six months in anyway. It was just supposed to be a quiet little trip to get out of Charlotte for a bit. The place is in this tiny hamlet a little north of Georgetown, so a great central location for sightseeing and stuff. But if you want to just stay in and keep it low-key—"

"Don't take this the wrong way, bro," Tucker interjected as they started across the street, "but low-key is not a word I would use to describe your ex. Unless you're using the word low-key to mean something else."

"Does your wife know you have such a dirty mind?" Max cracked a grin and shook his head. "Anyway, that was the reminder about checking in, and it's too late to cancel without losing the full payment. So that sucks a bit."

They walked in silence the rest of the way to their building, dodging tourists, construction workers, and other office staffers taking their lunch breaks. Once they entered the relative quiet of the elevator, Tucker nudged Max and said, "Maybe you should still go."

Max turned, eyebrows raised. "Alone? To a romantic bed-and-breakfast?"

"Why not? You've been working like a dog the past couple months on those new accounts, and you could use a little time away. Besides, you said it was a quiet area with plenty to do nearby, and I would think you'd already asked for the time off when you booked the trip in the first place.

Plus, you said you can't get your money back." The elevator doors slid open, and Tucker stepped out first. "It might be good for you."

Max frowned with doubt, but Tucker had already started down the corridor toward his office before any response came to mind. Sighing, Max headed in the opposite direction to grab a hot cup of coffee from the breakroom before returning to his desk and the account reports waiting there for him.

Maybe I should go. Tucker wasn't wrong; Max had been up to his neck in paperwork and client meetings for weeks, often working late into the evening and over weekends as well. Nothing out of the ordinary for an investment banking analyst with aspirations of making top dollar by the age of forty. At least, that's what he told himself when the thought of spending a lifetime in this career plunged him into doubt and gloom. And while it sucked that his relationship with Tiffany had crashed and burned so spectacularly before they hit the three-month mark, he had been excited about the trip for its own merit when he initially booked it.

The breakroom coffee looked unappetizingly stale. Max dumped it and started a fresh pot, and while it percolated, he opened the travel app on his phone and found his booking. The manager had sent him a message to confirm receipt of the check-in details for Monday. His thumb hovered over the screen for a few seconds.

As the coffee maker gurgled its final drops into the pot, Max typed, *Sounds great. See you Monday!* and hit SEND. Then, just for kicks, he opened his preferred job recruitment app and scrolled through the search results for senior-level banking jobs in Georgetown, South Carolina. Thoughts swirling, he clicked on one that sounded interesting—and looked like he might get a quick response—and started the application.

Chapter Two

Despite the warmth tumbling from the space heater in the corner of her office, chills overtook Vivi as she listened to the family lawyer relate the final details of her inheritance. She had expected some tangles in taking possession of the Ever Rest Inn, the sprawling bed-and-breakfast she'd managed for her late great-aunt for the past ten years.

But this—

"Two mortgages?" she repeated, her voice hollow as Mr. Bauer lowered his notes.

"Plus the outstanding bills from the new water heaters, the kitchen renovations, and the roof replacement after Hurricane Ian hit in 2022." Mr. Bauer spread his hands. "I know it's a lot, Vivian. I recommended the inn and its property be placed in trust so that other means could be used to settle Loretta's finances. But you know how she was."

Vivi nodded, tears springing into her eyes. "She always thought she would have time to take care of it later."

Mr. Bauer plucked a tissue from the box on the corner of Vivi's desk and handed it to her, waiting while she dabbed at her cheeks. "Not to be flippant, but *you* have some time. A couple months, at least, to go over things with a good financial advisor and come up with a plan. Right after Loretta died, I filed the paperwork to pause mortgage payments during probate, and the request was accepted. So you don't have to worry about that until everything is settled out."

"That won't help with the other bills," Vivi replied, wiping the moist tissue across the tip of her nose. "We have maybe two or three bookings over the next month. Things won't pick up until mid-May, when schools start letting out for the summer. But if I don't figure out how to pay things off…"

Mr. Bauer handed her the file folder containing a copy of her aunt's will, financial statements, life insurance policy, service invoices, and mortgage paperwork. "People want to be paid for services rendered, as you know. I can send over recommendations for someone who can help you figure everything out."

Vivi nodded, murmuring a thank-you as she and the lawyer stood. She shook Mr. Bauer's hand and escorted him in silence to the side door of the inn, the one reserved for staff, family, and business. He paused there and turned to her, putting a kind hand on her shoulder.

"I've been doing this work for the Ravanelle family for decades," he said. "Your aunt built something lovely here—something I don't blame you for wanting to save. She left the inn to you because she trusted your instinct and your judgment. Loretta might always have thought she had more time, but she knew she didn't have forever. She was a smart woman, if a stubborn one. Probably why she held on so long. But you're the owner now, not just the manager, and you have to decide what to do."

"What would you do?"

Mr. Bauer sighed, his hesitancy to put his thoughts into words obvious. "If I were in your shoes, I'd sell. It would pay off the bills and avoid defaulting on the loans."

Vivi grimaced. "What else would I do with my life, if I'm not running the Ever Rest?"

"You're a smart young lady," Mr. Bauer said. "And you've been successful at managing this place for the better part of ten years. Longer, if you figure in all those summers and school breaks when you worked alongside

Loretta. If running an inn is really what you want to do with your life, then I have no doubts you'd find somewhere else to work." He swung open the door and stepped out onto the side porch. "But I don't think you'd be as happy anywhere else."

"You just said you'd sell if you were in my shoes," Vivi reminded him.

Mr. Bauer chuckled. "That's true. But I'm not in your shoes, Vivian. *You're* in your shoes. At the end of the day, you must be content with the decisions you've made. If you want to save the Ever Rest Inn, there are ways to do it."

Vivi thanked him again and watched for a few minutes as he strolled down the garden path toward the back gate leading to the alley behind the guesthouse, where he'd parked. Once Mr. Bauer disappeared around a clump of camellia bushes, she shut the door and heaved a sigh. Then she headed toward the front of the inn. Other than the distant shuffling from upstairs where her two per-diem employees were cleaning a guest suite in preparation for this afternoon's arrival, only the quiet creaks of an old house permeated the air. Around her, above her, beneath her, the structure of the inn seemed to reach out, as if seeking a reassuring embrace that its future wasn't on shaky ground.

She settled for a few firm pats to the archway leading from the downstairs hall to the two-story foyer. "We'll figure it out. I promise."

Chapter Three

Max drove slowly down the shady tree-lined street, leaning over the steering wheel as he strained to make out house numbers along the way. He had vague memories of coming here with his parents as a kid, but twenty-some years had changed both the look of the neighborhood as well as the accuracy of his recollections. On their first visit, his dad had circled the block three times before he'd found the place, his mother's exasperated "That's it right there!" punctuating the search.

A chuckle bubbled in Max's throat at the memory. Determining from the GPS that he was close enough, he pulled into an open space along the curb. The weather was pleasant for mid-March, the faint smell of salt drifting in the afternoon air. He couldn't remember how far this place was from the ocean, but the breeze hinted at sandy beaches and breaking waves. Or maybe it was just his imagination calling up the happy family vacations along the coast and the scents that went along with them.

After pulling his suitcase and computer bag from the trunk, he strolled up the sidewalk toward the Ever Rest Inn. The house numbers were easier to see now, and within five minutes, he stood at the front gate of an old three-story house surrounded by a wrought iron fence. Max paused to take in the sight of the wide porches, the upper one accessible from the second floor through two sets of double doors that probably led to bedrooms. The white siding and contrasting black shutters needed a coat of paint, but the worn look of the building gave it a welcoming charm—an old friend beckoning him in for a glass of iced tea while insisting that nothing had changed since the last time they'd seen each other. Tall trees shaded the front lawn, and Max knew from the pictures on the travel app listing that the backyard and garden were similarly shaded. Even in summer, visitors to the inn could find a cool place to relax with a book or a drink—two things he hadn't enjoyed since his busy season had started at work in January.

A book and a drink sounded pretty good right now.

His suitcase thumped up the porch steps as he approached the front door, which stood open behind the weathered screen door despite the cool air. A little hand-painted sign tacked to the wide trim read *If the door's open wide, please come inside!* Chuckling at the instructions, Max did just so and found himself in a side two-story foyer facing a small reception desk tucked into a nook beside the angled staircase.

A young woman sat behind the desk, fingers clattering at an unseen keyboard as she scanned the contents of a computer screen. She stood and pushed a pair of cat-eye glasses into her hair like a headband when the screen door shut with a bang behind Max. "Welcome to the Ever Rest Inn."

She smiled expectantly at him, feathery dark eyebrows raised above hazel eyes tending toward green and ringed with long lashes. Her hair, the tight, neat coils nearly black but shot through with hints of reddish-brown, haloed around an oval face that looked like something out of a dream— fresh, bright tawny skin that probably turned bronze in the summer, and full pink lips, currently pulling to one side in an amused smirk, that would be heaven to kiss.

Now where had *that* thought come from?

"Hi. I'm . . . Max." His voice stuck for a second as he gathered his seemingly scattered wits. Waxing poetic about strange women wasn't his thing, no matter how beautiful they were.

Her smile settled back into place. "Max Andersen?"

He blinked. "Yeah. How did you—"

"You're the only arrival today, and since you have a suitcase, it wasn't hard to figure out. We don't usually get drop-ins asking about a vacancy this time of year." She cocked her head to one side, as if glancing behind him. "Do you want me to show you up to your room now, or are you waiting . . .?"

His reservation was for a double occupancy. "No, it's just me." He paused. "That's okay, right?"

One eyebrow curved upward again, curiosity playing on her face. "It's not a problem. I'll make a note to adjust your breakfast options. And you probably want to cancel the dinner for Saturday?"

He'd forgotten about the add-on for a romantic meal served out on the garden terrace if the weather cooperated. For his part, he couldn't have cared less about a romantic dinner. But Tiffany had balked at the idea of staying at a B&B over a higher-end hotel until the news about dinner had convinced her. She had probably expected him to take things to the next level if she got him across a candlelit table from her. Another bullet inadvertently dodged—but those thoughts were for the past, not the present. "Can we leave it alone for now?"

"I can refund it or apply the amount to a different upgrade." Her eyes narrowed slightly as she studied him.

Max studied her in turn, suddenly unnerved by the sense that he'd seen her before. Even more disconcerting was the rising feeling that sharing a romantic dinner on the garden terrace with *her* would be the perfect end to his trip. "Let me think about it."

The curiosity faded from her expression as she retrieved a small ledger from a drawer and set it onto the desk, facing him. She opened to a marked page and handed him a pen, tapping a line halfway down with one neat and naturally manicured nail. "You'll be on the second floor in the northeast corner suite. Sign here, and then I'll take you up."

Scrawling his name on the indicated line, Max stole a glance at her, still trying to place her. "I have some fond memories of this place."

She closed the ledger and whisked it back into the drawer before turning to the small cabinet affixed to the wall beside the desk. "Do you? I'm sure this is the first time you've ever checked in with us."

"As an adult. I came here a few times with my parents when I was a kid."

A noncommittal noise came from her as she opened the cabinet and reached inside.

"I remember the owner, Miss Ravanelle. I think she had a sweet spot for me." At his words, she froze, one hand still raised with a key dangling from her fingers. Something shifted in Max's stomach, realizing he may have touched a sensitive nerve. "Is Miss Ravanelle around? I'd love to visit her while I'm here, see if she remembers me at all."

The woman swallowed, her throat working for a moment. Then she shoved the key into his hand before snatching what looked like a set of master keys from a decorative bowl beside the computer. "I'm the owner now, and the only Miss Ravanelle around the Ever Rest Inn. Shall I show you up?"

Without waiting for a response, she slipped from behind the reception desk and started upstairs. Max lowered the pull bar on his suitcase and grabbed the handle, hurrying up behind her. Despite taking the stairs two at a time, she was halfway down the hall when he reached the landing. He quickened his stride, but she disappeared inside a front bedroom before he could catch up. By the time he got to the doorway, she was already circulating around the room, pushing open the sets of green damask curtains at each window to let in what late-afternoon light remained before sunset. Then she unlatched the double doors leading to the upper porch before crossing to the ensuite bath and switching on the light.

Max waited until she faced him again. "Hey, if I said something wrong—"

With a sigh, her shoulders drooped. "No, I'm the one who should apologize. I'm not usually like that, and certainly not to guests. It's just . . ." She hugged her arms around herself and strolled to the middle of the floor. "Aunt Loretta died about a month ago. Things are still a little raw."

"I'm sorry to hear that, really." Max stepped farther into the room. The urge to do something comforting bubbled—something like rubbing her arms or squeezing her shoulders, maybe even giving her a hug—but that would be even more awkward than the exchange they'd already had. Still, the forlorn look in her eyes tugged at him. "I remember her as being the nicest lady I'd ever met, outside of my own family."

She gave a short laugh, a sound of agreement. "Aunt Loretta could make anyone feel welcome. I'm normally better at it than this, I promise."

"I'm sure you are." Max extended his hand. "Could we start over?"

After a moment, she accepted his handshake. "Sounds good to me." She dropped his hand, closed her eyes, and gave herself an exaggerated shake, tipping her head back and pulling in a deep breath. Then she opened her eyes again and fixed him with a bright smile. "Welcome to the Ever Rest Inn. I'm Vivian, and if you need anything during your stay, you can text me at the number on the bedside table. Breakfast is served at 8:30 in the kitchen instead of the dining room, since you're the only one here. How do you like your eggs? I'll attempt anything, but your best bet for properly cooked is over easy."

"Over easy's fine," he replied with a lopsided grin. "Any suggestions for where to grab dinner tonight?"

"There are lots of options in Georgetown—you really can't go wrong. But there's a great barbecue place on Highmarket Street that won't be too busy this time of the day."

Silence dropped over the room as they stared at each other. Max briefly wondered if he should ask her to join him for dinner but thought better of it. "Thanks for the recommendation. I'll check it out."

Vivian nodded. "I'll leave you to get settled. I lock up around nine o'clock, but your room key will get you in the front door. Just make sure you throw the deadbolt again when you come back in, if it's after that."

"Will do."

After another slightly longer-than-was-comfortable pause, Vivian murmured something that may have been "See you in the morning" and headed for the door. Max watched her go, wondering if this familiar stranger was meant for more than hospitality. The feeling lingered as he lifted his suitcase onto the bed to unpack.

Chapter Four

Bacon sizzled in the covered griddle pan as Vivi surveyed her opponent—the two eggs waiting to be cracked into a second skillet. She could cook for herself, but she was less picky about burnt edges and slightly underdone middles. It never made sense, financially or otherwise, to bring in an actual chef to handle guest meals between Labor Day and Memorial Day, other than the weeks bookending Christmas and New Year's. Aunt Loretta had been more talented and at ease before the stove, and as she took a deep breath and cracked the first egg into the waiting pan, sadness twinged sharply around Vivi's heart.

Squeaky floorboards in the back hallway signaled her guest's arrival. She spared just a glance over her shoulder as Max ducked through the kitchen door. One of the features of the old house was a propensity for less public doorways to hang a little too low for most modern men. Even Vivi had to stoop to get through a couple of them on the third floor, and she was hardly above average height-wise.

"There's fresh coffee on the sideboard—help yourself." Turning her attention back to the stove, she told herself the sudden bottomless feeling in her stomach was due to the stress of making sure the eggs didn't burn. It had nothing to do with the way her guest's T-shirt showed off his physique.

Or the fact that she'd placed him as soon as he'd walked in the door yesterday afternoon. Twenty-two years had turned a gangly preteen into a tall, athletic man with the sort of chiseled features one tended to see on brooding high-end fashion models. Despite the season, his light brown hair bore streaks of blond, but not the kind that came from a bottle. Coupled with the tan on his arms and face, they were evidence of an abundant time spent in the sun. He had the build of someone who preferred running and swimming over lifting to stay in shape.

But his blue eyes were kind. They always had been, even when they'd been kids and he had helped Aunt Loretta ease her loneliness and worry. Still, his gaze had matured along with the rest of him, and she hadn't missed the subtle look of interest he'd given her when he'd checked in.

Vivi stepped away from the eggs long enough to drop a couple slices of bread into the toaster. Did Max remember her, too? Doubtful, or he wouldn't have looked at her that way, like staying here alone was no hardship if he could fill the empty space at his side with her company. Anyone who'd known her as a ten-year-old would describe her as mousey, shy, and forgettable. That is, anyone other than her parents, older brothers, and Aunt Loretta.

"That smells great. I'm starved."

The deep male voice, laced with the sound of a smile, broke Vivi from her musings in time to rescue the eggs from certain doom. She slid the eggs, miraculously unbroken, onto a waiting plate. Then she moved the griddle pan off the heat before lifting the lid, holding it like a shield for a moment to keep the bacon grease from splattering all over her. The toast popped just as she moved the bacon to a platter lined with paper towels, taking a moment to blot the strips with additional paper towels before grabbing four pieces with the tongs. After plating up the bacon and toast, she turned to the small table to find Max watching her with a half grin and that disconcerting glimmer of interest in his eyes.

Vivi set the plate in front of him. "Nothing fancy, but it'll fill you up."

"You aren't going to join me?"

"I ate earlier." She hid her surprise at the invitation by retreating to the fridge for a jar of the homemade strawberry jam Aunt Loretta had canned last summer. Her composure back in place, she brought the jar to the table and set it beside the crock of butter. "Do you need me to open that?"

"Nah. I'm a pro. My mom likes to can. My dad even expanded the pantry to make room for all her jams and jellies." As if to prove his point, he picked up the jam and popped off the lid with his spoon.

Vivi smirked. "I'm impressed. Usually, I have to use a can opener."

Scooping out a generous mound of ruby-red jam for his toast, Max glanced up at her. "Will you join me for coffee at least?"

That she could do. While Max dug into his plate with gusto, Vivi went to the sideboard to make her second cup of the day. Then she sat across from him at the small round table, aware of an intimate homeyness in the act of sharing a meal—or at least coffee—in the inn's kitchen. She studied him for a moment before voicing the question that had been bothering her since last night. "What made you decide to come on your own this week? You'd clearly booked a romantic getaway with someone special."

She expected some defensiveness or obfuscation, but he answered without hesitation, barely lifting his eyes from his eggs.

"She wasn't that special. And we aren't even together anymore."

"I'm sorry to hear that."

"Don't be." Max paused for a sip of coffee. "We hadn't even gotten to the three-month mark before she decided she was more interested in my roommate than me."

Vivi grimaced. "Ouch."

"I wasn't in love with her or anything," he continued with a shrug. "It was a bit jarring to come home from work and find them together . . . you know. On the sofa."

"Double ouch. I hope you got a new roommate."

He grinned, more amused than bitter. "And a new sofa."

Vivi chuckled at his tone. "You still could have canceled."

"I actually forgot," Max admitted, leaning back in his chair. "I'd taken the time off and everything. But with how crazy work's been the past few months, the whole trip slipped my mind until I got the check-in reminder on Friday. Since it was too late to get a refund, I took the advice of an office buddy and came alone."

"I'll try to be a good hostess, but I'm afraid you'll be a little bored."

"I think I can find ways to stay entertained." He gazed at her, lingering in a way that made heat tingle into her cheeks. "So, you run this place all by yourself?"

The inn was a safer topic of conversation, one unlikely to make her wonder if he knew how to do more than make a woman blush. "People come in to help prep rooms for guests, and we have a cleaning service, of course. I bring on an actual chef—well, a local lady my aunt knew since forever, who's a phenomenal cook—to do breakfasts during the busy season and pre-arranged dinners on request. Like the one you set up for Saturday. And Aunt Loretta until she got too sick to do much anymore. Now it's just me."

Max leaned forward at the catch in her voice, reaching across the table. For a moment, it seemed he intended to take her hand, but then he just rested his arm on the tabletop, his fingers a few inches from her wrist. "I really am sorry about your aunt. Does my being here make it harder to deal?"

"No. It gives me an excuse to putter around the inn, which both keeps my mind occupied and honors Aunt Loretta's memory. She loved this place and wanted it to outlive her."

"My parents and I came here three or four times when I was a kid," he said, easing back into his chair. "I always thought it was a cool house. Lots of places to hide."

"It was built in the early 1800s, so lots of nooks and crannies, for sure."

"Was it always an inn?"

Vivi shook her head. "My great-grandfather bought it for a song right after World War II, or so the family story goes. He planned on filling it up with kids, but after my grandfather and Aunt Loretta were born, he shipped off to fight in Korea and never came home. His widow tried to manage but had to do something to earn money if she planned on raising two babies on her own. It was a boarding house for a while, but when Aunt Loretta was a teenager, her mother decided to turn it into a bed-and-breakfast instead. My grandfather wasn't interested in ownership, so after he finished college and resettled in Columbia, the inn went to Aunt Loretta."

"And how did you end up in the line of inheritance?" he asked.

"My dad was an only child, and he followed in my great-grandfather's footsteps. Into the Army, I mean. He was stationed at Fort Jackson and met my mom when she was home for the summer after her sophomore year at Clemson. They got married right after she graduated and had my twin brothers the following year." Vivi took a sip of coffee, finding it the wrong side of lukewarm to be enjoyable. "Dad was active duty, so they moved around a few times. My mom stayed in Columbia to be near her parents whenever he was deployed. I came along a full fifteen years later—the surprise baby. I started spending summers here when I was ten."

She paused, waiting to see if he could make the connections without her having to go into the details of that first summer, the only one spent at the Ever Rest that she'd hated. The bright spot in that memory was the kid version of Max and the little-girl crush she'd had on him, alongside Aunt Loretta's soothing love.

He didn't seem inclined to remember her yet, so she continued with the pertinent facts. "I loved helping my aunt around the inn, and her dream became mine. My dad transferred to Joint Base Charleston when I was in high school and was able to get into a more permanent position with less chance of reassignment until he was old enough to retire. I went to Columbia to get a degree in hospitality from USC. I've lived here and managed the Ever Rest since I graduated. Aunt Loretta never married and had no kids of her own. So I guess I was just the logical choice." She cleared her throat and looked into her cup, giving the coffee a swirl while she considered how to proceed. "So, what do you do? For a living, I mean."

"I'm an investment banking analyst in Charlotte." He pulled a face. "Sounds boring, doesn't it?"

"Do you like it?" she asked, making a mental note of the possibility of getting advice about the inn's financial problems. *Her* financial problems.

Max shrugged. "It pays the bills. It seemed more exciting when I was in my twenties with a fresh new finance degree and big aspirations. My mom hoped I'd settle down closer to home in New Bern, but who wants to listen to wisdom at twenty-two? But now that I'm a little older and wiser, I wish I'd found something that didn't feel so much like a rat race."

"Hence the trip to the Lowcountry for a little R&R."

"I'm definitely looking forward to the downtime." His smile deepened as he swept a subtle, assessing glance over her. "But I'm open to suggestions for things to see and do."

That tingling warmth swept into her cheeks again and spread down her arms and into her fingertips. She needed to call the loan officer at the bank in Georgetown, where the inn's precarious mortgages were held, to make an appointment. But with Max her only guest and her breakfast skills taking up less than two hours each day, her calendar was wide open. "I can show you around, if you like."

"Like my own personal tour guide?" An intense curiosity flared in his eyes.

Was he actually flirting with her, or was her little-girl crush resurfacing to play tricks? Vivi swallowed. "I'll have to stay on top of my messages, but yeah. I don't have anyone else checking in this week, so I'm all yours."

If he noticed how pathetic she sounded in her own attempt to flirt, he didn't let on. "That would be awesome."

Flustered, she began gathering empty dishes. "I have a couple business calls to make this morning, but let's plan to head out for lunch and sightseeing this afternoon. I'll meet you at the front desk at eleven?"

"Looking forward to it." Max stood and tasked himself with putting the jam, butter, and creamer into the fridge, adding another note of homeyness to their interaction. "I'll see you in a bit then, Vivian."

"You can call me Vivi." She set his plate and the coffee mugs into the sink and faced him as he paused by the kitchen door. "Everyone does."

In response, Max gave her a wide smile that made her knees turn to jelly and ducked out the door.

Chapter Five

An unprecedented level of impatience and anticipation kept Max from doing more than wandering around the inn and garden most of the morning. Almost everything was as he remembered it from the last family trip, when he'd been twelve. The familiarity eventually helped him stop pacing from room to room, but it couldn't keep him from checking his watch every five minutes. He finally gave up around 10:15 and spent the remaining forty-five minutes studying the various photographs hanging in the foyer.

Vivi appeared a few minutes before their agreed-upon time, seemingly flustered as she hurried down the stairs in an ankle-length floral dress and khaki jacket. She smoothed one hand over her hair where she'd braided it back from her face, the mass of curls defying gravity on the crown of her head. For the second time since his arrival, he couldn't shake the feeling that he should know her from somewhere.

She paused when she reached the bottom of the staircase and met his gaze, and her face relaxed into an easy smile. "I see you're ready to go."

Max tapped a frame hanging next to the reception desk that held a black-and-white photo of a handsome Black couple. The man wore an

Army uniform with insignia Max had never seen before, even in history books, while the woman, dressed in a light-colored dress, clasped his hand and rested her head on his shoulder. "Are these your great-grandparents?"

"From their wedding, right before he shipped out to fight in World War II. He was with the 320th Barrage Balloon Battalion when they landed at Normandy on D-Day."

"I didn't know there were any Black soldiers at Normandy."

"His unit was the only one. A lot of people don't know about it because it's not commonly mentioned in school." She leaned over the reception desk for her phone and a set of keys, which she slipped into a small purse at her hip.

"All your calls taken care of?" he asked.

"I'm all yours for the rest of the afternoon."

His throat went dry, but he reminded himself that she was just being hospitable. Her benign statement had nothing to do with anything more than acting as a tour guide to keep him from being bored during his stay. She wasn't *his*; she was a complete stranger—their conversation over breakfast notwithstanding—and he hadn't come here looking for romantic entanglements. "Lead the way. I'll drive, you navigate."

Within five minutes, they were settled in his car and heading into Georgetown. Afraid of an awkward silence, he asked for more of the Ever Rest's history, which Vivi provided with an aplomb that revealed the deep love she held for the inn. She described the years of work her aunt had spent on the garden to make it feel like an English cottage garden, and how her great-grandmother had renovated a forlorn carriage house into a cozy two-bedroom guesthouse after she'd been widowed. She'd lived there with her young children once she had turned the family home into a bed-and-breakfast, and Loretta Ravanelle had never moved back into the main house after her mother had died.

"Is that where you live, too?" Max asked when she paused to indicate a good place to park on a downtown street.

Vivi shook her head. "There's a little suite of rooms on the back side of the second floor that you can get to from the stairs behind the inn office. It's like my own little hideaway, but there's a connecting door in the upstairs hall. It's a buffer between me and the guests, but I'm right there, just in case."

"Now that you're the owner, do you think you'll move to the guest house?"

"I'm . . . not sure." She pursed her lips. "Other than when I had to put together an outfit for the funeral director, I haven't stepped foot inside since Aunt Loretta passed. It still feels so much like her home. I'm not sure I'd ever feel comfortable living there."

Max cut the engine and turned to her, another question at the ready. But she squelched the opportunity by opening her door and brightly announcing that they were only a block from her favorite lunch spot. By the time they were seated at a cozy table and their orders taken, he'd forgotten what he'd meant to ask her.

The conversation turned to lighter, less personal topics once their food came, and then with the bill came Vivi's question about his tourist intentions. "What's your usual slate of activities when you're on vacation? Nature, history, the arts . . . all of the above?"

"All of the above sounds good to me," Max replied, reaching forward. "Whatever you think is worth seeing and doing while I'm here."

Vivi put her hand out at the same time, and he ended up covering hers on top of the check presenter. They both froze for half a second, and then Vivi snatched her hand back. A shot of electricity raced up Max's arm, and a telltale flush inched across Vivi's cheeks as she lowered her gaze to her empty plate and started fidgeting with an unused fork. Max stared at her and slid the presenter toward him.

"How much is my share?" she asked when he flipped it open.

He didn't even glance at the total before pulling out his wallet. "It's my pleasure."

She straightened and shook her head, her eyes widening as he slipped his credit card into the holder and slapped it shut. "You don't have to—I'm happy to split it."

"There are worse things to spend my money on than lunch with a beautiful innkeeper." The blush deepened in her cheeks, and some self-satisfaction leached into his smile. The server came back for the check, and then Max folded his arms on the tabletop and leaned forward. "So what do you suggest?"

Vivi's lips compressed into a thin line for a moment before she spoke, hurt pride echoing in her voice. "I suggest you let me pay for the next meal. Or at least agree to split the bill."

His smile faltered. "Sorry. I guess it's just a habit of mine."

"To buy lunch for a woman you aren't dating?"

He sat back in his chair and regarded her. "Would it be so bad if this was a date?"

She blinked. "It's not, though."

"It could be."

The server returned with his card before she could respond, and once they were alone again, he plunged forward.

"Listen, Vivi. I know—or at least I get the feeling—that you've got a lot on your plate right now."

"You have no idea," she interjected with a short scoff.

Max spread his hands. "I'm here to get away from the grind, have a good time, and relax a little. You said I'm the only guest at the inn this whole week, and you don't really have anything else to do. Even if you feel like it's part of your job to be my tour guide for a couple days, we can still have a lot of fun while we're at it."

She stared at him, then nodded. "All right. But you aren't buying me any more meals unless we agree to it in advance."

"Deal." He stood and held out his hand. "Where to next?"

"I thought a walking tour of Georgetown would be a good start, since it's such a nice day," she said as they left the restaurant. "Depending on how far you want to drive, we could scoot down to Charleston tomorrow, or even Hilton Head. There are a few spots off the beaten path that might be fun to explore, or we can hit the usual highlights. It won't be real crowded this time of year, especially midweek."

"Charleston sounds good." He followed her across the street, inching a little closer to her side when they gained the opposite sidewalk. "I've heard there are some cool places on the sea islands around the Kiawah River that are good for hiking, too."

"For sure. So let's plan for an early breakfast and hitting the sites in Charleston tomorrow, then do some hiking on one of the sea islands on

Thursday. Kiawah or Johns Island." When he nodded his agreement, she gave him a small smile and gestured up the street. "Let's go this way about a block, and I'll show you one of my favorite museums . . ."

By the end of his third day rambling around with Vivi as his guide, Max could recall nothing about the colors of the houses on Charleston's Rainbow Row, the view of the harbor from the broken-down ramparts of Fort Sumter, the reason why Broad Street was so wide, or the damage done to the Calhoun Mansion, among other historic buildings, by Hurricane Hugo's storm surge. Neither would he have been able to describe the live oaks on Johns Island or anything he saw at the Heron Park Nature Center on Kiawah Island.

But once he and Vivi settled down on a bench looking out over the ocean in Kiawah Beachwalker Park, with sunset closing in to the west and a brisk wind buffeting them from the southeast, he could describe his touring companion to anyone who asked. The way she navigated the sidewalks of Charleston as only a seasoned visitor or local could, her hip swaying temptingly close to his whenever she skirted past someone walking in the opposite direction. The cant of her chin as she leaned toward him to point out an elusive waterfowl ducking behind a tree. Her peals of laughter at his discomfort the first time he stepped into the icy surf rolling up the beach, with a smile that could have broken up storm clouds had there been any. The way the sun brought the greenish tints forward in her eyes and highlighted the hidden shades of red coiling throughout her dark curls where they cascaded back from the light pink scarf she'd chosen for a headband.

Best of all, the soft caress of her palm against his as she tugged him toward the bench at the end of the third day, the touch all warmth and welcome and intimacy that not only made him wish for the thousandth time he could remember why she seemed so familiar, but also had his heart racing and his lungs malfunctioning.

"We won't be able to stay too much longer," she said once they melted, tired but satisfied from the day, into the park bench. "Everyone has to be out by sunset."

Max glanced at the lowering sun, figuring they still had another half hour or so before they had to head back to the car. "This has been fantastic. I don't know how I kept up with you. You packed so much in!"

Vivi tipped her head back with a small laugh. "You seemed fit enough to manage. I had you pegged as someone with a regular exercise regimen to combat the desk job."

"There's a difference between a daily morning jog plus hitting a fitness center at lunchtime and . . ." Max swept an open hand out to indicate the beach and the island behind them, encompassing the past couple days as well. "Do you have anything in mind for tomorrow?"

"Unfortunately, no." She sighed and grimaced. "I have a business meeting in the morning, and then I have to touch base with the family lawyer who's handling my aunt's estate."

Max shrugged and looked into the distance to hide his disappointment. "No worries. I have a college buddy who lives down in Savannah, so I'll see if he can meet up for lunch somewhere halfway. Maybe I can do a little solo tour of Hilton Head."

A sideways glance found her also gazing out to sea, worrying her bottom lip between her teeth. But before he could say anything, she abruptly changed the subject. "I have to ask because I'm just that curious. Of all the places to plan a romantic Lowcountry getaway, what made you think of the Ever Rest?"

"It's . . . a little hard to explain." Max draped his arms across the back of the bench, conscious of how easy it would be to slide close enough to hug her shoulders. "I told you how my parents came here with me when I was a kid for a few family vacations."

"For a while, the inn was popular with families," Vivi said with a nod.

"It's not like these were action-packed trips," he continued. "But I always just felt so comfortable and at home every time we stayed there. That's the main thing I remembered."

"Aunt Loretta had a way of making people feel that way."

"But when I was poking around for places to stay, the Ever Rest kept showing as the top result. And all these—" He paused, searching for the right words. "Warm feelings sort of bubbled up. It just seemed like I was getting some sort of message, like I *needed* to stay there. And as soon as I walked up to the gate and saw the inn, that feeling just . . . took over."

She peered at him. "So you think booking at the Ever Rest was meant to be or something?"

"I guess so." He looked out over the ocean again, grinning as a memory surfaced. "There was this one time—the last time my parents and I came, the summer I was twelve. It was the first time I complained about having to do a family vacation at all. I had more important things planned at home, you know? And there was one day when my parents really wanted to go do something we hadn't done before. I don't remember what, but I was not enthused. Your aunt told them over breakfast that I could stay there for the day and she'd keep me occupied, and they could go out exploring as a couple." He stretched his feet out and contemplated the toes of his sneakers while the memory spun. "I thought I was going to die from boredom, but your aunt kept me so busy. I think I weeded the entire garden before lunch, and then she spent the afternoon listening to me explain everything I knew about Pokémon. I'd brought my card binders with me. I thought I was so cool, but I was such a geek. And a girl was staying there, a couple years younger than me. Super quiet. But then your aunt got her to come out on the porch and help her play through a Pokémon game, and she—"

Max broke off, the sudden realization so crystal clear, he couldn't believe it had taken him this long. He twisted on the bench to face Vivi, who was staring at her hands, clasped in her lap, while a furious rush of color bloomed across her cheeks.

"I remember you," he murmured.

She licked her lips before answering, gaze still lowered. "Aunt Loretta thought it would be a fun way for me to practice my mental math. I hadn't done well with it in school the previous year. As I recall, I ended up beating the pants off you, and then you were nice enough to hang out with me the rest of the day."

He frowned. "How could I not match your name and face with that little girl?"

"I had glasses and braces, completely in that awkward preteen stage," she said, looking up at him at last. "And I'm actually not sure if Aunt Loretta told you my name. I know I was too introverted to introduce myself."

"You were pretty."

A shy smile played on her lips, revealing that he'd flattered her. "It makes sense that you wouldn't make the connection right away. We hung out for half a day twenty-two years ago, and since then I got my braces off and ditched the full-time glasses for laser eye surgery. I'm glad you finally remembered, or I was going to have to say something."

"We've both grown up since then." He swept a covert glance over her, matching the little girl in his memory with the woman beside him. "How long did it take you to recognize me?"

She met his gaze. "I recognized you the second you walked in the front door."

"Seriously?"

"I knew your name back then. When I saw your booking, I had a feeling it might be you. How many Max Andersens could there be in the world, let alone in the Carolinas? It wasn't about remembering you, because I never forgot you." She looked out over the water again. "It might have been half a day twenty-two years ago, but it was the best day of that whole summer."

Max would never admit it, at least not at age twelve. But the afternoon spent on the Ever Rest's back porch with the quiet, pretty little girl he now knew was Vivi had been his favorite part of that particular family vacation. At the time, he'd thought he'd seen hero worship in her eyes from getting to hang out with an older boy who thought himself too awesome for words. But looking back, his preteen hubris had kept him from seeing into Vivi's heart.

He slid closer to her on the bench, daring at last to rest his arm against the back of her shoulders. "What made it the best day?"

Vivi took a deep breath, her lips tight, before speaking. "I told you my dad was military."

"Yeah."

"His unit was deployed to Afghanistan just after Christmas. My mom and grandparents tried to keep things as normal as possible for me, but it was hard." She blinked rapidly, as if tears had suddenly sprung into her eyes. "My brothers were both out of the house, and I felt so alone. I was really close to my dad—still am—and it was the sort of deployment where we couldn't know exactly where he was, couldn't talk more than a few minutes on the phone once a week, and letters had to be completely devoid of anything that might give away his location or what he was doing." Her voice shook, and her chin trembled for a moment. "He'd been deployed before, so it's not like we weren't used to it. But my mom was especially stressed, and that just added to everything I was feeling. My grades were slipping, I didn't want to hang out with my friends, and nobody knew how to keep my spirits up. My grandparents suggested I spend the summer with Aunt Loretta, hoping she could help me. And she did, in her way. I fell in love with the inn that summer. And then, when you were so willing to hang out with me, it just—"

She faced him with an expression that seemed to indicate she had more to say but couldn't find the right words. Instead, she stood and brushed some clinging sand from the back of her pants. Rather than push, Max joined her as she started down the walkway heading back toward the parking lot. But he lessened the distance between them as they strolled along, letting his silence speak for him.

Chapter Six

The chain of the back porch swing creaked as Vivi eased it back and forth with one foot. She lay semi-sprawled across the throw pillows, the folder Mr. Bauer had given her with all the financial information tossed to one side of the seat.

The past few days with Max had been a welcome respite from all her worries, and her heart floated in a way it hadn't in a few years over the way he looked at her and found reasons to touch her. The awkward feeling of one-sided recollection gone, she found herself wishing he could extend his stay, even by just a few days. She'd been a silly, sad kid the last time he'd lifted her spirits, and childhood crushes didn't usually grow into anything real. But Max had admitted it felt like more than coincidence that the Ever Rest Inn had popped up as an option when he'd started planning his getaway. The operating budget didn't allow for advertising, so the inn wouldn't come up as a sponsored result anywhere.

Maybe he was never meant to come here with his ex-girlfriend. Maybe he was always supposed to come here to reconnect with Vivi.

The idea seemed a ridiculous fantasy. But Aunt Loretta always believed it was impossible to plan for anything that wasn't meant to be in the first place, and that greater powers would work to make the meant-to-be happen.

The back screen door squealed on its hinges, then banged shut. Vivi lifted her head as Max sauntered outside, his hands in his pockets.

"Did you get ahold of your friend?" she asked, sitting up.

"He's traveling for work, as it happens. So I'm on my own tomorrow after all." He crossed to the swing and started to sit before he noticed the folder beside Vivi. He picked it up, turning and lowering onto the seat. "This looks important."

Instinct had her reaching for the folder and wanting to hug it to her chest as if to hide it. Instead, she set it onto her lap and flattened her hands on top. "Probably the most important thing right now."

He shifted on the swing, tucking one knee up so he was sitting sideways. "Anything I could help with?"

"Actually . . . I could use a banking analyst right now. Or at least a good financial advisor." She took a deep breath and handed the folder back to him. "That's all the information about the two mortgages my aunt took out on the inn, along with some outstanding bills for renovations and repairs that were done over the last couple years."

"Are you sure you're okay with me looking at this?" he asked, frowning with concern.

Taking a deep breath, she nodded. "The estate is in probate right now, and our lawyer was able to get the bank to pause the mortgage payments until everything's finalized. But that's not going to help with the unpaid bills, or be a permanent solution to the mortgages. I'm meeting with the loan officer tomorrow morning, but I'm supposed to come up with a plan of action for how all of this will be settled out. Unless," she continued, her voice catching, "I decide to cut my losses and sell the inn."

Max's frown deepened. "You can't do that. This is your family's legacy."

"I know." She drew her knees up to her chest and hugged them, feeling very much like a lost little girl again. "But I have no clue what to do. Which is why I thought . . . maybe you'd have some suggestions."

Pensive silence settled over them as Max opened the folder and began perusing the paperwork. He gave a little thoughtful noise every now and then, mumbling to himself at one point and shaking his head at another. Finally, he snapped the folder shut and met her expectant gaze. "I don't think you'll need to sell. But you do have some steps to take with the mortgages. What time do you meet with the loan officer?"

"Ten o'clock."

He nodded. "I'll come with you."

Vivi sat up straight, planting her feet on the floor again. "You don't have to do that."

"You need a financial advisor. Well, you've got one." He stood, using both hands to gesture to himself. "He's pretty good, too. So if you have a general plan for the future of the inn, I can muddle through the specifics of the finances."

"But I don't have a plan," she said. "That's part of the problem."

Max nodded and started pacing. "Well, for starters, you need to get in touch with someone at the insurance agency that holds the policy for the whole property. At least some of the cost of the roof should have been paid out. And you need to sit down face-to-face with whoever did the renovations and figure out a new payment plan."

"With what money?" she asked, rising. "I'm breaking even right now in terms of running the inn. It'll get a little better once the busy season starts in another couple months. But there really isn't any savings. All of it went to pay the balance of Aunt Loretta's medical bills."

"As part of probate, you'll go through your aunt's personal belongings and catalog everything. Anything of value could be used to pay off debts."

Vivi's jaw dropped. "I—I don't know if I can go through her things and sell them off like that."

Max shook his head. "Probate doesn't really give you a choice. Anything that can pay off debts is essentially seized. Do you know if there's anything of hers with sentimental value?"

"Not really. Before she died, Aunt Loretta started giving heirlooms and things to people. Probably to avoid them being taken during probate, I guess."

"Probably. Gifting money to people is a little trickier to get around, but if she started passing out heirlooms and they weren't in her possession when she died, then that's a done deal." Max crossed his arms. "So you need a plan of action for the inn. Do you have any ideas?"

"None. I'm very open to suggestions, though."

"This isn't my wheelhouse," he continued, "so I'm just spitballing. But you need to probably bring in more than just bed-and-breakfast traffic. The gardens are amazing, and there are tons of rooms on the first floor that are all connected. You could do events—graduation parties, reunions, even weddings."

Vivi cocked her head at him, considering. "That's a lot of work."

"But people look for that stuff, you know? And you wouldn't have to provide all the bells and whistles, just the location. People can bring in their own vendors." He came to her and rested his hands on her shoulders. "And—hard as it might be—you could offer the guesthouse as its own accommodation option."

"I don't—" But she clamped her lips shut over the reflexive protest. It was a good idea, and one that could bring in extra money. She lived in the manager's suite as it was, and if she ever got married and wanted a space for a family, that could all be reconsidered. "That could work."

Silence pressed down on them again, and Vivi became hyper aware that Max hadn't moved away, still had his hands on her shoulders. She looked up at him, surprised to see a look of intensity tightening his features. He ran his palms down her arms and moved closer.

"Vivi," he murmured. "Just so you know, I think I have to kiss you."

Her lungs seized, but she squeaked out a pathetic, "You can't. It's against the rules."

Max gave a sideways grin. "There are rules against kissing the innkeeper?"

"No, it's the porch rules." She gestured weakly behind her, where she knew a kitschy sign hung beside the back door.

He dragged his gaze from hers and squinted to read the sign in the dim porch light. "The porch is for sitting, conversing, and contemplating. No hanky-panky, canoodling, or other shenanigans."

"Aunt Loretta had the sign custom-made."

A low chuckle rumbled in his throat. "What's canoodling?"

Vivi couldn't help a giggle of her own. "It's old-timey slang for making out."

"You know," he said, leaning toward her until their foreheads almost touched. "You're the owner now. It's your porch. You get to make your own rules."

Gasping at the intimate tone of his voice, she rested her hands on his chest. "Max, this is crazy. We don't know each other. You have a whole life in Charlotte that you're going back to on Sunday."

"A life I'm kind of over," he replied. "Besides, we've known each other since we were kids, right?"

"I'm not sure it counts."

"Why not?" He slipped his arms around her waist and pulled her close. "Vivi, I have no idea why you remembered me and I didn't remember you. Or why I felt so strongly about booking a stay here instead of somewhere in Georgetown or Charleston. But I feel like—I know—something real and special and important is going on here."

She leaned into him, reveling in the way she seemed to fit perfectly against him. "What, exactly, are you suggesting?"

"Besides some canoodling?"

She laughed, letting her arms slide up to encircle his shoulders and draw him down. "Sometimes things are meant to be, even when we don't plan on them. But I'm a planner, so I need to know your intentions."

"Well," he began, pausing long enough to brush the tip of his nose against hers, "after we get up to some completely innocent shenanigans right here on the back porch, we're going to look over all that paperwork and come up with a real plan. And tomorrow morning, after I cook you an amazing breakfast to say thanks for making this trip so awesome—and making me feel like I'm where I belong—we're going to meet with the loan officer at the bank and lay that plan all out on the table."

She tipped her head back until she could look into his eyes. Despite his slightly teasing tone, only earnest honesty showed in his gaze. And something else. Something more than interest, even more than attraction. She recognized it because it had been building in her heart since he'd arrived on Monday afternoon.

"But you do have to go back to Charlotte on Sunday," she reminded him.

"I have to check out on Sunday." Max closed the distance between their lips but refrained from making contact. "I don't have to go back to Charlotte if I don't want to."

Anticipation almost made her squirm. "Max . . ."

"I haven't enjoyed my job in a while. And I'm sick of the grind. I'm bored. I'm lonely and unhappy with my life. Maybe an extended vacation is what I need to reevaluate what I want. Though I already have a pretty good idea."

"This is crazy."

"This is me falling in love with you."

At that, the space between them disappeared. Vivi's heart nearly burst with joy, even while the very fibers of her being exploded in heat and desire. Her little-girl crush hadn't prepared her for this by any means, and she clung to him to keep him close, answering his kiss with her own.

Finally, when they came up for air, she shook her head and repeated, "This is crazy."

Max took her face between his hands. "I know it's a lot, Vivi, especially with everything else you're dealing with. And I can't explain it because I'm not the kind of guy who goes around talking about falling in love and making plans for anything like forever after only a few days. I promise, I'm not."

She smiled, realizing that he wasn't the only one ready to jump feet first into something insane. "Max, it's okay."

"I'll get in touch with HR tomorrow to extend my vacation, talk to some people, try to get something lined up so I'm not a total pauper in three months. I've actually already put some applications in for banking jobs in Georgetown and Charleston, and recruiters have started emailing and calling. But I want to be here. I want to help you figure out what's next, and after that—"

"Max." Vivi set her fingertips against his mouth, stopping the flood of words. "I've been in love with you since I was ten years old. We obviously need to do some real get-to-know-you work. But if you're in, I'm in. I don't know how many 'after thats' we'll have, or if we'll get to have a forever after.

But as absolutely insane as it seems, yes. Let's go for it." She kissed him again, then smiled against his lips. "Help me save the Ever Rest Inn. And then stay. I'll take down the 'No Canoodling' sign."

He laughed, a warm, deep sound. "Promise?"

She shrugged. "I mean, we'll have to pay attention when guests are here, but . . ."

Max silenced her with another kiss. Then, after a long, tight embrace, they settled down on the porch swing and bent their heads over the financials folder. Only days ago, nothing had seemed certain. But now, Vivi saw a solid future for the inn. And for the first time in years, the lonely little girl faded away, leaving behind the glow of hope and the nascent stirrings of a love that could last forever.

The End

About J. Lynn Rowan

A writer since childhood, J. Lynn Rowan is currently published in romance, historical fiction, and academia. When not writing, she enjoys traveling, cooking and baking, and learning and teaching history. She lives near Charlotte, NC, with her own Romantic Hero of a husband and their children.

Find J. Lynn Online:

Website: http://jlynnrowanliterature.wordpress.com
Newsletter: http://eepurl.com/bt5Er9
Facebook: https://www.facebook.com/JLynnRowan
X : https://x.com/JLynnRowanLit
Instagram: https://www.instagram.com/jlynnrowanlit/
Amazon: https://www.amazon.com/author/jlynnrowan

Goodreads: https://www.goodreads.com/jlynnrowanlit
BookBub: https://www.bookbub.com/authors/j-lynn-rowan

Work, Play, & a Folly Vacay

by Addie Bealer

Work, Play, & a Folly Vacay

by Addie Bealer

Recently retired from corporate life, free-spirited Lily has an entrepreneurial nature, a zest for life, and more ideas than organizational skills. A trial run of her new business goes slightly awry when she sorta maybe accidentally kidnaps Sean. He's a structured workaholic, a mature single guy whose week-long plans for company team building leave him sidelined.

After publishing a less-than-glowing review of her work, Sean can't seem to avoid repeated run-ins with the woman who tempts his logistical brain as well as his lonely heart. Lily's initial attraction to Sean leaves her wanting much more, until his attempt at helping her business model backfires on both of them. A better-late-than-never chance at love might be worth the steps each will have to take to close the distance between them.

Chili Pepper Rating: 1

Chapter One

"Lily Melancon, you get your chaotic butt back here and give me some direction. I won't fall victim to your harum-scarum paper-planning system and miss picking up a client again. Twenty-five years into this century, you'd think technology would be second nature to you by now." Josie Whelan, panting from the quick jog from her apartment a block away, lifted her dreads off her neck and fanned her face with an envelope. "Sweating in April isn't normal."

"It is around here. Summer starts early in Charleston." Lily might still make a quick getaway. In a rush, she ticked off to-do items on her abundantly ringed fingers. "New brochures go in the bin. First yoga clients are at eleven. You'll need to heat the studio and get releases signed. Pick up the Evanses at one thirty and drop them on King Street. I don't know when I'll be back. Late if things go well, early if not. Thanks for filling in on such short notice. I love you."

She grabbed an overstuffed tote bag and sprinted—proud that she still could at fifty-five—to her car, sandals crunching on the gravel drive and bracelets jingle-jangling.

For good luck, she reached up and touched the sign hanging over the front door of her business on Folly Beach. Lily's Pad. It made her smile. Her tour-guiding business and yoga/art studio allowed her to engage with her passions and support herself at the same time. She'd added classes on making soap and candles, as well as bath-salt creation. Putting her merch in other businesses around town naturally drew more clients to the studio.

"And I'm not harum-scarum. I'm spontaneous." Two decades in corporate America had been too much. Lily much preferred her second, post-retirement career as a free spirit.

She had enough time to drop off some flyers at the Folly Beach bed-and-breakfasts that supplied most of her customers. Then, she'd fill the car with gas on James Island and get to the seafood restaurant off Maybank to collect her last-minute client almost on time.

Clive had called in a panic from the Wind Charm Guesthouse, requesting help ASAP. But this morning she could only promise ASASCM (As Soon As She Could Manage). Clive hadn't given her any info other than that this guy couldn't make his scheduled activity for today. The Wind Charm's one shuttle van was on its way to the airport, and Clive didn't want to leave his guest stranded. She could handle that.

It gave her the perfect opportunity to beta test her latest money-making idea.

This business brainchild, Lily's Live Like a Local, was made for the visitor whose plans fell through at the last minute, or people who wanted to see Charleston and its environs from a road less traveled. The scheme? Avoid all the normal tourist traps and popular parts of downtown. Her clients would see the area like a resident and do what the natives did on a daily basis, eat where the locals ate, and participate in some community activities.

Not a bad idea. Not bad at all.

She just hadn't had time to pull something together before the call this morning. She'd wing it. She hadn't reached her mid-fifties without learning to improvise here and there.

Lily pulled up to a gas pump in front of her favorite convenience store. Terence's old blue Kia was parked out front, a sure sign she'd be having sweet potato pie for breakfast. Her mouth watered. She put the nozzle into her car and went inside.

"Hey, Lily." Terence's deep voice greeted her from behind the counter.

"Hey, T. Your grandma been baking this morning?" She put twenty dollars onto the counter for gas and another five, hoping . . .

"Yes, ma'am. She told me she made these extra sweet, just for you." He slid a plastic-wrapped aluminum tart pan filled with flaky crust and creamy filling across the chipped Formica. The bills disappeared under his big palm.

"You're telling stories again, Terence. She makes them the same every day for everyone, and that's why I love her." Lily took the wrap off the tart and bit into it while heading for the door. "Mmm! Not bad. Not bad at all. Ask her if she wants to be one of my stops. I need good places to bring folks."

"I'll do it. Where's Miss Josie today?"

"At the Lily Pad. You should go take her yoga class." Lily winked at the giant behind the register.. His crush on her friend and business partner ran a mile long and two years deep. She'd have to do something soon if those two didn't stop dancing around their obvious attraction for each other.

Lily hopped back into her car and headed toward the drawbridge on Folly Road. Only a few more lights before her turn. The crowds were bad and getting worse the warmer the weather got. Soon her quiet little slice of heaven would fill with people who weren't lucky enough to live there. She didn't blame half the country for visiting her adopted hometown. Heck, she'd been a tourist once too. Now she reveled in her permanent vacation. Now . . . ahh . . . it was home sweet ho—

Shoot! She almost missed it. Her tires squealed through the tight left turn. A restaurant that didn't open for breakfast was an odd place to collect a customer. No one was in sight except some old guy with a down-on-his-luck vibe. He was hunched over, so she couldn't see his face. His slumped shoulders, rumpled clothes, and stained bucket hat spoke of a rough life.

He's probably hoping the kitchen has a sympathetic early shift.

Lily parked and locked her car, letting her path to the dock go past the old guy. She tucked a few folded bills under his knapsack as she walked by.

━━━━━ ♥ ━━━━━

Sean Waters, CEO of Waters Craftech, Inc. and best-selling author of a best-business practices manual, was utterly defeated by his own livelihood. What a joke. He'd never hear the end of this at next month's shareholders' meeting.

Team-building excursions were supposed to be fun. Invigorating. He'd brought the entire management team to Folly Beach to get to know one another outside of the office and to give everyone a chance to explore one another's strengths independent of the demands of the workplace. Boy, had it backfired.

As a show of support for his new VP, he'd promised free reign to arrange the whole week. The guy had booked every day for the entire week on one boat or another. Sean hated boats. Boats hated Sean. They made him fifty shades of green.

His head still spun like a waterspout and his whole body floated on an imaginary unmoored jetty. How was that possible half an hour after leaving that waterlogged death trap and downing a couple Dramamine? If the B&B's driver didn't get here soon, he might pass out. He'd never fallen asleep on a public bench before, but today had broken him.

He moved his borrowed backpack along the bench to serve as a pillow for his swimming head. A few folded dollar bills floated to the ground. Must have fallen out of one of the pockets. Sean tucked the money into a zippered compartment of the backpack and lowered his head to his makeshift pillow.

Nope. That made the dizziness worse and his stomach revolt. He sat up. And what smelled? It wasn't the clothes. His best friend, a fishing guide, promised they'd been recently washed, even if they did look like something off a trash pile. Some waft of a too-sweet perfume or flower he didn't recognize drifted into his nostrils. He took the borrowed hat off his head and waved it in front of his face. Soon he'd have the courage to open both of his eyes. He hoped the horizon would stay still when he did.

The smell got stronger.

"Are you Sean Waters?" A voice veered toward cheerful. Too cheerful. And lots of tinkly, plinky noise accompanied it.

Finally. He hated the thought of standing again, but the bench had lost its appeal. He took a fortifying breath and instantly regretted it.

What is that smell?

"Please tell me you're the shuttle driver and that the van doesn't smell like that." He stood, slowly, lifting his head and opening his eyes last.

Before him stood a human garden. Bright green tank top with a leaf print, floral skirt that swirled around long legs, sandals with plastic flowers on the toe, and a white bloom tucked into curly hair spiraling around a long neck.

"I'll take that as a yes, and I don't know what the van smells like. The B&B's driver couldn't make it, so they called me." Her lips curved upward, but she didn't quite smile.

"Fine." He didn't feel well enough to be picky. Or polite. "But take it easy on the turns."

He stuffed his borrowed bucket hat into a cargo pocket and shouldered the backpack. She spun around and made all those colors and patterns sway nauseatingly in his vision. Sean followed her to an orange SUV. Of course it screamed out loud. Everything about this woman was flashy. Colors, scents. Her walk. She clicked and jingled and clanked with every step due to the ridiculous number of bracelets and chains she wore. She pressed the unlock button on her key fob an unnecessary number of times, making the car chirp like an angry bird.

"We can put your bag in the trunk. That'll give you more room in the back seat. There's a water and some healthy snacks in the basket—"

"Water, yes. Snacks, no." Sean couldn't muster the manners the situation required. He definitely couldn't handle the back seat after three hours on the boat from hell. He'd never been carsick, but why take the chance today? "I'll sit in the front."

She paused walking and chattering, thank God, but only for a minute. Unfortunately, the quiet didn't last once they were in the car.

"I'm Lily, by the way, one of your host's vendors. I'm sorry your plans fell through, but never fear." She seemed to have decided to ignore his rudeness and forge ahead, even though he'd reclined the passenger seat and closed his eyes. "Your day is about to take a turn for the better. Would you like to hear a bit about the history of the area while we drive to—"

"No." Sean grimaced at his curt answer.

Her voice wasn't the issue. It had a nice, soothing tone, almost husky. It was the perk that bothered him. Plus, he'd bet anything she had bathed in floral perfume.

He softened his voice on purpose. "And can you put a window down? The odor is stronger up here."

Sean heard her quiet intake of breath and slow exhale, like she was searching for patience by counting silently to ten. He'd have his assistant send an appropriate apology note and gift. He wished he could type that in the memo folder on his phone, but the thought of looking at a tiny screen in a moving car stopped him.

"Fine." Her voice took on a clipped tone. "Enjoy the quiet and I'll let you know when we're there."

For a blissfully long while, Sean reveled in the silence and the scent-free breeze that blew across him from the open windows. He may have dozed, he wasn't sure, but his stomach finally settled and the tranquilizing effects of the anti-nausea medication started to wear off.

"Here we are. Your first stop."

The cheeriness came back, and Sean vowed to act more like a decent human.

Wait. First stop?

Chapter Two

Lily had never had a client fall asleep in her car. This guy, though . . .

Clive had vouched for him, so she felt safe enough. Probably having a really bad day. Doubtlessly super disappointed his original plans hadn't worked out. Maybe hung over from too much King Street last night? Anyway, her ideas for letting him live like a local had come together while he dozed. After going to three of her favorite places, he'd surely have a better attitude.

He couldn't get much better physically. When in her whole life had she been this close to corporeal perfection? The man had to be her age or a couple years older. Salt-and-pepper hair, still thick and wavy. A jawline that could cut glass, even with the midmorning stubble. No sign of a paunch around the middle. Nicely muscled forearms visible below his rolled-up shirt sleeves.

Not bad. Not bad at all.

No wedding ring or tan line where one usually rested.

Stop it. Haven't you retired that part of your life? He's too grumpy anyway. Probably still lives in his mother's basement.

The thought made her giggle. This guy definitely didn't live in anyone's basement. She had the feeling he didn't usually dress so casually. Even in repose, he looked all wrong in scuffed deck shoes, baggy cargo pants, and a wrinkled sportsman's shirt. Okay, so she'd looked closely. No shame in appreciating beauty when she could. She'd never see him again after today.

"Time to go." She raised her voice a bit since he hadn't moved much the first time she announced they were at their destination—or one of them.

He brought his seat back into an almost full upright position. "Where are we?"

"Red's Berry Farm." Lily threw her arms as wide as she could in the car and sang the name of the farm in her best ta-daaa voice.

He looked out his window, then through the windshield, then back at her. "Why? And what happened to your . . .?" He gestured to his own head.

She pulled her visor down and flipped to the mirror. Well, crap. Of course the humidity and wind had taken her hair and tossed it six ways from Sunday. She got out of the car and shoved tendrils back into place as best she could while walking toward the entrance and chatting about the organic farming methods of her favorite strawberry grower. It took a minute to realize her client hadn't followed her.

"What are you waiting for?" She walked back to the car. Since he still wasn't moving, she bent down to talk to him through the window.

"I don't know why we're here."

"This is your first stop."

"My first stop of what?" The guy frowned at her.

"Of the day. Of the three things I have planned for you as you live like a local."

"I don't want to live like a local. I want to go back to the guesthouse and crawl under the bed. Then I want to get back to work since I can't do the things I came here to do." He checked his watch, muttering about flight schedules. "Is this some kind of scam? I'm calling an Uber."

"No! Don't do that." Think of the beta test. She needed a good review for her fledgling project. "Your host said your plans fell through and that you needed an alternative vacation experience. That's why he called me. For a different excursion."

Sort of.

He fiddled with his phone, looking like a male model version of someone who believes he's been kidnapped.

"I had an excursion. Turns out I'm prone to seasickness. I'm nauseous, dehydrated, and have a mean Dramamine hangover."

"Well, why didn't you say so in the first place?" Lily chuckled and waved both hands in the air, chasing away all his troubles, jewelry chiming in musically. She opened the hatchback and dug around in her tote. "Here."

"What's this?" He held his hand out.

"Ginger chews. Great for nausea. You're in the perfect spot on Johns Island to cure yourself." She started for the entrance again, hoping he'd follow. Her first time out on a Live Like a Local tour . . . Could. Not. Fail. "Anyway, strawberries taste as good coming up as they do going down. And these are the best on the island." She saw the farm's owner headed over to greet them. "Hi, Red."

"Glad you called, Lily. I've got several rows that ripened up this morning. Howdy, young man." Only Red could get away with calling a man who looked to be at least her age young man. At almost ninety, Red had outlived all his siblings and could still outwork everyone on the farm. "Come on in. Don't be shy. Berries are waitin' to be picked and ain't got all day."

Lily scooted through the gate, mightily relieved to see Sean Waters making his way out of her car. Even though he shook his head in what might be irritation, at least he had put his phone away. So his personality lacked charm. She didn't mind spending a day appreciating his other qualities.

Now, she just had to get him to the next two destinations and ask for a positive review. She could make that happen.

Red's was the best—and only—strawberry farm Sean had ever been to. After that, they stopped at a local library for an hour-long story time for adults. He'd been surprised at first when Lily told him about it, but it wasn't *that* kind of adult content. An older woman with a lovely speaking voice read from a memoir collection on topics ranging from the history of Johns Island to local ghost lore. It provided a pleasant respite from the heat and all that jewelry jangling. He sat in a deliciously cool room, ate Lorna Doone cookies, and thoroughly enjoyed himself, much to his amazement.

They ended the afternoon at Beachwalker County Park for an hour he'd never forget. When they pulled up to the kiosk to pay the entry fee, Lily turned to him.

"Um, I can't find my pass and I'm a couple bucks short. Can you give me two ones?"

"Are you kidding me? You didn't know you needed cash?" He dug around and found the ones he'd stuffed into the backpack earlier.

"Of course I knew. But I gave them to you when I thought you were homeless and might be hungry, and since that's not the case, now you can give them back."

He handed them over and shook his head. There was some sort of logic in that sentence somewhere. At least his temporary hostess was a good human. Then, as if she knew just the right medicine for a landlubber, Lily took him to a less crowded part of the beach. Her ever-present tote bag revealed chilled bottles of water, a sand-proof throw, sunscreen, and a portable Bluetooth speaker. She turned on some weird music, told him to apply the lotion, and handed him a bottle of essential oil to sniff.

"Peppermint will settle your stomach and chase away the cobwebs," she said. Then she invited him to sit there and enjoy the view or join her on a walk.

He chose the former. It still chafed that she'd corralled him without his consent, but he supposed the B&B had hired her for a reason. And he felt much better. Why not just accept his fate?

Staying behind on the blanket allowed him a good view of Lily as she walked along the water. Younger than him, but he couldn't tell how much. A little bit of gray mixed in her dark, curly hair. A few laugh lines and frown lines. Tall, lithe, confident. All the things he normally admired in a woman. But she gave a definite hippie vibe. Not his style. Too loosey-goosey. He liked polished. Understated and pulled together. Sedate. With all those rings and ankle bracelets and flowy clothes, Lily couldn't be characterized as sedate.

Anyway, what did it matter? His focus in Charleston was on his team, not a vacation fling.

Right?

Chapter Three

With yesterday's seasickness all but forgotten, Sean resumed his regular morning schedule. Up at five, coffee, five-mile run, shower, breakfast, conferences with production teams, and lunch at one pm precisely. A well-ordered workday. Predictable, steady, productive.

Sean opened the calendar on his laptop. The Yelp review he'd written for his unplanned outing yesterday was still visible. He frowned, tightening one corner of his mouth.

Lily's Live Like a Local tour is probably worth the money you will spend on it. The guide is knowledgeable and capable. Unfortunately, her strong perfume and distracting adornments diminished my ability to enjoy the day. I'd advise the proprietress to adopt a more professional mode of dress and to inform her clients of their destination(s) at the outset of the tour to avoid confusion and disappointment.

Too harsh?

No, it was honest. He closed the screen and checked his watch. Still enough time for a little work before his next activity. His assistant had arranged for the B&B to fill his afternoons while the rest of the crew enjoyed the water. He didn't want to offend his assistant or his host, so at two thirty precisely, according to the schedule he'd been given, he would present himself on the front porch. At least today's activity would be beneficial.

Despite leaving his room on time, a phone call delayed his arrival at the porch by five minutes. He eased the squeaky screen door open, tiptoed to the one empty space at the back of the crowd, and sat down cross-legged on a colorful blanket.

"Now that we're all here, let's begin by settling into stillness. We'll run through a few breathing exercises first, then move into some gentle muscle-lengthening poses."

You've got to be kidding me.

This woman was invading his life again? But gone was the wild-haired free spirit in flowy skirts. Wearing a form-fitting top and slim joggers, both in very sedate black, she had tamed all that glorious hair in a sleek, low ponytail. No bracelets, anklets, or potent perfume that he could detect from a distance.

He turned to his immediate neighbor. "Isn't this supposed to be a runners' stretch class?"

"It is," the young man whispered. "Don't worry, you'll catch on. Lily's great."

"Shh!" The older lady on his other side apparently took breathing very seriously.

He frowned at the young man and scowled at the lady. Well, there went another afternoon wasted. What did she have in her tote bag today? Incense and crystals?

"Are there questions in the back?" Lily craned her neck to see the last row.

Sean ducked his head and wished the screen door didn't make so much noise. He wasn't too proud to admit that he'd retreat if he could.

Maybe she hadn't seen his review yet. It wasn't all that bad.

"Now let's move to all fours and use that breath to guide your cat-cow flow."

It just wasn't all that good.

———— ♥ ————

Lily had known there was a chance she would see Sean again. He was staying at the Wind Charm where she led a weekly yoga class. She just hadn't thought he'd willingly sign up for ninety minutes in her company after being so curt when she'd dropped him off yesterday. Plus, his review had made it abundantly clear she wasn't his cup of tea. What was that old saying about faint praise? Well, he'd faint praised her right to the bottom of the tourist attraction barrel.

Probably worth the money, indeed. She'd show him professional. And she wouldn't offer any homemade bath salts to ease his aching muscles tomorrow either.

She looked around the room. All regulars except him. And all regular runners except Mrs. Flannagan.

"We're going to do a deep dive for you runners today. A little extra love for those of you who're signing up for the Ravenel Bridge Run. Mrs. Flannagan, you know how to modify, right, dear?"

Ninety minutes later, while her class lay in corpse pose, she had to hand it to the man—he didn't give up. She'd even reminded everyone not to push beyond their limit and to take a child's pose if they needed it. Either he didn't need it or he was trying to prove a point. She could respect that.

She expected him to be first off the porch after namaste, but he stayed put. Several people came to say thank you or chat for a minute, but as she put her smudging bundle and sound bowl back into her tote, Lily realized she couldn't avoid him. She gritted her teeth and walked to his mat.

"I'd offer you your money back, but since I didn't get paid for yesterday, you're out of luck." She swung her tote up to her shoulder.

"I see you've read the review." He got to his feet a little slowly.

At least he had the good grace to look uncomfortable. She didn't know if it was from today's class or yesterday's Yelp slam.

"I have. And so have hundreds of others by now. I guess I should take some of that as constructive criticism, but you attacked me personally and didn't give my business a fair shake. I hope you don't take any more tours while you're here. Lots of the guides are my friends, and sometimes their livelihoods depend on their clients' good opinions of them."

"Why didn't you get paid for the tour? Does someone owe you money?" He frowned at her.

"It was a trial run. You were my first Live Like a Local client." Suddenly, it sounded as if she had used him as a guinea pig. "When Clive said your day had been canceled and you needed a ride, I . . ."

Oh dear.

"You what? Do you mean to tell me you actually kidnapped me?" A vein near his temple ran into his hairline, right at a peppery patch, and it sort of throbbed.

"No!" Why hadn't she asked more questions? It had seemed like such a great idea at the time. Stranger in town, plans derailed. He needed something to do, and she needed a . . . guinea pig. "You seemed disappointed that your day was ruined, and I knew I could show you a good time."

He put his hands on his hips and raised his eyebrows at her.

"Not like that."

"My plans were canceled because I got seasick. Horribly, violently seasick. And all I wanted was a ride back here to recover in peace. Instead, you and your over-the-top perfume and noisy jewelry dragged me to hell and back—"

"Oh, please. You ate your weight in free strawberries and Lorna Doones. I had to drag your happy ass off the beach before they kicked us out at closing time." She shouldered past him through the squeaky door and down the front porch steps. "And you owe Clive fifteen dollars for today's class."

Hours later, Lily clutched her laptop like it was her lifeline.

"Oh, go ahead and respond to it," Josie advised. "You know you want to, and if it will get your mind off it, do it. We still have the rest of the week to prepare for. Remember I told you we need to sort out the scheduling before it gets busy. Your sticky notes are overwhelming the calendar."

"I know. The problem is, he's probably right about some of this." She gestured to the paragraph on the screen.

"People can be right and still not be jerks." Josie walked over and massaged her shoulders for a minute. "You know Terence would be happy to pay him a visit for you."

"Terence has never hurt a flea and won't start now over something this silly."

"True, but you have to admit his size alone would scare that man into changing his review."

"Speaking of Terence—" Lily tried every so often to nudge the two together. It had never worked. But this time, Josie had brought him up. "He asked for you again."

"You wouldn't know that if you didn't stop there every other day."

"Seriously, J." Lily caught her friend's hand. "He likes you. You like him. What's wrong?"

"I'm over that part of my life. I thought you were too. But look at you, mooning over that three-star review like some man broke your heart."

"My heart's only a little broken. I was sorta attracted to him. Don't change the subject. If there's no hope, you gotta let Terrence know. I think he's in love with you." Lily made a sad puppy-dog face and batted her lashes.

Josie looked out of the corner of her eyes and laughed. Sobering, she drew a long breath. "He's a nice guy. Too young for me. I'm in a good place, and I don't want another man cuttin' up my peace. I've got work and I've got Little Jo and I've got you. What more could I want?" She shrugged.

"Well, work ends by six every night, Little Jo is a dog, not a loving human to share your life with, and one of my friend duties is to act as your wingman. And girl, I'm telling you, that man is smitten. Give him a chance."

As Josie turned away, waving her hand to dismiss the conversation, Lily read the damning review one more time.

Well, she had begged him for an honest evaluation of his day. Even on the eighth read through, it didn't sting any less. If she hadn't been considering asking him out for drinks when she'd dropped him off, maybe it wouldn't hurt so much. She sighed. Time to put on the big-girl panties. She guessed she should be thankful that she had the opportunity for a public reply.

Thank you for taking the time to review this emerging business. As a fledgling enterprise, we look forward to working out all the kinks. We strive to give our clients the best service possible, and to that end, appreciate your reminder that many of our guests may be especially sensitive to odors and noise. We are currently working on a menu of stops for our guests to choose from as well as a "surprise me" itinerary for our more adventurous clients. As always, we appreciate open communication and honest feedback.

Not bad. Lily closed the laptop with a snap, grabbed her smudging sticks, lit them, and created a veritable cloud over her computer. Let that be the end of that.

Chapter Four

At happy hour on Friday, while his management team enjoyed another day of deep-sea fishing, something he couldn't fathom doing, Sean enjoyed an ice-cold beer at a beach-front bar.

"Another?" The young bartender held up a frosty glass, waiting for the nod to fill it.

"Why not? Nothing else going on."

"Then you might as well enjoy that retirement."

Cheeky bastard. A few gray hairs shouldn't signal the end of a career.

Retirement was a sore spot. What would he have if he didn't have work? The prospect of years and years with nothing productive to do with his time scared the hell out of him. Refusing to discuss it with his friendly local barkeep, Sean accepted his beer and swiveled his stool to take in the view.

An orange SUV turned into the lot and parked.

Noooooo . . .

Nowhere to run, nowhere to hide. How did that old song go? In the split second before she saw him, he wondered about the location of a back door.

Pull it together, man. It's not like you've never spoken to a woman before.

A very beautiful woman, who, under any other circumstance, he'd have asked out on a date by now.

The beautiful woman unfolded her graceful length from her car and carried a stack of hats into the establishment. She looked about as happy to see him as he could expect her to. He stood.

Silence.

They looked at each other, then away. Sean stuffed his hands into his pockets. He took them out and ran one hand through his hair. He lifted his chin toward the bar.

"Buy you a drink?" God, was that the best he could do?

"If it will make this situation any less awkward, sure." She slid onto a barstool and ordered. "Just one, though. I'm on the clock."

He must have looked as confused as he felt.

"I teach dance lessons here on Thursdays and Fridays, and the owner feeds me. Benefits both of us. But I can't drink and dance with impunity anymore."

Turned out, though, she could. Sean watched in amazement as Lily commandeered the microphone from the band, charmed all the restaurant patrons, passed out costume cowboy hats, and gave a mesmerizing demo of the "Cotton Eye Joe." She had everyone in the whole place on the floor.

Her jeans hugged in all the right places. Her boots made her long legs look even longer. The cowboy hat held her gorgeous hair up off her long, slender neck. Even the dozen or so bangle bracelets sounded like they fit right in with the band, turning her into a living, breathing tambourine. Finally, she took a break and made her way back to the barstool next to his.

"You really get around, don't you?" That didn't come out right. "I mean, you seem to be a Jean-of-all-trades." Better, but still not debonair-man-about-town suave.

Her sidelong glance spoke volumes, but she grinned.

Her slightly spicy vanilla fragrance danced around his pleasure receptors, urging him closer.

"It's so many jobs. How do you keep track?"

"My business partner asked me the same thing yesterday. I haven't decided what I want to be when I grow up."

She must be kidding.

"You're kidding, right?" He couldn't imagine leading such a helter-skelter life. No routine? No set schedule? It wasn't realistic. It wasn't practical.

The music stopped, and the band announced a fifteen-minute break.

"Look, Sean, I appreciate that you're trying to make us meeting up again less weird, but there's no sense sitting here pretending. Maybe under different circumstances, we'd've . . . " She paused, gave him a long, considering look, and came to a decision about some question she hadn't voiced. "I'm going to take my food to go. Enjoy the rest of your stay on Folly."

She picked up a couple of Styrofoam cartons that had been delivered while she danced and stacked the leftover cowboy hats on top.

"Let me walk you to your car." Despite everything, he wasn't ready to let her walk out of his life yet. He grabbed the hats and proceeded her to the door.

Outside, April had decided to act like spring again. A light breeze carried a salty mist from the beach, cool enough to make him feel the difference between the crowded restaurant and the parking lot. She'd parked close to the door, so the walk ended too soon.

"Listen, Lily, I want to apologize. I was out of line posting that review. I should have—"

"No, you were right. About some things, anyway. Like I said, it's a new idea, and I hadn't thought it through. And sorry about the class the other day. I hope you weren't too sore." She seemed about to say more.

"Are you kidding? I'd run a couple extra miles that morning, and your class was the best stretch I've had in months. I loved it." Was he gushing? Grown men shouldn't gush. "Look, I don't mean to butt into your business, but I'm pretty good at teaching organizational skills and helping people develop better time management strategies. I'd be happy to take a look at your protocols and offer some tips, if you'd like."

She shivered. She must be cold out here, away from the crush of the dance floor. He turned his body a bit to block the breeze. It brought him closer to her. They were almost the same height, nearly eye to eye. A man could drown in those gray-green pools.

Will she appreciate it if I make the first move?

"You mean when you aren't busy expanding your vast marine empire? How did you pick that line of work with your, um, condition?"

"I improve technology and security on ocean-going vessels. I can test all that in a lab or in port, so I'm rarely required to get on a moving boat." He rolled his eyes in self-mockery. "Ironic, I know. So do you want to take me up on my offer?"

"I don't think we'd gel." She held the screechy Styrofoam boxes between them like a flimsy rope bridge straddling the Grand Canyon, but stepped a bit closer. "In that department."

Some strange glint shone in her eyes. She cocked her head, measuring him up.

Well, damn. Naturally, she'll make the first move.

Sean willed himself to be still as her lips met his. She landed left of center—of course she did—and stayed a second longer than a peck, but two seconds shy of an actual kiss. Every nerve in his body sprang to life. Hell, everything sprang to life.

"Not bad. Not bad at all. Bye, Sean."

By the time he registered the loss, she'd slipped the hats from his hands and walked around to the back of her car before putting everything inside. Then, she slid into the driver's seat, started the engine, and drove away.

Chapter Five

What the hell was she doing? Lily picked up a brush and dipped it into her cup, then onto the watercolor palette beside her. Bold strokes of color slashed across the paper, as bold as her behavior the other night. Her many business ideas left no time for a man, especially that man. Her traitorous body disagreed.

But someone so straightlaced? So tightly wound? So structured? He'd called at regular intervals since that incident in the parking lot. She'd let it go to voicemail every time.

Coward.

Taking early retirement and walking away from the corporate world of HRT and convention sales had been the best decision she'd ever made. She'd opened Lily's Pad three months later and had never looked back. She was gloriously free of strictures of any kind. His mere mention of organizational skills and time management and protocols had literally made her shudder. She'd lived in that world for twenty-five years, and she wanted nothing more to do with it.

But him. Oh yes, she wanted more to do with him.

She wanted to do things that didn't involve spreadsheets or profit margins.

Dammit, she was a mature woman who could handle a fling. At least, she thought she could. She'd never been much for one-night stands, but the man only had a couple more days in town. If she planned on having no regrets when he left, she'd better do something. Fast.

The chimes over her door signaled the arrival of Lily's Pad open-studio-Sunday clients. She had confirmed reservations for six people, including one booking that'd been made through the Wind Charm. How silly for her heart to race at the mere prospect . . .

"Good morning."

Lily smiled at his now-familiar baritone. His salt-and-pepper hair waved away from his forehead, damp and slick as if fresh from a shower. She let that image of him, water coursing down his naked body, warm her insides.

"Good morning to you. I'm glad you're here." It was now or never. "If you don't have plans tomorrow, I'd like to steal you away for the afternoon. And maybe the evening."

An immediate and eager smile dimpled his cheeks and crinkled the corners of his eyes. Okay, this was going well. They could leave talk of organizing and scheduling and best practices behind and just be two people enjoying a mutual attraction. A brief, hopefully very physically satisfying, mutual attraction. That's all she wanted. Right?

"I'd be delighted. My schedule opens up after one. Actually, I was going to suggest something similar. I hope I'm not being presumptive. I've organized a little surprise for you."

There was that word again—schedule, ugh—but his whole face lit up when he smiled at her. Sexy as hell.

"It's settled, then. I'll pick you up right after lunch tomorrow." Lily let her hand linger on his arm after leading him to a place at the long worktable.

When everyone had arrived, Lily turned all of her attention to presenting the art project of the day—a landscape collage using as many different types and qualities of paper and fiber as possible. She lost herself in the messiness of it all.

When he could take his eyes off Lily, Sean studied the space. A crystal chandelier with mismatched baubles, lamps with scarves over the shades, gauzy curtains, a beaded panel leading to other rooms. There were fresh flowers in everything from mason jars to china cups. Rolled yoga mats and bolsters leaned against one another like tipsy best friends. Sideways stacks of paper and folders hid a fancy, expensive-looking old desk, its spindly legs practically calling out for help. Several sets of wind chimes hung around the studio, each one emitting a different tune when disturbed by the breeze from the many open windows or Lily's hand, which seemed to reach up of its own volition whenever she passed one.

A huge bulletin board near the exit sported flyers from every business on the island. Hell, she had a handwritten appointment schedule for multiple businesses on a paper wall calendar, for pity's sake.

And rugs everywhere—braided, shag, Persian, southwestern—in every color of the rainbow. All in all, it was a disastrous, ineffective mess.

And he could fix it for her. It was the least he could do after leaving that review online. Lily had already admitted her partner had needled her for more organization. And she'd provided the perfect opportunity. He'd have to get his assistant out of the upcoming watercraft nightmare.

Tomorrow would be a big day, especially if it ended the way he hoped it would.

Chapter Six

On Monday, Lily picked Sean up at one thirty. "Just so you know, this afternoon isn't part of my Live Like a Local tour."

"No? What is it, then?"

"This is me, Lily, getting to know you, Sean."

"So no Yelp review?"

"Absolutely not. Ready?"

"More than."

She took him to Morris Island Lighthouse and to see the Angel Oak. Later in the season, both attractions would be crowded, but the middle of a weekday in early spring was a good time to go.

They avoided talking about work in favor of letting the desire between them bloom. They shared music tastes (they both loved jazz), food preferences, and favorite movies (they both hated slasher films). Lily mentioned her brief stint as a married woman from ages nineteen to twenty, when she and her high school sweetheart had realized they'd never be anything more. Sean told her about a long-ago engagement that couldn't survive his work schedule. He admitted that he hadn't been enough in love to put the relationship first.

They held hands under the big historic oak tree. He put his arm around her shoulders at the top of the lighthouse, where the wind from the Atlantic whipped her linen dress around their legs, and they didn't say a word about what would happen later that night. But Lily's heart beat a staccato rhythm all day. She'd forgotten how anticipation and desire could make her mouth dry.

"Okay if I surprise you with dinner plans?" She put her car into park when they got back to the Wind Charm.

"Barring sushi, yes." He rubbed his hand over his rock-solid abdomen. "Seafood is wonderful when it's cooked, though."

She decided on The Royal Tern. Slightly upscale, it was the perfect place for that new little black number she'd bought on a whim. Even the fitting room lights hadn't diminished how good she looked in that dress.

Leaving Sean at the guesthouse after a short but promising kiss, Lily enjoyed the surge of excitement that coursed through her. Forget butterflies—she had a cyclone whirling around her midsection.

Minutes later, she pulled into Lily's Pad parking lot and got out of her car, intending to take the exterior stairs to her apartment. On the little patio, Josie was in deep conversation with Terence, who looked out of place on the dainty bistro set.

"Hey, you two. What's going on?" As if she didn't know.

Josie darted a nervous glance at her, then back at Terence. Terence ducked his head. Maybe she didn't know.

"Lily, I don't want you to be upset." Josie held up both hands and spoke in the soothing voice patient mothers use with challenging offspring.

"What happened? Is everyone alright?" Suddenly, this didn't look like a budding romance. It looked like they had bad news to deliver.

"I said it was okay to leave you a surprise in there," Josie said. "I never said it was okay to—"

Lily had promised to wait for Sean before claiming her surprise, but something about the look on Josie's face made her change her mind. She walked to the studio door and turned the knob.

Josie and Terence followed close on her heels.

Lily pulled up short at the sight that greeted her. She blinked, trying to make the scene before her resolve itself. Sure, she recognized her Louis XIV desk and worktable, but the rest of the space wouldn't reconcile in her brain.

The wind chimes hadn't sung when she walked in. Her silk-scarf-draped lamps had been replaced by matching stainless steel floor lamps with overly bright, glaring lights. She turned slowly, hardly believing her eyes. The bulletin board by the door where she paraded all her friends' business brochures and menus . . . gone. In its place, a wall-mounted Lucite display piece, with the contents arranged alphabetically.

Next to her desk, her very empty desk, sat a wheeled hanging-file frame, full to the gills of what she assumed to be her important folders, the ones she used every day and kept *on* the desk for a reason.

Two new matching sets of shelves flanked the doorway to the back rooms—where was her bead curtain?—one filled with neatly rolled yoga mats, neatly folded blankets, neatly stacked yoga blocks, and neatly coiled straps. The other held dozens of matching clear plastic boxes, all with tidy little labels, separating ingredients for the various things she made and sold: candlemaking supplies, soapmaking and bath-salt ingredients, lip balm and lotion supplies . . .

Her mason jars filled with greenery and her chipped china cups with early blooming wildflowers were nowhere in sight. But, a giant bunch of dyed mums in a generic commercial vase sat on a clear plastic table near the front door next to a printed sign that said "Welcome, please sign in." And there was a clipboard.

With a spreadsheet.

Lily kicked off her shoes and shuffled across a hideously ordinary gray low-pile rug. Everywhere she looked, the color and life and beauty were expunged, and the bland and expedient had taken its place. Her art supplies, all encased in Lucite containers, were stacked under the window, too far away to be accessible to the workbench. And on the workbench, two—TWO!—monitors. One was labeled "private," the other "public." A note in front of them read:

This way you can display something for your in-house clients while still keeping business operations out of view yet constantly accessible.

A little smiley face at the bottom of the note mocked her.

What the actual hell?

She turned in a slow circle. Josie and Terence were huddled inside the door—as much as T could huddle.

"What happened?" She lifted her arms and let them drop, defeated.

"Lily, I'm so sorry. I only let them in, I swear." Josie rushed forward, grabbed her hands, and squeezed. Hard. "I had no idea this would be the result."

"Them? Them who?" But she had a feeling she already knew who. She just didn't want Josie to say his name.

"Sean Waters"—and there it was—"called me last night and said he had a surprise for you, but he wanted to keep it a secret. He asked if I'd let his assistant into the studio this afternoon."

Lily felt the hot burn in the back of her throat and knew she couldn't stop the tears.

"One person couldn't have done all this in five hours." She gestured behind her, because she couldn't bear to turn and look at that sterile scene again.

There was no more Lily in Lily's Pad.

"When I came back from an aquarium tour with clients, a whole crew had come and gone, and a portable storage unit was parked behind the azaleas. You must have missed it when you pulled in." Josie gathered her in a hug. "Lily, I'm so sorry. I'll help you fix it tomorrow, okay?"

"Where are all of my wind chimes?" Lily sniffled and swiped at the tears on her cheeks.

Reluctant, it seemed, to deliver more bad news out loud, Josie pointed at a box on the floor labeled "discard."

Well. That's that, then.

"When Sean gets here, tell him I can't make it tonight." Lily picked up her shoes and dragged herself toward the back of the studio, heart aching at the absence of the bead curtain that always whispered so soothingly to her when she passed through it. "Terence, see if you can pull that damn plastic thing by the door off the wall, would you? And smash it."

"I'm on it."

She let the tears flow as she climbed up to her apartment. He didn't like her as herself. He liked the idea that he could remake her into something more appropriate to his finely ordered world. She'd known that from the beginning. This was supposed to be a fling anyway. Well, she flung that idea right out of the realm of possibility.

Chapter Seven

Energy hummed through his veins. Sean couldn't wait to see her again, smiling and standing in the middle of her freshly organized space. He'd placed an order with Ikea last night and had a truck there this morning to collect everything. Charlotte, North Carolina, was close enough to make the drive worthwhile, given the number of people at his disposal to handle the other details.

Her businesses could be a huge success. She had talent, personality, and vision. And he could help her scale her cottage industry with efficiency and profit. He should know. He'd written a best-selling book on the subject.

He splashed on a bit of aftershave, tugged his cuffs to the proper length below the sleeves of his lightweight sport coat, and pocketed his room key.

With a smile on his lips and a jazz number he now knew they both liked whistling through his pursed lips, he jogged down the steps of the guest-house and found the car his assistant had rented for him for the night—a sporty little convertible with enough get-up-and-go to whisk them from the restaurant back to her apartment in the blink of an eye.

At Lily's Pad, he spotted the mobile container, full to the brim of everything that fell into the out-with-the-old category, parked out of sight of clients. Sean pulled the convertible under a shady branch and walked toward the open door of the studio, anticipation making his heart race.

A commotion erupted inside the door. He quickened his pace. Two voices, a heated discussion. Approaching the door, he saw the back of a man—a big man—on a stepladder. Large and small pieces of clear plastic and bits of drywall littered the floor. Sean caught only snatches of conversation.

"Everything okay here?" He raised his voice to be heard over the argument. He didn't see Lily anywhere, and he breathed a little easier knowing she wasn't involved in the fracas. He stepped over the threshold, which put him directly behind the dude on the stepladder.

"I've got it." The voice was female.

"Ouch!" Ladder guy teetered on the step.

Sean barely registered the fact that an arm was swinging closer to his face before his world burst into a bright array of flashing color. One minute he was upright, and the next he was sprawled on his backside on the floor. Sharp shards of agony bounced from one side of his skull to the other. He brought both hands up and felt the slick glide of blood. The voices got louder, shouting over each other and his pain-filled gasps for air.

"Now look what you did."

"How was I supposed to know he was sneaking up behind—"

"Get off that ladder and pick that man up." The woman's voice got louder.

"It's not my fault he walked into my elbow."

"Which he wouldn't have done if you had kept still like I told you and let me get that splinter out."

"Fine. Where am I supposed to put him now? He's bleeding all over me." The big man had his arms around Sean's midsection.

Sean relived the wooziness he'd had that day on the airboat. Another voice entered the fray.

"What the hell happened? Sean?" Lily came into view for a second, then she got all blurry again. Why wasn't she dressed for dinner?

"Terence hit him." Was that Josie? The business partner? He hadn't met her, but he thought he recognized her voice from the phone. The three of them were moving him across the room, all shouting different instructions to him.

Keep your head back.

Pinch the bridge of your nose.

Breathe through your mouth.

He felt himself being lowered into a chair. He slid into the seat as easily as blood slid down the back of his throat.

"Somebody get a cold compress." Lily was close. "Josie, did you tell Terence to hit Sean?"

Who the hell was Terence?

"I didn't hit him on pur—"

"No, I didn't tell him to hit Sean. Your boyfriend got in the way. And why are you mad at me? He's the one you're furious with." Josie again.

Wait. What? Lily was furious with him? Why?

Someone pressed a cold, wet towel to his face. He tried to speak but choked on the blood running into his mouth. Shit. His head hurt.

"Yes, I'm furious with him, but I didn't wish him bodily harm." Lily sounded indignant. That was good, right?

"Listen, buddy, I swear I didn't hit you on purpose, y'hear? And when the police come, I'd appreciate it if you'd tell them so." Terence had an unbelievably deep voice.

Wait. Police?

"You're calling 911 for this scumbag?" Josie's voice kicked up a notch or two, incredulous. Sean decided he didn't like Josie. He did like the sound of 911.

"Yes. That's a lot of blood," Lily said.

"The face bleeds. That's a fact." Terence again.

He tried to sit up, to raise a hand, to be noticed for something other than the amount of blood he emitted. The trio, however, kept shushing him and pressing towels to his face and arguing amongst themselves.

"Yes, I need medical help at Number Six Second Row Rd, Folly Beach. A sixty-year-old male has . . . has a face injury. Yes, he got hit in the face. An elbow. Yes, I said elbow. Yes, he's breathing and conscious. Okay, thank you."

"I'm only fifty-eight." Sean doubted they heard him. His voice sounded strange to his own ears, and the towel muffled everything he said.

Lily sighed. "How's he ever going to get all that blood out of his expensive rug when I return all this stuff to him in that storage unit?"

He heard laughter on all sides. Then the paramedics came in and he gave up trying to make sense of anything.

Lily mustered a laugh for the EMT crew. They teased Sean about the raging black eyes he'd have the next day and helped make up stories that made him look like a hero rather than some old guy who got too close to the elbow of a giant who was afraid of having a splinter removed.

After the ambulance drove away and the nosy neighbors went inside, Lily didn't know what to do with herself. Or with Sean.

"Thanks for staying, Josie. You and Terence should go. Try to enjoy what's left of the night." She put her head on Josie's shoulder for a brief moment.

"Call if you need anything. I'll be here in the morning to help you get things back to normal." Josie gave Sean a disgusted look.

"Tell your boyfriend I'm sorry again." Terence had cleaned up the plastic brochure holder—which he'd smashed as instructed—and swept up the drywall dust with one hand. The other was bandaged, compliments of the EMT crew, as if he had broken a finger instead of having had a tiny sliver of plastic taken out of it.

Finally, it was just the two of them. Sean leaned back in a new swivel chair in her studio with gauze stuffed up his nostrils and an ice pack across his eyes and the bridge of his nose. He looked like hell.

"They said to take this painkiller." Lily picked up one of his hands and put the pill in his palm. "I'll get you a glass of water."

He grunted.

What now? She couldn't let him drive even the short distance to the B&B. Should he stay the night so she could watch him for signs of a concussion?

This isn't what I had in mind when I decided to sleep with him.

She returned with water and helped him sit up straighter. He put the ice pack down. It wasn't preventing the swelling. The state of her studio still made her heartsick, but she hated seeing him in so much discomfort.

"I guess we have a few things to talk about." Sean sounded like he had the worst cold of his life.

"I'm not sure there's much point. Our differences seem to outweigh everything else. Maybe today was so magical because we knew there'd be no tomorrow." Lily tried for a nonchalance she didn't feel. Dammit, she was genuinely attracted to this man, and not in a one-night-stand sort of way. That's why the whole studio makeover hurt so much. She'd been envisioning a future with Sean in it somewhere.

"I'd still like the chance to make this right. You may not believe this, Lily, but I've learned quite a lot from you this week. You've made me feel . . . freer, somehow. Like I don't need every minute of my life scheduled down to the millisecond." He shook his head, then winced at the pain the movement obviously caused. "I wanted to repay the favor. You gave me a little bit of what you have in abundance, but the only things I have in abundance are logistic and procedural skills."

"And money and staff and resources." Tears threatened again. She hated seeing the softer side of this man when she'd determined never to see any part of him again. "But you didn't even ask me, Sean. After taking me to task—online, no less—for blindsiding you with my surprise destinations for a day, you did practically the same thing to me."

He stood up and took a wobbly step, bringing them close together. Oh, it felt good when he put his hands on her hips. He bent his knees to meet her gaze. His face was turning colors in a blotchy pattern spreading out from the bridge of his nose. Red, purple, blue, and ugh, he smelled like antiseptic.

"Would it help or hurt my cause if I said I think we both learned something about the nature of surprises this week?" He sighed and dropped his hands. "I'll get an Uber. My assistant can get the car tomorrow morning. I'm truly sorry, Lily."

He pulled out his phone and squinted at it.

That sick feeling she'd had since seeing her new and improved atelier got worse. Would this be it, then? Would he walk away, leaving her with this stupid excuse for a studio and no fabulous memories?

"Wait." She put her hand on his phone. "This isn't how I wanted the night to end."

He paused, clearly unsure of his next move.

"How did you want it to end?" He tried to smile.

Boy, that looks painful.

"Actually, I didn't want it to end at all. I wanted to still be with you when the sun came up, and maybe for as long as you'll be in town."

"I can make that happen." He slid his phone back into his pocket and reached for her once more. "What's so funny?"

"You said, 'I cad bake that hap-ped,' and you look like you're wearing a puffy purple mask with a clown nose."

"Okay, well maybe it won't be the night of our dreams, but I don't have to go unless you want me to. I might need a short nap, though. That pain-killer is kicking in and kicking my butt."

Lily took his hand and led him upstairs before kissing both of his eyes oh-so gently as his head settled onto her pillow. Definitely not the night of her dreams.

But could he be the man of her dreams?

Chapter Eight

"Get it done ASAP. No, it's not a joke." Sean hung up with his assistant. She'd phoned him immediately after he'd texted her to come back with the entire crew first thing this morning and undo every single "improvement" they had made to Lily's Pad yesterday.

The sun sent colorful rays of light all around Lily's bedroom. Of course she'd have crystals hanging like curtains in front of all the windows. He put his phone down and walked to the bed. Lily stretched, long and sinuous, like a sleek cat.

"Good morning, sleepyhead." He reached out and smoothed a spiral curl back into place.

"Hey. Did I fall asleep during my first night-nurse shift? How's your face?" Her eyes were more green than gray this morning, like the ocean when the sun is high.

"I don't know. You tell me. It only hurts when I blink. Or breathe. Or move my head." All true, but at least the constant throbbing had stopped.

"You're less swollen." She sat up on the edge of the bed and pulled a sweatshirt over her head. "I'll make us some tea."

"No need. I've ordered breakfast to be delivered. And I'm ready to start my penance."

"Sean, what on earth are you talking about? You've been injured and drugged and you're still dressed for dinner. I'm making tea." She exited the room and started down the hall to the kitchen.

"Josie's on her way over to boss me around a bit." Following her, he grinned at her confused over-the-shoulder glance.

"Why are you up so early? Why are you so chipper in the morning? Why doesn't your purple face look any less handsome?"

"Flattery will get you everywhere."

She made tea, then he took her hand and led her down the stairs to the studio.

"Sean, I don't want to go in there again right now."

"Don't say anything yet." He stepped aside to let her take in the view. He'd been up for a couple hours and had made good use of the time. "I'm trying hard to impress a woman I think I could fall in love with."

For a long minute, she held his gaze. Hers softened and a smile played around her lips. Slowly, she turned so she could see the studio.

He studied the room, trying to see it with her eyes. The gray rug was history. He'd put the nicest of her old ones in strategic locations. The art supplies were still in their drawers but were now tucked up under one side of the workbench. He'd taken the stainless floor lamps, the grocery store flowers, and the sleek entry table out.

"My wind chimes." She looked ready to cry again.

That's what he had been hoping to avoid with all this.

Lily walked around the space, brushing every chime and running her hand across her beloved old wrecks of décor. It wasn't perfect, but it was a start.

Josie came through the front door with another armload of stuff. She still sent Sean sour looks every chance she got, but at least she'd agreed to help. The food delivery appeared at the same time as his assistant, followed by a small crew of furniture movers.

"We are all at your disposal, Lily. Tell me how to make it perfect."

Lily squealed at the restored bead curtain. She let it drift through her fingers and graze her body. How could he have imagined her without it?

"I'll tell you one way you can make it perfect." Josie shoved a box of scarves into his arms. "Talk her into keeping that tablet and mobile scheduling app. And stop her from bringing the giant calculator back in here for accounting purposes."

"Josie, would your job be easier if we implemented some of these changes?" Lily carried her tea to her Louis desk.

"My job. My life. Tax season." Josie glanced covetously at the oversized monitors on the worktable. "And it would be nice if people could shove their stuff into a cubby after they take a yoga mat out."

"Why didn't you say something before?" Lily's shoulders sagged as if realizing she'd been holding Josie back.

Could it be that Sean had an ally in Josie? Wait, hadn't she called him a scumbag yesterday?

"Lily, you had this place decorated before I came on board. I'm not going to tell you how you can or can't run your business or what it should look like." Josie looked pointedly at Sean.

"But if our processes were hindering your efficacy, you should have communicated that to me." Lily paused, looking at all the people waiting to do her bidding. "Sean, would you mind putting this on hold until after a brief staff meeting?"

"Take all the time you want. I'll go grab a shower. See you for lunch?"

She nodded.

He winked at Josie, who gave him the finger.

With Josie's help, Lily restored her studio, but not exactly to its former condition. Some of the upgrades were worth keeping. Sean's ideas were mostly good. Lily just didn't like the décor style his assistant had picked out. Which was why that young lady had been sent on a very important, very far away errand which kept her absent for the duration of the morning.

Finally, Josie left, the workers went back to wherever they had come from, the storage container was picked up, and a small mountain of things from her past had been donated to charity. Time to look forward.

Now, Lily wouldn't think about the studio or work or procedures or structure for the rest of the day. She had more important things on her mind. Having never in her life been in bed at noon, today seemed like a good day to start a new practice.

Her downstairs door latch clicked open and closed. Sean called her name.

"Up here." Gooseflesh rose on her bare arms. "But don't bother coming up if you're dressed."

His footsteps on the stairs stopped. Articles of clothing shuffled and swooshed and a knee or maybe an elbow bumped the wall. The footsteps resumed, softer but quicker.

Clad only in a wolfish grin, he stopped in the doorway and leaned on the frame, arms folded across his muscular chest.

Just as she had suspected. Not bad.

Not bad at all.

The End

About Addie Bealer

Addie Bealer is certain she should have sprung from an English garden in the early nineteenth century. She is a Jean Austen devotee and loves classic British literature, the poetry as much as the prose.

She is the author of several pre-published Regency romance novels; a short contemporary romance published in *Love in the Lowcountry, Winter Holidays Collection Volume 2*; and a collection of poetry, some of which has been published in online journals. She is a member of Carolina Romance Writers, Regency Fiction Writers, Romance Writers of America and its online chapter Hearts through History.

Born and raised in New Orleans, the most European of American cities, Addie now lives in South Carolina's upstate, where she is regularly confounded by her sewing machines or flummoxed by the huge messes in her art studio. She loves traveling with her husband for research, relaxation, and red wine.

Find Addie Online:

Website: https://addiebealer.com/
Email: addie@addiebealer.com
X : https://twitter.com/addiebealer
Instagram: https://www.instagram.com/addiebealerauthor/
Facebook: https://www.facebook.com/addiebealerauthor
Amazon:https://www.amazon.com/stores/author/B0BHXDWLH5/about

Consider it Done

by Victoria R. Benson

Consider it Done

by Victoria R. Benson

From York to the Yorktown… Presley falls for the most handsome and successful bachelor at a friend's wedding. Scarred from previous heartbreaks, she is in disbelief when Thomas shares her interest. A flame ignites and the two become the dream couple. However, when Presley leaves York for a week in Charleston with her best friend, she begins to wonder if she has cold feet or if their fire has died. An afternoon touring the Yorktown changes everything, and Presley is forced to reexamine her cooled heart.

Chili Pepper Rating: 1

Chapter One

Exactly when I decided I would never marry Thomas Mathews is a bit unclear. However, I believe it was the moment just before he asked me out on our first date.

Was our start a cliché? Probably so, because we met at a wedding. The instant I noticed him I became terrified, because I couldn't shake the feeling that he might also be noticing me. The man was the complete opposite of unattractive. It also helped that he was well-dressed and had a confident posture. What made me so uneasy, though, was the unnerving fantasy that I could possibly be the topic of his conversations. Dare I dream that such perfection would go out of his way to speak to me?

I continued spying on him from my table while trying to pretend that I was scanning the room beyond where he sat. Each time I did look at him, my blood pressure increased and my cheeks burned, because dang it, his eyes were on me.

This went on for a while—perhaps a few songs—until eventually someone in his vicinity must have given him the ole "go ahead" to approach me. My stomach tightened, my brain floated in my skull, my heart raced. And none of these happened in a good way. I was terrified. That handsome man was out of my league.

As soon as he stood, I turned my head and tried desperately to act like I didn't see him strolling toward me. Within a few moments, he was there at my side.

"Hey," he said casually.

Some invisible force placed its finger on my chin and turned my head to the right and up. I hoped my smile didn't look insincere; my inner human just wasn't interested in a meet-cute that was going to end with a one-night stand. For years, my heart had wished so hard for this type of situation. However, once faced with it, I had no idea how to handle it. I wanted to meet him, talk to him, dance with him, but I knew this would never amount to anything long term. My soul decided the instant our eyes met that, at best, we would only be a wedding fling.

"Hello," I replied.

"May I sit?" he asked, motioning at the empty chair beside me.

"Of course. Everyone else from this table is on the dance floor." I pointed to the bouncing group. "They probably won't be returning."

As he pulled out the chair and turned it so he would be facing me, he asked, "Why aren't you dancing?" When he sat, he was so close his knee lightly brushed my thigh.

Playing it cool, I picked up my water and sipped, then replied, "The bride's parents are friends with my parents. I don't really know anyone. Joining a group of unfamiliar dancing nancies just isn't my *jam*. How about you?"

Thomas snuffed a small laugh before replying, "First, great song."

I gaped. *He knows that song?*

Then he finished, "My situation is pretty similar to yours—our parents are friends. They all grew up in the same neighborhood. I only know the groom and his brother, and neither of them cares to dance with me right now."

Glad he had a sense of humor, I giggled, slightly shaking my head.

"What's your name?" he asked.

"I'm Presley."

He grinned and said in an amplified tone, "Ha! Like the king of rock and roll?"

"Mm-hmm. My grandma named me."

"She did a great job."

"And you? What are you called by those who have the pleasure of knowing you?"

"I'm Thomas Mathews."

"Hi, Thomas. It's nice to meet you."

"It is very nice to meet you too, Presley."

There was a pause between us before he stood and asked, "Will you dance with me?"

Pleading with the universe that this guy was a gentleman, I nodded and took his hand. We walked naturally to the dance floor and began swaying unnaturally to Journey's "Faithfully." In my mind, I was merely crossing paths with this guy. We were going to dance, maybe chat for a few minutes, and then part ways.

As our sway slowed, my gut knew what was coming next; he was going to make a polite excuse to rejoin his friends.

Presley, this isn't your person. He's not the one for you. He's too good for you. My eyes lowered, and I prepared to leave the dance floor alone with a forced smile.

Imagine my shock when he said, "Will you have dinner with me tomorrow?"

I looked up at him and his expression told me he was waiting for an answer. I tried to hide that the butterflies in my chest caused me to be suddenly short of breath. Smoothly, I replied, "That would be nice. Do you live here in York?"

"No, I live in Charlotte. Since tomorrow is Saturday, I was thinking we could go to Carowinds for a few hours, then go have a quiet dinner. I'll have you home at a decent hour. The drive from Charlotte to York is only about forty minutes."

The song had changed, but we stood still.

"That sounds fun. Sure. We can hang out tomorrow."

For the remainder of the evening, we danced, chatted, and sipped wine. I kept waiting for some bit of sarcasm to seep into his tone, perhaps he'd show a sign of interest in a lovely bridesmaid, or I'd catch a glimpse of a moment of flirtation with the hot bartender. My past relationships had taught me that men eventually reveal their true intentions. But Thomas never left our conversations. His eyes never strayed from mine. He was interested in me... and only me! I couldn't wait for the sun to rise.

Chapter Two

Our first date was invigorating, a relief from so many others. Thomas proved to be amusing, intelligent, polite, and quite frankly, the perfect guy. He was so endearing I forgot all my insecurities. Since no red flags were raised, another date followed, then another and another until we were together every weekend. Thomas gave me hope, and because of that hope, I began to dream that he might be *the* one.

I had moved back to my parents' house so I could focus on finishing the final year of my master's program, so when the weekend of our six-month anniversary approached, we decided to spend it in Charlotte. I drove to his apartment on Friday, and he had just gotten home when I arrived.

"I made reservations for us for dinner," he said before I stepped through the door.

"Sounds great!" I beamed and reached up for one of his signature seductive kisses. I loved how he always moaned when he kissed me. It was as if I was his favorite… well, everything: sweater, blanket, pillow, meal.

"I'll change," I said.

"I'll watch," he replied.

"No, you won't! I want to emerge like a sophisticated, sultry, irresistible goddess."

"Then you won't need clothes for that."

"Ugh!" I shoved his taut midsection and said, "I'll be right out."

He placed a kiss on my forehead and extended his arm for me to pass.

The compliments didn't stop once I reappeared wearing a strapless, knee-length, snug-fit maroon dress. My favorite was "Pres, how am I going to keep my hands from riding the waves of your every curve?"

I raised one eyebrow and said, "You only have to stop when we're at the restaurant."

"Yes!" he hissed excitedly, looking toward the ceiling.

I laughed as we hugged. He held me tightly, and I rested my head on his chest. I had allowed myself to fall completely in love with Thomas. He felt like home to me. Then, in an instant, my smile faded. A memory crept its way into my mind of a previous love, who was full of flattery but was seeing someone else.

"Presley?"

I jolted from my nightmare. "Hm? What?"

"You left me."

"No. I was just feeling tired. It's been a long week." I smiled and said, "Let's go eat. I've missed you so much. I want to enjoy our dinner and get back here so we can curl up and watch football."

Another kiss was delivered. "I may be the luckiest man alive."

"Don't you forget it," I said.

Thomas escorted me out the door and to his car. We drove hand in hand to downtown, and once we arrived at the restaurant, he splurged on valet parking. The valet opened my door and offered me his hand. By the time I was upright and on the sidewalk, Thomas was there with his elbow extended. We entered the restaurant smiling and with eyes only for each other.

The quaint little place was dark and intimate. We took our time enjoying wine, appetizers, and our meals.

After our plates were cleared, the waiter asked if we would be having dessert. I scrunched my nose and politely declined, but Thomas interjected. "Babe, it's our six-month anniversary—choose *something*. We can share it."

"All right," I replied, then I looked to our server and asked him to bring us anything chocolate.

Thomas laughed. "Chocolate is her favorite meal."

"He's not lying."

"I'll be right back," the server said.

Within a few minutes, a plate was placed in front of me, and my eyes widened. On the plate was a black velvet box. I looked at Thomas, and the joy he felt shone through his smile. "I don't recommend you eat that," he said.

I picked up the little box and opened it. Inside was a beautiful diamond ring. My jaw dropped as I watched the man of my dreams move to my side, lower to one knee, and propose.

He said, "I knew immediately— the first time I ever saw you— that I would marry you. Presley Ann Riggins, will you marry me?"

No woman has ever said "Yes!" as fast as I did. I jumped into his arms amid the cheers from those around us.

Life was finally happening. Our wedding was being planned, I continued focusing on completing my master's, and Thomas split his attention between entertaining me and performing his best at work. We lived a whirlwind romance.

Until… it all changed from a flowing river to a stagnant pond. The stolen moments in the throes of passion ended. Perhaps we settled into a routine, because everything between us became mundane. I was never sure if it was me or the idea of forever with one person. Maybe I had deep unresolved pain. Regardless of the reason, Thomas and I simply remained a couple, but in my mind, a very stale couple.

Chapter Three

A year later, with an engagement ring on my finger and a new puppy in my lap, a closing date on a house loomed in our near future. Sadly, the reality I faced was that I had allowed myself to grow roots in a situation where I felt like I no longer had a choice. Thomas and I were to be married in two weeks, and that was final. No one calls off a wedding two weeks before they are supposed to walk down the aisle.

To top things off, Thomas chose April first to be our wedding date. When he told me this, with a demure smile and loving support, I agreed, all the while wanting to scream, this has to be a joke. I had forgotten why I was marrying him, and I could see no way out of the relationship. My only solace was my upcoming bachelorette trip to Charleston.

My friend Milly and I were spending six nights at a bed-and-breakfast with a front porch view of the Battery park, White Point Gardens. Knowing I would be sipping coffee while watching the sway of the Spanish-moss-draped oaks; enjoying my daily walks next to the Ashley River where it meets the Atlantic; and shopping, dining, and sleeping late eased my stress. Wedding woes would not enter my mind, mortgage commitments would have no place in my thoughts, and our little Corgi… Who was I kidding? I *would* miss my puppy with all my heart.

Sitting at the foot of my bed nuzzling little Francis and placing the last of my toiletries on top of my sundresses, sandals, swimsuits, and shorts, I heard what sounded like a hundred feet plodding up the wooden staircase of my parents' nineteenth-century home. I grew up in a house that was built in 1850. I'd lived on Main Street in York, South Carolina my entire life until I left for college. My childhood home still had its historic décor and design, but what I have always loved most about it is that underneath its antebellum façade, a complete modern remodel had been done.

Three of my bridesmaids, Hansen, Carli, and Milly, rushed into my room.

"Are you ready?" Milly squealed.

Carli and Hansen plopped onto my bed.

"I am sorry Hansen and I can't go with y'all to Charleston," Carli apologized for what must have been the hundredth time.

"I understand you both have to work. I'm happy that both of you have found your dream jobs. Hopefully once I graduate in May, I'll find my dream job too. And Milly, we all know you'll land the perfect job soon. Besides y'all, it really is no big deal."

Hansen moved from her stomach to a seated position and scolded, "Don't even joke. It is a big deal! I fully expect you to be celebrating every moment of my engagement and wedding when I find Mr. Right."

I hid my cringe and instead smiled at her and kissed Francis between her eyes. "Perhaps I'm just feeling melancholy over the loss of my independence. It'll pass. I'm sure this week is just what I need to remind myself that this path is exactly what I've always wanted."

Milly placed her hand on my shoulder.. "Presley, you're living the dream. Stop letting your past poison your future. Thomas is not like the others. He is handsome, funny, affectionate, and he has a great future ahead of him. With him passing the Bar exam, companies are going to be bidding for him like a piece of real estate."

I shrugged.

"What is wrong with you, Pres? You found a great guy!" Carli said.

I wanted to bury my face in my pillow. I wanted to curl up beneath my blanket. I wanted to understand what was wrong with me. Holding myself steady and controlling the lump in my throat, I worked to keep myself together. I said, "Actually, Carli, he found me."

I know Carli could sense my strain. "Thomas is sensible and responsible," she replied.

"He is both of those things. But those aren't the words I want to moan or shout when we're alone in the dark."

All three of them laughed.

Hansen shook her head and held up her hands. "What do you expect, Presley?"

"I realize that on a scale of Quasimodo to Thor, Thomas is definitely closer to Thor," I said, "but he doesn't sweep me off my feet and fly me to another planet anymore. Things aren't like they were when we first met. Everything is about work or planning the wedding. What happens when there's nothing left to plan?"

"Ugh!" Carli responded. "Stop overthinking every detail of your life. There isn't a man out there who can fly you or any woman to another planet. Geez! Where do you come up with this stuff? You're not the first bride to have cold feet."

"Is that what's wrong with me?" I asked.

"Yes! That and all of your past insecurities. I thought you were over that stuff." Carli reached her arms toward me. "Now give me Francis, close your suitcase, and get out of here."

To Milly, Carli said, "Get her out of here before she does something she regrets." Then back in my direction, she added, "Do not talk yourself out of this marriage, young lady! You said yes to him for a reason."

She was right. I thought about how many times I jumped into Thomas's arms. My acceptance of his proposal was not out of obligation; it was out of adoration. I couldn't figure out why I was so hell-bent on sabotaging this relationship.

"Take her!" Carli said to Milly again—her final statement on the subject. "Force her to rest, and while y'all are in Charleston, remind Presley every day how great her life is."

Milly saluted Carli, and Hansen and I laughed.

Petting and squeezing Francis, I said, "Take care of my princess, you two. I know you'll be busy, but she needs snuggles, snacks, and smooches."

I let Francis lick my nose, then I handed her to Carli, who was rubbing her hands together in anticipation.

Milly zipped my bag and slid it from the bed onto the floor. She pulled up on the handle, pointed to my bedroom door, and said, "Let's go tour some houses, eat amazing food, and shop like there's no tomorrow! Maybe we'll even drive out to Folly so we can put our feet in the ocean."

"I'm ready," I replied.

A group hug was shared.

Down the stairs and out the front door we went. I was thankful that the topic of Thomas was closed. I was tired of how I had developed an indifference to him. The guilt was excruciating. He'd be working all week and would spend Thursday and Friday nights with his friends. Maybe the break would do us good. The time had come for me to focus on my final fling before tying the proverbial knot.

Chapter Four

Milly drove the first hour and a half and I drove the second. It was a sunny day, so we tucked our hair into baseball caps, put the top of her Mini Cooper down, and turned the music up. Passersby probably thought we were sixteen instead of twenty-six. It was probably best that Milly and I ended up as a twosome. We needed the time away more than Hansen and Carli did. Milly had been struggling to find a job despite weekly interviews. She had made it to the second and third rounds too many times to count, but that perfect position eluded her. We really needed to forget about adulting for a while.

We arrived at the B&B too early to check in, so we decided to stretch our legs and have lunch. Once the car was parked, we grabbed our purses and walked straight toward the waterfront. The aroma of the sea rode the breeze that lifted our hair and fanned through our clothes. I didn't know about Milly, but the tension in my neck eased and my shoulders relaxed. Sometimes we don't realize how much weight we put on ourselves worrying and sulking.

"Time to eat," she said.

I raised my eyebrows and replied, "Oh, yeah, food! Wait, not just food—seafood."

Milly countered with, "Mm, and Lowcountry grits, and fudge, and pie!"

Despite our raging appetites, we didn't rush. Every moment of our walk north on East Bay Street was treasured. The anticipation of each day of vacation gave me goose bumps.

Milly commented, "I'm not sure how, but I think the reason Charleston is always a top destination worldwide is the way everyone who visits here immediately feels like they've just returned home."

"Could be. Every time I come here, I think about staying. I wonder if I'd be able to find a job that pays enough for me to live here. Do you think an aspiring magazine editor could survive in downtown Charleston? Do editors make millions?"

"At least you'll have your MA with a specialty soon. Having a bachelor's in management seems to be too broad right now. I'm competing with people who also have years of experience."

It was not my intention to bring Milly down, so I tried to raise her spirits again. "You're going to find the perfect position, Milly. I'm sorry I brought up work. No more despair. My parents have given us a generous budget for this week's shenanigans. Happy thoughts, my sweet. Happy thoughts."

Once at Market Street, we turned left. Lunch was going to be at the Chill and Drill Pub. Crab legs, oysters, and mojitos were on our minds. We were seated on the tabby concrete patio and placed our orders right away. Our food arrived quickly, and while gorging ourselves, we reviewed our plans for the week.

"Monday, the Old Exchange and Provost Dungeon and shopping," Milly ticked off. "Tuesday, the museum and aquarium and shopping. Wednesday, plantation tours and, of course, shopping if there's time."

"Are you interested in a couple of home tours on Thursday?" I asked.

"Sure. And we'll plan a few hours at the beach on Friday."

"Sounds great. How about we go to Sullivan's Island instead of Folly so we can tour Fort Moultrie while we're out there?"

Milly nodded in agreement as she nibbled on a few more fries.

Lingering moments of silence followed, and her attention seemed to turn to the passers by. I knew that look. I knew I should brace for an inquisition. It irritated me that our pleasant afternoon was about to be invaded by either wedding or relationship discussions.

"Let it out, Milly."

She didn't hesitate. "We're all worried about you and poor Thomas."

"He's not 'poor Thomas,' he's just Thomas. And don't worry! We're fine."

"Exactly. You're fine. Do you still love him, though?"

"I guess so."

"Presley!"

"Please drop it, Milly. This is supposed to be my week to not think about the wedding."

"No. This week is about you dreaming of nothing but your wedding."

I covered my eyes with my hand and exhaled. "We will have a beautiful wedding. The details are set. I made sure there aren't even any last-minute items to track down."

"The wedding isn't my point. Thomas is."

"He is very happy and I will be too… again… someday… I'm sure. Now, I'm done with this conversation."

Milly didn't push any further. We ate silently for a while and then decided to talk about other things.

Enough time had passed for us to return to the bed-and-breakfast. After checking in, we went to our room. My parents had booked an entire carriage house for us. It was spectacular. Because of the historic registry regulations, many of its architectural features had been preserved. The walls were brick. The fireplaces were framed with their original ornate mantels. The upstairs bedroom had a high ceiling with exposed beams and French doors that opened up to an iron-lace-trimmed veranda. The parlor was adorned with antique as well as replica Victorian-style furniture. The walls that weren't brick were painted bright white.

"I love this house," I said in awe of all that surrounded us.

"Presley, you live in a house that is a lot like this one."

"No, it's not!"

"Uh, the only difference is that this one is in Charleston and your parents' house is in York."

"Well, they're still different," I countered.

In the upstairs suite, we unpacked and settled our makeup bags and cleansers onto the vanity. Since lunch had been so filling and our accommodations included a small kitchen, we decided to Instacart some groceries and get right to relaxing.

Streaming movies on the TV was our big plan for night one—most likely, all of the nights. We chose a nineties rom-com and swooned over the leading man, who was, of course unbeknownst to the leading lady, a prince.

Lights were out at eleven. Monday was a sleep away.

Chapter Five

We woke up, fixed coffee, relaxed on the balcony, and took our time getting ready. The day was young. For breakfast, we had a reservation at a high-end restaurant. All that was traditional South Carolina was on our mind and on the menu. For appetizers, we chose pimento cheese with dry toast and deviled eggs. Talk about mouthwatering delights! For our entrees, I had buttermilk biscuits with fried chicken, and Milly had the shrimp and grits. There was simply nothing like South Carolina cooking.

As planned, after breakfast, we perused the Market before heading to the Old Exchange. Wanting to explore on our own, we chose the self-guided tour.

"My dream wedding reception would be in here." Milly sighed as we turned about the upstairs ballroom. "It's awesome that the location of this building is original to the founding of Charleston. George Washington stood in *this* room. Pirates were held in the dungeon below us. There's so much history right at this single address."

I remained silent, also taking in the splendor but listening attentively.

Several hours passed quickly, and we had seen all we wanted to see there. We were in agreement that breakfast was still lingering, so neither of us was hungry yet.

"Let's go tour churches and graveyards," Milly suggested.

"Should we go back to the Market and find a book to help guide us?"

"Yeah."

At a booth, a saleslady selected a book on cemetery tours for us. We reviewed the map and started at the nearest one on Meeting Street. Thankfully, the graveyards are located at the churches, and most of the sanctuaries are open to the public. Touring the cathedrals was captivating as well.

As late afternoon arrived, Milly and I chose a side-street restaurant to eat an early supper.

Having my stomach full once again, I wasn't sure how much further I could push myself. "The day has caught up to me, but I do have one more idea if you're up for it."

"What are you thinking?" she replied.

"Chalmers is a few blocks away. I say we detour that direction so we can see the Pink House on our way back home. If we walk off our dinner, we won't feel as guilty snacking again in a few hours. After all, we have an endless movie selection awaiting us at the inn. We'll be sitting for the rest of the night."

"Sounds good to me."

Luckily, when we arrived at the Pink House, a tourist group was there. We stood near them and listened. The guide said, "This is the oldest standing house in Charleston. It was built in 1712." He went on to discuss its transitions over the past three hundred years. What was most interesting, though, was that he talked about the cobblestone street. "The stones that make this road are river rock. These stones don't exist in Charleston. All of these rocks were brought over from England. They were used as ballasts for the ships. When the ships arrived, the stones were unloaded and eventually used to build these streets."

Having heard enough, Milly and I looked at each other. No words were needed. We knew a sofa was our only desire. From our loitering position behind everyone, I took one last look at the remarkable little house. My eyes lowered from the rooftop to the front door to the stare of the tour guide. He winked at me. I flicked my fingertips at him, knowing I had been caught learning stuff for free.

The walk all the way back to our carriage house seemed to take hours. Once there, we dropped onto the couch and didn't move again until it was time for bed.

Tuesday morning's routine matched Monday's, with the exception of breakfast. Before we drove to the museum and aquarium, we took advantage of the meal the innkeeper prepared. Everything we saw throughout the morning and afternoon was educational. There was something not only peaceful but intriguing about the life forms that live underwater. You look out at a body of water like it's a surface, but an entire world is living beneath what we see.

The museum exhibits were filled with the beauty and the beastly of South Carolina's history: natural and man-made. The strength of all humanity, the harmony and adversity that exists between every life form, and the query that leads to discovery amalgamates to create all aspects of life as we know it.

It doesn't seem possible that anyone can leave a museum unchanged.

Our lunch conversation was consumed by our shared, though diverse, experiences on the day's outing. With full tummies and overloaded brains, a mutual agreement was made to nap. We returned to the B&B for a respite.

"I'm going to stay downstairs and check emails, Pres."

"Alright. I'm going to call Thomas. It feels weird not speaking to him for almost three days."

Instead of lying on the bed, I chose to sit outside. I pressed his name, then his number in my contacts. Thomas picked up on the first ring.

"Hey, babe," he greeted.

"Heeeey," I sweetly droned.

"Having fun?"

"Absolutely."

"Do you miss me?"

My nose scrunched. I replied, "Of course. Do you miss me?"

"Yes! I haven't seen or talked to you since Saturday. I didn't want to interrupt your trip, but I was starting to worry that you might be getting attached to the single life again."

"All is good with me. You have nothing to worry about."

"That's a relief. Do you want to talk about your adventures with Milly?"

"There's too much to tell. We can talk when I see you Saturday. Have you seen Francis?"

"Pres, I'm in Charlotte. I don't plan on driving forty minutes to check on a puppy that hardly knows I'm alive. Her attention span is like fifteen seconds. I'm sure she's fine with Carli and Hansen."

I chuckled. "You're right. You spend so much time in York that I sometimes forget you don't live there."

"I love you, babe."

"I love you too. I'm going to nap now."

"Oooh, that sounds nice. I'm going to read some more documents that would put a starving zombie to sleep."

Thomas is funny. I can give him that.

"Sorry you're so bored and I'm having so much fun."

"You deserve it. You've done a lot to get our wedding ready. Get lots of rest because next week is going to be like running a marathon."

I wanted to say, *"Ugh. Don't remind me."* What I did say was "I can't wait. It'll all be worth it."

"Love you, Pres."

"Love you too."

The conversation ended and I dropped my head back against the chair. I stared and daydreamed about my idea of the perfect man and what our relationship would be like.

The only thing that came to mind was passion in all its forms. I wondered if Thomas and I would get back there after we got married.

I shrugged. "Maybe it's me."

I got up from the chair, changed into shorts and a tank top, and crawled into bed. I fell asleep remembering my ex-boyfriend telling me that I was just not exciting enough for him.

Milly woke me up at six. The first thing I noticed was that my legs ached. The second thing I noticed was that my brain was lost in a time warp. I had no idea where I was or what day it was.

"I have something to tell you," Milly said. "Please don't get mad at me."

I sat up, giving her my full attention. "What is it?"

Grinning and clearly giddy, she said, "I got an email from a company that wants me to come for a third interview tomorrow!"

"Tomorrow?" I echoed.

"Yes. The company is in Rock Hill. I need to leave now to get home. I really need a good night's sleep. Are you angry?"

"No. You have to go."

"I'll come back as soon as I can."

"Milly, don't worry about it. I'll get a ride to a rental car company and drive myself home on Saturday. It'll be nice having this huge place to myself. Having you with me is certainly my preference. But…"

"I know what you mean."

"Well, get going! Good luck, drive carefully, and call me as soon as you get home."

"Find your joy this week. Warm up those chilly feet of yours."

I smiled. If I had responded, she may have started another whole conversation about Thomas.

She kissed my cheek and began frantically packing.

Once Milly left, it was quiet but heavenly. I started a home design season on TV, fast forwarded the boring parts, and paused at the makeover parts to take mental notes. The house Thomas and I were buying needed updating.

Around nine thirty, Milly called. "I made it to York safely. Have you reserved a rental car yet?"

"I'm glad you're safe. I plan on calling tomorrow to get a car. I've decided that the plantations are too far away, so I'm going to go to Patriot's Point instead."

"Oh, you'll love the Yorktown."

"Yeah, I'm excited."

"Well, my offer of returning still stands. If you want me to come back, just say the word."

"Milly, you do you. Don't give returning to Charleston another thought. I'm fine, I promise. As a matter of fact, I'm better than fine. I miss you, but I'm good by myself. Living with my parents doesn't give me much alone time. Focus on your interview and I'll see you in a few days."

"Thanks for not making me feel guilty."

"I wouldn't dare. Night."

"Night. Love you."

"Love you too."

Chapter Six

The most crucial components to feeling truly independent are having a job, a home, and a car. I had two out of three of those things for the week. In York, I had no job and no home of my own, but I did have a car. In Charleston, I was on cloud nine; I had a beautiful house on the Battery and a brand-new car, neither of which I had to pay for. My joy level had increased exponentially.

The drive to Mount Pleasant was a breeze. Driving over the Ravenel Bridge felt like I was on top of the world. What a wonder—a marvel.

At Patriot's Point, the parking lot was practically empty. Apparently, visiting landmarks during the middle of the week was ideal. There were no crowds. Milly and I had had pretty much every place to ourselves. Today was going to be no different. Exploring the Yorktown solo was going to be great. I smiled at the fact that both the aircraft carrier and my hometown got their names from York in England.

I followed the giant blue-and-white sign to the ticket office, circled through the turnstile, and was on my way up the pier toward the USS Yorktown.

"Miss! Miss! Blue dress with white flowers!"

The stranger was talking to me.

Figuring I had dropped something, I turned around and replied, "Yes?"

A young gentleman wearing name-brand athletic wear was jogging toward me.

"Is there a problem?" I asked.

"No. I just wanted to know where your bodyguards and entourage are?"

Ugh! Creep!

I was not nice. "Oh my gawd! Dude! You stopped me to puke that lame pickup line all over my happy mood?"

Spoiled, unemployed, trust-fund guy bent over and roared with laughter.

Before he erected himself, I snarked, "What are you, like sixteen? Shouldn't you be at school?"

Gasping through continued guffaws, he said, "No! I'm twenty-five! You look familiar. I thought you were that actress—what's her name? Uh, Princess Leia's mom? Natalie Portman!"

"Seriously? You're not gaining any ground, pumpkin. Though I gotta hand it to her. She is drop-dead gorgeous."

"Well, you look just like her. She's a lucky lady. She married Thor, ya know? If I could be anyone else, Thor's my man." He made a *click* sound and pointed his fingers at me like they were little guns. He then added, "You and I, we'd make a great Thor and Jean. Your name isn't Jean, is it?"

His immediate reference to the man of my fantasies had me taken aback. Was the universe telling me something?

Perhaps it was my pause that caused him to repeat his question. "Is your name Jean?"

"Uh, no. I'm Presley."

"That's much better."

"Thank you…" I raised my eyebrows, waiting to hear his name.

"I'm Logan and I am so glad I decided to come here today. Are you meeting anyone? Do you want to walk this place together? I'm a local and I've been here more times than I could possibly count. It's one of my favorite hangouts."

I waved my arms, gesturing to our surroundings. "This isn't a hangout, Logan."

"It is if you love all things pre-1989. Every decade prior to 1990 had its own style and heartbeat. They all had their own unique story to tell the generations of the past, present, and future. They produced quality work. Even the word vintage means 'quality of an era.'"

Pampered, workout guy suddenly sounded like a poet. He spoke with passion. It was exciting to listen to him, and he was absolutely right. My mind processed every point he made, and I wanted to hear more.

I asked, "Have you read every plaque and poster on this carrier?"

"All of them. If we stick together today, you'll learn more than you could gather on your own. Not that I'm doubting your IQ. I'm just saying that it's easier to hear the summary than read the entire essay."

He was speaking my language. "Are you a writer?" I asked.

"Not exactly. I could be, but I choose to educate the public with tours. My family owns a guide company named Live, Learn, and Love the Lowcountry. We're located downtown, off Meeting and not far from the Market. We live in the business district in an apartment above our offices. It's a decent-sized apartment, though. We also have a couple of small studios for staff."

"Impressive."

He snuffed a small laugh.

Knowing he was a tour guide reminded me: "Are you the guy who winked at me in front of the Pink House two days ago?"

"I knew you looked familiar. Yes! I saw you in the gift shop and seriously thought I knew you."

"Your 'entourage' pickup line was far more creative than the ole 'Don't I know you from somewhere?' line. I guess I can forgive you for that. Congratulations. Not only have you managed to redeem yourself but you've also won yourself an eager student for today's private class."

Logan grinned and rubbed his hands together like he was choosing between a steak and red velvet cake. He offered me his right elbow and said, "Milady."

We proceeded with synchronous steps.

"Do not make me regret this."

"Never. I will warn you, though. At the end of our time together, you are going to be head over heels in love."

I tugged on his exceptionally muscular bicep to halt our walk. "Logan, I'm engaged." I opened my hand that was gripped to him to show him my ring.

"Nice one," he complimented.

"Thank you. Keep in mind that today is about us having fun and hoping to get a true sense of what living on this ship would have been like. We're—well, *I'm* learning."

"I'll agree with you as long as you realize you can't stop me from really enjoying our time. I'll hold on to you today pretending like you're mine."

"Logan!" I scolded with a deep tone.

He placed his hand over mine and led me up the iron steps to the entrance.

"I'll show you the hangar, then the flight deck when we're done below. In my opinion, those are the best, so we'll save them for last. It's also more organized to start at the bottom and work your way up."

That method wouldn't have occurred to me, so I was already glad to have a professional at my side.

Logan showed me the berthing quarters with the racks, or bunks, for the enlisted men. We spent a lot of time in an officer's stateroom. Imagining that a man had lived there, worked there, planned there, missed his family there, gave me butterflies. The voices of thousands of men became white noise in my ears.

Logan asked, "Are you listening?"

"Yes. How did you know?"

"That's what I do when I'm here. I pretend to be part of their world."

When we explored the galley, the mess hall, and the wardroom, Logan talked about the foods they would have been preparing and eating. He talked about the class of soldiers for each post during each war era and how things have changed over the years. I hung on every word, fascinated. We then meandered our way to the aircraft storage hangar, which was just below the flight deck. Our time was nearing an end.

Like the rest of the carrier, the hangar was immense. This area, though, was wide open instead of partitioned, and its side doors opened up to the harbor. Logan told me about the airplanes on display and that the car on board would have been driven by an admiral on the ship. I was hearing him, but I was also getting tired.

"Can we sit, Logan? I think I've learned enough for today. My filing cabinets aren't just full; they're overflowing."

"Love the analogy. Yeah, we can rest."

Benches had been placed at the raised bay doors, with guardrails in front of them. We sat quietly, staring at Charleston on the horizon. It looked so small. Even the grand Ravenel Bridge looked like a toy. We were so small in the city, but the city was small when viewed from afar. The bridge was enormous, but from a very short distance away, it was no bigger than a pencil. Even photos of astronauts viewing Earth from space seemed like giants compared to our entire planet. Distance. Distance makes us seem important and our surroundings seem minute.

My thoughts were interrupted when Logan touched my hair. His warmth felt intrusive. No one had touched me in such an intimate way since I'd met Thomas. I didn't speak. I waited.

He began, "I know it's not my place to question your private life…"

"But you're going to anyway?"

"Yes. It's obvious that you and I have a lot in common. I want you to tell me the truth. Does your fiancé make you happy? You have a melancholy disposition, like you're living in regret. Is he everything you want? Are you excited about your wedding? I've never seen a bride this close to her wedding not in a constant state of cheer and celebration. They shout from the rooftops, 'I'm getting married!' They count down the days. But you don't seem to be doing any of that. Why?"

"The only reason you feel bold enough to ask me this is because you're developing a crush on me, Logan."

"That's not an answer."

"I never said I would answer you."

"Touché. You don't need to."

He continued stroking a strand of my hair. I didn't stop him. I needed and wanted to know how I felt about having another man that close to me.

Though I didn't dislike Logan's regard, in my heart it felt like betrayal. I *knew* it was betrayal. I had experienced that from the other side.

"Logan, I'm almost out of energy. Time to finish this."

Loud, deep groans echoed throughout the hangar as I struggled to stand.

"You're not eighty, Presley."

"Sometimes I feel it," I responded. "You're in better walking shape because you do it for a living. I'm exhausted because I've been walking nonstop for four days. I think I'll sit all day tomorrow."

He shook his head and smiled. "Come on. This way to the grand finale."

We climbed the last flight of stairs to arrive on the flight deck. Logan reached the top and offered his hand for assistance on the last steps. After he insisted on ladies first on the first set of stairs, I wised up to the fact that he was being less chivalrous and more scandalous.

I said to him, "You just want to try to look up my skirt!"

His chuckle overflowed with guilt but not regret.

On the deck, he once again offered me his arm and I took it. The plan was to see the airplanes, but we walked to the railing to look out over the harbor again. Fort Sumter was in the distance. Logan shared some Civil War trivia and local folklore, aka ghost stories, and I absorbed it all.

Creating a lull in the history lesson, Logan said, "Thank you for today, Presley. This is by far the best date I've been on in a very long time."

"This wasn't a date," I insisted.

"It was to me." He smiled sheepishly like he had gotten away with something.

"I confess that if I weren't nine days from my wedding, and you were on board—"

"I'm on board," he flirted.

"Anyway, as I was saying, I would definitely be interested in knowing more about you."

He took my hand from his arm and held it intimately. "Why does today have to end? Let me take you to dinner as a friend."

I couldn't believe that I was actually contemplating his offer.

"Presley?"

My eyes and heart could have jumped from my body. I looked over my shoulder and Thomas was headed toward us. The tilt of his head, the mild gape of his mouth, and the squint of his eyes showed apprehension, disbelief and extreme ire.

"Your fiancé, I'm guessing."

I affirmed Logan's assumption with a nod but did not look at him. I pulled my hand from his hold and said, "I might faint."

"You haven't done anything wrong," Logan whispered supportively.

Thomas was in our midst and we were a trio. He never took his eyes off mine. His expression let me know what he felt was pure disgust. We all three stood silent. I knew Thomas would speak first. He was an in-charge guy. All I had to do was wait for his instruction.

Not acknowledging Logan at all, Thomas simply pointed to the arbitrary distance. He didn't yell or seem threatening. He just ordered with no words.

My guilt forced me into obedience, and I heeded his request.

Logan remained in the exact position in the exact place. I knew he was going to watch our entire exchange.

Thomas followed me. I only stopped when I was confident Logan couldn't hear us and no one else would be interested in viewing the scenery from our location.

"You were standing too close to him, and he shouldn't have been holding your hand."

My eyes lowered like a child. My pre-Thomas insecurities returned. I couldn't look at him, because I had gotten too close to the edge. "You're right, but I didn't do anything wrong."

"You're here with another guy. I'd say that's certainly not a good decision."

"I'm not here *with* him. He's a tour guide. He was telling me the histories of everything in this area. That's all."

"And your hand, and the proximity, and the look in his eyes?"

Agitation grew. "So he's a flirt, Thomas! That doesn't make me a harlot!"

He placed his hands on his hips; his eyes scanned the distance between us and downtown.

Thomas took a deep breath and said, "Were you enjoying his 'flirtation'? Before you answer, put yourself in my shoes."

I'd had enough. I glared at him. The volume of our conversation had elevated. "Why are you here, Thomas?"

"I came here to surprise you! And I am very glad I did."

My cold feet turned into a hot temper. I had been compliant and easy going, but I was finally done. All I had held in for the past few months came out. I snapped. "You're here to surprise me? What a great surprise! It's almost as great as the surprise of choosing a house for us! Or buying me a dog! Oh! The surprise of reserving our wedding venue for April first! That was also a great surprise. Why would you choose April Fools' Day anyway?"

His eyes were saddened and slowly filled with tears. His expression told me he had thought that all of those experiences were gifts from him and therefore treasures to me. In reality, they were burdens. Even Francis, though I love her deeply, was very poorly timed.

He muttered, "I never told you my favorite song is 'I Fooled Around and Fell in Love.' I was going to surprise you at our reception by singing it to you."

I had hurt him. Seeing and hearing his pain was heartbreaking. I was still angry, though, so I asked again in a softer tone, "Why are you here? In Charleston, Thomas? How did you know I was at the Yorktown?"

Calmly, he replied, "I have a job interview tomorrow morning—a good job, with a corporate law firm. If they chose me, I was going to surprise you. I knew you were here because I called Milly." He raised both of his arms and shrugged. "Surprise…again."

Still frustrated, I rubbed my face with both hands. With extreme curiosity, I asked, "Wait. You sing?"

"A little."

Then, the compilation of the past six months of stress, confusion, repression, and ignorance eroded, and I said something I couldn't take back. "You should know that I've been trying to find a way to tell you that I don't want to marry you. I don't think I love you anymore."

The tears that had formed moments ago, finally rolled down his cheeks. He turned away from me and wiped his face. He turned back. "Exactly *how* have you 'tried' telling me you don't want to marry me?" he asked. "When did that conversation almost happen but get thwarted?"

I gaped, completely lost for words. I guessed that he avoided the love comment because he wouldn't have been able to continue the conversation at all. I regretted having this discussion in this place at this time.

Thomas shifted his weight to one leg and put his hands on his hips again. He was still in total control. Except this time, it was magnetic. The crisp white dress shirt, the pressed dress pants, the matching belt and shoes. His perfectly styled brown hair crowned a face that was adorned with crystal blue eyes. The whole package was my dream. Suddenly, it was like I was seeing him again for the very first time. I saw the man my heart had desperately craved. My attraction to him was so intense I could hardly breathe. He truly was the absolute love I wanted. The absolute love I needed. What had I done?

"You seem to have run out of ways to hurt me today, Presley. I'm going to save you the trouble of coming up with excuses or arguments or some other way to knock the air out of me. You said you want to call off the wedding? Well, consider it done."

A hand that I wanted to kiss was extended toward me with its palm facing up.

"All of this is so wrong, Thomas! We need to talk...rationally. I'm sorry."

His arm held steady. His eyes were serious. His posture was resolute.

I pulled my engagement ring from my finger and placed it in his hand. Before I released it, his skin barely touched mine. His fingers curled ever so slightly as if he was going to hold on to me. But he didn't. He took the ring and turned and walked away.

"Thomas!" My voice cracked when I called to him.

He paused and gave me his attention.

"Can we please talk? Let's go back to my hotel or go to dinner."

"I'm not interested. We've both said all there is to say."

I begged, "Will you please come see me after your interview tomorrow? We have to work through this. Please come see me."

"No, I won't. Enjoy the rest of your spring break."

"Milly left last night. We'll have time alone."

"I suggest you check out early and try to get some of your parents' money back. None of this can be undone now. I probably could have gotten over finding you here with some random guy, but I have no desire to get over what you just said to me. I gave you my heart the first time I saw you. We're supposed to be married in nine days, and you just said you don't love me anymore. I deserve better and so do you."

The click of his heels tapping the deck of the Yorktown was a sound I'll never forget. I watched him leave. Not wanting to make a spectacle of myself, I held my tears. The whole situation had weakened me, and I couldn't move yet. I leaned on the railing and let it hold me up.

Logan eventually stepped to my side. Wisely, he didn't touch me when he said, "Presley, I am so sorry. Can I walk you to your car?"

"Please don't," I replied.

"Okay. But listen, if you need anything, please call me. I'm having dinner at the Oakland Mill tonight. I'd—"

I interrupted whatever he was going to say next. "I won't be calling you or joining you for dinner, Logan. Thanks, though, for being so nice to me today."

When I stepped onto the sidewalk I saw he was still standing in the same spot. I sensed his attention was on me until I was out of sight.

The drive from Patriot's Point back to downtown was a complete blur. It's curious how we can find ourselves at a completely different location with no recollection of how we got there. My mind saw only visions of Thomas. Every significant interaction between us flashed without halt. His smile, his excitement, his laughter—all I could think about was Thomas Mathews.

The only joy I felt upon my return was that I had a separate space from everyone else staying at the inn. I didn't have to see or speak to one single person. My walk was lumbered. Holding my head up was laborious. Once the door was opened, my feet carried me up the stairs, where I collapsed on the bed and cried myself to sleep.

Chapter Seven

Thursday morning, I fixed my coffee and sat on the balcony, wrapped in my robe and with my feet tucked under me. Rain fell steadily in the chilled air. Eating was not going to be an option for the day and perhaps for the weeks to come.

It was seven thirty. Thomas's interview was sometime before noon, so I said a prayer for him to get all he wanted in life. He was very rational and reasonable. I knew he'd be able to compartmentalize our relationship and keep it separate from his work. He'd get the job, no doubt about it.

Another cup of coffee comforted me, and possibly another. I lost track of time thinking about how I had never deserved him anyway.

My future was a blank slate. Tears no longer fell, but depression had taken hold. I wondered if I would finish my last semester. I wondered if everyone would snub me for canceling our wedding. I wondered if I was going to have to pay my family back for all of the expenses. I wondered if I was going to have to live in my childhood bedroom for the rest of my life. Ugh, the dark thoughts would not stop.

A heavy fisted knock on my door interrupted my pity party.

"Presley!"

Logan? Is that Logan? What's he doing here? I told him I don't want to see him.

Feeling frustrated because his presence would do nothing but exacerbate my situation, I wiped my face as I walked down the stairs. I prepared a brief but firm get lost request.

I opened the door, and to my utter surprise, Thomas was there. He was so handsome in his suit. His eyebrows raised, and he said, "I hope I'm not fooling myself by thinking you said some things you didn't mean yesterday."

The tears that had dried up poured once again. I didn't speak. I reached, clasped his wrist, and pulled him into the house. "Come upstairs with me, please."

In the bedroom suite, I removed his blazer and hung it in the closet. "Take your shoes off," I whispered. I climbed onto the middle of the bed. "Sit with me."

He sat.

"Talk, Presley. I'm here to listen."

A couple of weepy gasps preceded my confession. "I thought I meant it when I said I didn't want to marry you. Certainly, you've felt that we've grown apart. You and I seem to have lost our connection. We've just been going through robotic motions that people go through, except what I felt changed from love to indifference."

"I came over here so you could tell me I'm wrong, but you're going to reassure me all over again that you don't love me?"

"No, Thomas. That's not what I'm saying. I do love you, so much. I think I needed you to show up for me. Maybe the insecure me took over these past few months and I was just self-sabotaging us."

"Show up? I'm here, Presley! I've been here since our first glance."

"I know. It was me. I hurt us so you couldn't hurt me."

Thomas looked confused. "I don't understand you."

"I need you to...to..."

"What? I can't read your mind."

I scooted closer and placed each of my legs on either side of him. I then slipped the knot from his tie and unbuttoned his shirt. My hands went under his T-shirt and caressed the immaculate muscle tone he kept hidden from everyone but me. He was a masterpiece.

Close to his mouth, I whispered, "Be here for me, Thomas. Help me."

He pressed his lips to mine quickly and accurately. He leaned in, I leaned back, and he seductively placed himself on me. Knowing where this was headed, I broke our kiss.

"What's wrong?" he asked.

"Will you marry me?"

"Are you asking me to be your husband?"

"I am. And you are never going to believe this, but I happen to have a huge wedding production planned for next weekend. Not only would you be perfect for the leading role, but you're the only one I want starring in my show."

He laughed. "That is quite the coincidence, isn't it?"

"Well? Will you marry me, Thomas?"

Instead of an answer, he grinned, pulled my ring from his pocket, and said, "Will you marry *me*?"

I nodded as he placed it back on my finger. "Consider it done."

Thomas made love to me that morning like it was our first time.

Lying together, I said to him, "It's been so long since we've done that. I thought you weren't interested anymore."

"Presley, I'm a man. I'm always interested."

I snickered and shared my feelings. "Well, after we got engaged six months ago, you seemed to lose interest. Waiting for you to pursue intimacy with me became numbing. I got worried that you didn't really want me anymore and indifference set in. Today, though, you're completely different."

"Indifferent? Numb? In some ways, I may seem different to you, but I'm the same person."

"You're not the same at all. Can't you feel it? You had to be challenged and I had to be rejected for us to realize we needed to work this out. Today—right now—I can't imagine letting you go. However, when I woke up yesterday, I felt trapped."

Resting beside me with his head propped in his hand, he said, "I do see that you've changed. Your words are powerful. Until I saw you with that other guy yesterday, you've been passive. I tiptoed around you for fear of scaring you off. I planned every milestone for us because I was trying to keep you committed. Heck, I never even let you know that the real me has an infinite arsenal of F-bombs."

I rolled from my side to my back, laughing. "That's hilarious. When did you plan on dropping that on me?"

"I wasn't sure."

"Thomas, I need you to know that I wasn't with another guy yesterday. I was touring an aircraft carrier with a complete stranger who happened to be very entertaining. That was it."

"I believe you. So you don't regret accepting an engagement to me?"

"No, of course not. I just lost us because I lost me. We never have to go back to where we were, though."

I kissed him and lured him back to me.

Chapter Eight

Around noon, we were both very hungry. We showered and dressed. The rain had stopped, at least for a little while, so we walked up East Bay to find a nice place to eat. When we were on the battery walkway, facing the water, I threw my hands in the air and yelled, "I'm getting married!" I understood what Logan meant. I did want to scream it again and again.

Thomas and I were in love and engaged again. We spent those remaining days in Charleston celebrating our pre-honeymoon. It was almost better than our actual honeymoon. *Almost.*

Thomas sang at our wedding reception. I have to say that even if the events of the previous week had not occurred and I would've idled my way down the aisle, Thomas would have won my heart forever with that single surprising act of love. His talents would never cease to amaze me.

Milly didn't get the job in Rock Hill. I was secretly pleased because I had a much better plan for her. I researched Logan's family business and saw they were hiring. I contacted him and set them up on a blind date. Long story short, she now has a job and a place to live, but the truth of it is, she is moving to Charleston to be with him. I knew they'd hit it off.

Thomas got the job he interviewed for that week. Despite the pain in his heart, he worked his charm in the boardroom that morning. I was very happy about that. A change of scenery was exactly what I needed. I preferred to spend my vacations in York. It made the moments with family and friends sweeter when you had fewer of them to savor.

My degree was complete, and I got a job working remotely for an interior design magazine based in Alabama. We found a great condo to rent that was within walking distance to Thomas's office, and thanks to my job, I got to stay home with Francis. Though the road to wedded bliss had been bumpy, all was well with us.

The exact moment I knew I was going to marry Thomas Mathews was perfectly clear. It was just before he took back my ring. Perhaps I had it coming. But sometimes you really can't see how blessed you are until the blessing is taken away. That lesson was a tough one, but I wouldn't change it for the world.

The End

About Victoria R. Benson

A native South Carolinian and graduate of USC, Columbia, Victoria now lives in Idaho with her husband of twenty-eight years. They have two adult children and are enjoying life as empty-nesters. Victoria has been an educator for eighteen years, teaching all grades from fourth to seniors in high school. Seven years ago, a passion for writing revived and Victoria heeded the inspiration. She authored her first romance novel. Since then, Victoria has published ten novels and contributed to three anthologies.

Find Victoria Online:

Website: https://blackdressbooks.com/
Facebook: https://www.facebook.com/blackdressbooks
Facebook: https://www.facebook.com/vicki.dentbenson

Instagram: https://www.instagram.com/victoriarbenson/

X : https://twitter.com/blackdressbooks

Amazon:https://www.amazon.com/Victoria-R-Benson/e/B081GB6HS7/ref=aufs_dp_fta_dsk

Goodreads:https://www.goodreads.com/author/show/20432723.Victoria_R_Benson

BookBub: https://www.bookbub.com/authors/victoria-r-benson

Moonlight in Moncks Corner

By Janie Gordon

Moonlight in Moncks Corner

By Janie Gordon

Martin's temporary "I do" sweeps Olivia out of her parents' control and offers her a fresh start—free of drugs, dominance, and pressure to continue her superstar legacy. But what can Olivia offer Martin?

A vacation in Moncks Corner offers a reprieve, time for reflection, yet another gift from Martin. But Martin's childhood girlfriend, paparazzi, and an omnipresent alligator muddy the waters, leaving Olivia more confused than ever.

Can she find her direction and release Martin from the kindness of their marriage? Or will she discover forever love instead?

Chili Pepper Rating: 1

Chapter One

A muumuu, enormous and shapeless, billowed around a body labeled "voluptuous" by the tabloids. Olivia shrugged at her reflection in the dresser mirror. At least the shocking orange, pink, and lime-green folds promised anonymity as she traveled with her temporary husband. Four dresses, all tent-like, had arrived yesterday, along with shorts, shirts, dresses, lingerie, pajamas, jewelry, and a wide-brimmed hat. Her favorite purchase was a blue bikini—scraps of material that matched her eyes. Would he even notice?

Martin called from the kitchen, "Ready to go soon?" Within a minute, he stood in the doorway watching her, a smile teasing the corners of his mouth. "Don't you look…colorful?"

Olivia snatched an orange headscarf and pink sunglasses from the dresser. "I look fabulous. Thank you for noticing." She returned his smile as she covered her blonde hair. "You'll thank me later when the paparazzi aren't swarming. I can see the headlines now: "Missing Movie Star Found in Moncks Corner."

"I don't think anybody will recognize you there." Martin folded his arms and seemed in no hurry to stop staring. His green eyes held that cherished look again. If Olivia didn't know better, she'd imagine real feelings under that rock-solid exterior.

But she did know better.

Olivia filled the space with chatter. "Remind me why we're going to a tiny South Carolina town. I mean, we could go to Charleston for charm, Hilton Head for pristine beaches, or anywhere with a spa and nightlife."

"You wanted to get out of New York, and Moncks Corner will slow us both down."

"You mean it will slow *me* down." Martin's dedication as a director was legendary even at the youthful age of thirty-two, but he also insisted on long breaks between films, telling the press that everyone should have a work-life balance.

Olivia, however, didn't know how to relax. She'd been making films since the age of five, always pushed forward by her parents. Until now. Now she had absolutely nothing to do.

He changed the subject, as she knew he would. "You've been out of the hospital less than a week." A frown did nothing to hide the beauty of his rugged face. He ran a hand through his already messy black hair, a sure sign he was uncomfortable.

Olivia stepped closer and looked up at him, this man—her husband—who had insisted they get married five days ago to break her parents' hold on her. With her father's zombie medications finally out of her system, Olivia wanted to believe she saw the world more clearly. But a clear view didn't mean she liked everything she saw. It would take massive effort and time to turn her life around, find her way out of the mess she'd helped create, and call a "redo" at the ripe age of twenty-two. Life had already started to harden her.

This vacation might soften the edges.

She rested her hand on his forearm, once again reveling in the warmth of his skin, the strength of him. He'd been her champion since the award ceremony, where her childhood director had accosted her in an isolated dressing room. In the two years that had followed, each time her life took a dark turn, Martin had shown up, her anchor to a solid, gentle world. Now he was her husband. They told themselves the marriage would dissolve her father's conservatorship, a battle they'd left in legal hands. Maybe that's why Martin had insisted on leaving town rather than sit and wait for the final word.

Martin covered her hand with his, still frowning.

Olivia was torn between wanting to reassure him and needing to confess her infatuation. What would he do if she flung off her muumuu and climbed up all six feet four of him? No, her ego couldn't take another rejection. "I'm okay," she whispered.

When Martin took a step back, the shadow of rejection again fell on Olivia's heart, and she dropped her hand. Her smile was all teeth—as fake as their marriage. "How the hell did you come up with such a minuscule town with no redeeming features? You must *really* want me bored to tears!"

Martin turned away, leaving the room colder. "It's where I grew up."

Behind his receding back, Olivia covered her mouth. *Crap.* So much for getting closer to Martin. Her plan to entice her reticent husband, blind him with her sparkling personality and perfect—and purchased—assets, faded to black.

After a loud, bumpy flight in a plane barely big enough to hold Olivia's four suitcases, they arrived at an airport in the middle of a field. Martin held her arm until her feet hit the hard-packed dirt of the runway, puffing dust on her Gucci sandals. A small terminal boasting "Berkeley County Airport" crouched among silvery hangars filled with small planes and a tractor. Thank goodness an Audi waited for them under the glaring sun, promising luxury and comfort for the bulk of their week-long vacation in Small Town, USA.

Olivia marched toward the car, confident that either Martin or his pilot friend would deposit her suitcases into the car. She needed some cool air, a firm mattress, and a drink. A swarm of tiny black bugs surrounded her in a cloud, some charging up her nostrils, while others chose to drown on her sweaty face. She batted them away, sputtering, "What the hell?"

Martin's deep chuckle—a little less sexy in the watery heat—rolled toward her as she fought to open the car door. He called out, "That's not our car. Over here." He carried her suitcases toward a red truck painted in rust and dented like used aluminum foil. He tossed her bags in the bed and opened the passenger door for her.

Olivia rolled her eyes but scrambled into the truck, entangling her feet in the miles of fabric surrounding her. "If I'd known we'd be riding in such style, I'd have worn my tiara." She'd never tell Martin, but she actually owned nine tiaras, each worn at one of her movie premiers.

With a laugh that sounded like he was thoroughly enjoying his vacation, Martin boosted her into the truck with one hand on her bottom. "Up you go, princess."

After sweating for exactly seventeen minutes, bumbling past establishments called Dollar General, Wendy's, and 7-Eleven, they passed a sign for Lake Moultrie and arrived at Short Stay, a title that probably reflected travelers' suggestions. The hotel reminded her of *Schitt's Creek*, and as charming as the show was, she didn't want to spend a week there. She spared a glance at her silent companion. His smile hinted at reminiscing, and Olivia wondered if Martin had grown up on the lake. "Is this where we're staying?" *Please say no, please say no.*

"A little farther." Martin smiled at her and reached for her hand, his first deliberate touch all day. Olivia tried not to squeeze his fingers to hold him in place. "The house is on the lake. We'll have our own dock and a boat."

Olivia pictured a clapboard cabin that might fall over in a stiff breeze—not that the town seemed to have a breeze. Heaven forbid the little black bug clouds blow away. A boat might be fun, but Martin could be over the moon about a rowboat, like the one he'd used as a kid. Holding on to her husband's hand, she stared forward and braced herself for a short stay.

Martin turned down a driveway shaded by trees Olivia couldn't name. Around the bend, a manicured lawn previewed a pale-blue two-story bungalow with a white porch. Palms and indigenous trees flanked the idyllic house, and flowering shrubs tucked against one another below the porch railing. Circular stepstones meandered from the driveway to the steps below a red front door.

"Martin," Olivia exhaled, eyes wide as she surveyed their perfect vacation spot. He had rented well. As soon as the truck shuttered to a stop, Olivia tossed her glasses and scarf onto the dash, jumped out, and ran around to the lakeside view from the house, where a screened back porch overlooked a wide expanse of lake, a dock, and a white ski boat. Cypress trees and damp tree trunks stuck out of the water, most of them close to shore.

She called back over her shoulder, "It's perfect! I love it!"

Like a kid finding hidden treasure, she turned back toward the house, eager to share her discovery with Martin.

There, separating her from safety and all that is holy, a long, thick monster opened its mouth to reveal rows of prehistoric teeth.

Chapter Two

Olivia froze.

The eight-foot alligator squatted on short legs a few feet away. Behind the scaly monster, Martin came into view, but Olivia couldn't look away from the slitted mud-brown eyes.

The creature lunged.

While she watched her doom approach on surprisingly fast claws, it suddenly moved backward. The spell broken, Olivia looked up to see Martin clutching the creature's tail. The reptile jerked its body sideways, massive muscles bending back toward Martin with open jaws. A deep pink maw yawned, ready to snap shut on flesh.

Olivia's scream cut through the slow-motion struggle as Martin appeared to redirect the gator away from him and back into the water. All of his focus was on the task.

The gator snapped inches from Martin's hand.

In her own ears, the screaming continued. She leaped forward, determined to save Martin through a field of red and the pounding of her heart.

Martin shoved her back and bellowed, "No!"

The gator writhed again, bending and flexing to reach his captor before turning away and scrambling toward the murky water. For now. Any second, he could twist toward Martin again.

In one swift motion, Martin released the tail, scooped up Olivia, and sprinted toward the house.

When the screen door slammed behind them, Martin released his hold on Olivia, but she clutched him around the neck, repeating, "No, no, no, no" with her eyes squeezed shut.

"Olivia." He spoke quietly. "Olivia. You're safe. It's okay."

She buried her face in his neck and mumbled, "Okay?" Her mind raced to catch up with the pumping adrenaline.

"Yeah, you're okay." Martin gently pulled her arms down and set her on her feet, where she swayed. "If it happens again, just clap your hands and make some noise."

Her mouth dropped open. "*Again?*"

Martin pulled her to the porch swing. "Sit down. You look like you might fall over." He sat beside her and braced an arm around her shoulders. "Sometimes we see a gator or two near shore. They usually don't bother people much."

"Until they do! Did you see the look in his eyes?" She shivered. "Those beady, slitted eyes." She buried her face in her hands. "He tried to eat you!"

"He was just protecting his territory."

Olivia jumped up and glared at Martin. "He can have his territory! I'm out of here, and there's nothing you can do to stop me." She stalked toward the screen door and stopped, frozen again and refusing to turn around. "Um, can you get me to the truck?"

When she glanced back with wide eyes, Martin grinned. The nerve.

Olivia forced herself to add, "Or get my purse so I can call for a car."

She expected him to argue and braced herself to be fierce. He stayed seated and calmly said, "That's a good idea."

"What?" Was this some kind of trick?

He stood but stayed a few steps away. "Let's get out of here. We can have an early dinner." With a close-lipped smile, Martin punched in a code to unlock the house. "Come on, we'll walk through and leave by the front door."

Obediently (for now), Olivia trailed behind him, her head down, already planning a return to New York. When they reached the raised front porch, she stopped short on the top step, searching the lawn for her reptilian rival. "How do you know—?"

Martin scooped her up and carried her down the steps. He didn't put her down when they reached the truck but opened the door and deposited her on the seat before closing the door. Olivia watched the ground behind him for any sign of danger.

After Martin was safely inside the truck, Olivia closed her eyes and took deep breaths. If Martin thought she'd change her mind after a fancy dinner, he was dead wrong. Dead. She shivered. They had almost died. Olivia put on her scarf and sunglasses, more as a barrier to hide her fear than her identity.

Ten minutes later, Martin parked in front of a diner labeled "Music Man's Bar-B-Que." The plain red stucco facade and black awning foreshadowed what Olivia found when she stepped inside the swinging glass door. Red checkered plastic tablecloths covered round tables lining the right side of the room and picnic-style tables running through the middle. The white walls were covered with faded black-and-white pictures from the fifties and sixties, interspersed with red posters for the University of South Carolina and signs that screamed, "Go Cocks!"

On the left side of the room, a sneeze guard announced a buffet with macaroni and cheese, coleslaw, green beans, rolls, and several kinds of meat. What the restaurant lacked in style, it made up for in food, if the tangy, rich odor of smoked barbeque was any indication. Even though it was only six o'clock, an ungodly early hour to eat dinner, the place buzzed with conversation and clanking forks.

Martin called out, "Jim! Y'all have room for two more?"

Y'all? Olivia had heard the word from TV evangelists and Texas politicians, but it seemed like a foreign language from Martin's lips. She looked up at his profile while he waved at a couple in the corner.

After Jim seated them at the only open table, he smiled at Olivia. "Hey, pretty lady. What are you doing wasting your time with this guy?" Jim laughed at his own comment and turned to Martin. "How'd you snag this one? Tell her you're a big-time New York director?"

Martin grinned. "Yeah, and she bought it." He glanced down at the paper menu and pushed it aside. "Can you bring us two barbeque plates when you get a minute?"

"You got it!" Jim ambled away, stopping to talk to other customers as he went.

Olivia leaned forward. "If you think a plate of meat is going to change my mind about leaving, you—"

"Martin!" A pretty brunette laid her hand on Martin's shoulder and stood too close. "I didn't know you were in town! When did you get here? How long are you staying?"

"Hey, Debbie." Martin smiled at the petite woman, nearly pulling a growl from Olivia. That hand needed to leave his shoulder, and Debbie needed to step away from *her* husband. Oblivious to the tension, Martin turned his body to face their guest. "We just got here today." He gestured toward Olivia. "This is Olivia. Olivia, this is Debbie."

Olivia peered up through her pink glasses. "So I gathered." When Martin cleared his throat, she added, "Nice to meet you." But it was a lie. And that nubby-fingernailed hand hadn't left Martin's shoulder.

Debbie pulled up a chair beside Martin and sat. Surprisingly, she didn't feel the plumes of heat radiating from Olivia. The eager woman continued her intrusion. "We have to get together!"

Over my dead body.

"It'll be like old times." Debbie blushed prettily. "We could go out in the boat like we used to."

Over her *dead body.* Accidents happened on boats, didn't they?

Debbie waved a hand toward the room but didn't turn away from Martin. "Mike is over there eating his second plate of mac and cheese." She rolled her eyes. "We got married just last year." With a playful slap on Martin's bicep, she added, "I finally gave up waiting for you."

Why wait for a boat? Debbie might choke on a roll. Especially if Olivia crammed it down her throat. Enough was enough. Olivia reached across the table and covered Martin's hand with hers, smiling at him. "Probably the best thing, since Martin married *me*."

Debbie's smile faltered, but she recovered quickly, stammering, "Well… that's perfect. We could all go out in the boat tomorrow. It'll be a party. How about ten? We'll bring some beer." For the first time, Debbie stared at Olivia, a challenge in her eyes. "Unless you're the jealous type."

Olivia sat back. "Not at all. A party sounds fine. But we spend mornings in bed." Take *that*. "So let's say noon."

Debbie bounced up. "Great! Martin, I'll call you later, but we'll plan on noon." She turned to Olivia. "I hope you know how to waterski. Martin and I won a contest in high school!" The woman actually leaned down and kissed Martin on the cheek, lingering there a second too long for Olivia's taste.

To Martin's credit, he didn't glance at Debbie's pert little butt as she walked away, white shorts shifting side to side with each exaggerated step. Instead, he smiled at Olivia. "If you like barbeque, you'll love this food."

As if on cue, Jim arrived with two plates overflowing with ribs, coleslaw, baked beans, and Texas toast. He sat down two tall red plastic cups full of what he called "sweet tea."

Without another word, Olivia picked up the ribs, ripped one from the rack, and bit into the sweet caramelized meat. It was heaven, and she was ravenous. Halfway through her fourth rib, she looked up to find Martin grinning at her. "What?" she asked.

He handed her a stack of napkins and pointed toward his chin. "You have a little something…" When she wiped the sauce away, Martin gestured around his mouth. "And a little more…"

His obvious enjoyment lifted Olivia's mood. Here she sat, a handsome man in front of her, great food, and she was safe, with her whole life ahead of her. Amazing what a belly full of good food will do to a bad attitude.

After dinner, Martin drove her through town and pointed out his favorite hang-out spot as a kid, which was a Hardee's fast-food restaurant. They stopped at a store called Piggly Wiggly, a name that sounded like a greased farm animal, where Olivia helped Martin pick out groceries. Shopping right out in the open (with a disguise, sure) was exhilarating. By the time they got back to the cottage, dusk was falling, easing the heat by a few degrees.

Martin parked the truck and exchanged a glance with Olivia. Like a child asking for a treat and expecting a "no," he asked, "Will you stay?"

Chapter Three

A fist squeezed Olivia's heart. She sighed. "Fine. I'll stay. For now."

Her reward was Martin's broad smile. He jumped out and came around to her side before opening the door and extending his arms to carry her. "Ready?"

"I can do it." When Martin dropped his arms, Olivia warily looked behind him, scanning the yard. "What are the chances?" She slowly lowered one foot to the ground.

"Gators are usually more active from dusk to dawn." He said it matter-of-factly, like the news was no big deal.

It was definitely a big deal.

Olivia's leg shot back into the truck. "Maybe a piggyback ride."

Martin turned around, and she climbed on. The muscles in his back tightened as he reached down and held her legs in place. This position was a new slice of heaven, offering intimate contact in key areas that pushed fear to a corner of her mind. The only thing better than Martin's back was his front.

And his voice.

His eyes.

His smile.

Olivia shook her head and climbed down when they reached the front door. She mumbled, "Thank you."

"Any time." Martin used the keypad to unlock the house, then swung open the door, waiting for her to enter first.

The foyer opened to a living room and kitchen with marbled counters and steel appliances. An island held six stools with low backs. Beyond the kitchen, soft white furniture was set against white walls and a row of sliding glass doors that opened onto the screened porch. Pine end tables, a coffee table, and a hutch were brushed in a white ash wash. The effect should have been cold, stark, but instead, the overstuffed couches welcomed relaxation, and the walls glowed with the pink light of sunset.

Martin called out, "I'll get our stuff from the truck. Be right back." After two trips and depositing bags down the hallway, he returned.

Olivia asked, "How did you find such a great place? Did you stay here when you were younger?"

"All the time." Martin went to the kitchen and produced a bottle of white wine and two glasses.

Olivia pulled off her scarf and sunglasses and explored the room, leaning down to study pictures on the hutch. A smiling couple held fishing poles; a little boy sat on the dock with a toddler; a tall teenager stood beside a dark-haired girl, both dressed for the prom. The teenager looked familiar.

Those eyes, that smile.

"Martin!" She turned as he handed her a glass. "Is this your house?"

"Not exactly. It's my parents' house. We spent summers here."

"Are they still in town?" Olivia was torn between wanting to meet his family and wanting him all to herself. Already she had to share him with Debbie tomorrow.

"No, Mom and Dad are traveling. I think they're in Paris this month. And my sister lives in Raleigh with her husband and kids." He sat on a couch, and Olivia sat across from him, still holding his prom picture.

She examined the photo again. The dark-haired girl smiled and looked up at Martin adoringly. "Was this your high-school sweetheart?"

"That's Debbie."

White-hot jealousy, completely unreasonable and unwanted, shot through Olivia. "I didn't recognize her. She's aged since then."

Martin continued as though immune to snark. "We dated throughout high school, but we met in middle school."

Olivia squinted at the picture. Yes, she could see it. The girl in the picture had hair to her waist and a deep tan, but the essence of the adult she'd become showed through. She carefully set the picture onto an end table. "Middle school. That's a long time together." A very long time. And clearly, Debbie was as adoring now as she was then.

Martin smiled and looked over Olivia's shoulder as though remembering the years. *Damn it.* He refocused on Olivia. "I fell for her in the eighth grade, when she taught me how to kiss." He shook his head and laughed at the memory.

Olivia clamored to bring him back to the present. "Did she do a good job?"

"You tell me." He raised his eyebrows and laughed.

"I don't recall." *Liar.* They had kissed only a few times, but Olivia remembered every second, every nuance, every touch. "And besides, each woman has different needs." She tossed her hair back. "I have my own preferences."

Martin squinted at her. "Is that right?"

A gulp from her glass left Olivia coughing. She tried to recover her dignity. "Of course."

"Show me."

"What?" First the *y'all*, now this. Was he the same man who had refused to consummate their marriage, fake as it was? Now he was all but asking her to kiss him. Should she take the bait?

Slowly, carefully, she put down her glass and stood, straightening her awful muumuu. Her heart thudded at the base of her neck. Without breaking eye contact, she came to sit beside Martin and took his glass away, then placed it on the coffee table like it was made of the most delicate crystal.

Martin turned his body toward her, eyes holding a challenge. He murmured, "What do you like, Olivia?"

She reached a hand up and stroked his five-o'clock shadow. Her voice almost betrayed her as she exhaled, "I like it slow." Olivia leaned forward and touched her lips to his, closing her eyes to focus on the gentle pressure. He didn't respond, but he didn't stop her. She moved closer. Again, she pressed her lips against his, breathing in his scent—the smell of soap, pine, and *Martin*. She didn't pull away as she said, "Kiss me back."

Immediately, Martin applied pressure to her lips, pushing back against her advances until they joined equal forces.

Olivia broke contact with his lips to align her body with his. Closer. "Put your arms around me." He did. "Now do what I do." She kissed him and lightly bit his lower lip, testing the resilient skin between gentle teeth. He inhaled sharply, all the encouragement Olivia needed. "Your turn."

As instructed, Martin bit her lip at the end of his kiss. When she would have pulled away, he touched her upper lip with his tongue before flicking just the tip between her lips. Olivia opened to receive him, but he pulled back. His ragged breathing told her he was not unmoved by their lesson.

She stroked his cheek again. "Your tongue. I want to taste your tongue, but I'll show you how I like it first." After reaching her arms around his neck, Olivia tilted her head and kissed Martin with closed lips before touching his mouth with her tongue. "Let me in."

He opened his lips enough for her to slide her tongue inside and taste his mouth. Slowly, she pulled her tongue away, only to push it in again in an ancient rhythm. A small sound escaped her mouth without her permission, and neither did Martin ask permission when he sucked her tongue gently before releasing her.

They stared at each other in the near darkness. "Olivia, I don't think—"

"Your turn," Olivia whispered. A low thrumming vibrated through her, filled her up, ripened her for his touch.

Before her words faded from the air, Martin pulled her close again. He first kissed her lips, then he pressed his tongue inside, where she welcomed him with gentle sucking. Her mouth felt hot, ready for the rhythmic thrusting he offered her. She inhaled a jagged breath. *Don't stop.* His body burned under her touch. His shoulders, his biceps, his legs.

Somehow, without planning to, Olivia found herself stretched out on top of Martin. In a primitive dance, she wanted—desperately needed—as much of their bodies touching as possible.

Under her, Martin groaned like he was in pain, the kind of sweet pain that led to release. Olivia's heart beat a flush all over her body. Her skin throbbed. Light seemed to flash around her, creating a rainbow of colors behind her closed eyelids.

Martin sat up, holding Olivia securely by the shoulders. He growled, "What the hell?"

Olivia's eyes flew open, and she shook her head to clear it. Lights continued to flash.

Muffled shouts of "Olivia!" filtered through the closed windows. "Olivia! Can you give us a quote? Olivia! Why are you in Moncks Corner?" Several people knocked on the windows, rattling the glass under their fists.

Chapter Four

Martin stood in front of Olivia. "Your bedroom is at the end of the hall. Why don't you unpack? I'll get rid of the reporters."

She did as he asked, leaving him to clean up the mess. The idea of confronting those reporters deflated her, leeching her motivation and confidence. Martin to the rescue. Would it always be this way? Some measure of shame followed her down the hall, where she found a four-poster mahogany bed covered in a white down comforter and light gray chairs in a corner reading area. Her luggage was beside the bed, lined up neatly like soldiers ready for battle. She unpacked quickly, throwing clothes into a mahogany dresser.

The drone of distant male voices drifted throughout the house. Olivia sat on the bed and waited. And waited. Quickly bored, she stood and examined herself in a full-length mirror and nearly laughed out loud. Her hair was a tangled mess, and her muumuu was worse for humidity and sweat. Her entire body felt sticky. Olivia lifted an arm and sniffed underneath. A faint but unpleasant odor wafted up, bringing with it the crush of embarrassment that she'd been making out with Martin ten minutes ago.

A white-and-gray en suite held a whirlpool tub. Olivia started the bath water then stripped before stepping into the tub. Heaven. Warm water inched up her body as the faucet ran, and when the tub filled, she turned on the jets and submerged to her neck. Her head buzzed with the day, from the overwhelming heat to Debbie to this evening's make-out session, before settling on Martin.

Martin, out there saving her yet again.

He hadn't even asked her if she wanted to deal with the reporters; he just shooed her away and fixed it. Even though she should be grateful, Martin's take-charge attitude told Olivia what he thought of her; she was still weak, still recovering from all of her bad decisions.

Images of her first marriage flashed through her mind like a merry-go-round ride on acid. The quickie Vegas wedding, the torment of infidelity, the depression. Going home had seemed her only choice at the time, but her father's imposed conservatorship had led to drugs and long months at the institution.

Olivia dipped her head under water and exhaled, willing her mind to quiet. As she slid up again, a new thought bubbled to the surface. What if Martin was right? What if she really did need his help? What if she wasn't capable of dealing with her own life? She could vow to give in right now and let Martin hold the reins. No doubt he was successful, with the film industry clamoring for him to sign on as director, a blockbuster guaranteed. He sure knew how to run his own life. Martin was confident, competent, and determined—all that Olivia was not.

Mentally and emotionally defeated, Olivia bathed, pulled on under-wear and a T-shirt, and closed the bedroom door. This day needed to end. She stretched on top of the cool down comforter, staring at the ceiling and listening to the sounds of Martin locking doors, turning off lights, and showering.

Finally, the house was silent.

Still wide awake, Olivia padded into the kitchen for a glass of water. Soft moonlight drifted across the porch with each passing cloud. Olivia slipped out and paced behind the windows, where the reporters had ambushed them. A profound loneliness echoed inside her heart. Finding no peace, she returned to the kitchen and looked toward the hallway.

Before she could talk herself out of it, she tiptoed to Martin's room and turned the handle slowly. His large form lay still. Heart racing, she approached the bed, but he still didn't move.

Unable to see his face, she leaned close, closer, until she nearly touched his nose. "Martin."

"Olivia," he responded in a thick, sleepy voice.

"Can I sleep in here?" She still whispered because that's what a person does when sneaking into a bedroom.

In answer, he lifted the covers. Olivia climbed in, curving her body away from him, while he covered them both with a blanket. His soft T-shirt smelled like a fresh shower. She sighed.

"What's wrong?" Martin spoke softly near her ear.

"Just thinking about the reporters…and my parents…and people I've worked with." The darkness suited Olivia's mood, and it hid her silent tears. "Everyone wants something from me." She pressed back against him. "Except you."

Martin pulled away from her and stuffed a pillow between their bodies before holding her again. His breath was warm on her neck. "Go to sleep."

Olivia closed her eyes, trying to sleep through the suffocating quiet. And Martin's arm draped across her shoulders was doing nothing to calm her libido. She whispered, "Are you awake?"

"Mm-hmm," he growled in her ear.

"Thank you for marrying me."

His arm tensed. "You're welcome."

"Let me thank you." She reached back and pulled the pillow from between them, pressing herself against him.

"You just did."

"You know what I mean." She wiggled her rear end. "Be my husband."

"It's not real."

The pain in her heart sucked her breath away. Olivia waited for him to say more. Instead, he pressed the blankets between them.

Minutes ticked by.

Martin's breathing didn't deepen and soften. He was as wide awake as she was.

When the hurt became a dull ache, giving way to anger, Olivia blurted, "I can't *wait* for the divorce papers to come through." Yes, anger was better. "This must be torture for you—stuck with me day after day, but I remember the deal. Our marriage had one purpose—to save me from my parents. I get it. Crystal clear. Martin, the hero. Martin, the saint." She pushed aside his arm and sat up, ready to bolt. "Are you not attracted to me *at all*?"

Before she could stand, Martin's arm shot out and pulled her down to lean half of his body over her. Even in the darkness, Olivia could see his shadowed face inches above hers. "Not attracted to you?" The hardness against her leg spoke louder than his words. "I'm no saint." He crushed her mouth with a kiss that broke all the "go slow" rules she'd taught him.

Chapter Five

Olivia's arms reached around his back, deepening the kiss, matching his anger with her own.

Too soon, Martin broke the kiss and tucked his face against her neck, breathing like he'd sprinted across a finish line. "You're making me crazy, woman."

Olivia stroked one hand down his back, exploring the contours of taut muscles. "Then talk to me. Why can't we have some fun?"

He turned to lay beside her, one arm across her stomach. "Because I don't want payment, and I don't want fun." His chuckle lightened the mood. "I mean, I do like fun, but not like this." He kissed her cheek, lingering there. "Stay here with me."

He didn't ask for much, and Olivia didn't want to leave the warmth of his bed and his body. She curled against his chest. He held her there, one hand on her head as she tucked under his chin. As she finally drifted to sleep, she either heard or dreamed his soft, "Stay with me."

—— ♥ ——

The next morning, Olivia woke to an empty bed at dawn but stalled until ten o'clock, when she heard Martin moving around and the heavenly aroma of bacon filled the house. Yesterday, she had realized she needed his help; she needed his strength, just as he'd been strong enough for both of them last night. He was probably right. A fling would only complicate things and be one more damning piece of evidence that she made bad decisions.

Throwing back the covers, she took a deep breath. In her bedroom, she pulled on shorts before joining Martin in the kitchen with a wide, aren't-I-a-good-actress smile. Two steaming cups of coffee waited on the counter.

Martin turned from the stove and smiled like the sun had just come up. "Good morning." His cheer was a bit much in the face of Olivia's self-revelation. But if this was her destiny, so be it.

She smiled with half of her heart. "Morning." A sip of coffee did wonders for her mood, and she couldn't deny the eye candy in front of her in the form of Martin's broad shoulders and muscular chest pressing outlines into a snug T-shirt. Leave it to Martin; he acted like he didn't know how drool-worthy he was. If Olivia had to turn over control of her life to someone, at least it was a man who was fun to look at. And kiss. She grinned. Things could be worse.

Martin turned to her and set up plates on the island. "Hungry? I have eggs, bacon, and sausage."

"That sounds great, but no sausage for me." Olivia waited a beat to see if Martin would fill her in on last night with the reporters, but he remained silent, as he usually did. "So…"

He looked up, giving her his full attention, bless him.

"What happened last night?"

"You slept in my bed." He grinned.

A blush leaped to Olivia's cheeks, not because she had slept with him but because nothing else had happened. "I meant with the reporters. How'd you get rid of them?"

He shrugged. "I just asked them politely to leave us alone."

"That's it? It was that easy?"

"Pretty much." He shrugged again. "And I might have called the sheriff. We went to high school together."

"Of course you did." Olivia smiled.

"I told them you were on vacation and relaxing, that's all." He smiled. "And I might have pulled a Sonny from *The Godfather* and destroyed their cameras." He held up his hands in mock surrender. "No pictures."

Olivia's childhood tutor had marinated her in movie trivia, often abandoning geometry in the process. "Did you throw money at them like James Caan did when he improvised that scene?" She wished she could have watched the reenactment.

"No, but I was tempted." He laughed. "That's where the sheriff came in. I told him to bill me."

"Perfect!" He really did know how to handle everything. "Are we still boating today?"

"Yeah, Debbie and her husband, Mike, will be here by noon. But Debbie is always early, so I'll start getting the boat ready after breakfast."

Olivia hated that Martin knew Debbie's habits, but at least the husband would arrive with her. Surely she wouldn't fall all over Martin while her husband was watching—although Olivia was well aware that some couples liked to share. Today promised to be as challenging as yesterday. Olivia wanted nothing more than to crawl back into bed, read a good book, and drift off to sleep when her eyes got heavy.

Two hours later, Olivia found herself floating on Lake Moultrie watching Debbie lean too closely to Martin as she pulled another beer from the cooler. The tiny woman wore a yellow bandana top and a thong that showed off her tan and her rear end at the same time. Mike, a balding, loud man with a beer belly that seemed his pride and joy, took every opportunity to touch Olivia's thigh and compliment her on her figure in "that mouthwatering bikini." To his credit, he managed to drink beer faster than his wife, which was an impressive feat.

Martin had steered the boat far from shore and killed the engine. "Who wants to cool off?" He peeled off his T-shirt.

Good grief. Olivia had suspected muscles; after all, he was hard to the touch, and his physique pressed through the T-shirt. But she hadn't expected the rock-hard six-pack now revealed in all its glory. When did he have time to maintain that? If he wasn't on the set of a movie fourteen hours a day, lately he spent time at her side, not at a gym. She glanced at Debbie, and sure enough, she also stared at Martin, her mouth gaping open like a beached guppy.

Martin moved to the edge of the boat.

"Wait!" Olivia lunged toward him and grabbed his arm. "You're not going *in* there, are you?" Her imagination already had him legless, a massive alligator slithering away with its prize.

He looked confused, looking back and forth from Olivia to the calm water. "Yeah. Want to join me?"

Holding tighter, she shook his arm. "Did you see the size of that alligator yesterday?" With her free hand, she pointed to the water. "In *this* lake!"

Behind her, Debbie laughed and dove in. Martin covered Olivia's hand with his. "They don't come out this deep or far from shore."

Debbie splashed the water toward them. "Come on in, the water's fine!" Then she screamed, "Shit! Something's got me! Something's got me!" Her gales of laughter pierced Olivia's fear, leaving behind anger hotter than the unrelenting sun.

Mike drawled from his perch at the back of the boat, "C'mon, Debbie, take it down a notch." In response, his wife floated on her back and pouted.

Martin ducked his head and kissed Olivia briefly on the lips before promising, "I'll be careful."

Olivia dropped her hand and watched Martin dive in beside Debbie before resurfacing a few seconds later with a shake of his head. For the next twenty minutes, Olivia leaned over the edge and policed the waters around Martin, ready to warn him the second she saw a scaled tail or slitted eyes. Her heart raced faster every time he ducked his head under water. Behind her, Mike sang "A Country Boy Can Survive" as loud as his beer-sodden voice allowed.

When Martin and Debbie climbed back into the boat, Olivia looked toward shore, already anticipating the ride back, a shower, and a glass of wine. They had been on the lake for an hour, and even with sunscreen slathered on exposed skin, she could almost feel herself cooking. Instead, the rest of the party decided to water-ski for the next several hours, punctuated by swimming when the boat stopped. Olivia plastered a smile onto her face. If this made Martin happy, she wouldn't ruin his fun. But neither would she dip a toe in a lake filled with mortal danger. It took all of her effort just to keep an eye on Martin, as though her diligence would protect him from harm.

In the end, hunger saved the day, and Martin took them back to the dock and tied up the boat with Debbie's help. Mike was too drunk to do more than weave across the lawn. When the boat was secured against the dock, Olivia took Martin's extended hand to step out.

Debbie stood behind Martin with her arms crossed. "Well, bless your heart."

The words sounded kind, but the sneer on Debbie's face told Olivia otherwise. "Um, thank you."

The two women walked up the dock, leaving Martin with the boat. Debbie leaned close to Olivia, breathing beer breath on her cheek, and asked, "How'd y'all like the little gift I sent over last night?"

"What gift?"

"The reporters." Debbie leaned closer and bumped Olivia's arm. "They couldn't wait to see the famous Olivia Knight."

Olivia stopped walking. She couldn't patrol for alligators and argue at the same time. "What? Why?"

"You think I didn't recognize you in that lame disguise? Even people in little ole Moncks Corner have TV, and some of us even go to the *moo-ving pictures*." She dragged out the last words like they were foreign to her. "You're not better than me just because you make movies."

Enough. Something inside of Olivia snapped to attention, ready for the fight. "You're right. I'm not better because I make movies. I'm better for a hundred other reasons." She raised her chin and turned to walk away, peering ahead of her for a scaled visitor.

A hard shove knocked Olivia off-balance, and she teetered on the edge of the dock. *No!* But it was too late. She splashed into the murky lake.

Chapter Six

Olivia flailed in the shallow water. *What's the rule? What do I do?* She yelled, sputtered, and clapped her hands, intent on scaring away any gators sliding toward her. No question, today was the day she'd die. Something scraped under her knees. *This is it.*

Martin lifted her from the water, carrying her like a child being taken to bed, and deposited her on the dock before hoisting himself up beside her. She trembled and clung to him, arms around his neck.

Debbie had pushed her in—had actually pushed her into dangerous water.

Martin kept his arm around Olivia as they walked to the house and onto the back porch. Pungent lake water dripped into her eyes and down her body, cooling her off for the first time all day. Mike was asleep on the porch swing, and Debbie had the decency to avoid eye contact.

Pressed against Martin's side, Olivia felt the rumble of his growl even as the words left his body. "Debbie, be glad you're a woman."

Debbie faced him, a smile teasing one corner of her mouth. "Oh, I am, sugah." She put one hand on her jutted hip, a clumsy effort to look sexy that only showed how drunk she was. "I bet you are too." She cut her eyes toward Olivia and looked her up and down. "Too bad this one is just a *kid*."

"You haven't changed since high school, and that's not a compliment." He held Olivia tighter.

Debbie swayed unsteadily but kept talking. "Oh please. I'm on social media. I know how screwed up she is. Typical child superstar gone bad. Why are you—"

"Olivia is my *wife*, and I was brought up to know that means something." He leaned down to kiss Olivia briefly on the lips. His voice softened when he spoke to her, "I need to drive them home. I'll get a ride back." To Debbie, he muttered, "Then our friendship is over."

In the hour Martin was gone, Olivia took another long bath, this time concentrating only on *not* thinking. She turned on music, sang out loud, and ran through old movies in her head—anything to crowd out her musings about life. She dried off, pulled on a T-shirt and shorts, and drank a glass of wine. After another harrowing day, it was time to sit down and talk with Martin about securing his help. He was a powerful man in the business, and acting was the only life she knew. With him by her side, she felt more secure, safer, and one day, maybe even loved.

Martin walked into the living room looking exhausted. For the first time, Olivia realized the day might have been a challenge for him too. He held up two paper bags. "Hungry?"

Olivia took the bags from him and smiled, hoping to ease his day. "Famished. But why don't you take a shower while I set up plates and a drink. Feel like a beer?"

He exhaled and slumped forward slightly. "That sounds fantastic." He rewarded her with a grin. "Thank you."

Warmth radiated through Olivia, fueled by helping Martin for a change.

By the time he came out in clean shorts and a T-shirt, Olivia had sandwiches plated, a glass of wine for her, and a frosted glass of beer for Martin. He smiled, his damp hair messier than usual, like he had dried it with a towel and run his fingers through it.

While they ate, Olivia made small talk and worked up the courage to broach her future. Finally, after clearing the plates and pouring each of them another drink, Olivia invited Martin to join her on the cozy couches. She sat across from him, earning herself a raised eyebrow.

He waited.

"I want to talk to you about my future."

Martin nodded and drank from his glass.

"Can you put me in your next movie?" She knew he had the power to do it, and he was always starting a new project.

He nodded again. "I can."

Olivia exhaled and sat back, sinking into the plush cushions.

Martin asked, "But why?"

"It's all I know how to do. I'm a good actor. Some would say great."

"I would."

Olivia smiled. "Thank you. So that's what I'll keep doing."

"Is that what you *want* to do?"

"I guess." She shrugged one shoulder. "I could ride your success and not have to think about it." Truer words were never spoken, but Olivia wished she could take them back, just the same.

After a pause, Martin asked, "Where's the fun in that?"

"I'm sure we could make it fun." Olivia winked and smiled, hoping to lighten the moment but also remind him that she was willing to reward him with an object of value.

He set his beer on the table beside him. "Olivia."

It wasn't the good way people call a name; it was the bad way, all hard and final at the end, the way her father had said her name when she'd misbehaved.

Martin took a deep breath and breathed it out slowly. "I can't—"

"Never mind, never mind." Olivia jumped to her feet. "I don't know what I was thinking."

Martin stood too. "Let me finish. I can't think of anyone I'd rather work with." He coughed lightly. "And the other stuff too." He walked toward her, and Olivia's heart beat faster with every step. "But what do you want to do?" Now he stood in front of her and lifted her chin to meet his gaze, repeating, "What do you want?"

You. I want you. But Olivia knew what he meant. He was asking her to consider the thousands of possibilities for her future and choose one. Or two. Or more. But so many possibilities made her head hurt.

"I don't know." It was honest…and mortifying.

Pulling her down on the couch beside him, Martin said, "Right now, at this point in your life, the entire world is wide open. You have money, intelligence, beauty, and charisma. You're so young."

She didn't feel young. She felt tired and overwhelmed. "But what about—"

"The past?" He shook his head. "What would you tell a friend who lived the childhood you lived?"

Her eyes filled with tears, but they wouldn't fall unless she blinked.

Martin took one of her hands between his. "Decide where you want to live, what you want to do, who you want to be. Then surround yourself with experts who will help you get it done."

Olivia blinked.

"Don't cry, honey. You'll break my heart." Martin wiped away her tears.

How could he not see what a mess she was? How inept she was? She threw up her hands.

"Martin, I'm impulsive."

"You get things done."

"I'm stubborn."

"You're strong."

"I'm spoiled."

"You're perfect."

She laughed as she rolled her eyes to heaven. "You're nuts."

"How about this?" Martin asked. "What makes you happy? What excites you?"

You. But he wanted a harder answer. She was almost embarrassed to say, but she decided to trust Martin. "I like pretty things, like clothes. Even as a little girl, I loved jewelry, perfume, fashion." She grinned, warming to the idea. "I think I might be good at it."

Martin smiled, pride radiating and giving Olivia confidence. He said, "You could do a lot with that. You could go to design school, or you could focus on the business of it and start your own company."

Cautious joy rose up, pure and hopeful. A career in fashion. She wasn't drawn to designing her own line, and the idea of returning to school didn't thrill her, but she saw the possibilities of this path. Ideas fought for space in her mind, tumbling over one another like puppies just learning to walk.

Olivia jumped up and paced. "I could showcase new designers and their work. We could do competitions, shows, and marketing—maybe even getting into high-end boutiques. And they'd all have the Olivia Knight brand." She spoke faster. "I'd need to find lawyers, accountants, office staff. Oh! And an office. No, a *suite* of offices."

"And an image consultant." Martin broke through her rant.

"Huh?" Olivia whipped around to stare at Martin. "You don't like my image?"

Martin laughed out loud. "I love your image. But if you're going to become a brand, everything you say, do, and wear will be part of it."

He was right. She needed to be deliberate in her decisions, especially if she meant to change her public image of child movie star with famous parents. To wipe it away, she needed to choose every nuance of herself with care and always show the public the new person she'd become. The brand.

She nodded once. "Yes, you're right." A smile beamed from her flushed face. "I have so much work to do!" And she couldn't wait to get started. "Do you mind…"

"There's a computer in the drawer over there." He waved his hand toward the hutch. "Password and Wi-Fi are on a sticky note." Martin stood and approached Olivia, looking down at her with that cherishing look. "Have fun." Then he kissed her on the cheek.

Olivia closed her eyes briefly. If he had kissed her on the lips, she would have abandoned her research for the night, hoping for another bout of the kissing game. But new ideas are fragile; if they aren't nurtured, sometimes they break or just fade away, becoming too nebulous to remember why they were so exciting in the first place. Olivia wanted to nurture this idea before it got away.

Stepping back, Martin ran a hand through his hair. "I'm beat. I'll leave you to it." He walked down the hall and quietly closed his bedroom door, leaving Olivia alone with her thoughts.

Now what? How do people start a business—a brand—from nothing? How should she remake herself? She had so many questions. Then it occurred to her that questions were the first step of her journey, and that was okay.

After brewing a pot of coffee and opening the computer on the counter, Olivia sat down to plan a life.

At seven o'clock the next morning, Martin shuffled into the living room. Olivia looked up, but the vision before her blurred after a sleepless night of internet deep dives. The entire computer desktop was filled with files that held notes about business classes, accounting firms, fashion designers, and ideas for Olivia's brand.

Martin rubbed her shoulders, and she leaned back against him. He asked, "Were you up all night?" His voice held concern.

"Yes," she sighed. His hands seemed to melt into her aching muscles.

"What did you learn?"

"That I'm in way over my head."

"You just got started."

"Exactly."

Martin dropped his hands.

"Keep rubbing." She leaned forward and rested her arms and head on the counter. "Please."

With a chuckle, Martin resumed the massage. "Okay, if you had a friend who wanted to do this, what would you say?"

"I'd say start with one thing. Like deciding on a public image." In the silence, Olivia sat up and turned to Martin. "Oh! Right." How did he do that? Make everything simpler with his presence. "But right now I need some sleep."

"Go get some rest. I'll go fishing, so the house will be quiet."

Olivia rolled out of bed with crusted eyes and flattened hair. She had barely moved for seven hours. After splashing water on her face and pulling her hair into a ponytail, she wandered to the living room. A glance through the windows showed that the boat was gone, which meant Martin was still out. The place felt empty and too quiet without him, but Olivia had work to do. Sleep had solidified insights into her persona, and she realized she had to define who she *wasn't* as well as who she was.

> She found a scrap of paper in the kitchen drawer and made a list.
> *Independence from parents, prior roles, and acting*
> *Competent, confident, strong attitude*
> *Looking her best in public at all times—no more muumuus*
> *Savvy business woman*
> *Champion for hard workers, especially those with less power*
> *Signature color of white*

The color would follow her everywhere, from white clothes to a white suite of offices. Her future designers would be encouraged to use a rainbow palette, but Olivia would always wear white with the exception of accessories. Before she'd fallen asleep, she assumed the choice was defiance based on her mother's signature black clothing, but as Olivia looked around the living room, she recognized the inspiration. She put her list on the coffee table and dropped onto a couch, stretching her arms across the back and smiling.

The doorbell intruded on her thoughts, a persistent chime that sent Olivia padding to the front door and swinging it open wide. The smile she had plastered on her face melted.

"Good afternoon, Olivia," said her father.

Chapter Seven

"What are you doing here?" Olivia felt caught, like she wasn't old enough to be at a man's house without a chaperone. Her father's blue suit and crisp white shirt underlined his "adult" status.

"Where are your manners? Aren't you going to invite me in?" Before she could decide, he brushed past her and studied the room with obvious disdain. "*This* is where you choose to vacation?"

"I like it." She followed behind him. "How did you know I was here?"

He graced her with a glance before sitting, uninvited, on a couch and crossing his legs. "I received a call from a reporter who knew I'd pay for the information." He waved a hand toward the couch across from him. "Sit down. We need to get some things straight."

The screen door slammed, and Martin entered through the back door. He looked from Olivia to her father and back again, a question in his eyes. "I see we have a visitor."

Before Olivia could respond, her father said, "Indeed. If you could call Olivia's father a visitor. I've come to bring her home. Her mother and I are concerned for her welfare."

Old habits die hard, and Olivia nodded even while silently pleading with Martin for help. Fear coursed through her, bringing with it a prickly sweat. Did she have to go home? Hadn't marrying Martin broken her father's conservatorship? Terror froze her heart. They'd screwed up. Soon she'd be back on the meds that devoured her memory and motivation.

Martin's calm response eased her fear by a millimeter. "That's up to her." He touched Olivia's shoulder. "I was saving this as a surprise for our last vacation day, but hold on." He walked down the hall and quickly returned with a large manila envelope and handed it to Olivia. "These papers formally dissolve the conservatorship if you attest that you married me without duress while you were in the hospital. All you have to do is sign them."

Still in shock, Olivia slowly opened the envelope and pulled out a sheaf of papers. She shuffled through while Martin retrieved a pen from the kitchen. What did all these pages mean? Was she truly free?

A cough brought her attention back to her father. He stood with his hands on his hips. "Don't you dare. Your mother and I created you, molded you, into a valuable commodity. You will *never* make it on your own."

To his credit, Martin didn't say a word. He stared at Olivia and waited. But maybe her father was right. She had made some bad decisions in the past, decisions that had brought her back to her parents. Should she actually walk away now?

The documents felt as heavy as Olivia's heart. She sighed and dropped them to the table; the puff of air disturbed a scrap of paper.

Her list: *Independence from parents.*

Olivia's father rounded the table with his arms outstretched. "You know we want what's best for you." The hug she'd craved as a child finally came, bringing with it a regression to the scared five-year-old girl who wanted to trust. "We can help with your future."

Martin choked out, "Olivia." It was a plea.

But she'd made up her mind—or at least the frightened child in her had made up her mind. She laid her head on her father's shoulder. "I'm going home." Defeat coated her mouth with metal.

Olivia's father guided her toward the front door, but Martin blocked the way.

"Wait, let's take a minute. Olivia, what about your plans?"

She shook her head and turned away, leading her father toward the back door. "I'm not strong enough."

Martin didn't follow them. If he had, Olivia would have heard his footsteps. He was letting her go.

"Eeeee-yah!" her father shrieked, frozen at the bottom of the steps. The scaly stuff of Olivia's nightmares crouched a few feet from her father, mouth wide, rows of jagged teeth protruding, slitted eyes focused on prey.

Olivia jumped in front of her father, clapping her hands and yelling, "Not today, Satan! *Go! Go! Go!*" The gator backed away and slithered into the water, thick tail swinging lazily through the muck. With the danger past, her heart raced, sending a buzzing through her head.

She turned back to her father, who held his chest and breathed heavily. Leaning in, she asked, "Are you okay?"

He panted. "I will be." Crouching until he sat on the bottom step, her father looked up in wonder. "Where did you learn that? Who *are* you?"

Cicadas buzzed. In the distance, a boat whined across the water.

"I'm *the* Olivia Knight. Independent, competent, and strong." She reached for his arm and helped him up. "It's time for you to leave."

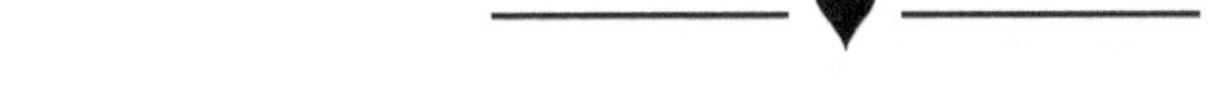

Martin lined their suitcases by the front door and poured Olivia a sweet tea, a drink she had grown to love almost as much as she did Lake Moultrie and Moncks Corner—their vacation spot, and forever the place where she toddled her first steps on her own. They would leave early in the morning, but tonight was for saying goodbye.

"Back porch?" Olivia asked, smiling up at her husband. Ice clinked against the frosty glass as she led the way to their porch swing.

Moonlight filtered through the trees and hinted at shadows in the darkness. The couple sat side by side in silence, unable to read each other's expressions or body language and instead relying on words and touch. Martin put his arm around Olivia's shoulders, and she leaned back against him.

His chest rumbled when he spoke. "Ready to go home?"

"I'm ready." Ready for the next chapter, the one not yet written. "I'll look for my own place when we get back."

"No hurry." He sounded end-of-vacation sad. "Stay as long as you want." A gentle kiss pressed against her head. Martin inhaled. Olivia felt the steady *thud, thud* of his heart beat against her back.

Olivia put her glass on the floor and shifted to sit in Martin's lap. His arms held her securely in place as she rested her head on his shoulder and closed her eyes.

She would miss sleeping in his bed every night, even though he insisted on stuffing those damn pillows between them. They'd touched and kissed and laughed in the living room, the screened porch, the lake. But never the bed, where it would have been too easy to give in. They had talked about the future and even the past—the parts Olivia was willing to relive.

She'd miss it all.

"Can we play 'what-if?'" Olivia spoke quietly, not wanting to break the spell.

"Sure."

"What if I stayed?" She held her breath. "With you."

"Depends on the reason. A safety net?"

"No. Not anymore."

"Then why?"

"I don't know yet." It was the truth. Olivia could have told Martin she loved him, but that kind of trust takes longer than a week to build.

A frog called to its mate.

Olivia waited. It was his turn, and she refused to fill the air with words.

"What if..." he started.

She remained perfectly still.

"What if we stayed married?" His throat sounded dry.

Olivia knew how much the question had taken out of him—this generous, loving man.

She grinned into the moonlight, watching it play across the lake. Had it always been this beautiful? For right now, in this moment, everything felt right and good—maybe for the first time in her life. Her mind played through fantasies of Martin as her husband. What that would look like, what it would mean.

Behind her ear, Martin exhaled, "You're killing me, woman."

In answer, Olivia stood and reached for his hand, pulling him to stand beside her. She led him through the quiet house and into his darkened bedroom. She crawled into bed and lifted the covers as an invitation as he had done for her. And, just as he had asked on their first night here, she whispered, "Stay with me."

The End

About Janie Gordon

Janie Gordon writes contemporary romance with strong female leads and supportive female friends. She grew up in Moncks Corner, South Carolina and has remained a fan of small southern towns. Her first book, *Random Husband*, is a romantic comedy about a social-media search for love, available on *Amazon*. Her second book, *Olivia*, is a gritty novel of survival and true love. Her short story in this anthology, *Moonlight in Moncks Corner*, tracks Olivia's vacation and a turning point in her life. Read the rest of Olivia's adventure on *Amazon*. For more stories and happily ever afters, follow Janie's social media accounts.

Find Janie Online:

Website: JanieGordon.org

Instagram: https://www.instagram.com/janiegordonauthor/
Facebook: https://www.facebook.com/janie.h.gordon
Amazon:https://www.amazon.com/stores/Janie-Gordon/author/
B0CSVG3VX6

IOP Connection

By Elaine Reed

IOP Connection

By Elaine Reed

College best friends Lila and Gabriel have a decade-long tradition of spending the Fourth of July at Gabriel's family beach house on the Isle of Palms. This year in particular, Lila needs a break, but Gabriel's tag-along guest is making that difficult.

But then Cash, Gabriel's good-looking neighbor, turns up. Both artists, Cash and Lila strike up an informal business partnership, and distract each other from who and what's irking them. Gabriel encourages Lila to have a beach fling, but there could be more at play for Lila and Cash.

Chili Pepper Rating: 1

Chapter One

Lila had met Gabriel at their college's freshman orientation. Before their first semester was over, they'd declared each other their ride or die, and every Fourth of July since, they'd gone to Gabriel's family's house on Isle of Palms. This year was no different. Except…

"Y'all! I can't believe we're here!" Henry, a new friend of Gabriel's, had come along. He spun in the driveway as though he'd just finished the makeover montage in a movie.

Lila gritted her teeth and actively worked to ignore him as she tossed the cans he'd left in the backseat and helped Gabriel unload the trunk. She gathered her tote and the messenger bag with her art supplies. A client had requested custom designs for wedding stationery and Lila had big ideas for something hand drawn. The sea air and the beauty of nearby Charleston was supposed to influence her. And then—

"Now what?" Henry called.

Lila glanced at Gabriel and lifted her eyebrows. *Now what?* They'd just arrived. They hadn't finished unloading the car and this man-child was asking, *Now what?* Lila kept quiet. Henry had attached himself to Gabriel after Gabriel had given a guest lecture at Henry's college. Gabriel could answer the stupid question.

Gabriel lifted a suitcase, best described as a craft project gone wrong, from the trunk. The afternoon sun glinted off haphazardly placed mirror tiles and glitter glue. "You can carry in your stuff." He set the suitcase onto the gravel driveway and retrieved his own duffel bag before slamming the trunk closed.

"But Gaaaaaaaaaaaay-briel! I'm the *guest*." Henry pouted. He actually stuck out his bottom lip and pouted.

Gabriel heaved a sigh.

"You're not going to—" Lila stopped herself when Gabriel took Henry's garish suitcase, attempting to carry it in one hand and their cooler in the other. "Stop." She slung her tote over her shoulder and hefted the cooler with both hands. "Get the door."

"Lila," Gabriel said. "I can do it."

"If I have to stand out here and listen to Henry ask a million questions and never wait for an answer, I'm gonna lose my shit."

Gabriel walked with Lila to the small portico in front of the house. She set the cooler precariously close to Henry's foot, debating whether she should've given into temptation and "dropped" it on his toes. Gabriel set Henry's messy suitcase between Lila and the cooler.

Henry jumped, too short to reach the top of the doorframe, and slapped it. "Why aren't the keys here?" He squatted next to a concrete planter packed full of dirt and tried—and failed—to lift it. "Keys!" he called, as though they would bound to him like a puppy.

Lila stared at Gabriel, silently asking why he'd let Henry come along. Was it worth it? Would this man-child torment them all week? Would she face legal consequences if she convinced Henry to hold a live firework in his hand?

Gabriel pursed his lips, meaning his answers were: I felt bad, probably not, probably so, and do we really want to deal with the drama of Henry experiencing any kind of injury?

Lila shrugged. "You're right."

"Right about what?" Henry asked. He hopped in place, his hands over his zipper like a child waiting to use the toilet.

Gabriel shook his keys. "Putting the sunscreen in the cooler. No one wants to put on hot sunscreen."

Henry ruffled his brow. "You two are weird. I hope when I've been out of college forever, my friends aren't this weird."

"You should be so lucky," Gabriel murmured. "Finish your degree before you make judgments."

Lila followed Gabriel into a small vestibule, where he opened an inner door.

"Bathroom is there." He pointed to a room by the foyer.

Henry hurried in and slammed the door, then yelled, "There's no light!"

Gabriel looked to the ceiling, as though collecting himself before he answered. "There's a pull string next to the mirror."

"A pull?" A squeal echoed throughout the little foyer. "Found it! How quaint!"

Gabriel set his duffel down and retrieved Henry's things. "Maybe this'll be a shark attack weekend."

"One can only hope." Lila put the cooler near the kitchen while Gabriel took Henry's suitcase to the room where she usually slept. "Excuse me, sir. I'm *not* sharing a room with Henry."

"Take the big room upstairs. I can't find the keys for that balcony, and the last thing I need is Henry turning it into his personal apartment." Gabriel stashed his bag inside another bedroom. "He already echoes too much. God help us if he was in a big room."

Lila loaded her arms with cans from the cooler. "In college, I would've snuck all kinds of awful men up that private staircase. Now I'm guarding it. Where did I go wrong?"

"You set some standards and held them." Gabriel opened the refrigerator, systematically taking the drinks from Lila and lining them up on the shelves.

"Not sure why I thought *that* was a good idea." Lila continued to pass drinks and snacks to him while Henry, fresh from the bathroom, harassed Gabriel over the sleeping arrangements.

"Why do we have to stay down here? We can't leave Lila alone and *unprotected* upstairs." Henry clutched imaginary pearls.

Lila patted Henry's head, then slung her bag over her shoulder again. "My resting bitch face is lethal. Plus, you and Gabriel are guarding the front door. I'll be plenty protected."

"I should booby trap that entryway."

Lila rolled her eyes and strode to the vestibule that the family had added when they'd built the second floor. "The stairs already do that."

"The stairs? What's she talking about?"

Desperate to escape the conversation, Lila jogged upstairs—careful of the trick step—and went to the bedroom at the end of the hall.

As Gabriel told it, they'd added a private balcony with stairs to the room at the far corner of the house so one of the uncles could take an early morning run on the beach without waking anyone. The main door often stuck, and the family had decided not to fix the squeak after Hurricane Hugo had blown through almost forty years ago.

They'd considered the squeak a badge of honor. Plus, it had let the parents know if someone was going to the beach unsupervised. On the downside, it also alerted the children in the house that someone was leaving, likely going to the beach, and that often created a tidal wave of floaties and beach pails rushing toward the door. Hence the discreet second entrance.

Lila set her bag near a side chair. The rooms on this floor were huge. Hers had a queen bed, a sitting area, and a crib and changing table. Gabriel's older brother often threatened to get whichever woman he was currently dating pregnant to make use of the crib and tease the parents and grandparents about the "no sharing until you're married" rule that still stood. No one knew why. All the "kids" were at least in their thirties now—some married with their own kids. Those who weren't single lived with their partners. Until they got to the beach.

The other room had a queen bed, plus a set of bunk beds. When the rest of Gabriel's family was here, that was the room Lila and Gabriel shared, though they most definitely were not married, nor had they ever dated. Lila had fond memories of staying up with Gabriel long after the parents and grandparents had gone to bed and giggling themselves to sleep over any and everything. Technically, this wasn't *her* family home, but it might as well be. Technically, Gabriel wasn't her brother, but he might as well be too.

She checked the locks on the balcony door: there was a regular deadbolt and a double cylinder deadbolt that required a key to unlock it from either side. She undid the regular lock and opened the door. The windmill palms around the balcony were overgrown and mostly shielded it from the street view, but they were trimmed against the house, leaving the little porch and its spiral stairs accessible. Lila grinned. She had an escape route from Henry. She closed the door and locked it, then went to the big main deck—the best feature of this house.

It was another spot where she and Gabriel had spent countless hours. They'd entertained his parents' friends. Insulted his brother's friends. Laughed hysterically with their own friends. She got a cloth from the nearby bathroom and wiped off the table and chairs. A large dining room table lived downstairs, but unless it was storming, they usually ate up here. With a view of the beach and the sound of the surf, it didn't get much better.

Now that she was here, Lila knew this was what she needed to finally push past her breakup. Despite almost ten years together, her ex-boyfriend had never come to this house. Early on, there'd been scheduling conflicts, and then later, excuses. Which was just as well. Lila carried enough ghosts from that relationship. She didn't need any of them waiting for her here.

"Watch the stair," Gabriel called out.

"What stair?" Henry asked, followed by the clatter of his fall onto the landing. "Why did it jump out at me?" He squealed as much as he talked.

Lila laughed, putting away the cleaning cloth. "It's the one after that gets you."

"What do you mean?" Henry dusted himself off and stood, looking a few blinks away from another pout.

Gabriel cleared the stairs. "The second step from the top is higher than the rest."

"And even when you're prepared for it, sometimes you still trip because your brain kinda expects the next one to be just as high. But it's regular height," Lila said.

"Short compared to the one before it," Gabriel added.

"I'm gonna tumble all the way down, aren't I?" Henry asked, his voice laced with overdramatic sadness.

"Yes," Lila said while Gabriel said, "It only gets you on the way up."

Henry blinked fast and glanced back and forth between them. "Well, which is it?"

Lila stared at Gabriel, willing him not to clarify. *Let me have this one thing,* she mentally pleaded.

Gabriel shrugged. "You won't know until you make a trip down."

"You've brought me to a deathtrap, Gabriel Cupik."

"No." Lila opened the screen door and stepped onto the porch. "The stairs are booby trapped for my safety."

Chapter Two

After Lila had gotten her things settled in her room, and Gabriel had finished Henry's tour of the house, they all met in the kitchen to figure out dinner. Gabriel took out the ancient takeout menu from his favorite barbecue place, The Notorious P.I.G. Henry squealed at the name, then selected enough food for ten people.

While Gabriel placed the order, Henry noticed the oversized *Beauty of the Beach* crown that lived on top of the old rarely used box TV. Gabriel's cousin Stephanie had won it when she'd been fourteen—one of the boy cousins had entered her as a joke. She'd left it at the house to remind them of her triumph.

"Oh my gosh, ohmygosh!" Henry hopped and clapped his hands. "Is touching allowed? Can I put it on?"

"Yeah, of course." Lila picked up the crown, untangling it from the TV antenna, and put it on Henry's head, making sure it was centered and secure in his thick, dark hair. "It coordinates nicely with your suitcase." She meant it as sarcasm, but Henry's shy giggle coaxed a smile from her.

"Food will be here soon," Gabriel announced. He beamed when he noticed Henry. "Congratulations! You're gay!"

Henry's face lit up. "Thank you!" He laid his hands over his heart and looked heavenward. "If I'd known I'd get such a joyful proclamation, I would've come out in high school."

"When did you come out?" Lila asked.

"Last Christmas," Henry said, eyes glassy.

Lila realized Henry's exuberance probably had a lot to do with the fact that no one here would think twice about who he dated, let alone make him feel bad about it. She cleared her throat. "You're a spectacular queen. Let's go drink on the deck."

Gabriel lifted a bottle of wine in each hand. "Hear! Hear!"

"Wait!" Henry threw his hands into the air. "We need more crowns!"

"That's the only one," Lila said.

"Hang on." Gabriel ducked into the foyer and returned with two beach pails, each a different shape at the bottom. He flipped one over and balanced it on his head, a tiny bit of sand dribbling out. "Few royals can make a castle with their crown."

Lila nodded and reached for the other one.

"No." Henry shook his head so violently that he almost lost *Beauty of the Beach*. "I have the finest beach crystals. You two in plastic will not do."

Gabriel looked at Lila. "Can you draw us some?"

"Oh! Yeah." Lila went to the small kitchen and rummaged through the drawers. "Is there any tape?"

Gabriel dug it out and used it to gesture. "Let's drink on the deck while you craft bespoke royal finery."

Lila opened a new bottle of wine and topped off everyone's glasses, admiring the crown she'd drawn for Gabriel on the pages of her sketchbook. She'd carefully folded and assembled them and even dug out her watercolor markers for extra flair.

Henry sipped his wine with his pinky out. "Now that I know about the Scandinavian blood on my mother's side, I'm changing my name. I need to honor my roots." He squeezed his eyes shut and squished his lips into a duck face.

Gabriel gave Lila a long look, his paper tiara crooked. He widened his eyes as if bracing himself, then directed his attention toward Henry. "What did you have in mind?"

"Well." Henry wiggled his shoulders. "Thor is a little too on the nose."

Lila choked on her wine. "Please tell me you're joking."

"What?" Henry asked, drawing out the word and pitching his voice higher at the end. "Thor's a perfectly good name."

Gabriel passed a napkin to Lila. "You're too swarthy for it. What else is on your list?"

Henry touched his crown and smiled. "Odin."

Lila turned to Gabriel and looked at him as if to say, *Where did you find this guy?*

Gabriel rubbed his forehead, which meant, *He attached himself to me. I'm innocent.* He took a deep drink of his wine, clearly ignoring the hopeful anticipation that danced across Henry's face.

"Well?" Henry pressed.

Lila gestured to Gabriel. "His house. He gets to answer first."

Gabriel gave Lila his revenge glare, then addressed Henry. "Erik is a Scandinavian name."

"Erik?" Henry cracked the *K*.

"Yeah, with a *K*. Well-known Scandi name."

Henry closed his eyes and scowled. "Don't try to cute it up. Erik is boring."

"Wait, if you change your first name to Odin, what will your last name be?" Lila asked.

"Theodorou. Duh."

Lila tilted her head. "I thought you wanted to honor your Scandinavian roots."

"I do."

"Isn't Theodorou Greek?" Gabriel asked.

"I'm not giving that up, darling. Look at this *gorg* complexion." Henry framed his tan face with his hands, fingers stretched wide.

"Hello!" someone called from the street. "Are you the three queens on the upper deck?"

"Oh!" Henry hopped off his chair and ran to the railing, then leaned over it dramatically. "Yes! And you are?"

"Helping your delivery driver."

Not recognizing the voice, Lila joined Henry at the railing. "Oh."

The man balancing a large box of food and two paper bags looked close to Lila and Gabriel's age. He wore beach basics: cotton shorts, a tee with his sunglasses tucked in the neck, and flip-flops. His slightly too long, slightly curly hair, his fresh tan, and his smile caught her eye. That smile probably held a thousand fascinating stories.

"I know, right?" Henry said in a stage whisper.

Before either of them could say more, Gabriel appeared on the driveway, greeting the man.

Henry spun and faced Lila, his back pressed against the railing and lower lip stuck between his teeth. "Do you think he's single? And gay? Bi? Bi-curious? Try anything?"

Lila sized up the guy, wondering the same things. He looked vaguely familiar, but she couldn't place him. Didn't matter, anyway. "This is Gaaaaaaaaaaaay-briel's house. He gets dibs."

"Uh!" Henry flapped his arms once and stomped to his chair before throwing himself in it with all the drama he could muster while holding his crown. "Isle of Palms? No. Isle of Gabriel. Not fair!"

Lila shook her head. "Did Gabriel call you and say 'Henry, I'm going to the beach for a week—join me,' or did you latch on to him in a public place, ask about his plans, and add yourself to the itinerary?"

Henry huffed.

"Well?" Lila circled the table, eyeing Henry the entire time, then took her seat, as regally as one with a paper tiara could. She raised her eyebrows and drummed her fingers. "Should I guess?"

Henry huffed again, arms folded tight against his chest. "The second one."

"Thought so." Lila patted Henry's shoulder. "Gabriel has dibs."

"What about you? Don't think I missed your comment in the car about having seniority."

"Gabriel and I have been friends for almost fifteen years. You've been in the picture fifteen minutes."

Henry narrowed his eyes. "All that means is you're old."

Lila shrugged. She might be ancient in Henry's eyes, but she was very much enjoying her thirty-second year.

"They're on the stairs." Henry ran his ring fingers over his eyebrows. "Can I flirt shamelessly, or do I have to compete with you?"

"Do your worst. I'm not looking for men."

"Ooh!" Henry brought his shoulders to his ears. "Women then?"

Lila sighed. "Sadly, no. My current status is: disappointed that I don't eat pussy. And so's my pussy."

Henry tipped his head back and laughed uproariously. "At least we have that in common. Though *I'm* not disappointed."

She didn't want to be amused by Henry, but Lila still cracked up.

"Cash is joining us for dinner," Gabriel announced as he and the man came out to the deck. "Cash, meet my bestie, Lila, and that's Henry."

Lila and Henry waved.

Gabriel took the box and set it in the middle of the table. "Cash's place is down the street. He's an Everett."

"Oh!" Lila grinned. "Margo's brother. How come we haven't met before?"

"I'm usually here at Thanksgiving." Cash set a bag next to the box. "And the few times we've overlapped, Oliver kept me away." Cash scratched his head in a way that should've been lame, but given the history of the families in this area—and his smile—it was kind of cute.

"Why is your brother always such a pain in the ass?" Lila asked Gabriel. Maybe if she'd met someone who looked like Cash a few years ago, she would've made her ex an ex much sooner and saved herself a ton of bullshit.

"I bet he was trying to help Mom get us together when she was in denial about being a gay-boy mom."

Lila rolled her eyes. "Oliver's not that altruistic."

"True. It's probably that he never got over the fact that you're *my* friend, not *our* friend." Gabriel directed Cash to an empty chair between him and Lila.

"Lame." Lila stood and unpacked the box, moving containers around to make room for everything.

"Cash." Henry batted his eyelashes as he spoke. "Is that name Scandinavian?"

Cash opened the delivery bag on the table. "Nope. Not sure where it's from, but it's been in my family forever, and I'm pretty sure none of my people could handle a Scandinavian winter."

"Mm, don't knock it 'til you try it, sir."

Gabriel leaned across the table, blocking Henry's view of Cash, and handed a jug of sweet tea to Lila. He looked at her as if to say, *I wish we could shut him up.*

Lila shrugged, which meant, *I tried while you were gone.*

"What happened to the original driver?" Lila handed out paper plates and packets of cutlery.

"I think he was overwhelmed," Cash said. "He's a college kid who took the job for the summer and doesn't know the IOP. He called for directions and was told to look for queens on a deck and had no idea what that meant. I was there for my order. I volunteered to help."

Henry waved his arm in the dramatic way that Lila realized was simply how he did things. "Now, what will I do with my tip?"

Lila made herself a pulled pork sandwich. "You keep it in your pants, Odor."

"Ah!" Henry gasped.

Gabriel laughed into his mac and cheese.

"I don't get it." Cash sounded casual and unassuming but looked suspicious as he opened a container with a huge rack of ribs.

"Lila besmirched my name!"

Cash squinted. "I thought your name was Henry."

Henry harrumphed.

"Henry's considering changing his name to something Nordic. I pointed out the dangers of going with Odin." Lila caught Gabriel's gaze. "Personally, my vote is for Björn."

Cash snickered. "Like the baby carrier. Nice."

Lila raised her glass to Cash. He winked and raised his glass in return, which earned him a flirty smile.

"Lila!" Henry whisper-yelled. He pointed his head toward Gabriel, his eyes wide.

Not acknowledging Henry's reminder, Lila said, "Gabriel has a suggestion?"

Gabriel tasted his Brunswick stew and thought for a moment. "Mads."

Lila pointed at Gabriel. "Yes! Yes. Mads fucks."

"What?" Henry asked.

"That movie. He's a retired hitman or something," Lila said.

"*Polar*," Gabriel supplied.

"Yes. *Polar*. He's a hitman, or used to be a hitman, I don't know. But people are spying on him and he's an older guy, maybe fifties, and one night while they're watching him, he takes a woman home, and he really shows you how it's done."

"Athletic fucking at its finest," Gabriel said.

Lila closed her eyes, remembering the scene. "Yes." She drew it out in a low voice.

"That's the first time I've been truly jealous of an actor." Cash's words pulled Lila out of her reverie.

She gave him a once-over. "You look athletic."

"Lila!" Henry shouted.

"What? He does!" Lila threw up her hands to show her innocence. Well. Her lack of intent.

"Didn't you row crew in college, Cash?" Gabriel asked.

Lila grinned at her friend as if to say, *This is why we're besties.*

He mirrored it, meaning, *It really is.*

"Yeah." Cash cleared his throat. "But I have a name suggestion."

"Hit me." Henry perched on his seat, hands gripping his knees.

"Seriously," Gabriel said. "Hit him. Hard."

Lila didn't bother to hide her laugh. As serious as Gabriel sounded, he'd never let harm come to Henry, or any of them.

Cash peeled a rib off the rack, another adorable grin gracing his face. "Spock."

Henry, Lila, and Gabriel exchanged glances, deathly silent.

Cash cleared his throat again. "Sorry. It means wheel maker. The name is tied to *spoke*. Never mind. It was dumb." He took a giant bite out of his rib.

"Cute *and* a nerd." Henry wiggled his fingers. "In several ways!"

Lila caught Cash trying to hide a blush. She pushed her plate away and picked up her sketch pad.

"He needs a crown," Gabriel said.

"On it."

Chapter Three

For at least the millionth time since they'd met, Lila acknowledged Gabriel had been right. This room—and its private entrance—was perfect for her. She could leave the house when she woke and avoid Henry. Did he squeal first thing in the morning? She didn't want to know.

She'd walked half a mile when an unruly head of slightly too-long hair caught her eye. As she got closer, she realized Cash had a sketchbook in his lap, and she wasn't sure if she should be excited or wary. Obviously, Cash knew she could draw. It was a nice coincidence that he could too. But was he one of those guys who had an attitude—any kind of attitude—about art? The island was big enough that if he was, she could spend the next fifteen years staying out of his path. It hadn't been difficult so far.

"Most people face the ocean when they sit out here." Lila plopped down next to him, not waiting for an invitation. Better to find out fast if she needed to avoid him.

"You've seen one ocean, you've seen them all," Cash said in a wry tone.

Lila gasped.

"But these bracketed eaves will eventually get remodeled away. I need to capture them."

Lila adjusted her sun hat and leaned against him to peer at his work. "This is lovely." He'd captured the house in pencil, using both sharp and soft lines to highlight the details. She ran her finger along the edge of the pad, desperately wanting to touch the drawing to feel how real it was but also respecting his effort and staying far enough away to avoid smudging.

"Thanks." Cash gestured toward the structure. "Documenting the changes to the properties on the shore has sort of become a hobby."

"Do you sell them?" The question was borderline offensive. Hobbies weren't meant to be profitable, but it was a knee-jerk response for her after a lifetime spent convincing her parents that art was a viable career.

"Nah." Cash looked her in the eye. "Are you telling me you never draw for the hell of it?"

Lila pulled the wide brim of her hat over her eyes, then let it snap back up. "Guilty. But not usually this early."

Cash grunted and added to his drawing. "It's a holiday week. If I try this later, there'll be too many distractions. Little kids asking, 'Whatcha doin' mister?' and wondering if I can draw them a picture."

"And naturally, you do," Lila said.

Cash handed her another sketchbook. "Yep. The parents wouldn't let the kids take these."

Lila flipped through the drawings, laughing at some, awing at others. He'd turned most of the kids into adorable fish, mermaids, or shells. He had even drawn a kraken. "Afraid you were doing the art equivalent of busking?"

"More likely I needed a shave and they thought I was homeless."

Lila scoffed. "Meanwhile, you're living in a house worth millions."

"Fringe benefit of coming from a long line of beach people." He scratched his pencil along the page, adding grass around the house. "The property you inherit is worth far more than you are."

The flat tone of Cash's voice had Lila shifting her position to face him. "That's bullshit. What's prompting that?" He'd been so calm and laid-back last night. Had even worn his paper crown home and had given off "this is where I'm meant to be" vibes. Now she noticed the lines between his eyes and his toes curled tight against his flip-flops.

"I'm between jobs. Took a risk." He dropped his sketchbook in the sand and drew his knees to his chest. "Not sure it's panning out."

"I know we just met, but I need more detail than that."

"I'm an architect."

"That explains the passion to capture the eaves."

"Come on." He nudged her shoulder with his own. "They're a knockout. I know you see it."

Feeling sheepish, Lila shrugged. "Sometimes it's hard for me to appreciate the details when there's all this… bigness to get around." She gestured toward the row of oceanfront homes, most of which were three stories tall and wide enough to fit the profile of two houses. Why did it frustrate her so much? She had all the advantages of this place and none of the responsibility. Still, every time a house was razed and replaced with a beach mansion, Lila mourned it as though she'd been born and bred on the island.

"I get it," Cash said. "I really do. About a year after I graduated, I went back to school to get my master's in preservation architecture."

"To save the details."

"Exactly." Cash picked up the book he'd tossed aside and flipped back a few pages. "So many small elements with function and beauty. And we replace them with—" He gestured at the air.

Lila nodded. "Blech. They replace craftsmanship with boring, blah shit that may be functionally successful but looks uninspired."

"Yes." He patted her leg, then quickly removed his hand. "So, I studied and earned the extra degree and applied to every architectural firm in Savannah, Bluffton, Jacksonville, St. Augustine…Nothing."

"Not even an interview?"

"One of my professors got me one at a small Savannah firm. They thought I'd be a good match. As a recent grad, I knew all the latest techniques. I still do. Especially the new preservation techniques. I watched their interest fade as I spoke. It was demoralizing."

"What did your prof say?"

"Would it be terrible to endure it for a year or two until they had a preservation project?"

"And?"

"It wasn't hard the first year. I survived the second without too much angst." Cash set his sketchbook down again. "But they were shifting the business. Big on remodeling. Not so much on preservation. I thought I could carve out a niche by showing customers the impact of saving original elements in their remodels."

"Seems reasonable." It was similar to what Lila had done as a young designer. Fresh out of college, she'd taken a job with an ad agency and done alternate versions of her assignments to show her skill and vision. It hadn't helped her there, but a few years later, when one of the partners left for a creative boutique, they'd invited her to join them.

"They closed their preservation services."

"I'm sorry."

He shrugged. "It's okay."

"Is it though?" If Lila had to face that level of disappointment, she wouldn't be able to call it okay.

"I got severance. Now I'm shooting my shot here."

"And you have a place to stay. You don't have to commute to Savannah or get a hotel."

"I can't commute to Savannah anymore. My roommate's getting married, and they bought a place. The lease was almost up. It felt like the right time to start fresh."

"Do they need wedding invitations? I know someone." She pointed to herself.

Cash laughed. "I'll ask."

"Thanks." Lila looked him over again; he didn't seem any more relaxed after telling her his career woes. "What are you doing for money?" Another bold question, but with her parents' persistent concerns, Lila tended to have several backup plans and streams of income. Her mind already spun with possibilities for him.

Cash raised his eyebrows. "Aside from making errant deliveries for the barbecue place?"

Lila smiled. "Yeah."

"I tend bar here and there, take an occasional catering gig. Not having to pay rent helps."

"Why aren't you selling your drawings?"

"Why would I?"

Those three words unlocked two levels of trauma for Lila—her parents fretting about starving artists, and her ex's obsession with career growth. Well, *his* career growth. She'd found out too late that hers hadn't mattered to him. She stretched her arms out in front of her and cracked her knuckles. Time to bring Cash to the dark side. "Your work is great. You could make decent money even when there isn't a bar gig. You can sell them online and skip sweaty bills on the beach or distracted parents venmoing the wrong person."

Cash squinted at her. The "hmm" he gave her dripped in skepticism.

"Here." Lila took out her phone and navigated to her Etsy store. "I design invitations, announcements, personal stationery, that type of thing. I'm at a firm, but I list designs they won't like, or that I create on my own time. Most sell as digital files. I've been doing this long enough that I have a steady side income. Spring and fall are my best seasons—weddings and holiday cards."

Cash complimented Lila's designs as she scrolled through her shop and explained her offerings. Then he flipped through the sketchbook with the houses in it. "I'd have to color them."

"Maybe. Lots of people like black and white, though." She put her hand on a page with a drawing of The Battery. "This one." She took a few photos with her phone, zooming in on ornate details. "I'll list this in my store. If it sells, you have a new option. If it doesn't, who cares?"

Chapter Four

"What do you mean, I'm not a *buyer*?" Henry squealed the question in the middle of the King Street antique store, causing a clerk to scowl at them.

Lila cringed, wanting to disappear.

"Shh," Gabriel admonished.

"Why won't anyone answer my questions?" Henry fell into his default pout pose.

"Charleston is one of my most favorite places," Lila said, her voice low. "But there is a *vibe*." She raked her gaze over Henry and his jean shorts. "You don't have it."

"A vibe?" Henry turned to Gabriel, looking aghast. "A *vibe*?"

Gabriel grabbed Henry's shoulders. "We love you—"

"Do we though?" Lila interrupted. She was willing to tolerate Henry, even accepted that he could be amusing. Love was a bridge too far.

Gabriel cleared his throat. "We accept you as you are. But the people who spend money in this store don't wear cutoff jeans and threadbare T-shirts."

Henry slammed his hand to his chest. "These are beach clothes. You told me. We were going. To! The beach!"

Gabriel cracked his neck and looked at Lila, lips pressed into a thin line, which meant, *I told him we were coming into town.*

Lila scratched behind her ear, which meant, *He can't hear you over all his squealing.*

Gabriel nodded. "Henry."

"Odin!" Henry put his hands on his hips.

Lila rolled her eyes. "Odor. When you're in the posh shops, you have to look like a buyer. You want to wear jorts? Fine. But you need a polo shirt and a belt. Flip-flops instead of slides. Boat shoes might be better."

"He's too young and not from here for boat shoes," Gabriel murmured.

Henry threw back his shoulders and lifted his chin. "I don't know what's more insulting." He gestured toward Gabriel. "You, or"—he turned a withering glance toward Lila—"the disrespect."

Lila grinned. "*Now* you're vibing."

Henry flapped his arms. "But what does that mean?"

Movement in front of the store window caught Lila's attention. She focused in and smiled. "I love that they still do that."

"Do what?" Henry followed Lila's gaze and sucked in a breath when he saw a group of Citadel cadets jogging past in their PT gear. "Ohhhh." He moved toward the door, gaze firmly out the window. "Excuse me!"

Lila and Gabriel laughed as Henry marched outside and called to the students.

"If we buy him a polo, he'll have the vibe down," Gabriel said.

"Do we have to?"

Gabriel shook his head. "He's not a buyer, anyway."

Henry's head bobbed along the storefront, then he turned and followed the joggers' path.

"We should probably keep an eye on him," Gabriel said.

Lila nodded and followed him out. "At a healthy distance, though."

"Naturally. We need private time so you can tell me about your beach and bang."

Lila stopped in her tracks, jaw dropped. "My what?"

Gabriel snickered. "You've been going to the beach first thing every morning. When you get back, you're too relaxed for the ocean to have been the only thing working on you."

Lila gasped. "Gabriel!"

"Don't tell Henry. He's hoping Cash is at least bi."

Lila shook her head and resumed her walk down the street. "I don't know if he's bi and there's no banging on the beach." Lila gave her best friend an annoyed glance.

"Maybe you meet on the beach, then go to his place."

"Gaaaaaaaaaaaay-briel." Lila leveled a dead-eyed stare at him. "No."

"I'm trying to encourage you! Get yours!"

Lila smiled in spite of herself. "The simple fact that he didn't repeat some overblown story he'd heard about me from a friend of a friend who plays poker or basketball or jogs the same paths as my ex is a win."

"No," Gabriel said. "It's a start."

A squeal, followed by a shouted command, and then another squeal of "Come back, I won't bite! Yet!" had Lila and Gabriel exchanging another glance.

"We gotta stop him." Gabriel sighed.

"Yeah."

Chapter Five

Lila sat in the backseat, tapping her foot relentlessly. They were stuck in traffic at Shem Creek, waiting at the light for the third cycle, trying to get to Shrimp Boat Lane. Even though the car was air-conditioned, it was hot and humid outside. Added to a day in Charleston with Henry, and him now singing at a very high volume, she was done.

Did she like the song that was playing? Not really. Did it deserve Henry purposely rewriting the lyrics to mostly be what he thought was silly but was actually annoying? No. Did she fantasize about knocking him out and tossing him into the creek? Maybe.

Lila pushed out a breath and caught Gabriel's gaze in the rearview mirror. "Poe's is near the water too."

"It's on a different island," Gabriel said.

Lila tilted her head back, which meant, *So what, we'd be moving.* "It's ten minutes away."

"Not in this traffic." Gabriel raised his eyebrows, which meant, *You're not helping.*

Lila glared at him. Her complaint wasn't with the restaurant but with Henry's inability to stop making noise. She needed a win. Since she couldn't muzzle Henry, this was her battle. "We have to go to Vickery's every time we're here?"

Gabriel rolled his shoulders. He was ready for a fight too. "Yes."

If Lila could turn her eyes into lasers, she would.

Henry seemed oblivious to them and intoned, "Gay men. Gaaaaay men," along with the song.

Lila pressed her fingers against her temples. She was at capacity with Henry's bullshit. "Come on, Odor. It's okay not to sing."

Henry glared at her over his shoulder and yell-sang, "Take me to drag! Worship like a straight at the hem of my gown!"

Done with Henry, Lila opened the door. "I'll go put us on the list." She climbed out of the car, Henry's squeals fading as she shut the door.

By the time she made it to the host stand at Vickery's, she was calmer, but nowhere close to calm.

"It's at least an hour wait," the host explained. "Unless you want to sit at the outdoor bar."

Lila looked down at herself, sweat glistening on her skin, a small river trickling between her breasts, and sighed. "Sure."

The host entered the phone number Lila gave. "All set."

"Hang on." Lila stole another moment in the air-conditioning. "Can I get a drink without a table?"

"Downstairs."

Lila wove throughout the crowd and made her way to the bar on the ground level. She asked for whatever they had with the best ice-to-alcohol ratio, then texted Gabriel with her location and the wait time for their table—still over twenty minutes.

"I promise I'm not stalking you." Cash stopped next to Lila, a beer can in his hand. "I stopped for gas."

Both pleasantly surprised and unhappy with the timing of Cash's appearance, Lila tried to smile, but she knew whatever expression her face made, it wasn't happy. "I'm not sure there's enough ethanol in that to power an engine."

"What's wrong?"

Lila sipped her icy drink as she tried to fix her face. She liked Cash, and if this was any other vacation, she'd be all in for a fling. But his family knew Gabriel's, and after sitting through too many first dates where the guy rehashed bullshit he'd heard about her, she couldn't do it. She was tired of hearing about herself. Tired of the humidity. And real fucking tired of playing as nice as she possibly could with Henry.

"Cash!" Henry's squeal proceeded him. "Do you know what this woman did?"

Cash looked between Lila and Henry, then leaned toward Lila. "Whatever he says, you're gonna tell me what really happened later, right?"

"It may be obscenity-laden."

"Counting on it." Cash dropped an arm along the railing behind her, not touching her, but she liked it. It felt like a shield. "What did she do, Henry?"

"Odin." He tapped his chest and winked before taking a deep breath. "She got out of the car!"

Gabriel joined their group with a daiquiri in each hand, one with a sizeable spray of fruit hanging off the rim. He gave that one to Henry. "People get out of cars."

"In the middle of the road?" Henry yelled, causing other patrons to look.

"He's so not a buyer," Lila muttered. "I *told* you. I put us on the list. Less time to wait."

"Smart move," Cash said. "It's packed out here during holiday weeks. I came on a boat, and getting to the dock was a challenge."

"You have a boat?" Henry's eyes grew and his pitch rose as he spoke. He practically panted while waiting for an answer.

"It's the family boat. It stays with the house."

"I've never been on a boat before." Henry bit the end of his straw in a coquettish way and batted his eyelashes.

Lila fisted her free hand, but it wasn't enough to curb her temper. "Stop inviting yourself places, Odor. You wanna ride a boat? There are like, seven tour companies a sneeze from this spot."

Henry threw back his shoulders and narrowed his gaze at Lila. "Someone's hangry."

Lila had never seen someone sip a big fruity drink with so much sass. She finished off her drink and set the cup onto the railing with a little too much force. "There are not enough crab cakes in the world to calm me down right now."

As Henry squealed another come-back, Gabriel and Cash both intervened. Gabriel pushed Henry toward the railing, pointing to something on the horizon, as Cash pulled Lila close, steering her through the bar.

"Let's go to my boat."

Once they were through the crowd, Cash took a step back, giving Lila space. The airflow was nice, but she missed the sense of security she'd had when he'd been in her space.

"This is me." He nodded toward an older pilot boat.

Lila raised her eyebrows at the ornate cursive along the side. "*Swim Shady*?"

Cash shrugged. "My mom was trying to be cool. Everyone hates it, but we can't change it."

"Mm. It's bad luck to rename a vessel."

Cash stepped onto the stern and held out his hand. "Have you been on a boat before?"

Lila finally laughed. "Not only have I been on boats, I even know how to swim."

"Fancy lady!" Cash flashed a bright grin. "Come on."

He ushered her onto the craft and gave her a quick tour, along with a bottle of ice-cold water.

"Are yous leaving?" a guy on a pontoon boat called out. His sunburn was so severe it stung Lila.

She glanced at Cash and nodded.

Cash waved to the guy. "Yeah! One minute."

As Cash climbed onto the pier and moved to the bow of the boat, Lila set aside her water and followed. "Toss me the rope."

He did and then went to the stern, where he untied that rope and stepped onto the rear deck.

Lila secured the rope around the bow cleat and then relieved Cash at the stern. "I got it. You get out of this slip."

"Normally, I'd make a joke about getting out of slips, but I suspect Henry's ruined that."

"You are correct!" Lila finished with the rope and joined him at the wheel. "But I usually like a good slip joke. Ropes too. You good with knots?"

Cash laughed. "I'm good with knots and nauts."

Lila winced. "You were hot until that so-called joke."

"Sometimes, *Swim Shady* has a stronger influence than I realize." Cash glanced at her as he steered the boat away from the dock. "Should we stay nearby so I can drop you off when the table's ready?"

"Doesn't matter when it's ready. I won't be."

"Henry's that bad?"

Lila sighed. She'd promised Cash an explanation. As much as she wanted to pretend the whole day with Henry hadn't happened, it might help to talk about it. Even if it made her feel shrewish. Whatever. He'd asked.

"Henry is fun in small doses," Lila said. "Preferably when there isn't an audience."

"How did you guys meet him?"

"Gabriel did a guest lecture at Henry's college in Greensboro. He's a special breed of geek who's on the cutting edge of cyber security. Henry was at the lecture and leeched onto Gabriel."

"I can see that," Cash said.

Lila retrieved her water bottle and rolled it along the back of her neck. "At first, I thought they were dating. Henry's ten years younger than us. It shouldn't be an issue, but it just felt" —Lila pushed her hair off her face as the breeze picked up— "seedy. It felt seedy. Henry hasn't been out long. It felt like if they were together, they'd be taking advantage of each other."

"Gabe doesn't take advantage of people."

Pride surged through Lila. Gabriel most certainly did *not* take advantage of people, and it warmed her to know that Cash held him in high regard. As he should.

"Gabriel is as good as they come. He knew Henry needed connection and community. He's become kind of a mentor, and Henry seems to be doing really well." Lila squeezed her palms against her temples for a moment.

"But also, if he could model more of Gabriel's understated style, I wouldn't be mad about it."

Cash laughed. "Don't feel bad about being overwhelmed with Henry."

"Maybe I'm jealous."

"Is Henry taking up too much of Gabe's time and attention?"

Lila rolled her eyes. "Gabriel and I can exist without being the center of each other's lives. Sometimes it's damn inconvenient, but we can do it." Lila paced the length of the ship, then stopped next to Cash. "I need recharge time. Henry just goes. We reached a point today where I wasn't capable of going anymore."

"So you got out of the car."

"Yeah. I feel like an asshole."

"You're not an asshole. You've sold six of my drawings and given me a new lease on my career." He smiled and tipped his head toward her. "And you drew us each crowns because Henry wanted it. And Gabe loves you. Honestly, that's the best endorsement a person can have."

Lila sniffled. "Gabriel is pretty great. I won the lottery with him."

"Why do you call him Gabriel?" Cash asked.

"It's what he prefers."

Cash tilted his head. "Really?"

"Yeah. Though these days he favors Gaaaaaaaaaaaay-briel."

Cash laughed, then patted the captain's chair. "Take a seat. I'll show you how to drive. And when you're good and distracted, you can tell me all the wild shit Henry did today."

Lila laughed and hopped onto the seat.

Cash got close, explaining the controls, and showed her where the 'no wake' zone ended. Given how sticky hot it was, his proximity should've bothered her. Instead, it was a balm. He smelled like salt and charcoal and, somehow, he knew how and where to touch her, or hint at a touch. He brought her out of her head and got her focused on the moment rather than the ick that plagued her. Eventually, he leaned against the dash. "Now, tell me Henry's wild tales."

Lila stretched her neck, enjoying the open air and the peace she found on *Swim Shady*, even with holiday partiers floating around them. "We were in an antique store today, a pricey one, and Henry had a meltdown because the staff ignored him." Lila focused her gaze into the distance, working hard to not roll her eyes. She wanted to so badly, but even she had grown tired of it. "Which was fair. He wasn't there to shop. Gabriel and I struggled to calm him down until some Citadel cadets jogged by."

"Uh-oh."

"Henry took off when he saw them. Gabriel and I followed at a leisurely pace, which was a mistake."

"Were police involved?"

Lila banged her hands against the wheel. "Yes!"

"Seriously?"

"No one got arrested, but I'm not sure what would've happened if Gabriel and I hadn't been nearby. The cop lectured Henry about how 'Those young men don't want *your* attention.'"

"Oh shit." Cash grimaced.

"I know!" As annoying and inappropriate as Henry had been, Lila had been truly angry with the cop. She'd taken that moment to use her "white woman" power to intervene. Then Gabriel had come in for the kill, letting the cop think he and Lila were a couple, until he gave a coy smile and slid his hand into Henry's back pocket and steered him away. It'd been glorious. "Gabriel and I set him straight, so to speak, and then we redirected Henry toward the car. Only to find another pack of cadets a few blocks away."

"But it's so hot!" Cash pushed his hair back. "How can they run on the hot pavement? They must've been dying out there."

"Right?" Lila sipped from her water bottle before pressing it against her cheek.

"Did Henry get in trouble again?"

"No, but they asked him to a party tomorrow. Totally made his day. Now we have to go." As *Swim Shady* cleared a group of boats, Lila turned into a quieter area. "Wanna drop anchor? I won't worry about my violent hand gestures so much." Really, she wanted to be able to make eye contact while they talked.

Cash chuckled. "Sure." He took over and got them anchored.

"A public meltdown." Cash ducked into the cabin and returned with more cold water. "A run-in with the police, party invitations possibly from people not old enough to drink—that would exhaust anyone."

"Honey, that's just the beginning."

Cash sat on a bench along the bow. "I'm waiting."

Lila drank in the sight of him—relaxed, settled into his tan, the setting sun shining off his hair. If she hadn't been thoroughly aggravated with men, this one would be fun. She sat next to him and drank deep from her water. Her phone buzzed. "One sec."

Gabriel: Table's ready. Unless you're all set with a boat and bang.

Lila immediately glanced at Cash, relieved that he wasn't reading over her shoulder.

Lila: When did you become such a perv? Eat without me. I'll meet you at the house.
Gabriel: That wasn't a no to boat and bang.
Lila: PERV

It definitely wasn't a no. But it also wasn't part of her plan. She enjoyed the possibility, though. She wanted a relaxing break from her life this week. Henry made that impossible. Cash, on the other hand...

Lila cleared her throat. "Where did we leave off?"

"Citadel party."

"Right." Lila sat up straighter. "That pumped new life into little Odor and he did. Not. Stop. Talking. From the time we pulled him away from the cadets until Gabriel turned on music in the car. Then he started singing."

"He truly never stops."

"Nope. He was loud and off-key and thought he was funny but wasn't. And then we got stuck in traffic, and he was yelling more than singing, and I couldn't anymore."

Cash squeezed her shoulder. "I get it. You wanted to hang out and get inspired and you wound up wondering if you'd have to bail out Henry."

Lila leaned against him. "Thank you."

Cash wrapped an arm around her, giving her a half hug. It was probably wishful thinking, but did he kiss her head? Why wish for that, anyway? She had her own room, but she didn't really have privacy on this vacation. Not with Henry around. He'd broadcast everything. Rent a billboard if he could. No, better to enjoy Cash's company and thank him for the quiet interludes he gave her.

She pulled back with a new resolve. "I have a proposition for you."

"Really." He stretched out the word, and his tongue darted over his lip so fast she almost missed it.

Lila raised an eyebrow. Cash had been friendly and flirtatious, but not like this. This was interesting. "It's not a sex thing." Unfortunately.

Cash resumed his king-of-laid-back posture. "Whatever it is, I'll probably do it. You said you'd try to sell one drawing and we're over six. I trust you."

Lila beamed. "Good, because it's about the drawings."

"I picked up some colors today. I can branch out."

"Cool. I've got another branch for you." Lila flipped her hair over her shoulder. "Prints."

Cash wrinkled his forehead. "Prints?"

"Yeah. I got an inquiry from someone asking if there were prints, because they liked a sold-out design."

"How did they know it was sold out? Don't they come down when they sell?"

"Marketing, baby." Lila shimmied her shoulders. "You wanna go out tomorrow and find a print shop with nice paper stock and make copies of your work?"

A slow smile spread across his face. "That is the sexiest proposition I've had in a while."

Lila laughed, another layer of aggravation melting away. Skipping dinner had definitely been the right decision.

"Now *I* have a proposition for you."

"Bring it." Lila rubbed her hands together.

Cash moved to face her. "Help me set up my own Etsy store?"

"Yes!" Lila made a tiny squeal, then slapped her hand across her mouth.

Cash laughed, tugged her hand away, and held it. "I won't tell Odor he's influencing you."

"Thank you." Lila relaxed and leaned into his chest. "I hope you include a few of your beach-monster pictures."

"You mean of the kids?" Cash wrapped his arms around her.

"Yeah."

"Sure, but I also have nature drawings. Wanna see?"

"Duh!"

Cash nudged her before he stood and went into the small cabin. He returned with an oversized sketchbook. He opened it and handed it to Lila, a marsh drawing front and center.

"This is beautiful. Did you do this today?"

"Yeah. After the first few drawings sold, I figured it wouldn't hurt to have a couple that weren't buildings." He turned to the next page.

"Oh, we definitely have to make copies of this dolphin."

"I'm gonna add color first." Cash fidgeted and then collected the empty water bottles. "Want another?"

"Sure." Lila didn't look up from the sketchbook. She turned page after page, impressed and inspired by his work. When she reached blank pages, she flipped back to the beginning. "Oh." She took a closer look at a nude. "Hmm."

Cash returned and held out a water bottle to her. "Ah." His tan couldn't hide the blush that stained his cheeks. "You weren't supposed to see that."

"So this is me." Surprised, flattered, intrigued. She wasn't sure how to respond; she just didn't want to make it awkward.

"Sort of." Cash scratched his forehead. "I drew it when we were all on the beach yesterday."

"I had a swimsuit on. With a rash guard."

Cash took the book and closed it. "I know. I guess it was…wishful thinking."

Huh. With Henry's constant pondering over whether Cash was interested in men, it hadn't occurred to her that Cash had been thinking of *her.* Naked. Had Gabriel been onto something with his 'beach and bang' encouragement?

"Well, one thing's for sure."

"I need to take you to a crowded place so you're not stuck on a boat in the middle of the water with a creeper?"

Lila shook her head. "If you're gonna sell that, you definitely need your own store."

Chapter Six

"Let me out here." Lila grabbed the car door handle and pointed to a driveway a few down from Gabriel's house.

Cash slowed but didn't stop. "No, it's pitch black."

"It's not far. If the guys see you pull into the driveway, it'll be a whole thing."

He stopped and looked at her, his expression serious. "Gabriel'll be glad I made sure you got back safely. I can handle Henry."

Lila sighed. Gabriel was constantly on her case about her personal safety, especially at night. "Then park and walk me. *You* can handle Henry. I don't want to."

"Deal." Cash parked the car and met Lila at the hood. "Text Gabriel to distract Henry."

"I can get in without them knowing."

Cash lifted his eyebrows. "Henry seems pretty nosy."

"Oh, he is. But look." She led him to the near side of the house with the secret stairs and showed him the opening in the plants.

"How long has this been here?"

"Gabriel said they added the second floor before Hurricane Hugo. So thirty, forty years?"

"This is amazing." Cash shook the banister and peered up the curve of the stairs. "Metal, old, silent. Incredible."

"And very convenient." Lila took half a step toward Cash. After his drawing and admission, coupled with her own thoughts, maybe she'd consider sneaking a man up after all.

His hand dropped from the railing onto her hip, and he squeezed, eyes sparkling. "I'll text you the appointment time for that specialty printer."

"Don't color anything that's been sold."

Cash rolled his eyes and leaned over her. "I know, boss."

"I like that." Lila stood on tip-toes, wrapped her arms around his neck, and kissed him.

He kissed back like he was memorizing her, his hands sliding to the middle of her back and pulling her closer. "What was that for?"

"I wanted to." Her phone buzzed. "Don't move." She kissed Cash again, then read her message.

Gabriel: Balcony & bang?

Lila: Cockblock

She didn't want to let Cash go without another kiss, so she gave him one. This time, she pressed their hips together and hummed at what she felt. Balcony and bang had potential. Another *buzz*. "We've been found out," she whispered.

Cash sighed. "I should go."

Covering her whimper as they separated, Lila said, "And work on my drawing. My nipples do *not* look like that."

Cash looked at her chest, blushed, and closed his eyes. "That was mean."

Lila kissed him one more time. "Maybe a little."

Chapter Seven

Lila: Wanna go to the beach with me?
Gabriel: No Henry?
Lila: Nope
Gabriel: On my way

"When did you start storing champagne in your room?" Gabriel asked as he topped off his drink.

Lila snickered. "I got it at the marina store yesterday."

"Your brilliant mind prevails again. Mimosas and Cheerios for breakfast. Amazing."

"Right? Sounds weird, but it works. I think the orange juice brings it all together."

Gabriel clinked his cup against hers. "Thanks for skipping your beach and bang for me. I needed this."

"There has been no beach and bang. Or boat or balcony bangs."

"Why the fuck not? It's clear he likes you." Gabriel kicked sand at her feet.

"No shacking up at the beach." Lila kicked sand back. "Remember?"

Gabriel took the small bottle of champagne and moved it where Lila couldn't reach. "You've lost your mimosa privileges."

"Says the man who's also not getting laid this week."

"Yeah, but I got some recently. You don't want to forget your moves."

"I was with my ex so long I need new ones. There are probably tons of things I'm ignorant to now."

"I'll get you a subscription to Pornhub."

Lila propped her head against his shoulder. "That's love."

"Seriously, though. Why no banging?"

Lila sat up and took a handful of Cheerios. "I don't know. Maybe the family connection. Plus, all the shit I've heard about myself since the breakup. This place is our refuge. I don't want your mom being all 'Lila, please abstain this weekend' or whatever."

"How would my mom find out?"

"Oliver."

Gabriel put the champagne bottle back between them. "I forgot about that messy bitch."

Lila laughed. "I love it so much when you call him a bitch."

"Forget Oliver. You and Cash are into each other. If you want some adult vacay fun, go for it. If it becomes news, I'll block it. Or spin it. Call out Oliver's jealousy." Gabriel tossed a Cheerio and caught it in his mouth. "Yeah, I'd enjoy that."

"Good morning, sun-burn buddies," Cash called from behind them.

"I am not burning!" Lila said.

"SPF 700, my friend," Gabriel added.

"Yeah, but you're not wearing your floppy hat." Cash nodded at Lila. "And there's no beach umbrella."

Gabriel held up the champagne bottle. "We carried more important things."

"Uh-oh, do I have to haul you two home?"

Lila stood and dusted off sand. "Nah, it was just that one little bottle. We're good."

"What are you celebrating?" Cash asked.

Gabriel smiled. "Each other."

Lila nodded. After a moment, she said, "You ready to build that storefront?"

"If you are."

Lila glanced at Gabriel. "What can I take back?"

Gabriel shook his head. "I got it. Go make money."

It should have only taken an hour to get Cash's digital store set up, and maybe technically it had, but Lila lost track of time while they worked. Cash had given her a guided tour through his creative brain, telling her what had prompted each of his drawings, what he'd been trying to capture, which details on the buildings stood out to him and why.

The alarm on his phone startled her out of a daydream about him working on a restoration project. The care he'd use. That *trill* broke the spell.

"Time to go," he said.

Lila shook her head to reset her focus. "Oh, yeah, of course. I'll see you later."

"Later?" Cash scrunched his face. "I thought you were coming with me to the printer."

Embarrassed at being caught off her game, Lila shrugged. "You know what you need."

He grabbed her hand and pulled her close, then guided her to the door. "I need your opinion while I make these decisions."

"Oh." She'd been ready, even hoping for a hug, maybe a quick kiss. Being directed to his car threw her even further off.

"When you mentioned this yesterday, I thought you meant we'd go together." Cash stopped and fidgeted. "Was I wrong? Do you have to be someplace?"

Lila shook her head again, this time to kick her brain into gear. "I'm on vacation. I can be anywhere I want."

"Do you want to come?" He blinked at Lila a few times.

Of course she wanted to come. What kind of question was that?

He pointed with his thumb over his shoulder.

"Yes." She looked around the room, desperately trying to reset herself. "Do you have everything you need?"

Cash wrapped an arm around her shoulder. "Yeah."

Chapter Eight

"That is the coolest thing I've ever spent money on." Cash held up a print copy of one of his drawings. "And it wasn't even much money."

"Where are you gonna hang it?" Lila asked.

Cash looked around. "I guess the refrigerator for now."

He laid the drawing across the kitchen table and stood back, looking proud. "I'll build a frame for it. Hang it properly when I'm in my own place."

Lila remembered her high the first time she'd seen her work professionally produced. It had been a surreal moment, and she was oddly emotional watching Cash have a similar experience. When her phone pinged in her bag, she dug it out and checked the notification. "You made another sale, sir."

He turned toward her, looking like he was about to speak, but he pulled her into a tight hug instead. "Thank you. It's nice to see that I have options again."

Wrapped in his arms, that sense of *safe* he'd given her the night before returned. She didn't know what to make of it, other than to savor it. She squeezed him tighter. This time, she wasn't imagining things. He kissed the top of her head.

"Any plans for the rest of the day?" she asked.

Cash didn't let her go but leaned back and captured her gaze. "I was hoping to hang out with you. And Henry invited me to that Citadel party. Did he bring clothes for a place like Republic?"

"Maybe that's what he and Gabriel are doing today."

"Do you mind if I go?"

"Not at all." In fact, inviting Cash had been the smartest thing Henry had done since Lila had met him. "It'll be nice to have a witness to confirm that I don't exaggerate when I talk about Odor." She stepped out of their hug. "Do you have any suits here?"

"Yeah, but I'll wear something I won't sweat in as much. I don't care if I look like an old guy. Did you bring a suit?"

"Only of the swimming variety." Lila winked. "I bought something sparkly yesterday. I'm set."

"Do you need to go get ready?"

Now *Lila* felt old. They had hours before that party. Her college self would've gone home, had a sandwich, taken a shower, exfoliated and shaved from head to toe, and gone into the type of prep that was probably standard for beauty pageants. Ten years post-college, and six months after ending a years-long relationship, she wanted to do other things before she went out. Not to mention, now she prioritized feeling good when she dressed up, not posturing. She wasn't sure when that had changed, but she didn't mind.

"We don't have to be there until after dark. We've got plenty of time. I thought I'd draw for a little while."

Cash tangled his fingers in hers. "Can we draw and hang out?"

"That's what I was hoping."

"Do you want to go somewhere?"

Lila dug through her messenger bag for her spiral sketchbook. "Here is fine. Get your stuff."

Cash disappeared for a moment and reappeared with an oversized book, like what he'd used on the beach.

She'd been thinking about this since last night and decided that even though Cash's and Gabriel's families were friendly, she could trust him. She sat on the couch with her sketchbook in her lap and took off her top and bra. Her nipples pebbled as soon as the air-conditioned air hit them. At least, that was the story she'd told herself, rather than acknowledge her nerves. When she finally looked up, Cash stood in silence, staring.

He cleared his throat. "Should I take my shirt off too?"

"If you want." Lila flipped to a blank page. "You need to fix my breasts in that drawing." She gestured toward herself. "Here's your opportunity." She hoped she sounded calm and comfortable, because as much as she wanted to do this, part of her screamed to cover up and pretend it had never happened. Maybe go back to Gabriel's and do that head-to-toe exfoliation routine.

Cash yanked his shirt over his head, then rearranged the furniture before he sat across from her at an angle.

"Do you want me to pose?" she asked.

"You're perfect as you are."

He meant it in an artsy way. No sooner had the words left his mouth than his pencil scratched across his paper. This was strictly professional. And somehow, that statement healed a bruise from her ex.

She'd always felt like she was striving in that relationship. Had something to prove. Someone she should be. A standard she'd had to achieve, even though she'd never known what it might be. Then one day this adorably sexy man had shown up and uttered the one phrase she'd needed to hear and hadn't even realized it. She stared at her page and willed herself not to react. If she reacted, she might have to explain. She didn't want to explain. She wanted to draw.

Chapter Nine

Lila did have a sandwich when she got back to Gabriel's. He and Henry hadn't returned yet, leaving her to relish in the quiet. She sat at the kitchen table working on her drawing when Henry's squeals told her the guys were back. She closed her sketchbook and cleaned up her sandwich as she braced herself for Henry.

"Gaaaaaaaaaaaaay-briel, you've seen the pictures!" Henry burst through the front door, shopping bags dangling from his arms like bracelets. "I have to go *big* tonight. Men in uniform." Henry fanned himself.

Gabriel maneuvered past Henry and deposited his own bags inside his bedroom door. "I don't think they'll be wearing their uniforms at this club."

Lila tilted her head. "Aren't uniforms mandatory unless they get special permission?"

"Lordt, I hope they don't have permission," Henry called as he walked into the bathroom. He gasped loudly and ran back out. "That room is twee!"

Lila looked at Gabriel, and she and her friend burst into laughter. The downstairs bathroom wasn't large by any means, but hearing Henry call it *twee* sent them over the edge.

"Why are you laughing?" Henry squealed. "Gabriel doesn't want to see Odin's spear swinging when I dash from the shower all the way across the house to my room."

Lila grimaced. Henry certainly knew his audience.

"You got me there," Gabriel said. "Mind sharing the upstairs bathroom, Lila?"

"It would be my honor." Lila gestured toward the stairs.

"Time to see to my ablutions." Henry collected the shopping bags he'd dropped in his fit of pique and sashayed into his room before closing the door with a firm *thunk*.

"I'm going upstairs before the spear makes an appearance," Lila said.

She put on what Gabriel had referred to as her moonlight dress, a shiny navy-blue dress with silver stars, a sweetheart neckline, and a swingy skirt, then stepped into a pair of coordinating sandals.

She filled her wristlet with the essentials, including a tampon even though she didn't need it, then knocked on the bathroom door. "My make-up's in there."

Gabriel opened the door in his shorts and an undershirt, half his jaw covered in shaving cream. "Do you need the sink?"

"Nah." She slid her make-up down the counter. "You hoping to go home with a man in uniform tonight?"

Gabriel swished his razor in water and shaved another line. "You know I've been seeing someone."

"It's not serious, though."

"Not yet. But the cadets need to graduate first." Another swish, another line. "You're single. Does Cash have a chance?"

"Maybe?"

Gabriel gave her a once-over. "You're not dressed like someone who's going out to chaperone a baby gay."

"Neither are you." Lila bent toward the mirror to apply her mascara.

"Deflecting." Gabriel rinsed his face and patted it dry. "Still worried about gossip?"

"Not really." She plunged the spoolie into the mascara tube and did the other eye. "Nervous, I guess. I was tied down for years. Can I handle a vacation fling?"

"If it helps, you can think of it as a vacation relationship."

Lila rolled her eyes. "Lame."

Gabriel shrugged. "He likes you. You're allowed to have fun, even if it's not for a decade."

Lila met his gaze in the mirror and gave him a sad smile that meant, *What if I don't meet his standards either?*

Gabriel's stern expression said, *Your standards are the only ones that matter.*

"I love you," Lila whispered.

"Love you too." He blew her a kiss and stepped out of the bathroom. "I'm gonna change."

Lila finished her hair and make-up, then went downstairs and waited in the foyer to avoid a sword sighting.

"You look hot, Lila," Henry said from the doorway.

Startled, she glanced up from her phone to find him looking surprisingly stylish in fitted slacks and a tucked in dress shirt, with an uncharacteristically subtle shimmer, open at the collar, with rolled-up sleeves. "Thanks. Your velvet shoes are a nice touch."

Henry slid a foot out and angled it, posing for her. "Are you glad I invited Cash? I bet he tries to take you home as soon as he sees you in that teeny dress."

Lila tugged at the hem. "It's not that small." She smoothed the skirt. "Is it?"

"No!" Gabriel called from the landing.

"No," Henry agreed, turning his chin to his shoulder. "But it *is* shorter than the rompers you've been wearing this week. Longer than your shorts. More suggestive, though."

"What do you know about suggestive?"

"I'm gay. I know *all* about it."

Lila couldn't help but laugh. If someone had told her earlier in the week that the person who gave her a blistering headache would also help her catch her equilibrium, she never would've believed it.

Gabriel finally came downstairs in a lavender button-down and sleek khakis. "Ready?"

"Aye, papi! Look at you!" Henry squealed.

"I thought you were Nordic," Lila said.

"We don't have an aye, papi equivalent, and *look* at this man!" Henry bit his finger. "He's giving me daddy issues."

"Do *not* call me daddy." Gabriel shivered.

"You're right. I should save it for the cadets."

Chapter Ten

"You look incredible," Cash said into Lila's ear as he rested his hands on her hips. "Is this okay?"

Lila leaned against him, letting that safe feeling wash over her. "More than okay." She turned in his arms and gasped. "You cut your hair!"

He grinned as she ran her fingers through the tidied strands. "You like it?"

Channeling the audacity she'd felt earlier when she'd taken off her top, she tugged on it. "It'll do."

He lifted an eyebrow, then kissed her cheek. "Am I reading this right? Should I call a Lyft?"

She brushed her lips against his. "You're an excellent reader. But we can't leave yet. Gotta make sure Gabriel and Odor are settled in first." She gave him a small kiss and nipped his lip.

"Okay. I gotta meet someone too."

"You do?" Lila led him toward the bar.

"Yeah. A guy at the barbershop has ties to a development group. They need a preservation architect."

"Shut up!" Lila jumped on him in a hug. "That's great news!"

Cash walked them the last few steps and deposited her at the bar, where he caged her in with his arms. "You got the ball rolling for me."

She ordered a drink, then put her attention back on him. "How so?"

"You snapped me out of my shit and got me moving again. People can sense sadness and desperation, you know?"

Lila nodded. "If it's any consolation, I didn't notice until you made the comment about the house being worth more than you." She stepped closer to him, brushing her chest against his. "Which is dumb. You're priceless."

He took the hint and kissed her, leaning into her and wiping her thoughts away.

She didn't realize her drink was there until Cash moved. She broke the kiss as he fumbled behind her. "Sorry," she said.

"Nothing to be sorry for." He signed the receipt and handed her the drink. "Dance?"

Henry squealed no less than three times while Lila danced with Cash. Eventually, Gabriel turned up to let her know Henry had been invited into a VIP room and he'd be following to "Keep Odin out of trouble."

"Pretty sure Odin *wants* trouble," Cash said.

"He can find it when I'm not around." Gabriel put a hand on Lila's shoulder. "You good? You guys want to crash VIP with me?"

"Honey, VIP is wherever you are." Lila gave him a half hug. She'd only had one drink, but she really did love Gabriel, and any excuse to show him was fine with her. "But Cash has to see a man about a house. We should stay out here."

"Okay." Gabriel waved his smartwatch at her. "I have my location on. You?"

Lila waved her small bag; she didn't wear a watch in the summer. Too sweaty. "Of course."

Gabriel popped a kiss on her cheek. "Later, kids!"

As he wove through the crowd, Lila turned to Cash. "I need to run to the restroom."

"Should I get you a refill?"

"Water for now, please."

"You got it." He smacked her ass as she walked away.

She hadn't been expecting that from him, but she liked it. He was leveling up their flirting too. Did condom machines still exist? She hoped there'd be one in the bathroom.

Once Lila emerged from the ladies' room—after trading her tampon for a condom—she scanned the club to find Cash. He stood at the bar, talking with someone Lila figured was from the group he'd mentioned. She sent a text that she'd be near VIP with Gabriel and went in search of her bestie. It didn't take long; she followed the sounds of Henry's squeals.

Gabriel stood by an alcove with a glass of champagne. Henry sat on someone's lap, squealing about men in uniforms.

"Trite," Lila said.

"On brand," Gabriel responded.

"Truth."

"Looks like you were having fun with Cash."

"Mm," Lila hummed.

"Where is he?" Gabriel asked.

Lila looked toward the bar, where she'd seen him last. "He's talking with a guy, hopefully, about a job."

"Nice." Gabriel bumped her with his shoulder. "A guy? You sure?"

"Yeah." Lila stretched the word out as a woman snaked her arm around Cash's waist and pulled him toward an exit. She looked at Gabriel. "Why?" She gestured wildly and champagne sloshed out of the glass and down her hand. She sagged and blinked as if to say, *Why?*

Gabriel grabbed her elbow. "Are you okay?"

Lila handed him the bottle and glass. "Yeah." Another glance in Cash's direction. He left through a side door with the woman. Lila checked her phone. No messages. She checked the door again. No Cash.

"What'd he say?" Gabriel asked as he set the broken glass onto a nearby table.

"Nothing." As her heart sank, she reminded herself that she hadn't intended to meet someone on this trip, anyway. Nor had she ever planned to go clubbing. "I'm not sticking around to see this play out." She moved toward the main doors.

"I'll take you home."

"No," she shouted over her shoulder. "Watch Henry." She'd never gotten out of a place faster.

Chapter Eleven

Lila was grateful she hadn't left her laptop at home for this trip. She lay curled in bed, bundled in blankets with the air-conditioning set to arctic, streaming *The Great British Bake Off*.

It wasn't so much that Cash had left with another woman. Lila had no claim to him, and even though she liked him, he was looking for work in Charleston. She lived in Asheville. This was truly vacation fun. Tonight, she'd wallow that it had ended a few days too soon. Tomorrow, she'd have fun with her friends. Cash would go back to being another IOP person. She might see him in passing during other visits. Probably not. It'd taken her this long to meet him.

Paul Hollywood had picked up a piece of kugel with his pocketknife when there was a knock at the door. Not the main door. *Her* door. To the balcony. Trying to convince herself it was Gabriel, Lila climbed out of her warm bed and crossed the frigid room. She shifted the curtain to see out the window. Shit. She pasted on a smile and opened the door.

"You found me!"

"I'm sorry." Cash looked concerned and a little confused, but earnest.

Lila stepped onto the balcony and closed the door behind her. "For what?"

"Gabriel said it looked like I'd left with another woman."

Lila nodded. "It did. Which you can do." She gestured between them. "We're not a thing."

"But I want us to be."

Lila squinted. What was she missing? Why had he left with someone else? "I...I need more information."

"The woman. She's one of the developers. She stumbled getting off the bar stool. Her partner had gone out to the garden, and after she fell, I figured I should make sure she got there unharmed." Cash pushed his hands through his hair, looking frustrated that it wasn't as long anymore. "When I found Gabriel, he said you thought I had left, so you did too."

Lila nodded. "That's what happened."

"And then Henry jumped on me. That guy looks small, but he is *solid*." Cash rubbed his neck as though trying to relieve the memory of the pain. "He yelled so much. I could only make out that straight men are the worst." Cash threw his hands into the air. "And sure, but I was trying not to be."

Lila covered her mouth as she laughed. After all the push and pull between her and Henry, all the headaches she'd had since they'd gotten here, it hadn't occurred to her that he would come out swinging for her.

"Maybe Odin really does suit him."

Cash stepped forward and took Lila's hand. "I'm sorry. I should've texted when I found them at the bar. Then you would've known it was a few people and they were going outside."

"You don't owe me anything."

"I upset you when the only thing I wanted to do was make you feel good."

"Thank you." Lila squeezed his hand. "I appreciate the explanation and you finding me instead of waiting until we bumped into each other again."

"Bump into you? I want to see you all the time."

"I live four hours away." Lila crossed her arms in front of her abdomen. "This is vacation fun."

"I don't have a job yet." Cash took a step toward her. "I can live anywhere. This can be any kind of fun we want."

Lila eyed him, taking a moment to decide her next move. She wasn't sure she wanted something serious yet, but she liked spending time with Cash. It would be nice to get to know him more. "I'd like more fun."

Cash took another step. "With me?"

She lifted onto her toes and gave him a small kiss. "I think so."

"You just made my whole summer." He wrapped his arms around her and squeezed her tight against him.

To her surprise, that safe feeling came back. "Wanna put on some crowns and sit on the deck until Gabriel and Odor get back?"

"Yes." Cash pulled back and moved toward the stairs. "Mine's at home. I'll be right back."

"You kept it?"

"Yeah." The look he gave her was almost exasperated. "I have something for you too. Gimme two minutes."

While Cash was gone, Lila adjusted the temperature on the air conditioner and set herself up on the deck. She giggled when she caught sight of Cash walking down the street, sketchbook in hand, and his Jughead-style crown atilt on his head.

"Front door's open," she called to him.

"Come into the light," Cash called as he climbed the steps.

Lila stood and went to the threshold, flipping on the hallway light.

When Cash reached the top of the stairs—after a small trip on *that* stair—he thrust his sketch pad into her hands, open to a drawing.

"What's this?"

"For you. I made it today."

It was the most beautiful portrait of herself that she'd ever seen. "You did this today? Just in one day?"

"Turns out, when you're determined not to ogle someone, you can get a lot done."

Lila spun on her heel and retrieved her own work. "Trade?" She handed him what she'd drawn at his house.

"You drew me."

Lila nodded.

"And I drew you."

She grinned.

"No way was I ever gonna leave with anyone but you."

She didn't know who reached for whom first, but she was back in his arms, bodies pressed together from shoulders to thighs, wishing the heat in their kiss would burn away their clothes.

Slamming car doors registered vaguely in the back of her mind, but she didn't care. She and Gabriel had caught each other making out before, though Gabriel was getting too good at interrupting.

"You good, Lila?" Henry's voice rang out from the driveway. "Those cadets are pretty, but I had to see if you were okay."

Lila laughed and walked to the railing. "Yeah, I'm alright."

"Ready for that big deck energy?" Gabriel called out.

Before Lila could answer, a pickup pulled in behind Gabriel's car, and three cadets got out.

"What are you doing here?" Henry shouted.

"You said party at the beach," one man answered.

Henry squealed.

Somehow, Gabriel produced an air horn, which put all the men, including Henry, at attention. "Beach bender, that way!" He pointed away from the house.

"Wow." Cash wrapped his arms around her waist.

"This is part of the fun if you stick around."

"I'm sticking." Cash pulled her against him as if to illustrate the point. "Definitely sticking."

The End

About Elaine Reed

Elaine writes contemporary romance and women's fiction. She lives in South Carolina's Lowcountry. When she isn't writing, she can be found exploring Charleston, taking in live music, and searching for shark teeth on the beach with her family.

Find Elaine online:

Sign up for her newsletter:https://www.elaine-writes.com/newsletter/
Website: https://www.elaine-writes.com/
Instagram: https://www.instagram.com/_elainewrites/
Facebook: https://www.facebook.com/elainereedwrites
Amazon:https://www.amazon.com/Elaine-Reed/e/B07YNCV6LP

Goodreads:https://www.goodreads.com/author/show/16599589. Elaine_Reed

The Blue Victorian

A Marion's Corner Story

by Robin Hillyer-Miles

The Blue Victorian

A Marion's Corner Story

by Robin Hillyer-Miles

Roosevelt wants to spend a well-deserved mini staycation on Sullivan's Island, in the Lowcountry of South Carolina, but her ex-husband wrecks the plans by making up the entire package he gifted her. After flying to the top of a tree to rescue a cat, she is determined not to have her holiday ruined. Roosevelt accepts the offer of an overnight stay from the grateful cat dad who also owns the blue Victorian, the house she's coveted since her teens. David might be the answer to her dreams and fulfill all her fantasies.

Chili Pepper Rating: 3

Chapter One

Roosevelt struggled to control her fifteen-year-old VW Bug convertible as she drove over the Isle of Palms Connector. The convertible top buffeted like it did when she followed too close to a semi-truck. *Whomp. Whomp*

When she discovered she could fly at the age of five, her parents teased that she looked like a hydroplaning car. Something she hoped would not happen today, as she he pressed all her weight into the driver's seat to help keep the car on the bridge. The wipers whipped with effort to keep up with the sheeting rain. She shifted to a lower gear and clutched the steering wheel.

The traffic signals at the end of the bypass welcomed her with green lights glimmering through the rain streaked windshield. She flicked the blinker to indicate a right turn. A cozy bed-and-breakfast awaited her arrival, and then the house tours began in—she checked the car's clock—ten minutes. She could skip all the other homes and see only the one, the blue Victorian, the house that had captivated her from teenhood.

GPS directed her to take a left after Breach Inlet, then the first right. The house number on the reservation sheet didn't match any of the houses. She pulled close to the mailboxes to read them in the now misty rain. One house number on a mansion-sized home almost matched. Two numbers flipped, but close. She blamed her dyslexia and pulled into the driveway of what must be the bed-and-breakfast. She cut off her engine, got out. A quick glance up and down the street showed no onlookers, so she levitated over the puddle next to her car and landed on the stairs. Her ability to defy gravity, if only for a hundred yards vertical, tended to keep her feet dry.

She shook rain off her coat and mashed the button. Her stomach grumbled, the sound competing with the doorbell sounding through the door. Her ex-husband had mentioned the B&B included a cocktail hour with light hors d'oeuvres each evening. Perhaps she could grab a bite before she headed to her dream house.

He'd been so happy, her ex, when she'd opened the envelope containing the ticket to the annual Sullivan's Island home tour. A tour that, this year, included the historic blue Victorian on a two-acre lot. The house she'd often driven by in her dilapidated MG Midget on her way to and from running a summer children's program throughout her college years.

The house spoke to her. Invited her to visit. Tugged at her heart as she'd maneuvered her stick shift down Middle Street, past Dunleavy's, the grocery store, Bert's Bar, and the laundromat. Her car would glide past her house so she could stare at the circular windows, elaborate fretwork, the turret, and the gabled tin roof.

Last Winter Solstice, while her ex explained about the bed-and-breakfast, Lincoln, her sister, interrupted with a sharp bark of warning. Roosevelt motioned at her sister to hush. Lincoln stomped off, throwing up her hands as she was wont to do when it came to Roosevelt's relationship with her ex. He grinned when Lincoln slammed the door and leaned in close to Roosevelt for a kiss. The tickle of his mustache drew her in, and their lips touched. She recoiled, remembering all the unfulfilled promises from their long marriage. The bedroom rules. The lights-on prerequisite. The must-have-just-showered necessity. The no-hair-below-the-neck requirement for her. The no-toys constraint. The never-a-big-O-for-Roosevelt result.

She'd confirmed the tour ticket the next day. Spoken to a young person who seemed confused but confirmed her reservation for the tour this fourth Tuesday in March. Her boss approved her days off. Two nights to explore her old stomping grounds and reacquaint herself with her favorite island. A staycation. A relief from all the stress of the hospital ER.

Someone approached. Shadows moved behind the tinted glass in the mahogany door of the bed-and-breakfast. The door opened, encumbered by the chain.

"Hello?" a small voice said.

"Hi. I'm here to check in for two nights. Is the manager here?"

"My mama is here."

"Can you get her, please?"

The door slammed shut, the chain rattling in the wake of the movement, and minutes passed. The storm raged anew behind her, and she glanced at her car to ensure it wasn't floating away with the expected King Tide. The air filled with the scents of salt, sea-foam, and a hint of pluff mud, that briny, dark, sulfide scent that brought joy to her heart. It smelled of home.

Her hair began curling into ringlets, which she should have known would happen and not paid the forty-five dollars for the fancy King Street salon's blowout earlier that day.

The wind scattered camellia and azalea petals across the lawn and drove down palmetto fronds that skittered down the street. A hammock swayed and creaked on the porch. A tricycle lay on its side on the sidewalk.

Wait. This isn't a bed-and-breakfast. She peered up and down the street. Double-checked her phone's GPS. Confirmed the address her ex gave her. A nonexistent address. He'd done it again.

Gaslighter.

No wonder he called earlier, begging her to forget about the tour and the overnight stays. First because of the weather, and then to guilt her into attending their grandchild's school event. A women's history month celebration and play. Important to Roosevelt. Not important to her freaking ex.

The door opened before she walked away.

"May I help you?" The woman looked to be in her late twenties—could have been her daughter's age.

"I think I have been misinformed about a bed-and-breakfast being located on this street." Roosevelt wiped wetness from her face, hoping it looked like rain and not the tears that began to fall.

"Oh dear. Yes. I think you've been misinformed. Maybe it's on Isle of Palms? I don't think our town council even allows bed-and-breakfasts on Sullivan's Island. I could be wrong. But I know there's none on our street. This was my grandparents' house, and then my parents', so I've lived here all my life."

"I must have my wires crossed. Sorry to have bothered you." She paused for a second to gather her thoughts.

"Are you okay? Do you need to call someone?" The younger woman took a step forward and placed a soft hand on Roosevelt's arm.

A snort of laughter escaped from Roosevelt. "Oh honey, thank you for your concern. I'm not that old. I can figure this out. I think I've been bamboozled. Please excuse me. You have a beautiful home."

She scooted down the stairs on her feet, since the owner watched her. She mentally thanked the person who had placed sandpaper runners on the steps, as she almost slipped halfway down and grasped at the railing so she would not automatically float to the ground. No need to let everyone in on her little magic. It caused too many questions.

She pretended to steady herself as she waved goodbye to the slender woman holding hands with a small boy who clasped a toy dinosaur. Both looked at her with concern in their eyes.

"That son of a…" She slammed her car door and put on her seat belt. It took time after starting the car to defog the windows, so she fumed for a minute. "At least I can still see the house. That, I confirmed."

The blue Victorian had come up for sale the year she graduated with her nursing degree from the University of South Carolina. She'd missed the open house due to her job and being young and stupid. Not that she could have afforded it or been able to place a down payment on it at that time. But she could have gone in, walked the floors, opened doors, peeked into rooms.

She took Middle Street to her dream house. She'd kept up with seeing it since college. Two years ago, she dined at Poe's Tavern last fall and attended a fancy postdivorce celebration with her sisters at The Obstinate Daughter, so those looked familiar. Dunleavy's Pub's ever-present green edifice brought joy to her heart.

The park upgrades looked good. And…she arrived. Picket fence surrounding the cropped lawn. A live oak taller than the house and draped with Spanish moss stood on the left of the porch. A palmetto tree on the right. A broken sidewalk led to the house that haunted her dreams.

Solar lights flanking the sidewalk flickered on because the storm made this six o'clock hour seem like midnight. No—she checked her car clock again—seven o'clock. The tours lasted from six to eight. She parked in one of the many empty spaces on the street. Each step closer to her house filled her heart with more joy. She opened the gate.

The gate bottom scraped on the sidewalk. The cicadas and tree frogs started filling the air with their song. A gale force of wind came from the ocean, silencing the wildlife and almost knocking her straight into the house. A vortex of a gust that flickered around her body, her face, her hands, her legs. She hung onto the fence as her feet lifted in the air of their own volition.

Then quiet, nothing, a void of sound, of touch. The vortex left as quickly as it came. A foreshadowing of the storm to come, maybe? Her father always said to get ready for a doozy of a storm if you felt swift winds followed by eerie calm.

She closed the gate, pulled her feet back to the earth, and focused on the view of her house.

The rain on the tin roof must have sounded as marvelous from the inside as it did at her cottage in Marion's Corner. The blue of the exterior, more faded than the vibrant blue of the past, came to her mind from recent memory, as it was difficult to see in the rain. Pampas plants screened the sides of the front porch from view.

Roosevelt walked up the sidewalk. No welcoming porch lights. Maybe the house lost power? No lights shone in the windows on either side of the door.

A man, silhouetted in the dark by the solar-powered landscape lighting, stood on the sidewalk. He peered into the branches of the live oak.

She walked behind him, cleared her throat. "Is this the line?" Her hands shook and she needed to ground herself before glee, excitement, and another blast of air lifted her to the sky.

"Line?" The man eyed her. Even in the now slightly lit yard, the full moon covered by clouds, he commanded attention.

She almost said, "Hubba-hubba" out loud. Tall. Built. Some gray in his dark hair. He wore jeans and a windbreaker. He looked back up the tree.

"Line for the tour?"

He looked down at her; he stood taller than six feet, a good foot taller than she, at minimum. A bubble of air filled her chest. Her feet lifted from the ground. Uh-oh. An inch. Another inch.

"Stop it." She used her arms as if she were in a pool and tried to touch the bottom.

"I'm sorry?" He crossed his arms. Uncrossed them. Dug into his back pocket and pulled out a phone as she elevated another inch.

Arms flapped as she shoved herself back to terra firma with such force she thought she twisted her ankle. Before menopause, she could control her ability to swim in the air, as her sisters called it. She took off not like a superhero—more Jean Grey than Superman. Legs always toward the earth, crown of the head to the sky, chest open to the planets. Then she'd swim, show off all the strokes they'd learned from their swimming instructors, but in the sky. Menopause hit hard and even on hormone therapy, sometimes she lost control.

She exhaled to the bottom of her feet and took in a sip of oxygen to speak. "The line to the house tour. Is there a group inside?"

"Oh. The tour? Last night's tour?" He gave her a quizzical look and then concentrated back on the tree.

She checked the paper ticket her ex had placed in the gift card, shining the light from her phone to read it in the impending dark. Checking the tour website, her fingers scrolled down the main website page to the listings of tour homes. Under today's date, it listed four houses. None on Middle Street. Two old officer houses, one on the Pitt Street side of the island at the intracoastal waterway, and the other near Breach Inlet. But not her blue Victorian.

Gaslit again by the master manipulator. Years of being told one thing and given another. Said to have misinterpreted what was said. She didn't understand. She was stupid. She needed to pay attention. She never did anything right.

"Did the date change? I had it down for this evening." She needed something to hold on to so she didn't float away. She walked over to the tree and pressed her palm on the trunk while she spoke. A wisp of Spanish moss wafted into her face.

He shone his cell phone flashlight in her eyes.

Chapter Two

"Sorry to blind you. Can you see my cat in that tree?" He aimed the flashlight into the long limbs of the live oak.

She let her eyes readjust to the darker night and looked straight up. A tail swished from side to side in a branch near the top. She pointed and he moved closer to her to get a better look. Each time he took a step nearer to her, the bubble built larger in her chest.

"Dang cat. Come down here. Treat?" He reached into his pocket and pulled out what looked like cat treats.

"Is the tree climbable?" She felt along the trunk to the first grouping of limbs. "I could probably reach him."

"Oh, no you won't. It's covered in Spanish moss and resurrection fern. The fern gets slippery when wet. My granddaughter broke her arm last year doing just that after a rain."

"Yikes. Okay. No climbing." She looked into the tree. Two eyes glowed near the top.

"Kitty. It's going to storm and the wind's going to carry you clear to McClellanville, you stinking cat. Kitty. Kitty. Get down here." His voice changed from mad to cajoling to sing-song and back to mad. The brewing storm kicked it up a notch.

"Meow." The cat moved up a limb.

"Stop climbing up." The man started to sound desperate.

"Meow." The cat's eyes gleamed in the light from his cellphone.

"Get down here." This time his voice broke.

Roosevelt moved to a vantage point that had a clear shot to the limb to which the trembling cat clung. The wind whipped and tangled her hair, and the bottom fell out of the sky. Buckets of rain gushed down. She tucked her phone into her purse and set it on the ground.

"What are you doing?" The man shielded his eyes and took a step forward, but the fury of the wind held him back.

She took three breaths. Long. Deep. Filling every crevice in her body. The bubble in her chest expanded. Her heels, the balls of her feet, her toes, left the ground. Her hands to her side, palms down, guided her to the exact limb where the small black cat clutched the wood.

"Here, kitty, kitty." She filled her lungs and reached out her hands. Startling the cat, she grasped it by the crook of the neck and held on to its feet with the other hand. With a rush, they swooped down to the ground. They landed with a *whoosh*.

Roosevelt stood, rearranging the cat in her arms so she didn't fall or jump out.

"Come inside." The man snatched up her purse, took her by her shoulder, and led her into the house.

Once inside, he ushered her to a plush chair by the roaring fire. The cat refused to leave her arms. He left the room and returned with a stack of towels.

"Let's get y'all dried off." He dipped his hand into his pocket and showed the cat the treats.

This time, the cat released its hold on the sleeve of her shirt. Her soaking-wet white shirt.

She took a towel and placed it in front of her chest. "She's a sweet kitty."

"Milo."

"Roosevelt." She held out her arm to shake his hand.

"The cat's name is Milo. I'm David. Nice to meet you, Roosevelt." He took her offered hand.

"Hi, David. I'm not usually this unfocused or drenched." The cat curled up into a bed near the fireplace.

"Me neither. Nice magic, by the way. I only fly in my dreams."

"Thanks. It's only helpful getting cats out of trees, though. And reaching the top shelves in the kitchen and grocery stores, but only if no one is looking."

"You don't receive the stipend?" He set the cat onto a bed next to his chair.

If someone had magic that would garner them more income doing a job than an everyday, run-of-the-mill person could earn, then they had to give away their gift for a government stipend.

"No. The test committee couldn't figure out how it gave me an advantage over other nurses."

At age twenty-five, everyone had a magical-abilities test, and after that, only a state supreme court order could change the verdict. Her testing center had been makeshift. When they called her into the room, she'd forced her body to lift no more than ten inches, fighting the rush and need to swoosh to the flag they'd attached to a basketball goal's backboard in the high school gym.

"Lucky."

"Well, the committee consisted of a bunch of old white guys, not the most brilliant humans on the planet."

He looked himself up and down. "You know I'm an old white guy, right?"

"I didn't mean you. You seem to have it all together."

The federal government meant for the stipend to give an easy life, but after trickling down from federal to state to county to city, much of the money got eaten up in service fees, leaving the recipient barely making ends meet.

"I take it you passed the magic test," she said.

"Never took it. I walked in and they said, 'Dismissed.'" He didn't look her in the eye.

"Why? Because you're a white male?"

"No. But I did have some friends who didn't even attend the test because their daddies got them out of it. So yes, I agree, the patriarchy is real. Back to you, do you have to hide your magic?"

"I have to be careful around certain people and parts of town because they'll accuse anyone of cheating just to be paid the bounty."

A bounty to tell on others who may or may not have lied on their test. Or showed diminished abilities. Sometimes age brings bigger powers, sometimes not. Hers had grown stronger but less controlled.

"I take it you're not afraid of heights then." He grinned at her.

She saw his face in full light for the first time. Dimples. A short-trimmed beard. Hair longer on the top than the sides—not military style, more like the young surfers you'd see at The Washout on Folly Beach.

"No, sir. Not afraid of heights." She nodded at him and then looked around at the house. The house she knew from her dreams. Once, in her teens, she'd flown over the backyard because Middle Street, at the front of the house, always had traffic. She'd seen a few bedrooms on what looked like an addition. Her presence made the hens in the yard flutter about, causing a commotion. An older woman walked into the yard to feed the chickens. She spotted Roosevelt and waved at her to come down. Roosevelt hid behind a tree instead.

But now she sat inside. Inside. The original hardwood floors gleamed. The corner of the kitchen island could be seen from her vantage point. A draft came from behind her as a door opened and closed. His wife must be in another room. She envisioned the primary bedroom being down the hall past the staircase to her rear.

He took the seat opposite her, and they dried themselves off.

She dabbed at her face. Her perfect outfit, her make-up, the expensive hair blowout, all for naught. No bed-and-breakfast. No tour. No staycation. She pushed on the arms of the chair and stood. Draped the towel on the back of the chair.

"My ex bought me tickets to the tour. I was going to make a mini staycation out of it. He got me two nights at a nonexistent bed-and-breakfast on the island."

He stood, but a frown crossed his face. "A bed-and-breakfast on this island? Not Isle of Palms? Mt. Pleasant? Maybe he gave you the wrong address?"

"No. Definitely Sullivan's." She sighed. "He'll talk his way out of this entire fiasco as usual. He plans something and then creates an emergency, so I never figure out that the nice gesture had no relevance. I'm not explaining this well. I guess I'll head back home. Thank you for the towel and the warmth of the fire." She held out her hand to shake his.

He took her hand in his and looked her in the eyes. "That's not okay. That's abuse."

A wave of warmth swept over her body. She swayed, righted herself, patted his shoulder. "I know. I know. I'm okay. I was done with him before—now I need to stand firm." But she couldn't set her feet under her. She couldn't stand. Her magic left her. She leaned down to pick up her purse. Dots formed before her eyes. Her stomach squeezed nothing, since she skipped meals today. She swayed. The floor reached up to slap her face, or it seemed that way as she dove for the hearth.

David grabbed her and kept her from tumbling. He pulled her into his arms to steady her. Made certain she was on her feet. "You okay? Need some water? Food?"

"I'm a nurse."

"Okay, Roosevelt, do you want to self-diagnose and not have me try and figure out what's wrong besides a hurt heart?"

"No. Sorry. I am a nurse, and I didn't eat much at all today in my eagerness to get here. I looked forward to going to the Sea Biscuit Café for breakfast and to Long Island Café for lunch. I wanted to walk the beach, see the sunrise, watch the pelicans on their morning hunts over the ocean. Hear the waves. Feel the sand beneath my feet."

"You can still do all that."

Her head touched his chest. His hard chest. The palm of her hand rested on his pectoral muscle. The heat from the fireplace or his nearness warmed her face. "His ploy to prove to me that I'm incompetent won't work this time."

"Good. What was his plan? To win you back? No one should ever treat you like that. Don't let him get away with it. I know we don't know each other, but I'll stand by you if you need help. Whatever his scheme, you saved Milo. You are our hero." He helped her sit back onto the chair.

"I am so not being clear. I haven't eaten since breakfast. I've been trying to get here. I kept getting interrupted by my ex, who was on a mission to keep me from coming to the house tours and the bed-and-breakfast, and now I see why he insisted that I attend our grandson's school event. Not a wish to spend time with me. It was an all-out lie to get me to stay home."

"Wow, he is a piece of work."

"He's an ass and a gaslighter. I should never have given him an inch. Now I need to head back home, to the Corner."

"If you need backup, I'm here. I have some resources I can share. Where did you say you live?"

"Marion's Corner, the small town north of here that sits between the Cooper River and Lake Moultrie. We hold a Revolutionary War reenactment every April." She wiped her brow.

"Ah, yes, Marion's Corner. Explains the accent. Food. I do have food. Loads of leftover food from last night. I bought food and wine for the tour, but then the organizer nixed it. The food. Not the tour. I have a ton of leftovers. I'll make you a plate."

"I can't intrude on you and your wife." It looked like they had an intimate evening planned with the fire. A silver tray holding a liquor bottle with crystal glassware sat on a side table.

"I'm a widower." His face didn't change expression.

"Oh, I'm sorry for your loss. I heard a door." Not married. No woman. Who had opened and closed the door? Roosevelt fanned herself with her wet shirt.

"Old houses make sounds. Do you want to borrow a shirt?"

"No, no. I'm fine. The fireplace will dry it soon enough. I love your old house."

She took a moment to enjoy the view as he walked toward the kitchen. His wet shirt clung to his muscles, and his pants molded to his legs. When he disappeared around the corner, she checked out her dream home. He'd decorated it with furniture that invited one to sit and stay awhile. It was showroom ready but livable and inviting. The front window panes shimmered with ancient blown glass. Her body relaxed into the cushions. She leaned her head back and admired the beadboard ceiling.

He brought her a glass of water and a white wine and set them on coasters on the table next to her chair.

"You sit and relax. Do you have any food allergies? Preferences?"

"I'm a pescatarian."

"Fish then, no meat?"

"Yes. But you don't have to fix anything for me. I can't believe I am imposing on you after Milo's adventure and your event with a house full of people last night."

"I like company. I don't get it often."

David went back to the kitchen.

The lights dimmed and then brightened. A door shut behind her. She gazed over her shoulder. No one was there. But the swish of skirts sounded across the floorboard. Milo ran from the kitchen, where he had followed David, and jumped into Roosevelt's lap. They both stared at the area the sounds came from.

David arrived with a platter of food and a couple of small plates. "Do you like cheese? I can't remember if pescatarian's eat cheese, so I brought some anyway because I love cheese."

"I love cheese too." She and the cat gaped at the spot across the room as the lights flickered again.

David looked in the direction they watched. "Grace, please meet Roosevelt. Yes, it's an interesting name. I'll ask her how she got it in a minute."

"Grace?"

"The house ghost. It—she's a lady from the late 1800s or early 1900s and she wears long skirts. Did you hear them as she passed you? I know she's in here because wherever she stands gets wavy, like the glass in the windows. See the chair, how it looks like it's out of focus? She's standing in front of it. She came with the house. She's harmless but curious. It's unusual that she showed herself to you. We have an understanding. The prior owners introduced us after I bought the house." He sat in the chair opposite her.

"How do you do, Grace? I have loved your house for years. I'm so grateful that David has invited me in to see it and sit in it. She's a beauty, this house."

"She's a lot of work is what she is. But she's a keeper. The house. Not the ghost." He started to serve the food, paused, glanced over his shoulder. "Grace is no work at all. She's pure delight. Would never wish her gone." He wore a *whoops* look on his face.

"I'm certain Grace is the highlight of the home." Roosevelt tried to appease the ghost as well.

"She's fine." He lowered his voice. "I don't know why I'm whispering. Anyway, she's still over there. She likes looking out that window. That's why the former owners planted the Pampas grass, to hide the windows from passersby. Too many questions from curious people who see her or catch a photo of something in my window and want to come show me their prize. We don't need all that attention."

"Good idea. Thank you for this wonderful assortment." She perused the platter he'd created with various cheese, breads, crackers, chips, olives, boiled shrimp, some kind of dip—maybe crab—and an assortment of fruit.

He handed her a dinner plate. "Dig in. There's more where this came from. The dip is crab. The caterer's a Gullah-Geechee food artist. It's unbelievable. She told me it's calorie-free." He winked at her and laughed.

Roosevelt's heart flipped in her chest. The sparkle in his eye, the deep dimple in his cheek, visible even through the beard. Her fanny tingled and she levitated above the seat. She looked to see if Grace noticed and realized at the same moment that she couldn't see the ghost's reaction, or even knew if ghosts reacted, and a giggle erupted before she could stop it. He didn't notice. So, she talked herself down, took a sip of the wine, and placed one hand firmly on the arm of the chair.

They dug into the food, and he refilled her glasses of water and wine. They chatted about grandchildren—his a girl, hers a boy—and how fast they seemed to grow. Faster than, somehow, their own children. Two hours sped by when she glanced at the mantel clock.

"Is that the time? I am so sorry to have intruded on you for this long."

"I've been thinking." He took her plate and set it onto the coffee table between them. "I have overserved you. You weigh what, around a hundred pounds? I can't let you drive home now. I have extra guest rooms that are guest ready. You planned on staying on the island anyway, right?"

"Yes, but…" He'd underestimated her weight by twenty pounds, but still. "You don't know me. I don't know you."

"The doors have locks, and there is an en suite bathroom in each room, plus a tiny seating area, and the rooms are separate from the house." He pointed behind the fireplace.

"Oh, but I—" She stood. Swayed again. This time from the wine instead of hunger and stress. They drank a bottle and a half of a sixty-dollar bottle of wine. Wine she eyed for a special occasion at her local grocer but could never purchase. He joined her with one glass and then switched to scotch, which meant she had an entire bottle.

"Yep. I'll show you to your room and then grab your bag from your car. I might move your car to the back lot so it's near your room, if you don't mind."

"Thank you." She handed him her car keys, then led the way to the back entrance, down a small hallway, past the enclosed porch she'd known would be there, and back into the open air onto a side porch that ran the length of three or four rooms on the right.

"Are you certain you haven't been here before?" David stepped behind her on the porch.

"In another life maybe." She touched the keys in his hand. "I didn't ask. Can you drive stick?"

"Yes, I can drive a manual. Here's your room—the furthest from the main house, so you don't have to worry about anything. Except the coyotes."

"I've heard about them harassing pets. Where's Milo?" She looked around their feet.

"Milo is in the house. He's wearing a collar that allows him in certain areas of the yard. He can climb up but not out past the invisible fence. But see, that's one of the reasons I'm happy to let you stay here. Your first thought was for his safety." He held the door open for her. "I'll be right back with your keys and bag."

She took a step toward the door, then spun. The maleness of him, the scotch, the outdoor scent that mingled with the fire's smoky odors, all made her want to lean into him. She placed her hand on his chest, hard and muscular, of course. How old was he again? Sixty-eight, he'd said?

"Thank you for letting me stay here. You've made a quite horrible evening into a delightful one." She stood on her tiptoes to buss his cheek.

But he moved to face her at the same time and their lips met. The initial contact startled her, but she threw care to the wind and wrapped her arms around his neck to kiss him deeper, harder, longer. The intensity increased and he pulled her body into his. His hardness hit her belly, and she rubbed herself against it.

"Hey." He pulled away a bit. "I'd like to continue this when we're both sober. Let me get your stuff. Lock your door so you feel safe, but I shall see you in the morning."

"Yes, sir." She pecked his cheek and took a few steps into her sleeping quarters.

A room the size of her primary bedroom loomed before her. She used the toilet. Tipped her fingers into a basket filled with travel- and sample-size lotions and creams that she could never afford. A knock sounded at the door. She opened it to find her overnight bag on the welcome mat with an azalea bloom resting on top of it.

The songs of birds woke her at seven o'clock. A quick dig in her toiletry case surfaced headache tablets, and the small refrigerator near the door held glass bottles of water.

She opened the window shade and looked out onto the back side of the double lot the house stood on. He'd parked her car in the nearest spot to her room. She made the bed and dressed. She wore her touring clothes, as Lincoln called them—a skort, a T-shirt, and a jean jacket with tennis shoes. In all the trips she'd taken with her sister as a tour escort or a guest, she'd worn this go-to outfit. It might not be the height of current fashion, but she thought she looked cute as she adjusted the tuck of her shirt before heading out the door. She tossed her overnight bag into the car and automatically headed in the direction of the main house, as if it called to her to return.

David met her on the side porch. Steam rose from the cup in his hand.

"Good morning. You look lovely. You booked a two-night stay, didn't you?" He came down the steps to the yard and handed her the cup. "I put stevia in it because I don't know if you like cream."

"I can't impose." She took a sip of the perfect cup of coffee handed to her by the perfect man. "I use Stevia—good guess."

"Stay another night, please?" David made a pleading gesture with his hands.

She laughed and nodded. Why not? That kiss last nice held a promise she'd like to see kept. No one expected her home until tomorrow anyway, and this would chap her ex's behind. He hadn't ruined her mini staycation. Even though he lied about his entire "gift" to her, she came out the winner. She got to sleep in the house she'd coveted for forty years.

And maybe she'll even sleep with the owner.

Take that, asshole.

David went to her car and removed her bag. "I'll drop this off in your room. You go inside and see Milo. He's been peeking out the window trying to catch a glimpse of you. When you walked out, he hollered at me."

Milo greeted her at the door, and she set down her cup to cuddle the cat. They snuggled and enjoyed the view out the bay window of the enclosed porch when David appeared.

"Milo. Are you being a traitor again? I feed you. I clean you. I keep your bowl filled with fresh water. Your litter box is pristine. And you let me hold you for seconds at a time." He came over and chucked the cat under the chin.

"He's a sweet kitty. This room might be my favorite. I've dreamt about it." The light streamed through the windows. She sat on a tufted window seat.

"It's got perfect lighting. The furniture can be moved around, except for where you're sitting. It photographs well. It's pretty popular." He took a seat across from her.

"Popular?"

"Um, it's been in magazines, you know? So, you never did tell us why you're named Roosevelt." David set his cup onto a side table and leaned his face into his hands.

"Didn't I?" Some of last night's conversation blurred in her head. She remembered he retired from investment banking. Grown up in Mt. Pleasant. Bought the house on a whim. He saw a realtor setting out the sign one day as he drove by. Made an offer right then. And boom. Owned a house he'd never stepped foot in.

"Roosevelt?" David got her attention. "Trying to remember why your parents gave you your name?"

Chapter Three

"Oh no, that's easy. They collected coins." She got up and wandered back to the entryway to find her coffee cup.

He followed her, took the cold mug from her, and headed to the kitchen.

"Let me warm that up for you. I often nuke my coffee because of Milo. He's a distraction." He placed the cup into the microwave and, arms crossed, focused on her. "Coins?"

"My parents had nothing when they got married in my grandparents' backyard. Someone gave them a huge glass jug, and everyone put their coins in. Whenever anyone visited, they'd add to the collection.

"Anyhow, Mom got pregnant with their first. They decided to take the jug to the bank to help pay for baby things. But the jug, heaped with coins, could not be picked up. They tilted it over. One coin rolled to the floor. A penny. So, they named that baby—my sister—Lincoln. And then they continued the tradition. So there's Lincoln, Jefferson, Roosevelt, Washington, and Kennedy. All girls."

"Interesting that they didn't name her Penny." He set her cup onto the kitchen island.

"Then I'd be named Dime, so thank goodness they didn't do that." She laughed, put down the cat, and took her cup in hand.

He leaned against the counter. "My parents did not use their imagination. We're David, Sally, and Tom."

"At least it's not Dick, Jean, and Sally."

"We did have a dog named Spot, though." This time, they both laughed.

"Let me close up the house and we'll head to the Sea Biscuit." David wiped down the quartz countertop and flipped off the coffee maker.

"You're going with me?" Her heart fluttered. She set down her coffee cup to ground herself with the counter. He looked delicious this morning. Golf shirt that matched the green of his eyes, darker khaki shorts, boat shoes with no socks. His legs kinda took her breath away. Strong. Muscular.

"Did I spill coffee on my shirt?" He looked down at his chest and swiped at it with the cloth in his hand.

"No, no. I was just thinking. Uh, I'm glad you're joining me for breakfast." She moved to the sink to rinse out her cup.

"Just set that in the sink. I'll be right back. I gotta grab a jacket. Lock up. Tell Grace we're leaving. Give Milo a treat. My car is out back near yours, if you want to meet me there." He nodded to the back door.

The ubiquitous crowd waited for seating at the restaurant. Everyone gathered in the spot of sunlight in the cool morning air.

"I never gave you the full tour of the house."

"Ha. How did I miss that? I've seen most of the downstairs. That's what was offered in the tour price, right?" Roosevelt adjusted her shades to see his face. She'd been a bit distracted the night before. The light of the day showed off his good looks. Other women her age, and younger—much younger— checked him out as they stood around in groups. Some whispered behind their hands. She could swear that a couple of women took sly photos of him.

"Full house tour and—what are we doing after this? Do you want to go to Station 16 and walk the forest trail? Have you been to Fort Moultrie recently? You said you worked there back in the day. We could go for a hike on the Awendaw portion of the Palmetto Trail or visit the Center for Birds of Prey." David stopped his spiel and straightened his shoulders. "Sorry, I don't get much company, and no one I know wants to explore."

"I'd love to do all of that and more, but I have a limited schedule. Let's do the fort, and if we have time, the forest trail. It's after eight, and the fort opens at nine, or it did." She checked her phone for the hours. "Yep, nine. So—breakfast, the fort, the trail. And then Long Island Café stops serving lunch at two but opens for supper at five…"

"We have great restaurants near my house too."

"Yes, but I've been to them for special occasions in the past couple of years. Maybe we can have a beer at Dunleavy's, enjoy a memory of my youth."

"We could have lunch, a beverage at Dunleavy's later, and then you can help empty more of my fridge for supper. How's that sound? Plus, the tour of the house will take some time. I might need a nap."

The look he gave her made her toes tingle and her feet lift off the parking lot. *Shoot.*

He stretched as if he knew how good he looked stretching. How it broadened his shoulders, emphasized the deep *V* of his upper body, made her heart dance.

More space appeared between the gravel and her feet.

The buzz in her chest grew larger. She tried a quiet burp, which used to work, like when Charlie and his great-uncle drank the fizzy lifting drinks in the chocolate factory.

"Are you trying to fly away from me?" he asked as he took her hand and brought her back to safety.

"Ha ha." She clutched his arm and cursed her gift.

The host called out his name and seated them at a two-top by the window. They flirted all through breakfast. Shameless. Blushing. Sharing a pancake. The server asked if they were on their honeymoon.

He told her about his plans for the house, which consisted of keeping it upright and inhabitable since he'd spent a ton on the renovations for the kitchen and bathrooms. She told him about her cottage, which could almost be a tiny replica of his home. The tin roof on her house in honor of the one on her dream home.

The ride to the fort, back on Sullivan's, included a detour to drive past officers' row. The structures housed military officers during the two World Wars.

"I can't believe I didn't tour the houses on my list last night."

"I can get you a private tour. I know the owners."

"Even for that one?" She pointed to a stunning example with a wrap-around porch.

"That one was not on the tour. But I play golf and ride bikes with the owner."

"Bicycle?" She would pay money to see him in a pair of tight bike shorts.

"Motor, darling. Motorcycles. I do have beach bikes in the garage, though. We could go for a ride. I need to put air in the tires first."

Now her mind was on him in a leather biker outfit and her riding on the back with her arms strapped across his waist and chest. Her hiney barely touched the seat from the excitement of the wind in her hair, reminding her of flying. She shook her head to clear it; she didn't need to get caught staring off into the abyss again. And he said Milo was a distraction. *Sheesh.*

They paid the park's entrance fee and perused the mini-museum and gift shop. She dragged him to watch the same history of the fort video that aired for forty years. A video where the narrator said damn three times in the twenty-two-minute film. She dug her elbow into his side at each instance, and they giggled like schoolchildren.

"I'm a bit surprised by the cussing." He'd bought a compass as a souvenir, in case, he said, he had to find her when she stranded herself flying. He fiddled with it while they waited to walk across the street.

"It's always cracked me up. Imagine sitting in the theater with fifteen kindergarten-aged summer campers and hoping their parents don't raise a fuss. Ah, the eighties and nineties."

"There's a grave." David pointed at the entrance of the Fort.

"Yes, Osceola, a Seminole. He was captured while negotiating a treaty. Under a white flag. Part of Andrew Jackson's Indian Removal Act. The

United States does not have a pretty history. Osceola died while held as a prisoner here." Roosevelt's voice caught, as it did every time she'd told this story to her summer campers back in the day.

They read more information on the plaque.

"And this fort gave South Carolina her flag." He pointed to the flag flapping over the fort.

"Yes. Back then it was named Fort Sullivan. On June 28, 1776, Colonel William Moultrie—wait, let's explore the old fort area, and I'll tell that story. Even though you kinda heard it in the film. It's one of my favorites."

They walked through the modern-day portions of the fort, checked out a few of the hideaways and barracks, until they reached the palmetto fort replica.

"Here we go. This, of course, is not the original, but it'll give you the right idea. So, Colonel William Moultrie commanded Fort Sullivan. He received word that the British would attack, trying to capture Charleston. However, the fort wasn't finished, so locals volunteered, and enslaved people were forced to chop down palmetto trees and stack them to create a makeshift fort. They packed and tossed sand between the logs. The British came and landed on Long Island, now Isle of Palms, and moored ships out there." She pointed toward the beach path.

"Interesting." David took a seat on a bench.

"Yes. The British began firing from the ships, and the story goes that the cannonballs, due to the spongy consistency of the logs, would either bounce off the palmettos and land on the beach or they'd get stuck between the logs in the sand. Anyhow, that was the first decisive battle that the rebels, as the British called us, won. It gave the budding potential government the hope and nerve that maybe, just maybe, they could win this thing."

"I got chills." David showed her the chicken skin on his arms.

"And Sergeant Jasper saved the fort's flag during the battle and reattached it. That flag, blue like their uniforms, with a silver crescent, became our state flag in 1861. The legislature added the palmetto tree then. The crescent is a mystery. It isn't a moon. Some say it's a military gorget—the thing they wore at their necks. I learned as a child that it was a Chinese symbol of strength that Colonel, soon to be General, Moultrie liked. Who knows."

"We have the coolest flag of all the states."

"The best. I also kinda like that there's no official flag and we see different shapes of crescents and palmettos on various flags. Keeps it interesting." Roosevelt took David's arm. "Let's walk down to the beach."

They kept un-accidentally touching each other. He said she needed to hold his hand so the wind didn't make her glide down the beach like a parasail. By the time they'd walked the fort's beach path to enjoy the ocean view, they became comfortable enough to stop and kiss a few times, losing themselves in the enchantment of history and each other.

They rushed through the last stop at the fort, General William Moultrie's grave, and hurried to the car to beat the lunch closing time for Long Island Café on Isle of Palms.

"White tablecloth service for lunch is never a bad idea." David tapped his beer to Roosevelt's glass of wine.

"Marion's Corner does not have a restaurant that does colossal Calabash shrimp like this." She pulled the tail out of the shell and popped it into her mouth.

"You don't use tartar or cocktail sauce?" He drenched his fried seafood platter with lemon and had been dipping everything into the white and red sauces.

She covered her mouth to speak. "I don't like to cover up the flavor."

He tossed a balled-up cocktail napkin at her.

David parked at his house, and they walked down the street to Dunleavy's Pub. They sat at the bar, surrounded by signs and license plates from all over, and sipped a beer.

David touched her arm, moved her hair aside, and whispered in her ear, "This has been a great day. Thank you."

This time, Roosevelt's arm hair stood on raised goose pimples. She rubbed her nose with his. "I'm enjoying my staycation."

They gave up their seats as a crowd moved into the small bar and restaurant. Holding hands, they explored the forest path at Station 16.

By the end of that walk, he draped his muscular arm around her shoulder, and they walked in step to the blue Victorian.

"What now?" She stood within his arms on the porch of her dream house. "House tour?"

"Excellent." *If it includes the primary bedroom.* Then she smacked her hand in her head for even thinking such a thing. But golly, the sensation of his hands on her body parts—her hand, her hip, her hair—made her horny. Best staycation ever.

They both said hello to Grace and gave Milo some attention. He offered the cat a treat. He made a show of telling her about the rooms she'd already seen—the enclosed porch, kitchen, breakfast area, living room, and half bath. The staircase took up most of the foyer, and he'd sanded and refinished the steps himself. He told her not to look too closely at the work.

He took her by the hand and led her to the back hallway to a guest room decorated for his granddaughter. A hall bath held mandala-designed floor tiles in greens and blues, which Roosevelt reached down to caress.

He led the way to the remodeled primary bedroom.

"Do you mind if I shut the door while we're in here?"

She shrugged her shoulders.

He held the bedroom door open and then snapped it shut behind her.

"I'm not trying to scare you, it's just that Milo crawls under my bed, and it's right near impossible to get him out."

I wouldn't want to leave either. Roosevelt cleared her throat and ventured into the primary bathroom. It held a clawfoot tub and a doorless walk-in shower. An armchair sat in one corner, with potted plants on shelves nearby. The toilet room held a regular toilet and a bidet.

"Fancy." Her daughter bought a bidet accessory online, but a solitary bidet seemed to be überposh. Best not to talk about toilet preferences when you first meet a man, though. "The stained-glass windows in the bedroom—where'd you get them?"

David walked her back to the bed. On either side hanging from the window frame were colorful panels depicting a lion's head that took up the entire window.

"This one, I found in an old barn in the Georgetown area. And this one"—he pointed to the other—"is new. A replica of its twin. The artist did a fantastic job, even if she told me that I hung the original upside down."

"It's not a lion?" She tilted her head. "It looks like a lion."

"The ribbon should be on the top, not the bottom. I think it's a tulip, maybe. But I like the lion better."

"I agree. Plus, you have a story about it. I love the way the light plays across the walls. Like a fancy spa or a high-end hotel." The bed's tufted frame headboard and the linens on it matched the colors in the windows.

He took a seat on the bed. "My mother never let me sit on the bed unless I was getting out of it or getting into it. Once we made the bed, we could not mess it up. So, I sit on my bed and toss around the pillows and read books and watch videos all in the comfort of this room." He bounced on the bed and grinned at her.

"Everything in here is perfect." She stood near him, and when his hands touched her skin, she fell into his arms with a kiss.

They never made it out of his bedroom except when he ventured out for leftovers and beverages and to feed the cat.

In the middle of the night, while sleeping with her back to her companion's belly, a hand touched her hip and pulled her toward him.

"Roosevelt?"

"Yes?"

"I like your name. Roosevelt. It feels like velvet on my tongue."

She shivered at his voice, and a warmth enveloped her. Her body inched above the bed.

"Don't take to the air again yet. This is the part in a romance story where we pledge our devotion to each other or we have an emotional experience. I want to give you that emotional experience. May I?"

She whispered her affirmative answer. Her body floated above the bed as if they played the childhood game. Light as a feather, stiff as a board.

He drew her down, his hand on her side. "I can feel your hip bone."

"You can? Oh, thank you." She made a move to face him, but he pulled her closer to his own hips and hard cock.

His finger caressed her from the dip of her waist to her hip to the section where her leg met her behind. He teased her bottom with swirls and rubs. She moaned and pushed herself closer to him. He used his free hand, the one he'd propped his head on, to move her hair to one side. The rush of the touch of his lips to the small space behind her ear brought tiny bumps of desire to the surface of her skin. Every fine hair on her body stood at attention, and a quiver started from her head and ended at her thighs. Her body soared above the bed.

He tugged her back and pushed apart her thighs to play with the inner folds between. She made an incomprehensible sound, another slight moan, a guttural need of her innermost voice. She reached to her back to guide him.

"No, ma'am. Let me enjoy the wetness, the warmth, the squeeze on my fingers…"

She clasped his fingers inside her. He held her close, his hardness throbbing between her butt cheeks. His fingers left, came back, spread.

She gasped.

"Yes, show me what you like, and now your clit. A tease? A tap? A slap? Oh, the spank…"

He made sharp, quick smacks, and she spread her legs for him.

She moaned a yes as the sting caused her to curl forward and then arch back. She leaned her head back and they kissed. He rubbed her labia and found her clit. The next second, a series of spanks. The heat between her legs and the beat of her heart melted her into a puddle of need and desire.

The urgency of her movements increased, and her brain couldn't comprehend whether to press forward to the touch of his hand or backward to reach his cock. She rocked back and forth to enjoy both sensations.

They melted into another deep kiss as he entered her from behind, pushing her forward until her breasts touched her knees. She leveraged a hand on the bed while he held onto her shoulder to help her meet his thrusts. The full-body orgasm came over her as soon as his moan of release began.

And he had a drawer full of unopened toys he said they could explore later.

The next morning, she found her suitcase in his bathroom, with plush towels beside it. Here, too, the most opulent assortment of hair and body accoutrements surrounded her. The couture-level experience made her want to move in.

She took extra time in the extravagant multi-head rain shower and wrapped herself in the luxurious cotton terry robe he'd draped over the chair for her. A top-of-the-line hair dryer hung from a hook near a sitting table facing an LED-backlit vanity mirror.

She couldn't resist a bit of snooping, and as she dried her hair, she slid open a drawer to find unopened boxes of expensive lotions and creams and high-end skin care tools. A red light therapy mask she'd seen used by celebrities sat in the bottom drawer.

She saw the door behind her open in the reflection of the mirror. She jumped and rotated on the stool. A ball of fur snuck across the floor. Milo leapt into her lap and rubbed his head under her chin.

She focused on the table, petting the kitten as she opened her make-up bag and sorted through her drugstore-brand products. She sucked her teeth. Looked in the mirror to meet Milo's eyes.

"There's no reason not to avail myself, right?"

She snuck a hand over to the clean-beauty high-end bottle of moisturizer that sat on the dressing table. She opened the top. Took a sniff. Sighed. Light, airy, clean scents that made her think of linens fresh off the clothesline in her grandmother's backyard. She let the cat smell it. He purred. She pumped out a dime-sized portion on her ring finger and took a deep breath.

Women with perfect skin who didn't have to wear make-up to cover flaws must bathe in this stuff. She allowed herself another pump and thought she heard her pores break out in a joyful tune when she rubbed in the potion.

Everything about this man is orgasmic.

She finished getting ready, made certain everything found its way back to where it belonged, and took the cat—who never bothered to hide under the bed—and her bag with her to the living room.

David greeted her with another steaming cup of coffee and took her bag to her car. When he reentered, she joined him in the kitchen, and he pulled leftovers out of the fridge before placing some in a to-go bag for her.

A knock came at the door. David excused himself and asked her to finish packing her container. Roosevelt couldn't help but overhear the conversation.

"Dad." Another deep male voice, similar to David's.

"Hello, son. Want to come in and meet my friend?"

"A friend? No. I, uh, I need to tell you to stop with the videos, please."

"May I ask why?"

"It's embarrassing."

"To whom? I never mention that I have a son or a grandchild. What's to be embarrassed about?"

"The subject matter."

"This sounds like a you problem, not a me problem."

"Dad. I am tempted to have you evaluated. You act like you're twenty-eight instead of sixty-eight. You spend more money on this monstrosity of a house than you do on your family."

The house rumbled, as if disturbed at overhearing derogatory remarks about itself. Roosevelt felt the floor shudder beneath her feet. She snuck closer to the door's opening.

"Son, none of this is your business. My money and what I do with it does not concern you."

"It's family money."

"Earned by my hard work. Not yours. Mine to spend as I see fit."

"That's what I mean. You squander money unwisely. You get on videos and make a fool out of yourself and my family."

"Would you like to meet Roosevelt? She's about to leave. I'd love for you to meet her."

"Does she have magic? I know you like to hang out with those who have a gift."

Roosevelt gasped. And the front door of the house flew open.

"It's really none of your business. I need you to leave. The house is ready for you to depart."

"That right there—thinking the house doesn't want me here. That's wild. Hanging with paranormal people is harmful." His son moved closer to David.

David held out a hand to his son in the stop motion. "Son. Go home. You need to get a grip. What brought this on?"

"I saw the latest video. It's a disgrace. You need to come with me to the bank to get me on your accounts so I can check your spending habits." The young man moved forward. Then he skidded to a stop. Made a painful guttural noise. Clutched his belly.

Roosevelt moved away from the door.

"I've sharted. This is your freaking fault." David's son grabbed at his pants and ran out the open door.

Chapter Four

Roosevelt peered around the corner and watched David close the door with a soft *thunk* and rest his head on the doorjamb. She touched the back door's knob, rubbed the cat on his head, whispered goodbye to Grace, the ghost, and slipped away.

Her hands shook when put her car into reverse to leave David and the blue Victorian. She waved as she passed the porch, saying goodbye to her house, Grace, Milo, the energy of comfort from the second she'd stepped over the threshold. How could it have been two short days ago? Had it been real? A glitch in the matrix? The few days seemed like a dream sequence. If her dreams contained hours of erotic entertainment and deep conversations.

Did David have a spending problem? Was he in over his head in debt? He'd made a video? What about? He couldn't be on one of those sex-for-pay sites. But you never know.

She'd spent years being bamboozled by her former husband, and the first time she found someone interesting enough to sleep with, he has secrets. Her dream house, pictured in her head as a pristine promise of hope and happiness felt tarnished, her crown crooked.

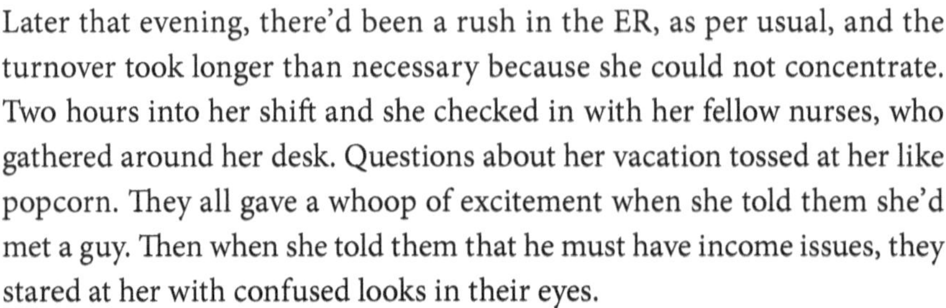

Later that evening, there'd been a rush in the ER, as per usual, and the turnover took longer than necessary because she could not concentrate. Two hours into her shift and she checked in with her fellow nurses, who gathered around her desk. Questions about her vacation tossed at her like popcorn. They all gave a whoop of excitement when she told them she'd met a guy. Then when she told them that he must have income issues, they stared at her with confused looks in their eyes.

"Why do you think that?" Carol, her oldest work friend, asked.

Roosevelt straightened the desk area. "His son accused him of making videos and frittering away money. He has a huge supply of super expensive lotions and creams on his bathroom counter. His skin does look and feel fantastic, though." The memory of her hands rubbing along his firm chest as he thrust into her made her squirm.

"But y'all, you know, enjoyed the sex?" Tamara tapped her pen on her chin.

She checked the area, leaned in, and whispered, "Let's just say he performed like a thirty-year-old, not someone more than twice that age."

Roosevelt thought she should leave out the levitation orgasms. Once, she'd touched his ceiling, she'd come so hard.

The heat in her face rose again when she remembered how uninhibited they'd both been about their bodies, their words, their actions, their laughter, their unabashed need for each other.

The receptionist buzzed their intercom. "Roosevelt, you have a visitor. I'm sending him back."

Everyone gathered closer to Roosevelt in anticipation. She could feel their collective breath on her neck and face. "Y'all need to step back. Practice social distancing before you forget how."

She walked toward the entrance to greet her visitor. The only visitors she ever had were her daughter, and only one other time, her son-in-law. She checked her watch—ten thirty. Not too late, but their little family started with the cock's crows in the mornings. She saw a tall male carrying a reusable grocery bag and a dozen roses headed down the hall toward her. She stumbled on the flat floor and looked at the group a few steps behind her. She shooed them away. They moved behind various objects.

"David. What a nice surprise. These are perfection." Roosevelt dipped her nose into the flowers while giving him a half hug.

He smiled at her and then glanced around. He noticed the audience and waggled his fingers at them. Two of the younger nurses ran over.

"Oh my gosh. I'm subscribed to your channel." Kelly clung to his arm.

Scarlett reached out her hand in greeting. "I must say, sir, I am proud of you. Not many men your age would have the gumption to do what you do on video for everyone to see. I showed my dad, and he acted like he wasn't into it, but I know he watches now too."

Videos? How do you spend money making videos? Were they about gambling? Did he travel extensively and have a travel vlog? That would cost a lot. That must be it. These videos were making him broke. Her ex had kept secrets about money that he'd spent carelessly. She could not handle another gaslighter.

"Roosevelt? Hello?"

The young women moved away, giggling.

David now stared at her with a twinkle in his eye. "Off with the fairies?"

"No. I, uh, appreciate you coming over, and these flowers smell delightful. But I need to get to work." She touched his arm, but her hand slid down to his hand, and it felt like home.

He gave her hand a squeeze. "I can take a hint." He leaned over and whispered in her ear, "I wanted you to know that I enjoyed every second we spent together, and I would love to take you on a real date, downtown, with restaurant food from a fancy chef." He kissed her on the forehead, then pressed his forehead against hers.

An audible sigh came from behind them.

David and Roosevelt laughed.

"Your friends want a recap." He walked away.

One of her co-workers jumped up and down with glee. Two scrolled on their phones as if they'd seen a celebrity and needed to tell the world.

"What?" Roosevelt set the vase down. "What? Do y'all know something I don't? He's a gambler, isn't he? A porn star?" That would explain a lot.

Scarlett shoved her phone in Roosevelt's face—a still shot of David with a title on the screen with a list of shorts, videos, and more listed under it. Scarlett pointed at the subscribers number, which read 1.16M. Dawn held up her phone, opened to his social media account—300K followers.

"He's an influencer," they both shouted.

"David?" She took both their phones and scrolled.

"His catchphrase is 'Your future self will thank you.' I have the biggest crush on him, and he's way old." Tina, the youngest of the nurses, peered over Roosevelt's shoulder.

"He's sixty-eight," Dawn said. "But he's hot."

"And doesn't show signs of spending money all willy-nilly. He talks about living a long, healthy life taking care of his retirement plan so he can enjoy traveling the world and his experiences in the Lowcountry and around the state. He's a catch." Scarlett emphasized her last words.

Roosevelt took a seat on the nearest stool. Relief flooded her. Then shame for thinking bad things about him. Yet the sense of relief came again—her chest opened, her heartbeat quickened, and hope sprung. The gurgle in her chest began. She held onto the stool with both hands until the effervescence subsided.

This relationship held the promise of a future. And he brought flowers. And delicious leftovers.

She caressed a rose petal and took a deep breath. Remembering the middle-of-the-night pull-over sex from behind. The orgasms. The spanks. She tightened her thighs. She laughed at herself.

Calls of an emergency began when the victims of a three-car pile up arrived.

The next morning, she struggled to keep the flowers, the food bag, and her purse in her arms as she walked to her car. Her ex leaned against her door.

"Dude, you're going to scratch my car. Get off." She hit the fob to unlock her door and tucked away her belongings. She meant to get in and drive off, but he held the door from closing. "Let go."

"Did you, uh, go on the tour?" He leaned into her personal space.

"Do you remember when I took out that restraining order on you? I can have that renewed. The judge doesn't like you."

"The judge is your sister's friend, and she should have rescinded herself from the case." He pulled the door farther open.

"It's a small town—everyone knows everyone—and it's recused. Rescind is what I would like to do with our entire relationship."

"You don't mean that. You're just overworked. You know how you get."

"No. I'm not doing this again. We're done. Finished. Kaput. You blew your final chance with the bed-and-breakfast false promise." She pulled at the door he held on to.

"Step away from her." A familiar rumbling voice spoke.

Her ex looked at David. "Make me."

"Sir, just move along. Now." David moved to the driver's-side door between Roosevelt and the threat.

The gaslighter took another step toward David. And another.

David made the stop motion with his hand.

Another stride toward the two of them from the ex. His face changed, though. Now he looked like he did the time he got food poisoning from gas station sushi.

Roosevelt stepped away from the car. "Go away, asshole."

Her former husband leered at her and lurched forward. His face turned a bit green. His hands shook.

David placed his left hand on her shoulder, and with his right, he forcefully pushed at the air with the stop motion again.

The ex clutched his belly and bent over. The smell of diarrhea and gas exploded from him. He clenched the back of his pants. Ran away doubled over with a dark stain running down his backside and legs.

Roosevelt got out of her car and hugged David's neck and kissed his cheek. "I think I figured out your magic. It's hilarious," she hiccupped in her laughter.

"It's only handy in emergency situations, and I try not to use it without cause. I discovered it in college when some drunk wanted to fight me over his girlfriend. Took me a bit to figure out that I made his bowels react with magic, not scared him into pooping." David giggled like a schoolboy.

"No wonder the magic testing committee dismissed you without seeing you perform. And that's why your son left in a hurry." She patted his back.

"Full confession, I didn't mean to make him shart. He got me angry, and I had a guest. My level of emotion triggers the intensity of the intestinal irritation. I wanted him to go away. I love him, so I didn't go full force. Sorry the argument made you run off."

"It was pretty intense. Are you okay? He accused you of…"

"His second wife is the reason he's so worried about money. Her collection of designer purses and 'fits have emptied their bank account on numerous occasions. That's why my granddaughter stays with me during her visitation time. And that's why the current daughter-in-law wants to scare me. She threatens me with never seeing my grand again if I don't give them more money. But she's the stepmother, and the real mother thinks I'm amazing."

"I do too. Why did you return to see me this morning?" Roosevelt caressed his cheek. A tear trickled down his face and onto her hand.

"Sorry." He wiped away the tear. "My magic also makes me emotional. I wanted to see your face again. And I don't know where you live or have your phone number. I meant to put a note on your windshield but found you in trouble instead. Should I follow you home? Make certain you're safe?" He hugged her and helped her into her car.

"I have to work tonight. I'm going to need some sleep." She rolled down the window.

"I might let you sleep. Can I tire you out first?" He leaned in and kissed her.

"Indeed."

"I'll follow you to Marion's Corner then."

"Speaking of following…" She showed him that she now liked his social media and video accounts.

"Ah, hope you aren't embarrassed by my topics."

"Let's see." She scrolled and read some to him.

"Foreplay, toys, and other fun things to do in bed. Exercise is good for the heart. Let's Explore Charleston. Why men should read romance: hint—it'll make you a better lover. Facial cream for men that won't break the bank. Wait, most of the stuff in your bathroom was high-end." Roosevelt showed him the screen.

"I use some of it, hard to resist. Companies give me stuff, and I do giveaways for my followers. I do not share with my current daughter-in-law, and that adds fuel to the flame. Maybe I should slide her a box or two, get her off the scent."

"Might be a good idea. And that explains the unopened boxes." She covered her mouth with her hand. "Sorry, I snooped."

"That's okay. Just know that turnabout is fair play. What's in your drawers?"

She led his hand down the front of her scrubs and spread her legs. "Wetness."

"Expect an inspection of your drawers then. We may not make it to your house." His fingers caressed her.

She pushed him away and adjusted her pants. "I can't lose my job for having sex in the parking lot. Get in your car and let's go."

"Looking forward to making you levitate in bed again." He hurried to his car.

The sun rose behind her on the ride to her dream home replica with a dreamboat following her. The car's wheels barely touched the road.

The End

About Robin Hillyer-Miles

Robin Hillyer-Miles is a South Carolina native happily living in the Lowcountry with her husband, son, dog, and two cats. Robin writes contemporary romance novels with a magical realism twist. She's a certified city of Charleston tour guide and has 300 plus hours in yoga instructor training. She's published in the Lowcountry Romance Writers Anthologies, Volumes 1 and 2.

Find Robin Online:

Facebook: https://www.facebook.com/RobinHillyerMilesAuthor
Instagram: https://www.instagram.com/rhillyer_miles/
Amazon: https://www.amazon.com/~/e/B07YN9P3T6

Finally Found

by Suzie Webster

Finally Found

by Suzie Webster

After a painful divorce, Megan embarks on a transformative journey to Charleston, South Carolina, a city steeped in history and charm. With a broken heart and uncertain future, she seeks solace and healing in the cobblestone streets and magnolia-scented air. What she finds in the arms of a local high school football coach is something she never expected.

Chili Pepper Rating: 5

Chapter One

Meghan

The minute I walked through the doors into the intimate lobby of the hotel I had chosen for my impromptu vacation, I knew I'd made the perfect choice. I'd considered a beachfront getaway but had always been more of a mountains kinda girl. But the thought of the mountains brought a bitter taste to my mouth. I didn't need any reminders of the many vacations I had taken with my ex, Julian, who was an avid hiker. After researching options that were a quick plane trip from my Northern Virginia apartment, I decided Charleston sounded like the perfect city to lose myself in. A town steeped in history, with beautiful antebellum homes, cobblestone streets, and restaurants that everyone seemed to rave about. I prayed there would be no reminders of my busy suburban life on the outskirts of Washington DC. I needed time to take a breath and forget about the pain of the last two years.

As the Uber drove me from the airport through the picturesque city streets that lead to my hotel in the heart of downtown, I could already feel the stress sliding off me, my shoulders feeling lighter as we traveled farther into town. With my cheek resting against the seat back, I watched as the colorful houses came and went from view, gas porch lanterns winking in the dusky light of the setting sun. I felt like I had disappeared into a postcard; it was exactly how I had imagined Charleston would look. I'd traded in the hiking boots I'd worn on my frequent hikes with Julian for my favorite well-worn Converse, and I couldn't wait to explore after unpacking my bags.

For the first time ever, I had no set plans, no obligations, and no one else I needed to even consider. It made my heart speed up a little, this sensation of being so untethered and alone. Back in Virginia, I had left behind my son, who was attending the local college, and my daughter, who was happy to spend a week with her father. He would no doubt spoil them with gifts and dinners out, desperate to be the favorite parent. It was ironic that he had no problem treating them to such luxuries after all the years of him controlling the purse strings on our spending, even with me contributing half of our income. But I refused to dwell on the past. This trip was a chance for me to rediscover Meghan Rose Brown—the girl who had once dreamed of becoming an illustrator, a writer of children's stories, and a world traveler, among so many other things I had never done.

I walked through the large antique doors of the boutique hotel I had chosen and admired the beautiful touches in the small reception area. I caught the eye of a balding man behind the tall ornately carved wooden reception desk. I felt like I had traveled through time to the turn of the century, when furnishings were rich in color and overstuffed with down feathers that invited you to sink in with a good book and a cup of hot tea. The man at the desk gave me a bright smile, his brown eyes sparkling warmly as I made my way over, my small suitcase trailing behind me over the thick antique rug.

"Welcome to The King's Court Hotel," he said as I set my purse on the top of the desk.

"Thank you." I returned his infectious smile, feeling a small spark of excitement in the pit of my stomach. I could hardly remember the last time I had felt that sort of emotion. Five years ago? Six? When Holly had won her first medal in gymnastics? Maybe when Seth had made the junior varsity football team?

"Are you checking in with us today?" His voice had a slight hint of a Southern accent, and everything about him seemed to fit perfectly in this space. From his well-groomed mustache to his colorful bowtie, he seemed like a character in a movie set in a quaint hotel in a southern city decades in the past.

"Yes," I responded. "My name is Meghan Brown and I'm checking in for a week."

He typed a few things into his computer, the only modern convenience in sight other than the phone sitting next to it.

"Ahh, here you are, Mrs. Brown."

"Ms.," I quickly corrected. "I'm not married."

"Oh, I am terribly sorry, Ms. Brown." He gave me another smile before looking back at his computer. "Well, it would seem that this is your lucky day. We overbooked the room type you selected, so I've upgraded you to a king suite overlooking our gardens at no additional charge."

"Oh," I said with a start. I felt another jolt of something that resembled happiness. This was not normally the way things went for me. At least not in recent years. Things like free room upgrades only happened to other people. This had to be a good omen for my trip. "Wow, thank you. That's amazing." As it was, I had used a good portion of my savings to go on this trip, and I had booked the least expensive room I could find in this hotel.

"Of course, my dear. It's the least I can do after our mix-up. And I'll let you in on a little secret. This is my favorite room in the hotel. I think it will be perfect for you."

As the kind hotel clerk finished checking me in, I continued to look around the space. I had spent hours online looking at the various inns and boutique hotels in Charleston. I wasn't interested in staying in one of the chains or larger hotels. I wanted somewhere peaceful and quaint, and I could see that the pictures I'd seen online of King's Court hadn't steered me wrong.

I returned my attention to the clerk, who was in the midst of telling me about their rooftop bar and restaurant and the library where they served tea midday and wine in the evening before dinner. He directed me to the elevator and gave me my room key, which was a large gold antique key hanging from an ornate letter *K*.

I unpacked my bag and my toiletries in my gorgeous and spacious room with a stunning view of the gardens, which, even in late October, were filled with colorful blooms and dark green palms. Eager to get out and explore, I threw on a long flowy skirt and fitted top under my denim jacket and pointed my converse toward King Street. I had done a bit of research on Charleston before I'd left, and while I didn't have any set plans, I did have a list of places I wanted to visit, but since the sun had already set, I knew my options were limited tonight. I decided to walk over to a little French bistro I had read about that was a few blocks away. It had been open for forty years, and it seemed to be a beloved landmark in town. As I stepped out onto the sidewalk, I was surprised to see how much foot traffic there was on a Thursday night at seven o'clock.

Strolling toward the restaurant, I admired the beautiful shops lining the street. As I got closer to the restaurant, I would pass an occasional residence, many with wraparound porches, and nearly all had window boxes overflowing with flowers. Even the tiny yards were packed with greenery, and brick or stone walkways meandered up to the painted or stained wood doors flanked by flickering gas lanterns. After living in Northern Virginia my whole life, it felt like a time warp to be surrounded by so much historic architecture.

I turned onto Broad Street, and before long, I saw a swinging sign hanging in front of another beautifully restored Charleston single home. I immediately recognized the name of my bistro and walked inside. A beautiful woman with snow-white hair came over as I entered.

"Hello, are you planning to join us for dinner this evening?" she asked with a smile.

Before answering, I looked around the cozy space and noticed a bar with an empty seat over to my left.

"Is it possible to order food at the bar?" I asked.

"Of course, ma'am. Please follow me." She turned gracefully and led me to the open seat at the end of the bar.

As I climbed onto the high-backed barstool, I noticed a young man in the seat next to me. He turned as I sat down and gave me a friendly smile. I was immediately struck by his stunning blue eyes and high cheekbones with a smattering of freckles like he spent a lot of time out in the sun.

"Hi," he said.

And I blushed as those eyes looked me over with discernible interest.

"Oh shoot, I made you blush," he said with a chuckle. "I'm sorry, I didn't mean to stare. It's just, I'm in this spot almost every Thursday, and I've never seen you in here before." He reached his right hand across the bar top and held it out to me. "My name is Zach."

Not wanting to be rude, I slid my hand into his much larger one to shake it. His palm was callused, and his grip was strong but gentle, and his hand felt warm and strangely good wrapped around mine.

"I'm Meghan, and yes, I've never been here before. In fact, this is my first time in Charleston." I took my hand back to look at my watch and immediately wished I hadn't let go of him. Okay, now this was getting a little weird. He was a complete stranger, and yet, as his eyes scanned my face, I couldn't help but feel I knew him from somewhere. "I've only been here about an hour."

His eyes widened. "Oh, wow. Well, welcome to the Holy City."

He gave me another grin and I noticed a small dimple on the left side of his mouth. Damn but he was good-looking. Young, but really cute. I was beginning to wish I had taken a little more time with my appearance. Almost as if he could read my mind, his eyes twinkled as he waited for me to say more. Or maybe he was amused by my obvious social awkwardness.

"Um, yes, I read that it was called that. Because of all the churches, right?" Yep, totally awkward, which was not surprising considering it had been twenty years since I'd been single and talking to a man in a bar. Not that this was anything more than the Southern hospitality I'd heard so much about. A guy this handsome would not be interested in a forty-something divorcée.

Fortunately, he seemed completely unfazed by my inability to carry on a conversation and willing to carry it on for both of us.

"That's right. I see you've done your research. So, Meghan with the blonde hair and pretty green eyes, where are you traveling from and what brings you to our city?"

I felt myself blushing even more at his compliment. He was so amiable, but I again reminded myself that he was no different than all of the other overly friendly people I'd met since arriving in Charleston. Even my Uber driver had chatted my ear off the entire drive. As I looked into his handsome face, friendly and open, I decided to be honest about my reason for visiting.

Chapter Two

Zach

As I watched the beautiful blonde in front of me considering my question, her sad eyes simmered with interest as they locked with mine. All the noise of the restaurant seemed to fade away, and I found myself completely focused on her. I was on the edge of my proverbial seat waiting to hear what she would say. I couldn't shake the feeling that she was about to be someone important to me. I'd been sitting on this barstool nearly every Tuesday and Thursday after work for over a year, and I'd never had this kind of reaction to anyone else who'd sat down next to me. In fact, I couldn't remember my attention being captured so completely, period. Not here, or if I was being honest, not anywhere else. Even my longtime girlfriend—now my ex—had not evoked such a reaction on our first date.

Meghan—a fitting name to compliment her ethereal beauty—let out a soft sigh, and something like resolve settled on her face. Her lips compressed together, making them puff out, and I had the irrational urge to run my finger along her full bottom lip.

"Are you sure you want to hear this? It's honestly a little pathetic," she said, her lips curling in a wry smile.

"I do." I wanted to reach out and touch her hand resting on the bar top, but I wasn't sure it would be welcomed, so I resisted. From my peripheral vision, I saw the bartender approaching. "But why don't you let Tim fix you a cocktail, and then you can give me all the details while we enjoy a drink together." I kept my tone soft, feeling somehow like I needed to tread lightly. She felt fragile, despite her squared shoulders and unwavering eye contact.

She nodded without answering and turned to my favorite bartender as he approached. Apparently not missing the way my body was angled toward hers, Tim gave me a slightly raised eyebrow before taking her drink order and giving her a food menu. Over the last ten years, Tim and I had become friends, even meeting away from the restaurant to play golf or watch a football game at a local sports pub. He had become one of my first friends since moving here. He knew my history, my ex who had cheated on me with my supposed best friend, and my decision to focus on work and put dating aside, which had lasted successfully for the last two years, despite him and other friends constantly trying to play matchmaker. Meghan was looking at the menu with a cute little furrow in her brow.

I touched her hand to get her attention, and she looked up immediately, her green eyes wide. It was obvious she wasn't used to dining alone, much less in a strange city. Her nervous energy was palpable. I smiled reassuringly. "The chicken here is amazing. They have several different preparations depending on what you like. My favorite is the Provencal."

She smiled, and I found my mind already thinking about other ways to keep that smile on her face. She turned to Tim and ordered my favorite dish, along with a gin and tonic. I gave her another encouraging smile as Tim walked away, giving me a pointed look, which I ignored. I waited patiently for her to fill me in on her story. I needed to know what twist of fate had brought her to the barstool next to mine. Likely reading my expression, her contemplative look returned, and the smile disappeared.

Well," she said softly, her chin tipping up slightly, a defensive gesture that again had me wanting to put a reassuring hand over hers.

But I refrained, instead leaning back in my chair to give her space.

"I've had a kind of rough year. Actually, it's been a bit of a downhill slide for a couple of years now. I realized after a particularly unpleasant interaction with my ex-husband that I needed to get out of town for a little while. I can't remember the last time I had a vacation that wasn't centered around my children or visiting family, so I decided to go on a little trip and visit a place I'd never been. I love history and art, and after researching different options on the East Coast, I settled on Charleston. I wanted somewhere completely different from where I grew up. I'm from Northern Virginia, outside of Washington DC."

Despite her casual delivery, I could sense the sorrow in her words. I considered what to say in response to convey the empathy I felt without making her think I felt sorry for her. Because when I looked at her, all I saw was potential, and a person I wanted—no, needed to get to know better. In this moment, I would do anything to keep her sitting here talking to me.

"Here's the thing, Meghan. Why you came won't matter after today, because I think after a couple days in the Lowcountry, you will feel like a new person. I visited here ten years ago with a group of friends for a bachelor party, and something about this place spoke to my soul. When a job opened up here in my field, I threw my hat into the ring and never looked back." I winked at her. "Not that I'm saying you have to move here, but this place will heal whatever it is that is hurting you, that much I'm sure of."

I expected her to laugh at me. I mean, maybe I had piled it on a little thick. But I meant what I'd said. Moving to Charleston had changed my life for the better. She surprised me when she laid her hand on my wrist, the gesture taking me by surprise. Her eyes were serious as she responded.

"I'm not surprised, Zach. I felt a pull when I stepped out of my Uber today. I hadn't exactly decided what it meant, but it was almost as if I'd been here before. Like I was returning home after a long absence." She shook her head. "It's utterly ridiculous since I've never even set foot in South Carolina."

"It's not ridiculous. I felt something similar, and I'd never felt that either. My family thought I was crazy to leave my dream job and the home I'd lived in my whole life. But I knew Charleston was where I was meant to be. It took about a year for me to find a position worth leaving for, but I've never had a moment of regret. This place—it gets under your skin."

As Tim returned with Meghan's drink, she removed her hand from my arm. I gave him a dirty look at his untimely arrival, and he gave me a knowing grin and set Meghan's drink down in front of her. He let us both know our food would be out shortly—I had ordered mine just before she'd arrived—and he walked away, giving me a wink that I prayed Meghan didn't notice.

"So, what is it you do for work?"

I couldn't help but smile. My job was everything to me, and I loved talking about it. "I was fortunate to land an assistant coaching job right out of college after interning my last two years at a nearby high school. As soon as I graduated, they offered me a permanent position. I'm originally from Alabama, and my family bleeds for football—specifically Alabama football—and I played from the time I was five or six years old. I didn't have the talent to go all the way, but I loved the game so much, I decided to focus on coaching instead. I was here with the head coach only a year after I started the job, scouting a potential player who was moving to our town, and that's when I decided I needed to find a coaching opportunity in Charleston. I started out ten years ago as the assistant coach of the high school right here in town, and when our head coach retired a few years ago, they offered me the job."

She was smiling as I finished my story. "I can see by the way you talk that you are really doing something you love. I can imagine those boys enjoy playing for you. Your passion is obvious. I'm honestly a little envious. I have a great job at home, but it's never been much more than work for me. I would love to be able to pay the bills doing something I love."

I thought about my players and the joy it gave me to see them succeed. Not just playing the game but also in their academics and personal lives. Coaching was more than a job for me; those people had become my family.

Which made it easier to be eight hours away from my parents and siblings, who all still lived outside of Birmingham.

"What is it that you do for work?" I asked, suddenly wanting to know everything about her.

She sighed. "My job isn't very exciting. I started working at an accounting firm after high school. My boyfriend at the time, now ex-husband, was a junior in college when I graduated. He wanted to get married, so I decided to go to community college part-time and work to save money. After we got married, I finished school with an accounting degree. It seemed like the easiest thing because my boss at the firm I worked for offered to pay for me to finish my undergrad if I became a CPA. I got pregnant not long before I graduated, so I kind of dove headfirst into adulthood. Until two years ago, being an accountant, a wife, and a mom were all I'd ever known. Now I'm starting over as a single mom and a frustrated accountant." She gave me a smile, but it didn't reach her eyes. "I don't know why I'm telling you all this. I'm sure the last thing a handsome young guy like you wants to be doing is sitting next to a divorced single mom unloading her depressing life story while you eat dinner."

I grinned at her, trying to lighten her mood. "Did you call me handsome?"

Her cheeks turned pink, which seemed to happen often. It occurred to me that she likely wasn't used to someone flirting with her. It made me want to do it more. Before she could respond, I laid my hand on hers.

"I'm teasing you, Meghan. My default is to make someone laugh when they seem to be sad. But I am flattered that you called me handsome. And I doubt if I'm that much younger than you."

She raised an eyebrow. "Oh, yeah? How old do you think I am?" she asked, giving me a cute little smirk.

"Oh, no, I'm not getting caught in that trap. How about I tell you my age and you tell me how much older you are." She hardly looked older than 35.

"Fine. How old are you, Zach?"

"I'm thirty-two, but my birthday is Saturday and I'll be thirty-three."

Her eyes lit up and she gave me a victorious smile.

"Well, happy almost birthday. Also, Ha! I'm nearly a decade older."

It was the most animated she had been, and I wanted to fan the tiny spark I saw in her expressive face.

"It seems to me that maybe you need to hang around a fun young guy who can really show you the best of Charleston. I don't have any big plans for my birthday, and I would love to spend it with a beautiful single mother, showing her all the secret local places in my favorite city. I can promise you no one will suspect that you are a cougar on the prowl when they see us together." I sat back in my chair and waited for her response as I watched her realize that, yes, I had asked her out on a date.

Chapter Three

Meghan

My racing heart registered the fact that this gorgeous younger man had asked me out on a date well before my brain did. I stared at him, mouth agape. The crazier thing was…there was not one part of me that wanted to turn him down. Even the tiny voice saying, *This doesn't make sense. He's ten years younger and he lives in Charleston. This is going nowhere.* That voice of reason was hardly convincing, because as he sat there waiting for me to respond, his blue eyes sparkling and filled with fun, I knew there was no way I could say no. I needed this in my life right now. I wanted to spend more time with him, and I had promised myself I would be spontaneous and free on this trip.

"Yes…yes, I'd love for you to show me around your city, Zach." My heart lightened with every word. I could feel the smile spreading across my face, and I couldn't look away from his answering grin even as the bartender set our food in front of us, clearing his throat to get our attention. I wasn't even embarrassed to be caught staring. Something about Zach had me so caught up that my usual inhibitions seemed to have disappeared.

The rest of the evening went by in what seemed like seconds. Several times, I wanted to brush aside the dark curls that fell on his forehead as he talked animatedly about everything from football to his love of animals and even his family back in Alabama. He did the best job distracting me from the mess I'd left behind at home while still asking pertinent questions about my life in a way that kept me from being too focused on the negative aspects. He asked about my hopes and dreams and led me gently down a path of self-discovery with such ease that when I left him, I was filled with a sense of hope for my future. His optimism was a breath of fresh air, and I felt like I'd known him for months rather than hours.

Zach and I finally got up from our seats at the bar. It was after ten o'clock, and the restaurant was empty except for the staff who were cleaning up. Normally, I would've felt awkward staying after all the other patrons had cleared out, but I wouldn't have given up one minute I'd spent with this charming man. He'd brought me out of my shell with his gentle teasing and light flirting. I found myself flirting in return, and while it had been decades since I'd been in the position to flirt with anyone, I was amazed at how easy it was with him. My confidence grew as the evening wore on, and he leaned closer into my space. To my surprise, I found that I liked him there. It should've felt strange to be intimate with a virtual stranger, but it only felt good.

"Did you Uber here from your hotel?" he asked.

"No, it's only a few blocks, and I walked." We were now standing on the sidewalk out front, and the slight breeze cooled my skin, which had been heated all night.

"Wonderful. I can walk you back."

When I started to protest, he shook his head and held out his hand.

"It's not safe for you to walk alone at night, and it's foolish to call an Uber on such a beautiful evening. I'd love to take a walk."

"What about your car?" I asked, tentatively reaching for his outstretched hand.

He took my hand firmly in his. "I walked too. Where's your hotel?"

"It's The King's Court—a few blocks from here," I answered, goose bumps scattering across my skin from the feel of his hand wrapped around mine.

We began walking in silence, broken occasionally by a car passing on the quiet streets.

"This is one of my favorite parts of town," Zach said, looking over at me with a small smile. "It's peaceful here, a little further from the more touristy areas. I live a few blocks away, near Colonial Lake. Not long after I moved here, my grandfather passed, and I was fortunate enough to inherit a little money. I used it to buy a small rundown house in my favorite part of town, Harleston Village."

He continued, "I was raised in a family of very handy people who believed in fixing everything yourself when it broke down, so I was a jack-of-all-trades, master of none. I knew enough to be able to do most of my home renovations. Other than electrical wiring—I hired a local guy to help me with most of that aspect. I took down some walls to expand the kitchen and open up the living area, and I turned the three bedrooms into two. I never saw myself having kids, and most of my family prefers to stay in a hotel or Airbnb when they visit, so the second bedroom is an office that can double as a guest room for my friends who occasionally visit. There's an outbuilding in the rear that holds all my sporting gear and tools. Someday, I may turn that into a little studio or something, but the house is plenty for just me. It even has a driveway for two cars, which is probably the greatest luxury in town."

"That's amazing, Zach. You've accomplished a lot. Your family must be very proud."

He laughed. "I think they are, once they got over me leaving Alabama. I'm the only one who doesn't live in our hometown. My father is the unofficial mayor, and my mom knows every bit of gossip and is always excited to fill me in on what I'm missing. Lucky for me, my older brother and sister are both married with kids, so Mom's finally stopped nagging me about grandchildren."

I had been so caught up in his story that I hadn't realized we had reached my hotel. Zach turned to me, still holding on to my hand. He pulled me close to him, and with nearly a foot in height difference, I was forced to look up.

"How early can I pick you up on Saturday, Meg?"

The nickname caught me by surprise. The only one who called me Meg was my mom. But I decided I liked it. I wanted to be different for him. Someone new. I moved closer until the tips of my Converse touched his Adidas.

"Do you want to take me to breakfast?"

He released his hand from mine and slid it up my arm before following the curve of my neck and resting it gently on my cheek. Such an intimate gesture, but I found I liked it.

"I want to spend every minute I can with you, sweet Meg."

I knew he was going to kiss me, and the look in his eyes said he knew I wanted him to. My ex-husband's lips were the only I'd had on mine in over twenty-five years. I was filled with excited anticipation, and the nerves I would have expected were nowhere to be found.

He leaned closer. "Can I kiss you, Meghan?" he whispered, so close now, I could feel his breath against my cheek.

"Zach," I said, feeling I should protest and knowing I had no desire to. We had just met. This was not something I had ever done, even in my teen years, before I'd met Julian. I had always been so deliberate and careful. He waited patiently and a sigh escape me as I leaned in closer. His gaze on mine was so intense that I had to close my eyes as the words flowed from my lips. "Yes, please."

His lips were soft against mine at first—brushing side to side, tasting, teasing. I pressed in closer, reached up, and put my hands on his chest, which was warm and firm. He let out a small sound, almost a moan. His kiss became firmer, more demanding. I opened slightly and he tilted my head at an angle for better access as he explored my mouth with his soft full lips. His kiss was sensual, exploring, and his other hand had moved up to cup my other cheek, cradling me as he worshiped my mouth with his own. I couldn't ever remember being kissed quite this way. He held me with such care and reverence as we stood on the cobblestone sidewalk under the soft light of the motel entrance.

My heart raced in my chest, and my stomach tightened, a warm flush prickling the surface of my skin. Never in my life had I had a one-night stand, but I was already wondering how those large hands would feel exploring my body. What would the hard muscles of his chest look like as he lay back against my headboard in my cozy hotel room, waiting for me to join him on the bed?

As he pulled back, he looked into my eyes, and I could see some of the same thoughts flickering in his blue eyes, which had darkened to the color of the Caribbean Sea at night—royal blue with flecks of turquoise where the moon shined across the surface.

"Oh," I said breathlessly.

He chuckled softly, still holding my flushed cheeks in his hands as he looked at me intently.

"I will be back Saturday at nine o'clock in the morning, beautiful Meg. And I can promise you my dreams will be filled with no one but you tonight. I'm not sure why you sat down on the barstool next to mine, but I'm not about to let you get away so easily."

He pulled out his phone and handed it to me. "Put your number in my phone so I can call you when I get home."

It wasn't a request, more of a plea, and I immediately complied, my heart rate still faster than normal.

I handed him back his phone, and he grabbed my hand and pulled me into him, encircling me in an embrace that had our bodies connected from the top of my head nearly to my toes. I breathed in his scent, a mix of leather and fresh-cut grass, before sliding back and turning toward the door.

"Good night, Zach," I said over my shoulder, and our eyes connected. I knew the warm lust I saw swimming in his depths was mirrored in my own, and I immediately wondered how I would make it through another thirty-five hours before seeing him again.

Chapter Four

Zach

I had spent the last day and two nights counting the seconds until I could see Meg again. I'd had to hold myself back from walking to her hotel after my game on Friday, but it had been a long day, and I'd been tired. I had even considered inviting her to come, but I'd known I would be too busy to give her much attention and would spend the game worried about her and wondering what she was doing, instead of focusing on my job. The rational part of me also realized my enthusiasm might scare her away. And even though our time together was extremely limited, I was fully prepared to do whatever I had to do to make her realize that I was serious about her.

It seemed like madness that I had spent every minute I wasn't focused on my job and my players wondering how I could have fallen so hard for a woman in just a few hours. After telling myself I preferred to keep things casual in my romantic life, suddenly my thoughts about this woman were anything but. I'd hardly slept the last two nights, thinking about the way the streetlamps shone off her pale blond hair or how the green of her eyes changed when she was sad. Visualizing the way her skin had flushed pink and those green eyes had stared at my mouth just before I'd kissed her made my cock swell in my pants. I could feel her yearning, and it was like a drug I needed another hit of.

But more than the physical attraction, I wanted all the details of her story. I already knew the things that made her sad. Her failed marriage. Her children, nearly grown and ready to move on with adulthood. Even her job seemed to leave her so unsatisfied. She had mentioned her love of art and how she had recently started drawing again. She'd told me about her *scribbles*, as she'd called them. Little stories that she'd made up to entertain her kids when they were young. I wanted to hear them, to see her art. I wanted to see more of the smile that transformed her face every time it appeared.

I'd texted and called her as often as I could throughout the day on Friday. I called her after the game Friday night. Even though it was late, she had insisted she was still awake and wanted to talk. We had stayed up way too late talking, and I had never had so much difficulty saying good-bye. I had wanted to drive over and start our date at three in the morning. It made no sense, but seeing her again was all I could think about.

Now I was standing in the lobby of her hotel, impatiently waiting for her to come down from her room. I had the first part of the day planned, and I wanted to see how things went before we decided how to spend the afternoon and evening. More than anything, I wanted to show her my home, which I'd spent years fixing up with my own two hands. But I didn't want to make her feel pressured or get the wrong idea. Logically, we hardly knew each other, but logic wasn't in control right now, and she already felt like mine.

The elevator doors opened, and my breath caught in my throat as a beautiful angel drifted toward me. She was wearing the same well-worn Converse, but instead of a skirt, she had on fitted jeans that hugged her curves perfectly, along with a loose teal blouse that made those damn eyes stand out even more as they locked on mine. The smile that lit up her face gave me hope that maybe she shared some of my feelings and I wasn't falling alone.

I looked down at her as she drew close, and already, I wanted to pull her into my arms and kiss her until she could hardly breathe. I wanted to feel those panting breaths against my lips and explore inside her mouth with my tongue. I had spent the last two nights dreaming of her taste. I was ready to forget about sightseeing and drag her back to my house so we could spend every spare minute locked inside.

As all these wild thoughts spun in my head, she whispered, "This is crazy."

I pulled her close and looked into her upturned face. "It's not, Meg. It's fate. You were meant to enter my world, and at least for this week, while I have you, I'm not going to question it."

Her eyes scanned mine, searching.

I leaned down until our lips were millimeters apart.

"Can you do the same? Can you just let this day unfold without questioning who we are to each other?"

She let out the breath she must have been holding, and her voice quivered as she responded, "Yes."

I captured her mouth with mine, and it was a relief to feel her melt against me, arms encircling my waist. I could've kissed her for hours, but after a minute or two, and before I lost all sense of reason, I pulled back.

I took her hand in mine and led her to the door. "Come on, I have some breakfast pastries in the car because we're taking a little road trip to one of my favorite spots in the Lowcountry."

Ninety minutes later, after a scenic drive to Edisto and after demolishing the pastries and coffees I'd picked up from my local bakery, Meg and I were standing at the beginning of a long boardwalk surrounded by marsh. In the distance were woods, and behind us was the gravel parking lot where we had left my Jeep. I carried a backpack for our shoes, and in it was a small blanket in case we wanted to stop and sit. A large water bottle hung from a loop.

I took her hand, happy to have another reason to feel her skin pressed against mine.

"It's a bit of a walk to get there, but this place is unlike anywhere else in the country. Truly unspoiled and special. It's one of my favorite spots, and you can't access it within a few hours of high tide. Which is why we had to go light on breakfast. So we could come here first, when the tide was low."

As we walked the quarter of a mile to our destination, Meg stopped to check out the crabs scurrying through the marsh grass or admire a flower blooming in the pluff mud. I filled her in on the history of Botany Bay. How it had been a privately owned plantation until it was donated to the state as a wildlife preserve in 1977, but the owners had remained for many years after. I explained that it had finally opened to the public as Botany Bay Heritage Preserve in 2008 and was run by South Carolina's Department of Natural Resources.

As we approached the hidden beach cove, Meg's eyes grew wide. I watched her face as she took in the scene in front of us. "Oh my," she exclaimed, surprised delight dancing across her pretty face. "This is incredible, Zach. I don't think I've seen anything more beautiful. And the smells…" She took a deep gulp of air. "It feels like we have stepped into a fairy tale."

I pulled my backpack off my shoulders. "Here, give me your shoes and socks so that you don't get sand in them." Knowing where we were going, I had opted for flip-flops, a necessity for Charleston locals. Meg quickly untied her shoes and leaned against me as she yanked them off, along with her socks. Once my backpack was back in place, we clasped hands and moved into the softer sand leading onto the beach.

As many times as I had been, the same sense of wonder filled me whenever my toes sunk into the sand of this magical place.

I smiled as she oohed and aahed over the many trees stripped of their leaves and bleached white by the sun, scattered along the shore like a woodland graveyard. It was wild to see waves crashing against giant tree trunks and swirling around overturned roots that had kelp and shells clinging to them. And watching her delight was like seeing it all again for the first time.

"It looks different every time I come here," I told her. "Somehow, I expect it to be the same, but the power of Mother Nature changes everything."

"It takes my breath away, Zach. Thank you for bringing me here. I don't remember seeing anything about this place during my research of what to do in Charleston, so I never would have found it on my own."

"To be fair, it is a good distance from the city, and without a car, you probably wouldn't have made the trek. But it was the first place I thought to take you. Somehow, I had a feeling you would fit in well here."

I turned to look at her as the October breeze whipped her hair around her face. She looked like some kind of sea siren, and there was no doubt she had me under her spell. With her dancing green eyes and tanned skin, it seemed as if she had been made to live along the sandy shores of the coast. The idea of her in some boring suburban neighborhood was hard to imagine. In this moment, she looked wild and free—nothing like the sad woman sitting on the barstool next to me two nights ago. This right here was the girl I'd seen hiding beneath the surface, with a world of potential swirling in the mossy depths of her eyes.

After walking for a while, I pulled her over to a dry patch of sand that offered the perfect view of trees, sea, and sky. A cozy spot nestled between two of the largest trees that seemed to be growing up from the sand despite their bare, leafless limbs. I slid the backpack off my shoulders and pulled out the blanket, spreading it out on the sand. I sat down on it and patted the spot next to me. To my surprise, she dropped down immediately. I leaned back on my hands and stretched my legs out in front of me, and she surprised me again by scooting in closer until our thighs were touching. A soft smile still played on her lips, and her eyes were shining as she looked at me. She angled toward me and put her hand on my chest.

"Zach, I can't thank you enough for bringing me here. You have no idea how much I needed it."

I pushed the hair that had fallen across her cheek behind her ear. Any excuse to touch her.

"I'm so glad you love it as much as I do, Meg. Somehow, I knew you would."

I put a finger under her chin, lifting it so I could look into her eyes. "I need to kiss you in my favorite place. Are you okay with that?"

She nodded. "Yes, I am okay with that."

She had barely gotten the words out before I was dipping my head to kiss her. She tasted of salt and sweetness, the perfect combination to have the blood heating in my veins. Our other two kisses had been tamer, but I was eager to explore as I pushed my tongue between her slightly parted lips. She opened, allowing me access to delve inside, and our tongues tangled together, a perfect dance of eagerness and lust. She moaned against my mouth, and I pulled her onto my lap, grateful that the beach was deserted on this weekday morning. Botany Bay was rarely busy, but right now, there wasn't another person in sight.

She reached up and wrapped her small arms around my neck, leaning into our embrace, and her proximity allowed me to explore down the side of her neck, licking the sweet saltiness from her warm skin. She tilted her head to the side, giving me better access, and I let my hands wander from her back around to the front to slide up and cup her breasts, which she pushed eagerly into my palms. God, but kissing her was almost better than sex. I couldn't remember ever being so turned on from just kissing. The sounds she was making made me eager to see how she would respond to my tongue between her legs, which had me wondering if she tasted even sweeter down there.

As my mind swirled with all the possibilities of having her naked in my bed, she pulled away only to rearrange herself, so she was fully sitting on top of me with her knees on either side of my outstretched legs. Which put her pussy right up against my hard cock.

Chapter Five

Meghan

I should be freaking out right now. This was so far from the woman I usually was, the woman I had become over the last twenty years. Maybe once, long ago, I had felt this wild and free, but if I had, it was a long-ago dream now. But despite how I should be feeling, I couldn't get close enough to this man. Even with the cool breeze and public beach, I resented the clothing that separated my skin from his. Every part of him that touched me felt like a relief. His lips on mine were a revelation, filling me with a heady lust that I couldn't ever recall experiencing. My body had a mind of its own as I pulled him even closer and ground against the hardness pressing up against me, causing the most delicious sensations to course through me. I felt out of control, and I didn't even care. My need for him overpowered any sense of reason.

His fingers slid open the top buttons of my shirt, and he pulled down my cotton bra and slid his mouth down my breast. I couldn't hold back the loud moan as his lips encircled my nipple, and he sucked it hard into his mouth. The slight twinge of pain sent shock waves to my core, the wetness already seeping into my panties. I sunk my fingers into the hair on the back of his head and pulled him tightly against me, encouraging him. I writhed helplessly in his lap as he kissed and sucked first one nipple and then the other. He moaned as I slid up and down the hard length in his jeans. The friction was driving me mad, and I could feel an orgasm beginning to build. I didn't realize it was even possible to orgasm by humping someone when we're fully clothed, but damn if I wasn't right on the edge. As my movements grew more frantic, I felt him pulling away.

"No," I whimpered as his mouth left my breast.

He chuckled softly, sliding my bra back up and pulling my shirt back together to cover me up.

"This is not how I want to give you your first orgasm with me, my little sea nymph. And if we keep going, it's going to be an uncomfortable drive home for me."

I looked at him, confused, and he kissed the tip of my nose. "I can't remember a time when I was so close to coming in my pants, but you had me ready to lose it with those sounds you were making. You are too sexy for your own good."

Reaching down and buttoning my shirt, with a sigh, I bent my head and leaned it against his chest, my hands clutching his shirt. He rubbed his hands gently up and down my back in a soothing motion. I looked back up to see a crooked smile on his face and his eyes warm as he looked back at me.

"I can't believe I did that," I said, starting to climb off his lap.

His arms tightened around me, preventing me from moving. He leaned his head down and kissed me softly on the lips.

Pulling back, he spoke, and his voice was husky and flowed across my skin with the cool ocean breeze. "It wasn't just you, Meg. You had me completely out of my head. Whatever this is between us is all new for me. I know you're only here until Thursday, but I want to make sure that whatever we do, we do it because we both want it. I don't want you to have any regrets about the time we spend together."

"Zach, the only thing I'm going to regret is leaving. I can feel that already." The words slipped out of my mouth without a thought, and his eyes widened a little. Immediately, I worried I had said too much. But his next words crushed that fear instantly, and hope sparked my chest.

"I feel the same way, Meg. I can't even think about you leaving, and while the idea of how quickly I'm falling is scary, I'm not about to hold back. This thing between us"—he put a hand on my chest and then covered mine that was still holding his shirt—"it's worth exploring, and somehow, when we get to Thursday, we will have figured it out."

I knew my mouth was hanging open, because he put his fingers under my chin and gently closed it. "Trust me?" he whispered softly.

I nodded. "Yes, I have no idea why, since we hardly know each other, but I trust you with everything that is important to me."

His smile was blinding. "Good. Let's head back to the car. I'm going to fill you full of delicious Southern food, and maybe after you're nice and recharged, I can take you back and show you around my neighborhood."

He reached down and cupped my ass with his hands, scooting me closer, and he was still hard underneath me.

My breath caught in my throat as he leaned in and dragged his mouth up my neck to my ear.

The gravel was back in his voice as he said quietly against my ear, "And maybe after that, I can give you a tour of my house, and we can finish what we started before I cook you dinner."

Goose bumps had broken out across my skin at the thought of being truly alone with him in his house. I realized I wanted it more than anything I had ever wanted before. I reached my hands down and cupped his face, pulling his lips up to mine.

"Yes," I said before kissing him. I pulled back just a little and murmured against his lips, "Take me to your house and let's finish this."

"So how did you like Roxbury?" Zach asked as he navigated his Jeep throughout downtown Charleston's afternoon traffic. His hand was on my thigh and had been there much of the hour drive back from Meggett, where we had stopped at a cute local restaurant for lunch. I tried to focus on answering his question, but between our heated make-out session on the beach and his flirtatious attention at lunch, I was having difficulty concentrating on anything but the warm weight on my leg.

"Umm, my shrimp taco was delicious. And that blood orange cocktail was way too good. I think it's gone to my head a little."

He glanced over and gave me a sexy smirk. "Oh yeah? And here I thought our kiss on the beach had you light-headed."

I felt myself blushing. How was it so easy for him to tilt my world off its axis with just his crooked smile? I decided to see if I could do the same to him, even just a little.

"Honestly, I've hardly thought of anything else. I'm amazed I made it through lunch without crawling into your lap in front of that family of five sitting next to us."

He threw his head back and laughed, and my body filled with pleasure at his response. He gave my leg a firm squeeze, and I had to keep myself from squirming in my seat at the pressure. After the first couple years with my ex-husband, our sex life had evaporated to once-a-week appointments with very little spontaneity and certainly no amount of kink. Something in the way Zach handled me on the beach and was gripping my leg right now sent a message that he was comfortable taking charge. Every cell in my body was responding to that energy. It almost felt as if we were already a foregone conclusion, and any part of my brain that might object didn't stand a chance. I had heard stories of instant love and insane chemistry between two people, but I had never come close to that feeling…until now.

As we pulled down a narrow tree-lined street, I felt a change in Zach. He seemed to vibrate with happiness as we pulled into a driveway next to an adorable two-story house. It looked almost like a gingerbread house out of a fairy tale. The edge of the peaked roof was lined with ornately carved trim, and the wood siding was slate blue. The front door was painted yellow, and I would have been surprised to see such a bright, cheerful color on the house of a bachelor, but after spending nine hours with Zach, it seemed to fit him perfectly.

Zach came around and opened my door and helped me out of the Jeep. He led me up a stone walkway onto the front porch that extended the width of the house and held a swing in one corner. Like many of the houses I had seen, Zach's first-floor windows were lined with planter boxes full of greenery and a few remaining flowers. As he unlocked the front door, his other hand lingered on the small of my back. An intimate and sweet gesture that made me feel as if he didn't want to let me go.

As the front door swung open, he grabbed my hand and eagerly pulled me inside. I smiled at how excited he was to show me his home. I couldn't remember ever feeling this way about my brick colonial in Northern Virginia. But as soon as I took in the view of the tiny foyer leading into a cozy family room, my heart leaped into my throat, and I fell immediately in love with the beautiful, charming space. It was a sanctuary of vintage wood pieces and cozy, inviting furniture that made you want to snuggle up with a fluffy blanket and a good spicy romance.

I looked up at Zach to see him watching me intently.

"What do you think?" he asked, and I could swear his voice seemed to tremble.

"It's so welcoming and cozy. I love it, Zach. I understand why you were excited to show me."

"Come into the kitchen," he commanded, pulling me through the room, past a staircase, and to an opening off to the right. We stepped from the family room into a surprisingly large kitchen and eating area. Like the family room, it was eclectic and inviting. I could imagine friends gathered around the island while Zach cooked or mixed drinks. It was a home and a kitchen meant to be enjoyed and lived in. It was absolutely perfect.

I turned to Zach and pulled his large frame against me for a hug. After a second of surprise, he wrapped his arms around my shoulders and pulled me in close. God, but it felt so good in the safety of his embrace.

I looked up into his smiling face.

"What an amazing sanctuary you've built for yourself, Zach. You should be so proud. Anyone would love to live here."

His eyes seemed to touch every corner of my face as he looked at me with so much intensity that I wished I could read his mind. The smile was gone, but the light remained behind his eyes, and I had difficulty imagining it ever not being there.

It turned out, I didn't have to be a mind reader, because as he reached a hand up and stroked it down the back of my head, he spoke.

"How about you, Meg? Could you ever see yourself living here? I have a building in the back that I want to fix up, and I think with a few more windows, it could be a perfect art or writing studio."

I started to speak, and he put his fingers on my mouth and shook his head, a slight smile returning to his lips.

"I know what you're gonna say, but I need you to hear me out. I don't want to pressure you or add stress to your life, but I need you to know this before I take you upstairs and do all the things I want to do to your sexy body."

A shiver ran through me at his suggestion, but my stomach was already an explosion of butterflies over the impact of his words. I found myself locked into his gaze, unable to look away, my breath held waiting for him to finish.

"I know this seems insane; I would think so myself if I wasn't the one experiencing all these feelings that I've never felt for anyone else, Meghan—I mean, I am…falling for you. I know you're leaving next week. I know you have children and a life in Virginia. But I can't let you leave without knowing that, for me, this is not some fling with a woman visiting Charleston. For me, you are the one I want. The one I have been waiting for. It's crazy but I know this to my soul." He cupped my face with his hand. "So, please, Meg, tell me you feel the same. Tell me you want to find a way to make this work between us." His eyes suddenly filled with worry as his voice softened, and I could hear the emotion as he continued. "Because as much as I want to take you upstairs right now and show you just how much you mean to me, I can't do it, if there isn't a chance for us. If we sleep together, I'm going to have a really hard time letting you walk out of my life on Thursday. I know that after only a few kisses."

I waited before responding. I needed a chance to gather my thoughts. He seemed to know what I needed as he waited quietly. I could feel him. I could feel the rapid beat of his heart against my own as I stood still, wrapped up in his strong arms, the warmth of his skin seeping into my own. I ran my hands up his chest, feeling the flex of his muscles against my palms. He was a beautiful man, young and virile and in the prime of his life. I wanted to believe I was still there too. When I was with him, I felt like the younger, more hopeful version of myself.

"Zach." My voice was a whisper, and I was surprised to hear the sultry way his name sounded from my mouth. It felt so good rolling off my tongue, and hearing it gave me courage. "This is crazy, but you aren't alone. I feel something new and exciting. It's scary because I was married for nearly twenty years, and I've never felt this way before. I didn't expect to find you when I came here. It's hard for me to even believe I can have you, but damn it, so much of me wants this. I don't want to walk away either." I sighed, and his expression fell a little. "I can only promise you this week. There is so much I need to consider. My life…it's complicated. I have to think about my children—it's not just about what I want." I looked into his eyes, the beautiful blue clouded with disappointment. "Please, Zach, just give me this. I need to feel you. I need to know what it's like to have this." I gestured between us. "Even if it's only for a few days."

He stared at me hard for a moment. I could see him considering as I held my breath. I wouldn't push him for more if he said no. I would be devastated, but I would walk out the door and be grateful for the hours we had. It was too soon. No matter what my heart wanted, I couldn't make him any promises.

Without a word, he took my hand and walked out of the kitchen and to the bottom of the stairs. He turned and looked at me, and the emotion from earlier was gone from his face. I felt a tiny bit of sadness lingering, and I wondered if I was making a mistake. Would doing this hurt him? Was I being selfish?

"Okay, Meghan. If we only have a few days, let's make it count."

I followed him up the stairs, wondering if I was doing the right thing.

My heart trembled. My body was filled with a need I couldn't resist, and despite my uncertainty, I couldn't deny myself the gift of letting go. Maybe it was selfish, but I wanted to know what it felt like to have Zach inside me. I only prayed he wouldn't hate me when it was over.

We entered his bedroom, and it was larger than I had expected. I barely had time to register my surroundings before he was pulling me close. Any uncertainty I had felt evaporated when his lips met mine. The force of it caught me by surprise, but heat flooded my body, and I quickly matched his intensity. His lips devoured mine. Any reluctance I might have had was replaced by a desire so strong that nothing else mattered.

His lips moved from my mouth down to my neck. Our hands tangled trying to remove each other's clothes. I eagerly yanked up his Henley trying to get to the warm skin underneath; his fingers unhooked the button of my jeans. We both lifted our heads for air and looked at each other, panting. My fingers were still tangled in his chest hair, his shirt hiked up above his waist. He pulled down my zipper purposefully, and the sound of it echoed in the room. His face was flushed. His eyes were so dark they were nearly black. He reached his other hand behind me and wrapped his hand around my hair, pulling my head back so he could look into my eyes. His lips were swollen from the force of our kiss, and the way he looked at me had a storm raging in my blood. I wanted him badly. I didn't want to wait any longer.

"Take off your clothes, Meghan, and lie on your back in the middle of my bed."

I had never had anyone speak to me that way during sex, but I didn't hesitate. The tone of his voice and even his stern expression had warmth flooding my panties.

He released me, and I quickly obeyed, peeling off my jeans and panties, ridding myself of my socks, and then lifting my shirt and unhooking my bra, all under his heated gaze. As I crawled onto his bed and lay back against the pillow, he stood at the end of the bed fully clothed, looking at my body hungrily. I should've felt shy or embarrassed, but his expression had me wanting to beg him to join me. But I bit my tongue as he lifted off his shirt and began to unbuckle his belt.

I had seen his firm stomach earlier when I'd tried to undress him myself, but looking at him standing in front of me shirtless was a whole different experience. His skin was bronzed from the sun, and chest hair scattered lightly across his muscled chest. His biceps bulged slightly as he removed his belt and unzipped his pants. I couldn't stop myself from licking my lips as he pushed down his pants and underwear in one quick movement. His cock sprung free as he stood back up, and I drank in the sight of him, so young and virile. In my eyes, he was the perfect specimen and all man as he stood there his eyes stormy with lust as he stroked a hand up his hard cock.

Chapter Six

Zach

I should have sent her away. She was going to break my heart; about that, I had no doubt. Everything I had promised myself after my girlfriend had betrayed me had been thrown out the window after just a few short days spent with Meghan. She was everything I wanted, and this was all she was willing to give me. I wanted to be strong, but I couldn't deny myself this one night with her. And I knew this was all we would have. I couldn't continue to see her after tonight. It was going to be hard enough to let her go after I had tasted her. Just the taste of her lips had been enough to have me making foolish declarations. Being inside her might possibly break me, but I had to feel her wrapped around me. Just this once.

Her eyes beckoned to me, and the sight of her spread out on my bed was almost too much. Her full breasts begged for my mouth, and I could even see the wetness glistening between her legs. She was ready for everything I had to give her, and I would make sure my name stayed on her lips long after she left. I would give her a night she would never forget. Unfortunately, I knew it would be a long time before I forgot her as well.

I crawled up on the bed until my knees were on either side of her hips and my hands were next to her head.

I looked down at her pink cheeks and full lips, and the need I felt for her was so strong, it made my chest ache painfully.

"Zach," she whispered. "I want to feel you inside me."

I put a finger on her lips. "Not until I taste you. I have been dreaming about your taste for the last two nights." I leaned down and kissed her, catching the moan that had escaped at my words. I wanted everything with her, even if it was just for one night. I wanted to touch and taste every part of her until we were no longer able to stay awake.

I slid down her body, tracing every dip and curve with my lips and tongue. My fingers stroked all the places my mouth had been as she writhed and moaned beneath me. I could tell she wasn't holding back, and I relished every whimpered word as I settled in between her legs and flicked her full, wet clit with my tongue. As I prodded and teased her, she pushed up into my face, her body demanding more. Her scent and taste were even better than I had imagined. As she moaned above me, begging me with words she probably didn't even realize she was saying, I sucked her engorged clit into my mouth as I slid my finger into her wet heat. She bucked off the bed, letting out a scream as I slowly fucked her with my finger and sucked her even harder, loving the feel of her clenched so tightly around me.

I pulled my mouth off her and added another finger, pushing deeper and faster as she bucked against my hand.

I knew she was so close, and I leaned back down and sucked her back into my mouth, curling my fingers inside her with each stroke as she screamed above me, "Oh my God. Yes, Zach. Yes, please. I'm coming."

I let her ride against my face, enjoying the taste of her pleasure and lapping it up eagerly with my tongue. She was everything I had known she would be and more as she let go with a ferocity that surprised even me. My cock was rock hard and dripping, and I ached to fill her.

As she lay with her limbs loose and her head thrown back, I pulled away and leaned to get a condom out of my nightstand. Her eyes locked with mine, and she shook her head. My heart sank. She didn't want it.

"No, please." Her voice was raspy, and even as disappointment filled me, my cock throbbed at the lusty sound of her voice. "I ca-can't get pregnant, and I haven't been with anyone since my husband. Please, Zach, I trust you. I don't want you to use a condom. I want to feel you." Her voice was shaky, her eyes pleading as she looked at me.

I leaned back and pulled myself up her body, allowing our skin to rub together, the tiny beads of sweat coating her body making me slide easily along her warm skin. She felt amazing underneath me. "Are you sure?" I asked. "I haven't been with anyone in a long time either. I am definitely clean." I found that I wanted to be bare inside her more than anything now that she had said the words.

She put her arms around my neck and pulled my mouth down to hers. She seemed unfazed by her taste on my lips as she kissed me hungrily. "Yes, Zach, hurry. I need to feel you," she whispered against my lips.

Her legs widened as I pressed against her, finding her more than ready to take me. She raised her hips, giving me a better angle as I slid inside her slowly, relishing every inch as I filled her. I groaned as I felt her clench around me, and I dropped my face into the side of her neck, burying myself inside her completely. We moaned in unison as I pulled back out and pushed in more quickly this time. It was more than just the friction, the feel of her enveloping me—she was so much more. As I picked up my pace and she bucked up against me, I knew I wouldn't last long. She felt too good, and I was too far gone already.

"Can you come again?" I asked her, hardly recognizing the rough sound of my voice.

"Yes. Oh yes, you feel so good, Zach."

God, her words.

I kissed her then, needing to feel her mouth on mine as I thrust in and out more quickly. I pulled away and leaned back. I wanted to see her body. I wanted to see where we joined together. I needed to see it, just this once.

"Touch yourself, Meg," I rasped and she immediately reached between us and began to rub her clit.

The sight of her was almost too much as I tried desperately to hold off my orgasm. I felt her clench around me as she arched up against me, and I knew she was about to come, so I began to increase my pace, filling her deeply and angling to hit the spot I knew would send her over the edge.

"Zach, oh my God, yes. You feel so good, so, so good," she cried out as I continued to slam into her at a steady pace.

Her eyes flew open, and she locked her gaze with mine, and that look of ecstasy on her face sent me flying. My orgasm soared throughout my body, and I felt the telltale tingle at the base of my spine as I pulled her against me and filled her with everything I had for the first time. As I cried out, I was filled with a deep and penetrating pleasure I had never felt before. I tried not to think about the fact that it would likely be the last.

I sat at my kitchen island sipping on coffee that had long since grown cold. I didn't know how long I had been here; I only knew that my mind was blank and my body was numb. I couldn't let Meghan leave until I had had her two more times. Her screams had bounced against my thick block walls as I'd brought her to orgasm after orgasm. I remembered how she had looked up at me as she had taken me into her mouth for the first time, so eager to taste me, and I had nearly come just from the sight of her between my legs. After we had exhausted ourselves, we fell asleep in each other's arms. And maybe that was the reason it had been so hard for me to send her away this morning. Waking up to her snuggled against me, her leg over mine, her soft breast pressed against my shoulder, was a Heaven I'd never known I needed.

I had planned to make her breakfast and talk, try to convince her to give us a chance, even if it was long distance until we could figure things out. But she must have read my mind, and she made it clear that she could not give me any more than this week. For her, this was nothing more than a passionate fling. It was all she was able to offer. I told her I couldn't do it. That last night would have to be all we had.

Any more would be too hard for me. She was kind and said she understood. I could read the disappointment on her face. I offered to make her breakfast, but she refused, saying it would just make things more difficult. She took her clothes into my bathroom and got dressed. When she came out, her face had been blank, her eyes no longer readable. And maybe that was for the best. Not being able to read her expression made it easier to believe she didn't feel the same. It made it easier to let her go, knowing she didn't return my feelings.

I dropped my forehead down onto my arms in front of me on the counter. It sucked to have had this happen again. But this time, I had no one to blame but myself. I had gotten swept away by an affair that had had no chance of working out. There had never even been a possibility of a happy ending. But the truth didn't make it hurt any less. Especially as my mind flickered through the memories of our brief time together. My chest ached knowing I would never see my beautiful sea nymph again.

As I lay across my kitchen island feeling sorry for myself, I heard a knock at my door. I sat up and looked at my watch. It was only nine o'clock, and I wasn't expecting anyone. The knock came again, and I dragged myself out of my chair and made my way to the front door. I didn't really have the energy to deal with friends, and I hoped it was someone who had come to the wrong house.

As I pulled open the door, I was surprised to see Meghan on my doorstep, still wearing the clothes she'd left in two hours ago.

"Can I come in?"

Her voice shook with nerves, but I didn't respond, just swung the door wide and gestured for her to come in. I racked my brain, wondering if maybe she'd left something behind, but I hadn't noticed anything when I'd made up the bed after she'd left.

She walked in and kept going into the family room before taking a seat on the edge of my sofa. Her fingers were clenched together on her lap, and her face was pale, her eyes wide as she looked up at me. I felt myself softening as I recognized the anxious look on her face. I couldn't help but want to make everything alright for her. She seemed to bring out the protective side in me. I wanted so badly to pull her into my arms, but I leaned against the doorframe and waited instead.

Chapter Seven

Meghan

Zach stood there and looked at me. For the first time, I couldn't tell what he was thinking. My palms were sweating in my lap, but I was determined to say what I had come here to say, and I prayed he would believe me. I had spent the last two hours walking through the streets of downtown Charleston. I had walked along The Battery, enjoying the way the sun hung low in the sky and flickered across the water. The sidewalks were fairly quiet as I wandered throughout the more residential part of the city. It was Sunday morning, and most people were likely at home still sleeping, getting dressed for church, or making a big Sunday breakfast.

I thought about my life, as it was. I thought about my children, who loved me but were ready to begin their own lives as they entered adulthood. I thought about the years I had given up for them and for Julian. The parts of myself that I had let slip away as the years had gone by. Julian had never given up on his dreams, and when he'd decided he no longer wanted to be married, he'd left without a backward glance, forcing me to pick up the pieces and put together a life apart that would cause the least amount of damage to our children.

And now, for the first time, I had something in my life that I wanted more than anything I could remember. I had a tiny flicker of hope growing inside me. The dreams I had laid aside so long ago were beginning to come back to life. And there was this man. This beautiful, kind, sensual man. Yes, he was younger than me. Yes, this was so very fast. And yes, I still had things to settle at home. But I wanted him. I wanted this. And I had to tell him; I couldn't leave without letting him know how I felt.

I took a deep breath and stood up, then walked over to Zach, who still lingered in the doorway. He looked at me cautiously as I laid my hand on his chest, needing to feel his warmth through his T-shirt. The way he had made love to me, cared for me, and had even let me go, filled my heart. I was so full of him; I could hardly feel anything else. As he looked at me, his blue eyes began to soften, and hope filled his expression. It seemed impossible to love someone after such a short time, but what I already felt was so much more than I had ever had with Julian. His warmth wrapped around me and made me feel safe, and finally home.

So, I took a deep breath, and I began.

"I don't want to leave, but I will have to for a little while. I do have responsibilities at home, but in nine months, my youngest will graduate, and she's already been accepted to a school in North Carolina, so I will be even closer to her if I'm here in Charleston. Other than my children, who are nearly grown, there is nothing keeping me there. So, yes, as insane as this is to say, I want to try and make this work. I already know leaving you on Thursday will be hard, but if there's still a promise in your heart for more, I'm going to run toward that promise and do all that I can to keep you."

I was surprised to realize that my vision was blurry as I looked at him through tear-filled eyes. What I saw reflected back at me told me everything I needed to know. I knew people would think I had lost my mind, but nothing else mattered. Nothing but this man standing in front of me, words of love yet unspoken but still swirling around us as real as if we had both said them aloud. Everything else would work itself out. It had to, because for the first time, I felt something that had been missing for a very long time. And even as he leaned down and captured my lips with his own, and I felt that zing of electricity cracking between us, it was there, almost like it had been waiting all this time. It was me, I realized. I had finally begun to find myself again.

As he whispered the shortened version of my name over and over against my lips, I reached up around his neck and let him pull me up into his arms. Wrapping my legs around his waist as he carried me out of the kitchen and toward the staircase, I felt nothing but happiness. Happiness for a future I had never believed I deserved. It was because of him, his sweetness and his light, his confidence in who I was, that allowed me to see myself through his eyes. Finally, I was beginning to find the me that had been there all along.

The End

About Suzie Webster

Suzie Webster - Gypsy, Storyteller, Relentless Dreamer, Foodie, Happy Wife, Cool Mom of three.

Why did Suzie Webster start writing romance novels at age forty-nine? To Inspire women to realize that they are the owners of their life and that it is possible at any age to turn their story into a journey filled with laughter, steamy romance, and adventure just like their favorite book. Throughout her many careers from Northern Virginia to Charleston, Suzie has always loved mentoring and supporting other women who are trying to live the life they want and deserve.

She has loved writing since childhood, and weaving stories is another way to share the message that love always wins. She is supported in her own journey by her very patient and tolerant husband Drew, who is always the inspiration for her sexy leading men and her three kids, Ryleigh, Percy, and Reese, who never fail to keep her on her toes and put her in her place.

When she's not traveling (her favorite hobby), she can be found curled up with a good book and a tasty cocktail, preferably tequila.

Find Suzie Online:

Website: www.suziewebster.com
Facebook: https://www.facebook.com/suziewebsterauthor
Instagram: https://www.instagram.com/suziewebster_author/
X : https://twitter.com/suzieQcanwrite
Amazon: https://www.amazon.com/Suzie-Webster/e/B07SGR7Y96?
Goodreads: https://www.goodreads.com/author/show/18874438.
Suzie_Webster

THANK YOU

Life and love, experience and imagination, all play leading roles in any good book. The women of Carolina Romance Writers bring all of that and more to the table. We meet online every month to improve our craft and strengthen our community. We encourage our members' efforts in their chosen genres, and we collaborate on large projects like this anthology. We organize in-person get-togethers at least twice a year. We are loosely headquartered in Charleston, SC, but our members hail from across the Carolinas and beyond. Our membership includes published authors, pre-published authors, and industry professionals

The proceeds from this anthology sustain our efforts to support experienced and aspiring authors through education, connection, promotion, and professional development. To learn more about us or to explore membership, please visit our website:

www.carolinawomenwriters.com

We hope you enjoyed *Love in the Lowcountry: Vacation Collection*. Please consider leaving a review of this anthology on Amazon, Goodreads, or the site where this anthology was purchased.

www.ingramcontent.com/pod-product-compliance
Lightning Source LLC
Chambersburg PA
CBHW022019300726
48970CB00003B/957